LEGACY AND A GUN

JOHN HOLMES

SOCCIONES

© Copyright John Holmes 2019

All rights reserved.

John Holmes has asserted his right under the Copyright, Designs and Patents Act 1988 to be identified as the author of this book.

No part of this publication may be reproduced, distributed, or transmitted in any form or by any means, without the prior written permission of the author, except in the case of brief quotations embodied in critical reviews and certain other non-commercial uses permitted by copyright law. For permission requests, contact the author.

ISBN: 9781099743757

Cover design & typesetting by Socciones Editoria Digitale
www.socciones.co.uk

1
A LEGACY

For the thousandth time, I watched the video of my father falling downstairs carrying a tray of roses. Like every other time, it struck me as funny, full of pathos and plainly odd. There was a man in his thirties, who looked only vaguely like me at that age, smartly dressed, nose in the air at the top of a staircase, and then suddenly and silently he fell.

I hadn't even known the film existed until quite recently, when my nephew told me about it after my sister died, but he could tell me nothing of its origin. She'd assured him it was the only decent thing the old man ever did, and she had destroyed every other trace of him. There was no-one to ask about its origin now, and this eight-second video, absurd as it was, would likely remain the only thing I had that marked my father's existence.

Over the years, I'd become preoccupied with the way history forgave or condemned a person, until some new evidence arose and history would then be rewritten, and the condemned would be forgiven, or the favoured found guilty. My father's history, such as it was, would probably never be rewritten, this eight seconds preserved in cyberspace his only legacy. I knew virtually nothing of him or what he'd done. In fact, I knew more of what he hadn't done: he hadn't followed his father into politics, he hadn't served in the armed forces, he hadn't been much of a father and was never even seen in the family home from about my third birthday onwards. He had not made enemies that I knew of, had not been successful in his mining company career, and had not been a spectacular failure either.

I knew my grandfather better. He was the leader of the country for twenty years and was that curious political creature: the elected dictator, until he died in office in circumstances forever in dispute. Little of his rule remained in the public mind, but the controversy over his death lived on. With his demise, for me the notion of the heroic leader died.

For a moment, I was back at the presidential palace as a little boy. My earliest memory remained especially clear. It was one hot summer when the flies were relentless. They seemed to mock us with their persistence, and I felt sorry for the servants in their fruitless efforts to control them.

Now, fifty-odd years later, I was with my wife Serena in a new apartment in a smart suburb of a foreign capital. As exiles we had been in this country for three years, never settling, like restless caravan dwellers, never accumulating more than we could abandon with the next move. The brochure for the latest flat claimed for itself 'touches of Hollywood glamour', but cynically all we could think this meant was the desultory palm trees and the kidney-shaped pool, which we never saw anyone put so much as a toe in. We were never comfortable anywhere, and certainly not here with our random collection of furniture of faded luxury. In our mid-life reveries, we convinced ourselves we would return to the old country one day, and we never tired of our nostalgic talk but always concluded sadly that going back was impractical. We were well used to the irritations of a peripatetic lifestyle and of calling someone else's property "home", but here the fact we could hear the conversations in the apartments around us meant that we never felt entirely secure.

2
RESTAURANT

Serena had found a new Italian restaurant for us to try in a side road off the main city square. She was a sucker for the new and ostentatious, even if sometimes unashamedly tacky, and this place had arrived on the 'fine dining' scene with the epithet 'seriously stylish', courtesy of a paid-for article in the local newspaper. The seats were leatherette in pastel colours, there was soft jazz, a modest menu, and few customers. I could not imagine it as a restaurant I would frequent often because my preference was for old bistros where the waiters knew my name and favourite dishes, and they would feel relaxed enough to tell me their news, and I could, in my pretentious way, refer to a table in the corner as my 'office' for welcoming my guests. But such a precious arrangement was not practical in the capital; it was not safe to have a regular eating place because, as expatriate critics of the dictatorship back home, we were always potential targets - and creatures of habit were the most at risk of all. Yet in a restaurant with customers so scarce, such as Serena had brought me to, it was impossible not to feel conspicuous. Fortunately, 'long arm attacks' on expatriates were uncommon, although not so rare as to justify ignoring the risk.

As our meal progressed, I began to warm to the place: the waiting staff were attentive and the food was unfussy and tasty. It had been recommended by one of Serena's Ladies Circle friends, who'd been prompted to try it after reading the same paid-for article I'd seen. This friend had also imparted some disturbing news.

'There's a Rat on the loose,' Serena announced in a theatrically hushed voice. Luckily, the two well-heeled women at the nearest table did not overhear her or they might have run out shrieking. *Rat* was the term we used for those of our compatriots who had slipped into our adopted country with the intent of killing us exiles, for which a dirty reward would, if they were fortunate, be payable. Exiles were known as *Birds* by those who'd forced us out, and we'd coined *Rats* in response.

'So what exactly happened?' I asked her.

'Someone I'd never heard of. Can't recall the name. Shot in their home.

Just a few streets from us.'

'Worrying, but are they sure it couldn't have been a domestic situation?'

'Family? Seems not. Been living here years quite happily. Similar to other cases. Two men involved.'

'I don't know what to say.'

'I do,' she said firmly. 'I've decided I need a bodyguard.' At this she threw back her fading blonde locks for effect.

We'd discussed the subject of bodyguards before, and, out of what she considered parsimony, I'd rejected the idea. Irritated at having to revisit it, I summoned all the reasons against it I could immediately bring to mind: privacy, the false sense of security, inconvenience and, of course, cost. Finally, I said, 'Three years in exile with no attempt to attack us.'

'You know I've always felt unsafe. Anyway, think about it. But please don't take too long - there's a new danger out there - or I'll have to go and hire one for myself.'

'Will the Ladies Circle have a recommendation for that too?' It was a catty remark but she'd rattled me.

'Not funny.' She frowned with such affected gravity that I couldn't resist a smile. She ignored me: 'And I want us both to have guns. I assume you haven't bothered with that precaution either.'

'I have, actually,' I said.

'Get *you*. Since when?'

'I've had it for a while.'

'Really? Where do you keep it, then?'

'Under our bed. It's not loaded, though.'

'What is it?'

'A Glock. Glock 19. Nice and versatile, as they say. Handy. Are you sure I didn't tell you? What good am I? But an ex-military man caught without a gun, well, you know, that wouldn't sound good.'

We were silent while the waiter removed our plates. Then she said, 'I'm thinking of taking lessons. Why isn't it loaded, by the way?'

'The same reason you want a bodyguard: for your protection.' I was trying to make light of it.

'For my protection?'

'Yes. If we have a drunken row and you start throwing stuff around, there'll be no tragic accidents.'

'That doesn't even bear thinking about,' she said, not even half-smiling, perhaps because of the notion of her getting drunk, which she always maintained had never happened in her life. Then she brightened at my rather weak attempt at a joke: 'I think I'd rather take the risk, thank you, and feel secure the gun is loaded. So, you will get us bodyguards, won't you? I don't want to be stuck in the flat the whole time, afraid some goon is going to attack me any minute. And I'm sure you wouldn't want me there all the time.'

On that last point we were agreed at least.

3
SOLDIERS

That evening, I was watching an old war film and feeling sorry for myself when Serena came in, late as was usual these days. After she'd sat down, smelling of wine, she said, 'What's up? You seem out of sorts.'

'I just feel lost,' I replied mournfully. 'I feel like I've lost my edge. Exile is getting on my nerves. It's been building up as the months go by.'

'I've noticed it,' she said. 'I feel it in myself, but I see it more in you.' She pointed at the TV screen where a gunfight was ensuing. 'I think you miss all that.'

There was something in what she said. I liked to think I was born a soldier, that soldiering was in my blood. I looked for a role model to my grandfather, who'd enjoyed a successful military career before he entered politics. It had then skipped a generation, my father having avoided national service, only to return with me.

'As you know, I tried other things,' I said. 'Engineering, journalism, even teaching, but none of them worked out for me. I like to believe I was a good soldier, though.'

'If you weren't good, you wouldn't have risen through the ranks like you did. And you enjoyed it.'

'I did.'

She understood my love of it, although I didn't think she understood why. I never lost the excitement of combat. I never gained any pleasure from killing people, but firing a gun at an enemy while he fired at me was the most exhilarating experience I'd ever known. That and the intense comradeship were the things I never found replacements for in civilian life. But being a soldier's wife did not suit Serena. Too much uncertainty, she said. She was therefore relieved when other ex-military figures encouraged me into another exacting career: politics. Over seven years, I held various roles in government, chiefly the role I ended up in - that of defence minister.

'You miss making decisions as well,' she said. 'Decisions that affect people's lives.'

'Yes.' I laughed ruefully. 'Making decisions about my own life was always the hardest bit.' Resolving major conflicts was what I relished, since they presented the toughest challenge, but this was also the thing that had got me, and more importantly the government, into trouble.

As was the case with the other cabinet ministers at the time, I fell foul of one man in particular, a soldier like me, a man we never called by his real name but referred to disparagingly as the Smooth Killer. I had always been loyal to the government of the day, be it of left or right, and both as soldier and in public office, but when the Smooth Killer came to power in a coup, loyalty counted for nothing, for he was determined to sweep away everything of those who preceded him.

When I mentioned that one of the characters in the war film vaguely resembled him, Serena said, 'He's such a national embarrassment. Who would seriously want a man like him to represent the nation? He'd never win an election. Vile man. Pathetic. Looks like a pug, thinks like one too.'

'I used to think that dictators secretly wanted to be loved, but he seems immune from that. He's a walking gift for the satirist and the stage comedian - if they can stay unnoticed.' Indeed, such was his dissatisfaction with his own appearance, that it was said that any jokes about it put him into uncontrollable rages and spontaneous violence.

'I still can't believe it happened,' she said. 'The coup, I mean. So swiftly executed. You have to have a lot of preparation to be that quick.'

It had taken us all by surprise. One minute we were driving home from an enjoyable dinner date, and the next we were arrested.

'"Under suspicion" is their favourite expression,' she said. 'No charges. Too cowardly for that, the bastards!'

So had followed ten months of house arrest, ending with the choice of exile or gaol. We chose exile. It wasn't a difficult decision. If house arrest was intolerable, gaol was unthinkable. Besides, there was always the risk that Serena's tongue would get us both in even worse trouble. She routinely berated the military police guarding the house and exploited every opportunity to tell anyone who would listen, about the new president's limitations. Exile to another continent had offered us a life we imagined would be safe from whatever threats the Smooth Killer might dream up, although, increasingly, events were eroding our sense of security.

4
RUSSO

I met my old friend Russo at his market stall in the centre of town. He had the usual collection of ethnic bric-a-brac, which he himself disparaged as 'rubbish, basically,' and the ratty-looking women he tended to hire - faded glamour, cheap perfume.

I recalled the first time I'd seen him in the context of a fellow exile. He was a hustler then, running a couple of girls, shuffling the odd loan, turning counterfeit cash for local hoods. He was living on his wits, feeling ashamed whilst putting a brave face on it. Back home, he'd been a journalist, highly regarded for his accuracy and investigative ability, not to mention a sweet turn of phrase, but here he'd resigned himself to creating a new career from the discarded items of modern life. It was one of the Smooth Killer's first actions: to arrest the journalists - and anticipating this Russo had fled just in time.

We went to a café popular with young students writing their debut novels. I asked him about the latest assassination Serena had told me about.

'The killer was one of ours, too,' he said.

'Aren't they all?'

'In the past, some came here on a specific mission, but recently they've been people already settled here. This was one of the latter, every bit as worrying. He was an inveterate gambler. Inveterate and not very successful.'

'Hence the new profession,' I said. 'But how do you know he was a gambler?'

He tapped his nose. 'I wasn't a bad journalist, was I?'

'No, of course not. Besides, you probably know everyone in our community.'

'I still have my newshound's eye.' He leaned forward and lowered his voice, 'I was in here a few days ago, and there was a man I recognised who served under Old Smoothie but got fired. A Finance Minister for a while. Anyway, this fellow ran an insurance racket.'

I had that sensation of forgotten knowledge being nudged back into memory: 'Oh, I think I vaguely recall that little weasel.'

'Yes. He persuaded Old Smoothie to go along with his scheme. If you do that, of course, you have got to get it absolutely right. So, supposedly two hundred million dollars' worth of cargo was sent in transit up the coast on an old tub. Not surprisingly, it sank in the mildest of storms.'

'OK. I think I see where this is going.'

'So, anyway, the insurers in New York, doing their due diligence, sent divers in. What they found was not military hardware at all, but a load of old scrap metal, which had already been blown to bits in an explosion.'

'Before the storm, obviously.'

'You got it. So the police started poking around and our friend made a dash for it. Washed up here with a price on his head. Amazing what cosmetic surgery can do these days, but I know it's him.'

'And what exactly is he doing here, apart from hiding?'

'He lives frugally, on the face of it, but he must have something stashed away from his halcyon days. His girlfriend's a beautician and a sex therapist, and they've set up a blue movie business.'

'Talk about landing on your feet! So is this character dangerous?'

'He's the kind would love a presidential pardon - "Can I do anything at all to clean up for you, Your Excellency?" - so I would say so, yes. If I see him again, I'll surreptitiously take his picture. I wish I'd been quicker last time. I mention him because he's the kind of creep who's around these days.'

I told him about Serena's desire for bodyguards. I asked him about a support network for our exiles he'd once told me about. 'Would they provide them?' I asked.

'They would,' he replied sagely, 'but I wouldn't recommend it. Who's to say it isn't infiltrated with Rats by now? And some of the security agencies are fronts for the local Mafia, and I certainly couldn't recommend *them*.'

'I'm a little out of touch, aren't I?' I said.

'I think that's because you haven't had to worry about an attack since you've been here. And maybe also, without knowing it, you've gone a little soft, if you forgive me saying so. Anyway, I'll get back to you with some hired muscle. I need to be back at the stall. I've just remembered that there's a man coming, hoping to sell me a splinter from the Holy Cross of Jesus.' Seeing my expression, he merely added, 'Don't ask!'

5
TIME IN GOVERNMENT

Late that evening, I saw an interview on TV with a former local politician whose autobiography had just been published. He'd had a controversial career, and the interviewer posed some tough questions. I was impressed with the way the politician confidently deflected any question that might embarrass him.

Waiting for Serena to return from her evening out, I fell asleep on the sofa for a few minutes, during which time I dreamt that I was put on trial over my political career. Instead of one prosecutor, however, I had a series of accusers, none of whom I recognised from real life.

The first critic, a man dressed in what appeared to be farming clothes, said, 'Your government was heartless. You cared nothing for the poor.'

In response, I found I was unable to speak. I was determined to defend myself, but as I tried to say the words no sound came out. I feared I was about to be found guilty for want of a defence, when a woman stood up. It wasn't Serena and vaguely looked like a woman I knew called Andrea - oval face, dark slicked-back hair - who'd served in the same government as me. She turned out to be my advocate. She said, 'The government could have done more, but this man showed great humanity.' This was sycophantic nonsense, but it appealed to my vanity and sounded convincing.

Next to make an accusation was a soldier. He said, 'As defence minister he was too soft.' This stung me. It was my deepest fear that people thought me weak.

My advocate made the case that I was there to avoid conflict, not merely pursue it, and besides, military campaigns on my watch had gone well. She did her best, but I felt there was a hollowness about her argument. The fact was, I'd been defence minister when the coup happened, which I saw as a personal failure.

Finally, another woman stood up, probably a teacher, and she criticised me for 'a lack of imagination'.

This time, my advocate was strong in her rebuttal: 'Others in the cabinet looked to him for his imagination, since none of the others showed signs of possessing this precious gift, and we were all too aware of this. As a consequence, he became an engine of ideas on all manner of subjects, all of which were warmly received.'

I thought this was going rather well, but then the judge unexpectedly intervened, saying, 'But those ideas were never used, except as a foil for other ministers' own agendas, which were always, through the use of intricate reasoning, to essentially leave everything exactly as before - a slight movement of the same old furniture, pretending to themselves they were embracing change.'

My advocate sought to intervene at this point, but the judge raised his hand to indicate he would not be interrupted, 'For them it was all about power and holding it at all costs, rather than using it to make the country a better place to live in. True, he clashed with them over this, but to them it was merely jousting. Their collective lack of foresight secured their removal - and his.' I thought to myself: is this man ever going to stop? He was destroying me. He continued, 'Of course, this is my own view of events, which is entirely biased, and there are other versions, including other versions of my own, all with the same inevitable conclusion.'

Allowing no further comment from anyone else, the judge then announced, 'Accordingly, I find this man and the government he served in guilty of incompetence, weakness, hubris, and a fatal lack of imagination.' A woman then started screaming from the public gallery. I instinctively knew it was Serena and could see she was armed with a shotgun.

At that moment, I woke up, feeling both aggrieved and depressed at the proceedings, and cheated at not discovering what Serena could do with the gun. I poured myself a glass of port, drank it straight down, and then went to bed.

6
HIRED MUSCLE

Russo promptly arranged 'hired muscle' for us. Whilst I was still not entirely convinced of the need, I accepted it was best not to take any chance with our security. I could also see an unspoken benefit in that I was beginning to suspect Serena was having an affair, having noticed not only more instances of 'I'm staying overnight with a girlfriend,' but more disappearances in the afternoon than before, and so protection could easily double as surveillance if necessary. This line of thought also led to the notion in my mind that Serena's insistence on the appointment of bodyguards might in itself be an act of deceit, trying to steer me to the conclusion that she could not possibly want another person with her all the time, if what she desired was more privacy for secret assignations. I knew her well enough to believe her not incapable of such a deception.

The two bodyguards arrived together. They were young, not tough-looking but tall and lean, exuding a quiet strength. Zico was mine, an angular-faced Slavic blond, just the sort Serena probably fantasised about, whereas hers, Julia, was also blonde, with high cheekbones and blue eyes. I immediately liked them both, but, at the same time, I would not have wanted to be on the wrong side of either of them in a fight.

We had an informal chat about what we thought we needed, their capabilities and experience. I was cautiously optimistic that they would prove ideal for us. Once the brief initial meeting was over and they'd gone, Serena said to me, 'Trust you to be assigned the handsome young man. I would have rather liked to be able to show him off - the Ladies Circle would think he's my gigolo. That would be a joy.' I could only smile weakly. 'They don't exactly look like our children,' she added.

'We can always pretend,' I said, though not keen to dwell on this subject, since Serena had been unable to have children herself, much to her private distress. I hardened my heart: part of Zico's responsibilities would be to report back whenever Serena told Julia she didn't need her. I'd cook her goose in its own fat, I said to myself.

7
EXILE

I went over in my mind the implications of our recruitment of bodyguards and to what extent it could change my admittedly rather languid approach to life in exile. We were used to bodyguards from my time in public office, but I'd thought, perhaps naively, that in exile we would not be at realistic risk. I was mulling this over as I watched a news programme on which appeared a report about an exile being shot (although from the programme's perspective he was called an 'immigrant'), and a debate followed about the 'migrant issue' and whether the normally tolerant hosts were at last running out of patience.

I felt I would have liked to speak up for the exiles, misunderstood as we believed we were. We often wished to be inconspicuous, but could never entirely achieve it. Even though we dressed like the locals, spoke the same language as they, enjoyed the same jokes, frequented many of the same restaurants, followed the same teams, we were still always apart, never quite fitting in. Even if we never opened our mouths to speak, we gave our otherness away by some (to us) imperceptible sign. Amongst the locals, even the most rackety good-for-nothings gave themselves airs in our presence, whilst even the most kindhearted and sophisticated would say to us, 'So tell us why you're here.'

Now and then, usually following some reported crime or other, the locals noticed us exiles a little too closely and found us an increasing nuisance. 'Keep the foreigners out,' we'd hear sometimes; 'Throw foreigners out,' someone would utter in the street and, in our minds at least, 'Death to foreigners,' would logically not be far behind. We were seen as representatives of a nation too stupid to prevent autocracy, too backward to avoid despotism and purges, and an unwelcome and all too real reminder that chaos, whilst it might be well hidden, was always close at hand. But, we reminded ourselves, we were here by right, not charity. The irony was that this new country was not even richer, either materially or culturally, and most of the rich were foreigners anyway, and there were millions of poor people too. There were merely more people in the middle here. 'A nation of pigs and dogs' was how Serena rather ungraciously described our hosts, although she'd used the same expression privately for people in the old country as well; indeed, many times in the past. In truth, no country could be good enough for her. It was something in her nature made her like to remind the world that every apple had its worm, every summer had its pestilential flies, and every land, be it of eternal peace, uninterrupted balmy weather, and blissful hosts, would still not measure up to her ideal.

We, and those of our fellow expatriates we knew, felt we were living in a kind of psychological ghetto, a feeling of, at times, intense isolation, although in our case it was to some degree self-imposed, for we had taken pains to stay as aloof as possible from the gossip and tittle-tattle from home that might otherwise consume all our time. Not that we had given up on our country; indeed, in our private world we waited for a time of reckoning, even recompense, whilst scarcely believing that such a time would ever come. We still imagined ourselves as having, even in our absence, an enduring significance back home, whilst all too aware we meant nothing here. We were unlike the opera singer who, in the old days, lived at the end of our street, and who three years ago had seen her husband, now deceased, arrested at four in the morning, never to return; yet despite, or perhaps because of, her predicament, she had persisted with her career, now singing in venues far more prestigious than any her home country could have offered. And we were even more unlike the younger exiles, who hungered most of all. We assured ourselves that if we were younger, we too would see this new life as an opportunity, as even some of our contemporaries did, but Serena and I felt stuck, as though caught in mid-air between two trapeze bars, emotionally in neither one place nor the other. We deplored our lack of ambition, our burnt-out talent, passing our time dreaming up strategies for imaginary political parties and make-believe laws for a country we knew in our hearts no longer existed, even if it ever had.

The old country was not going to give us another chance. It had never welcomed its exiles back, but in our most resilient dreams the despised Smooth Killer was certain to fall, and whoever replaced him would feel compelled to invite us back in. And in my wilder moments I thought how in every age our country had needed a military hero to save it, and now and then I even fantasised that I could become the latest saviour, recognising, however, that such a saviour invariably ended up as the latest despot. I had learned from history and knew the value of patience. I could hold myself in readiness for the time being, quietly, telling no-one of my grandiose ideas, not even Serena or Russo, whilst openly maintaining my regular practice of marksmanship skills at a target range, something I'd always done, even when in government; only when under house arrest had it been impossible. It only needed one glance in the bathroom mirror, however, to remind me I was too old to fulfil such a fantasy, although perhaps not too old for the skills of the solitary sniper that I could still imagine myself one day using to impact the theatre of politics.

Compared to most of my compatriots abroad, I was outwardly doing well. Why, for example, was Russo, for all the sharpness, even brilliance, of his mind and his investigative skill, buying and selling tat in a rundown market? And why was he living (to quote his own words) in 'elegant but lonely squalor'? And what of the old wretches I often saw, living out their tepid lives in rat-ridden, derelict streets, incognito or merely forgotten ('Been there decades,' according to Russo), despised by their reluctant hosts in a country whose government made a show of falling over itself to stay neutral regarding the Smooth Killer's antics? On any given early afternoon when it wasn't raining, I could find my countrymen sat sullenly on rotting benches in a desolate city square, trying to ignore the smell of the local food, greasy and overcooked, thick in the air around them, amongst the brightly-dressed office workers and itinerant sales reps who, unluckily for them, had no smarter place in the sun to spend their lunch break.

As the weeks and months trickled by, we came to the quiet conclusion that exile would be permanent. Seeing the old country on TV and in the newspapers being destroyed from within, and feeling powerless to do anything to prevent it, weighed heavily upon us, confined as we were to the odd letter to the press or dry comment on social media, as well as the occasional call to a former associate, who was no better placed to know anything than we were.

We received word now and then, sometimes weeks later, of the most recent death amongst former associates and old friends, most of whose funerals we were prevented from attending, since to attempt to do so was to invite arrest. Such sad news stirred nostalgia in us for the ambitions we once held and brought to mind stories of otherwise forgotten conflicts. Telling ourselves lies about how good the old country was, we clung to our myths about it (even about things we'd despised at the time), or rather, they clung to us like old, indestructible moss, we scarcely realising they were myths, always with eyes to the past because the future was too unclear and too unappealing. Amnesia was the way out for many, drinking themselves into oblivion. Meanwhile, the richest amongst us dawdled through life in idle and unsatisfying luxury, with all their carefully preserved grudges and resentments intact, and the oldest merely sat around, trapped in their uselessness, drifting towards death.

As regards the employment of bodyguards: although it had not been my idea, I could see they would have a value beyond the physical benefits. They would serve as a constant reminder of our own mortality and this might wrench us out of our languorous ways. Moreover, if we needed bodyguards, and I now conceded that a clear-eyed, neutral assessment would confirm we did, it meant there was something in ourselves to protect and, thus, our lives had value. If there was nothing of value in us, there would be nothing to protect.

8
SURVEILLANCE

On the first day of service of what Serena grandly called 'our security detail', the two of them checked all the rooms for surveillance devices. They found none, although disconcertingly Zico quipped, 'To be honest, you'd hardly need them here with these thin walls.' This comment caused Serena to grimace and reinforced the feeling in both of us that this apartment, for all its 'Hollywood hints' and kidney-shaped pool, was not a home we should make permanent.

It was only a couple of days after they'd started at the (according to Russo) 'specially low rate' of $200 a day for the pair of them, that Julia remarked to us, 'We've noticed you have a friend outside.'

'Oh no!' I immediately opened the lounge curtains. Sure enough, as I did so a black car with tinted windows pulled away from its parking space across the street. I scrambled for a pen to write down the registration, but found the number had escaped me.

'Don't worry,' Zico said, smiling. 'I took a photograph. It's registered to a company.'

'Are you sure they're watching this place?' I asked, then noticed Serena's face was a picture of barely repressed panic.

'Pretty much sure, yes. They're not very good. They sit there up the street, never exiting the car, never doing anything to suggest they might have some legitimate business. We will always check your car for devices anyway.'

'What sort of device?' Serena asked nervously.

'Tracking devices. Also explosives.' Zico's matter-of-fact tone unnerved her even more.

'My God!' she exclaimed, shaking.

'Serena,' I said, 'it's no different from the old days back home. Bombs were a part of daily life there for a while.'

'Yes,' she replied, 'But that was almost a war situation with terrorists running about. It was a fight for the soul of the nation. But why now? The idea that evil people are trying to do it to us now is totally outrageous.'

I was tempted to remind her that this was the reason for securing Zico and Julia in the first place but thought better of it. She wasn't in the mood for cool discussion. That the 'evil people' might have been watching the apartment every day and we hadn't even noticed it, was not something she could allow herself to contemplate.

'Of course, we might be wrong,' Zico said hurriedly, rather transparently trying to rescue the situation, but a little too late.

'I trust your instinct and I thank you for telling us,' Serena replied portentously. 'It is just another cross I'll have to bear, but I will carry it - with all the others.' And with that she retired to the kitchen to make tea, which was her customary way of securing the final word.

9
INSECURITY

One evening, after Zico and Julia had left for the day, Serena was sat half-watching the TV ads when she sighed, 'Well, I don't know how long I can put up with all this!'

'All what?' I asked her.

'It's this bodyguard business.'

'Bodyguard business? But it was your idea. You insisted.'

'I know, I know. It was my suggestion. But now we've got them, I'm really not so sure. I don't know about you, but I feel like a prisoner in my own home sometimes. Except it's not our home, is it?'

Her gaze flicked disapprovingly over the various items of furniture, each bearing witness to our temporary status, none matching, none to her taste, nor, for that matter, mine.

'It reminds me of when we were under house arrest,' she continued. 'Oh, I shudder at the memory of that!'

I could empathise with her regarding the flat, although I suspected there was more to her change of heart about the bodyguards than she was letting on.

'How do you find Julia?' I asked her.

'She's very pleasant, but it's not like when we had bodyguards before.'

'It's not like then because we didn't have to pay for them ourselves.'

'No, I mean, you had one of the top jobs in government, and they were part of what went with it. Life was busy - it's not, now - and everything we were doing seemed worthwhile.' She gave the room another imperious sweep of her eyes. 'And we weren't in such *reduced* circumstances. Here I feel trapped but without the trappings, if you get my drift. In the old days, if someone tried to attack me - I say "tried" because they would have failed - as you know, I can take care of myself - it would have been a national event. Here no-one would be in the least bit bothered. Incidentally, have you ever seen a police car around here? They only go out when some TV presenter can't find their phone, and then they roar over there in convoy for a photo opportunity. It was in the papers. If something happened to me, they wouldn't even open a file. At least, back home, with all the backhanders they got, the police would actually turn up. Here, I think they're bribed to do absolutely nothing. Oh, I can't believe the depths we've sunk to! And the way things are going, we'll carry on sinking, I don't doubt it.' Her face was filled with tears. If it wasn't for the wrinkles she could have been a girl of ten.

'So Julia's OK then?' I asked, keen to nudge her off her self pity.

'I suppose so. Can't say I have any real criticism... yet. Not exactly taxing work.'

'Oh, I have to disagree,' I said.

'But I thought it would be one of ours, or a local. I can't read her mind. No idea what she's thinking. And what do you disagree with about it not being taxing work?'

'Because they have to be all ears and eyes. You know that. Zico may look half asleep, but he's as sharp as anything. Russo found them for us. He knows what he's about.'

'Well, that explains a lot. You didn't tell me he was involved. I should have guessed. That little hustler!'

'He got us the best deal going and, I must say, I'm very happy with the arrangement,' I declared gamely.

'But I'm not. And why isn't there someone here now?'

'No need. A security man's downstairs all night. Seems professional. Certainly should be for what we're paying for this place.'

She was unimpressed: 'I bet if you went down there at one or two in the morning, you'd find him fast asleep. You know he drinks.'

'OK, but remember, if there's any trouble...' I parried.

'Oh, yes, your precious - what is it? - Oh yes, your precious Glock.' She pointed vaguely in the direction of our bedroom. 'You told me it's not even loaded. What use is that? If someone wanted to force their way in here, it would take them ten seconds to waltz past that deadbeat downstairs, run up here, and our front door's not going to stop them.'

'It would slow them down.'

'Barely time to say your prayers. And by the time you've got your gun sorted out, I'd be lying there dead, shot through the heart. A victim of terror. And even then it would take the police a week to get here! But at least I would have died in a democracy. No, if we're going to have bodyguards, we should do it properly. If I'm at the tennis club and Julia's in there with me, who's keeping an eye on the street? I think we need two bodyguards each in the daytime and at least one at night.'

'That'd cost a fortune!' I protested. She gave me a look of shock, so completely artificial that it annoyed me. 'Alright,' I said, 'if it'll make you happy, I'll get you your own private army!'

'No need to be facetious. We're talking about life and death here.'

'I don't know why you're so worried,' I said. 'It's me they'd be after. Believe it or not, they probably don't know who you are.'

'Don't know who I am?' She sounded wounded, her forehead tilted back as though hit by a sharp stone. 'Well, if they shot you and left me alive, they'd soon find out! I'd be straight round to the Chief of Police's office and I'd demand to see him, even if they have to drag him out of his favourite brothel, and I'd say to him, "Look, whatever the Rats are paying you to do nothing, I'll pay you double to get off your arse and arrest these people - money no object!"'

Money no object. If her grandpa had known Latin, it could have been her family motto: *Nihil pecuniae*.

'Look, if we can't afford it,' she continued, 'why are we even living here? It's not as if we enjoy it. The building's so noisy, it's like living in a shanty town sometimes. All it needs is a scrawny chicken to wander in, or a few stray bullets flying in through the window. No, it's only a matter of time. I feel I can't go on living here. And since we can't go home, we should at least move somewhere safer.'

'The countryside?' I suggested, knowing it wouldn't suit her.

'No, that would be intolerable. And those pretty-looking places by the sea have all kinds of problems. And what would I do there? No, I have to live in a city. Somewhere like Italy - perhaps Rome or Venice. At least they have a decent culture. I've been thinking I'd rather take on a new identity. That's what they do with crime witnesses. And that's what we are essentially: witnesses to the theft of our country by a gangster. Oh, it makes my blood boil with rage to think of that odious man...'

'The Smooth Killer?' I interjected.

'Yes, who else? Running the show. Running it into the ground, more like.'

She had got herself into a state again, so I poured us both a whisky.

'Thank you, darling,' she said, lighting a cigarette. 'By the way, those fancy panic button things, GPS and all that, they've given us...'

'Yes?'

'I can't abide them. If I tell Julia I don't need her for a couple of hours, I don't want her being able to know where I am. I should be allowed *some* privacy.'

'OK.' I was non-committal.

'I mean, I'm sure the two of them share secrets. I've heard them gabbling away in a foreign language, knowing we can't understand them.'

'They're supposed to be discreet,' I said. 'It's pretty fundamental to their training.'

'I know, but, after all...'. She leaned back theatrically, taking a long drag and blowing out the smoke forcefully. 'After all, to take an entirely hypothetical example: if I was having an affair, I would like to think Zico wasn't able to blab about it to you.' She paused, as if taken aback by her own candour, but I caught her glance checking my face for a reaction. She was testing me, telling me she knew that I knew. Well, God bless her, but the fancy panic button things were staying.

10
OUR FRIEND

At Russo's request, I met him in a bar after he'd packed up his business for the day. It was a surprising request, in that customarily we met in the morning or early afternoon at his market stall and went from there to a nearby café.

I noticed, when we'd sat down with our drinks, that he was not as relaxed as usual. He'd told me on the phone he had a couple of things he wanted to talk to me about.

The bar was quiet with just a few people, mainly office workers finished for the day.

'You should see it on a warm Friday evening,' he said. 'Absolutely buzzing. So how's the hired muscle working out?'

'Zico and Julia are great. I'm happy, they're happy (so far as I can tell), and the only one who isn't is Serena.'

'That's a shame,' he said.

'Yes, she says it cramps her style. We don't have them all the time anyway. For instance, Zico's not here right now. He's a good man. The thing I particularly like about him is that he's not ex-army. Incredibly focused and alert, but very calm at the same time. With a former soldier, you never know what you'll get. It can be like having an attack dog. No, seriously, they can get bored easily and can't wait to rip into someone. We had one like that in the old days. I think he'd been a mercenary somewhere. If he went with Serena on a shopping trip, she'd come back a nervous wreck. He nearly caused an international incident once - got in a spat with one of the King of Somewhere's bodyguards. After that and two other embarrassing incidents, we had to replace him. Even then, he argued like the Devil; he turned up drunk, and Serena chased him down the street with an antique malacca swordstick she'd just bought. The neighbours were all cheering - they were terrified of him.'

'Is she having an affair, by the way?' he asked.

I paused, taken aback by his question, then said blandly, 'Pretty sure she is.

More or less admitted it.'

'How are you about it?'

'Truthfully, some days it breaks my heart. Nostalgia, you know. Other times, I feel excited. Maybe her lover's rich and she'll give me a divorce. Someone else can pay for her designer dresses. She lives in the past, I'm afraid. A past where money doesn't matter.'

'Well,' he said, 'you did well to get your bodyguards when you did. The way things are going, everyone we know will want them.'

'Why, because of our friend, Old Smoothie? What's he up to now?'

'They call it his *exceptionalist* phase. He's like an old-fashioned monarch: in his own world, by his own rules. Those ministers who tell him the truth are sacked because the truth's too awful, and those who lie to him are sacked or worse when he finds them out. He knows that there's few dictators die peacefully in their beds. He wants Congress to give former presidents immunity for past actions...'

'For when he's one himself.'

'Right. And the last flickering lights of opposition are secretly doing whatever they can to prevent it. At the same time, he has more military purges than some people have enemas. There won't be any military hierarchy left soon. You never know, you could get your old job back.'

I sniggered, unsure which job he meant, not that I cared much.

He continued, 'He's convinced there'll be a coup attempt and it will be financed from here.'

'Much as I hate him,' I said, 'I wouldn't wish it on the country. They might get someone worse. I nearly said "We might" then. I still have that attachment.'

'So do I,' he said sadly. 'It never goes.'

'So, old friend, what is it you wanted to talk to me about? Unless it's you Serena's having an affair with.'

He blushed slightly, and for a brief moment I forgot the incongruity of this notion. He laughed, 'I declare my innocence! She's a good woman, though. I like a woman with spirit.'

'Well, you didn't invite me here to talk about politics either. We can still do that on the phone. You know I'd see you anytime - I'm not exactly busy - but I sensed when we spoke that you were worried about something. Not like you at all.' I looked straight into his eyes, which were those of someone who hadn't slept properly in days. 'What's on your mind?'

'I'll get some beers,' he said, immediately getting to his feet.

'My turn,' I protested.

'No,' he insisted, and as he reached my side of the table on his way to the bar, he said quietly, 'I fancy standing for a bit. Do you mind?' When we were at the bar, he said, 'Don't look round, but I think someone's following me and they're here now. People have been at the stall when I'm not there asking questions about me: where I go, who do I know? I don't like it one bit.'

I bought the beers and then said, 'I'm not comfortable at the bar because of what you've told me. Let's go back to where we were sitting.' As we walked back, I took a quick scan of the room. When we'd sat down, I said, 'Is our friend the one in the long coat, with the newspaper and the Coke he's hardly touched?'

'Yes,' he said.

'OK. I'm going to assume he can read your lips, but I'm sure he can't see mine. If he moves around at all, tap your nose. What is it you want - just to know, or also what's behind it?'

'The former.'

'OK. You could confront him, although I wouldn't. He'd just deny it and you'd be none the wiser, but he would. Give me a couple of minutes to think and, as there's the two of us, we can do a routine which will prove if you are being followed. Well, no bookmaker would give you odds. Up for it?'

He nodded. He looked so vulnerable at that moment that it felt strange to me. It reminded me of how usually it was *he* who had all the answers, knew the right contacts and the ways to get things done. But his blind spot was that he thought he was immune from political events. It was as though, as a former journalist, he saw himself as a mere observer of such things; he couldn't see that even the observer was never completely neutral. Thus, the idea that he, ostensibly a non-politician, might attract hostile surveillance, was something he couldn't cope with.

While I worked out the routine in my head, he told me a story about a woman who'd brought a stuffed ostrich to the stall to sell, a Jack Russell terrier had attacked it while they were discussing the price, and an altercation with the dog's owner had then ensued. Afterwards, I said, 'OK, I'll tell you the routine and if anything's unclear, or doesn't make sense, just say "Really?"'

I went through it, and when he said 'OK' I began the routine itself by offering him another drink. He demurred after checking his watch, said he needed to be somewhere else, and stood up.

I said, 'Come on, just a quick one for the road.'

He reluctantly acquiesced and sat down. I went to the bar and bought a large beer for myself and the small one he'd insisted on. We took our time and talked about nothing. I thought we might as well make our friend suffer, which was a little risky because if he got bored he might just walk out, which would be a disaster with nothing resolved. Then Russo made another performance of getting up, looking at his watch, and declaring a little loudly that he needed to be on his way. I stood up and said, 'See you soon,' and shook his hand. As he was about to leave, he pretended to answer his phone and then ran up the stairs to the exit.

Less than thirty seconds later, I watched our friend, the potential 'snout', leave, walking awkwardly like someone wanting to run but constraining himself from doing so.

After another half minute, I left. I was not convinced Russo was being followed, but if he was, my main concern was how he'd deal with knowing it.

11
ROUTINE

As I sauntered up the steps to the bar's exit, I couldn't resist a feeling of quiet pride. In only a few minutes I'd devised a routine which, if Russo was being followed, would confirm it within an inch of certainty. He was pleased with it, and this had settled him. The only point bothering me was that the plan started with him as someone ostensibly in a hurry, but then required him to some extent to dawdle. My error. One moment, a creation was perfect, a work of genius; the next, it was flawed, perhaps even mediocre. Moreover, the long, straight street, bright, clear and relatively empty an hour ago, was now overcast, rain-threatened, and busy with cars and pedestrian commuters. Most worrying of all, there was no sign of either my friend or his suspected follower. I let my eyes acclimatise to the bustle, but there was still no sign. It had only been a minute - where were they? The thought flashed through my mind, followed by a thud in the stomach, that I'd fallen for one of the softest sucker punches of my life (and I'd taken a few): the man in the long coat was not some lowlife earning pennies following a stranger around, but a hired killer. I cursed my stupidity and began to panic for my friend. To make the situation worse, neither of us was armed - Russo never took even the most reasonable of precautions, and I hadn't seen the need for a weapon on this occasion. We were two prize dummies, especially me: one of my oldest and best friends had sought my help, and my fancy plan in response had put him in greater danger than before. He was nothing on the political scene now, but, at least amongst us exiles, he was high visibility and well-known. His harmlessness was his protection, but it was a false one: if you wanted to spread fear in a community, who better to target than someone with no apparent clout that everyone knew? In my mind, I was at his funeral, delivering a eulogy whilst keenly and secretly aware that my stupidity had led to his demise.

I felt the first raindrops on my hatless head, and they were almost a gentle relief. I studied hard all the people I could see: their hair, their height, their gait, a few obscured by umbrellas. I walked down the street in the direction I'd told Russo, a hundred yards or so down one side and back on the other, staring into every shop doorway and alleyway and every side-street as far as

I could see. Nothing. Frustrated, the only answer was to phone him and thereby break the routine, which did not allow for us to talk to each other. I had to know that he wasn't bleeding to death in a garden or car park somewhere. It was a long ring until I gave up and crossed the street to the bus stop to take shelter. As I was about to try again, my phone rang. It was him: 'Sorry about that, Boss.'

'Where are you?' I said agitatedly. 'Are you OK?'

'I'm in Mateos.'

'Mateos? What's that?'

'You know - clothes shop. They've got a sale on. I started looking in the window, like you said, and saw some lovely shirts - bright colours but not garish and at knockdown prices - so I went in. Some real bargains. Just settling up when you rang. You OK? Sound a bit breathless.'

'No, I'm fine.'

'Good. Only I feel very relaxed about it all now. Your plan - your routine as you call it - is brilliant. I suddenly feel in control. This is actually quite fun. Shame about the rain. Got my hat. You?'

'No.'

'Buy you a cap while I'm here? Some nice sporty ones. Would suit you.'

'No thanks.'

'Yes, I feel so much better after our chat. You had it all covered.'

'Thanks.'

'I feel, if they want to waste their time following me, then let them. I'll waste their time for them. They're not going to kill me, are they?'

'No.'

'I'm not worth them wasting their bullets on. They'd want them back. I'm a nobody.'

'I'm glad you feel better. So you're not really bothered if they're following you. Good. I can't see our friend anywhere, so I think we can call it off for today.'

'The routine? Oh no, that would be a shame. After you went to all that trouble, I'd still like to know. It's a good plan, and we should see it through. I'm quite enjoying it, actually. Bit of a laugh, don't you think?'

'Bit of a laugh, yes,' I replied, trying not to sound glum. I ended the call confused: glad at my friend's improved state of mental health, but feeling a hundred years old. I brought my focus back to the task. The absence of the snout proved nothing. He most likely went home. I kept my eye on Mateos while briefly enjoying the din of a rock band practising over a nearby electrical shop.

A now be-hatted and happy Russo finally emerged on the street with a bright yellow carrier bag. At least I would't lose him. As for the snout, there was still no sign. I'd give it five more minutes. The street was quiet again - less commuters, the rain easing off.

After a minute, I was startled by the sight of the man in the long coat stepping out of a small wine merchants, at which he'd ostensibly bought nothing, only a few yards in front of me. I only hoped he hadn't seen me earlier looking for Russo. I watched as he walked briskly in my friend's direction and then suddenly slowed down. I sent Russo the signal - two rings - and he speeded up. So did the snout. This was more like it. I sent another signal. Russo slowed, looking in a window. The snout, however, did not. He was almost level with Russo and then disappeared into Starbucks. What was that about? Puzzled, I let Russo loiter, gradually wandering out of probable sight of the coffee shop. It would be better if he crossed the street, but the flawed plan didn't allow for that. I could ring him again but couldn't face hearing about how much fun he was having. The snout stayed in the coffee shop. Maybe he knew what we were up to, or wasn't a snout at all. In vain, I watched every person leaving Starbucks. I was about to call it off when my gaze caught a man walking briskly from the coffee shop and then slowing down for no apparent reason. I started ambling down the street so I could keep him in view, but stopped before Starbucks in case the man in the long coat, Snout One, was on the lookout from there. Russo was still idling, but the new man, who I believed was Snout Two, had speeded up and was about to overtake him, at which point I turned and hurried back to the bus stop.

Still nothing resolved; only theories. I took the first bus, remembering to keep my back to Starbucks as we passed it. I travelled two stops, by which time the bus had passed both men. I got off the bus and waited at the stop, momentarily relaxed, the rain having eased, but became immediately alarmed on finding Snout Two standing right next to me - a young man with short but untidy blond hair and gaunt features. I could feel my anxiety at being unarmed revive. Russo by now was opposite us, outside the Bulstrode Bar, supposedly talking on his phone. I walked about fifteen yards on to a taxi rank and positioned myself next to a fake Rolex salesman, whilst listening partly to a young woman playing a tin whistle and partly to a drunken argument between a smart-looking couple fresh from the races, while the smell from a nearby Chinese kitchen made me hungry.

After hanging around for a couple more minutes, Russo went into the bar; I observed Snout Two cross the road to do the same. I took the first available cab round to the front of the Bulstrode, gave the driver some cash, and got him to agree to wait for 'Mr Sloan', assuring him the gentleman in question would not be drunk. I sent Russo a signal, went inside and ran down the poorly-lit, musty-smelling stairway. Russo passed me, but we didn't acknowledge each other. At the bottom of the stairs was a swing door, and I made as if to stumble, thereby preventing any exit for a few precious seconds. I kept my head down and didn't look up when an angry-sounding man forced his way through and hurled himself up the stairs. I followed cautiously up. There, looking frantically up and down the street was Snout Two - no Russo, no cab, just a fresh wave of commuters. I took a photograph of him, then returned downstairs for a quick drink. Bit of a laugh? I was a nervous wreck. Afterwards, I made my way to the taxi rank for a car to take me to our rendezvous.

12
MR SLOAN

Twenty minutes later, I was being led to Russo's table at the expensive steak restaurant he'd chosen. I found him sitting in a private booth.

'So romantic!' I remarked.

'Inquisitive ears,' he said. 'Or should that be *acquisitive* ears?' When I'd sat down, he said, 'OK, my friend, what do you think?' I explained that it was pretty clear he was being followed. He was unfazed by this: 'It was an interesting experiment wasn't it?'

'You might say.'

'I like the moniker *Mr Sloan*. I felt decidedly and, dare I say, *deliciously* English posh. I might use *Mr Sloan* in some of my future business dealings. People might think I know what I'm talking about.'

'I shouldn't worry unduly,' I said drily.

'But I don't think I've ever spent as much time at shop windows, and I'd certainly never set foot in the Bulstrode Bar, that ponced-up place. Too much cocaine in there for an innocent like me.'

'How dreadful, my dear! You don't know the half of it, though, I'm sure.'

'But it was ideal for the taxi rank, I'll grant you that. Like I said on the phone, if you don't care that you're being followed it's actually quite fun. The only thing that still bugs me is: why me?'

It hadn't exactly been fun for me, but I decided I'd play along with him: 'OK, Mr Sloan, Sir, any dispute concerning your current business? Offloaded any expensive fakes recently?'

'No. Not at all. Nothing that would warrant surveillance on anyone's part.'

'OK, Sir, have you been hiding secret income from the taxman?'

'No.'

'Not fooling around with anyone's wife, Sir?'

'Only yours. I mean, no.'

'OK, Mr Sloan, any issues concerning our dear president, His Excellency, the Smooth Killer?'

'No, although it was me that coined the name Smooth Killer in the first place, inspired, I think, by the Michael Jackson song *Smooth Criminal*.'

'No prizes for fancy erudition here, Mr Sloan.'

'Plus, I wrote a highly critical, but entirely accurate, article about him, on the way to the airport on my last day in the country. Since then, silence.'

'OK. Any truth in the story, widely touted, that you tried to seduce His Excellency's beloved daughter into evil ways?'

'Widely touted? Get lost. It was no more than a silly rumour.'

'You know how it works, Mr Sloan, Sir: today's silly rumour is tomorrow's history.'

'But I made it up myself.'

'That's even worse. You know spreading falsehoods is a crime against the state. You're lucky it's only surveillance.'

'Stop it. But why after so many years?'

'Never underestimate the abominable power of grudges, Mr Sloan. Or the abominable power of boredom. You can imagine him sitting in the palace saying, "Tell me, underling, who was that journalist creature who insulted me four years ago?" "Which one, Your Excellency? There have been so many; that is, there have been a few." "I don't know. There must be one who never went to prison who should have done. Well, find him, whoever he is." "Absolutely, Your Excellency."'

I paused, suddenly feeling thirsty. 'Sorry to be boring,' I said, 'but do we get service here?'

Russo, embarrassed, immediately called a waiter over, and after we'd ordered he said, 'It doesn't worry me as such - our friend, I mean. It just puzzles me. But enough of that...' He was holding my gaze tightly. 'I really wanted to talk about you.'

'Me? There's nothing to talk about.'

'Exactly. So, what are you doing these days?'

'I ask myself that every day. Then I go back to sleep until noon.'

I changed the subject, but a little later he asked, 'Ever think of going back?'

'The old country? No. The only person who'd care is our dear president. It'd be automatic gaol without charge. No, thank you.'

'But you commanded an army once. Hard to believe.'

'Thanks.'

'You could do it again.'

I began to feel alarmed. 'What do you mean - lead a ramshackle band of dissidents? You're joking. And don't you think the dissidents, many of whom will remember me from my Ministry of Defence days, would have something to say about it? I don't understand. What is this: *Your Country Needs You* week?'

'But it does need you. Not just you. People like you with experience and knowledge, who sit around regretting and wishing and feeling sorry for themselves.'

'Look, I did my stint, both in the armed forces and in the cabinet. When I was defence minister we won three quite limited border wars, none of which we started. I liked those little border wars. There were few casualties, and they kept the armed forces on their toes. Otherwise, they become lazy and corrupt. And you know as well as I do, that the borderlands are always a toxic playground for traffickers, gangsters and every kind of crook and shady dealer. The occasional skirmish kept it in check. We also foiled two attempted coups, and then, admittedly, things got murkier. The economy got in trouble, everyone on strike.'

'That time was awful.'

'It was. The Boss, as we called him, the president at the time, wanted to go in hard on the troublemakers, send in the troops and all that. I wanted us to negotiate with them. I was worried the country could spin out of control. You know what I mean: street violence, random killings, grievance riots, growing widespread unrest leading to possible civil war. The government dithered, and it was easy to see a situation of spiralling failure developing...'

'It was such a shame because that government did a lot of good.'

'Thank you. I like to think, despite all the problems, we did achieve something worthwhile.'

'Poverty rates down, literacy...'

'But the Smooth Killer was waiting for the right moment, and he pounced. The reluctant saviour. And the worst of it was that people *cheered*.'

'I know. That was heartbreaking. So, with hindsight, you blame the Boss?'

'I do. It was his fault, but it was mine too. I should have argued harder, I should have convinced him. Or I should have shut up. I feel guilty every time I think about it, which is just about every day. I tell myself there'd have been a coup anyway, but I don't believe it. Nothing I can do about it now, though.'

I fell silent as the waiter arrived with our drinks. Afterwards, Russo said, 'You say all this, but, think about it, you could be there now - false passport, disguise, fake story, hang out in the mountains until the right moment. It would only need one shot.'

I almost dropped my glass. 'It would only need one shot if my gun was pressed against his fat head - or I was very lucky. Even the best need several bullets, and I'm certainly not one of them. It's not like in a film where the gunman vaguely points in someone's direction and bang! - they fall over dead. Believe it or not, with all his security and whatnot, I'd never get close enough. What is this anyway: *Day of the Jackal*? Well, just remember, even with his fancy preparations the Jackal missed.'

'I suppose there's always bombs,' he said brightly.

'*Bombs*!?' My response, involuntarily rather loud, made me look nervously for signs that anyone had overheard me. 'I'm not a terrorist, for Heaven's sake! I can't believe this conversation. Bombs! Anyway, there was an attempt the other week, remember? Amateurs.'

'Just because it failed,' he said.

'No. They timed it wrong. Couldn't get close enough. Just when his rally started. Professionals would have waited till the end.'

'As a matter of interest, why would they?'

'Because, on a hot afternoon like that, after a couple hours of speeches everyone's a bit tired, irritable to some extent, security gets complacent because nothing's happened and they think nothing will, and everyone wants to get away as soon as possible. There's less attention to the little details, which is what security planning is all about, and there's confusion. It's in that little space of time that the target's a bit more at risk, and that can make all the difference. But, anyway, be that as it may, that kind of thing is not for me.'

At that moment, Russo was distracted by someone entering the restaurant. He told me this expansive-looking man in the grey suit was one of his best customers, and he mentioned a couple of deals they'd done together. When the gentleman and his party had sat down, Russo went over to greet him. They had a brief conversation, and my friend returned looking happy. 'Great guy,' he said. 'Wants me to find him some antique vases. I know nothing about vases.'

'When has that ever stopped you?'

He grinned. 'And he said to me, "Who's that sad-faced fellow you're with? Is he a professional mourner?" I said, "No, he's my bank manager."'

'Thank you.'

'So, anyway, you're still doing your target practice, aren't you?'

'Religiously. I force myself to do it. But I feel I'm losing that sharpness I once had. I'm aware of getting tired and slow, you know. When I married Serena I promised her papa that I'd always protect her. But it was her idea to get the bodyguards. She insisted on it, and she was right, even though nothing bad's happened yet. It was she who said the security where we live was suspect. She was right about that too. It turned out he was helping burglars get into the flats and taking a share of the proceeds. It's her protecting me now. I've never believed in the macho culture you and I grew up in, not since my teens anyway, but this reversal of roles doesn't sit well with me. Not what I signed up to, if you like. All I do these days is make sure she doesn't spend all our money. What sort of life is that?'

At this point, Russo startled me, slamming the table with his fist. 'So create another!' he said forcefully.

Although taken aback, I was unpersuaded: 'Is this what you spend your time thinking about? Is business so slow that you have all this time to think about what I should be doing?'

This rattled him. He began to redden in the face. 'Business is fine, thank you. All I'm saying is, someone needs to think about what you're doing. Look, whatever you do, just promise me one thing...'

The waiter now arrived with our steaks. 'Go on,' I said, when he'd left.

'If the chance comes along, whenever and however, for you to do something that makes a difference back home, that you'll take it with both hands.'

'Yes, if it makes you happy. Just so long as it doesn't involve hanging out in the mountains. My constitution couldn't take it.'

I tried a piece of steak but found it surprisingly tough. Russo was silent, apparently happy with his. I felt a little embarrassed by my rather obvious tetchiness a moment earlier, for he meant well. 'Don't get me wrong,' I said, 'I take on board what you say, in the sense that I don't want to be remembered like my father.'

'Oh, do you mean that video?'

'That video, yes.'

'But it's only ten seconds long. Why care?'

'It's eight,' I said. 'But think of it: it's all there is of my father. No photographs or anything normal like that. He had a low-level administrative job at a copper mine.'

'Nothing wrong with that.'

'No. But apart from that simple fact, all that exists is that video. I never knew him. He left before I was four. My sister, quite a bit older than me, hated him. That's, apparently, why she put this stupid video up on the internet as some weird revenge, having burnt everything else, every last trace. I only found out about it from my nephew after she died. You've seen it, haven't you?'

'Remind me,' he said.

'There's a man, my father, maybe in his thirties, in a smart suit and tie, all smiles, facing the camera, holding a large tray covered in roses, standing at the top of some stairs. He takes one confident step forward, and, sure enough, crashes straight down - tray, roses and all - and out of shot. It's had, last time I checked, 300,000 hits, probably over a thousand of them mine. People find it hilarious, and so do I, maybe because of his stupid expression - talk about pride before a fall! - but it's sort of sad as well. Why he was dressed up, why the damned roses, where it was, who filmed it, even how and why, whether he was injured, whether it was staged - are all things I'll most likely never know. I was estranged from my sister. She insulted Serena to her face once - probably something about her extravagant tastes - and, as you can imagine, Serena doesn't hold back in an argument. And with this exile business going on, I couldn't visit her when she was ill.'

'Maybe your nephew could take it down.'

'But that wouldn't seem right either. The fact is, he was a stupid bastard. Maybe it's the legacy he always deserved - but then, he's part of me.'

'But your grandfather, now, he had a real legacy,' he said, rather transparently trying to make me feel better, which I appreciated.

'Sure he did. But even that's conflicted. President for twenty years and very popular for most of it, but, as you know, he killed himself in office. He was being harassed over a sleazy story - implicated in an attempt on the life of an opposition leader.'

'Officially, he wasn't implicated,' my friend said. 'I mean, history absolves him.'

'Right. The scandal was probably a scam. The people turned against the opposition parties over it and they never got in. But for our own family, his death was a matter, not only of sadness, but also shame and even mystery. He was a fighter, and it seemed a rather extreme reaction to a baseless rumour. The irony is, without it the opposition would probably have won the election. Maybe he couldn't face defeat. All politicians lose in the end. So he was a great man, but his death tarnished his legacy for me. And maybe that's why my father stayed with his ordinary, boring administrative job and steered clear of politics. So when I think about all this stuff, I do wonder: what am I doing, just drifting and keeping my head down?'

I felt grateful to him for listening. We were both silent for a minute, and I attacked my steak with renewed vigour. Finally, Russo said, 'I need your advice on something.'

'Go on.'

'Well, you see, with all these people following me, not that I care, obviously...'

'Obviously,' I replied deadpan.

'Do you think I should invest in a gun, just in case?'

Even with my background, coming from him the question took me by surprise. 'I don't know. Ever fired one?'

He shook his head. 'Never did national service. I've got an ancient Beretta someone pawned off on me once.'

'Does it work?'

'Don't know. What sort of gun does Zico use?'

'He's never had to employ it in the time he's been with me, but it's what the American Secret Service uses. It's called a Sig Sauer. Never heard of it? I'll write it down for you. He calls it "the girlfriend". Then for special occasions there's "the wife". He calls it Israel's gift to the world - a mini-Uzi. But why would you want a gun: for when you're at home?'

'Yes, whenever.'

'I like Glocks, but in that setting a pistol can leave you outgunned. You might think about a shotgun for your home, especially a pump action one.'

'I've heard of that. Is it legal here?'

'God knows. But it's one of those things, that if you think you need it, you don't care whether it's legal or not. They say just the sound of the slide action will send your average burglar running out with nothing more than fresh stains in their underwear.'

'That sounds cool.'

'But the downside...'

He sighed. 'Always a downside.'

'Yes. If it's a professional killer, the sound will alert them to where you are. They might just shoot you through the wall. It's a dangerous world, my friend.'

'Hmm. So you recommend?'

'For now, I'd take that old Beretta to an expert and get some serious lessons in. Or hire someone like Zico to worry for you.'

'OK,' he said, and he took a serious gulp of wine.

13
REFLECTION

During the taxi ride home from the restaurant, after all the talk of exile and the risks of return, and triggered by the driver's noticeably intense focus on a boxing match on the radio, I was reminded of another car journey, three years earlier, when it had been a soap opera the driver was listening to as he took Serena and me to the airport after ten months of house arrest.

We had declined the other option: an indefinite spell in gaol without charge. We knew the government preferred exile because it was cheaper, and prison cells were needed for the protesters they arrested every weekend. Serena claimed a friend at the Ministry of the Interior could have obtained a reprieve for her (though not for me), but 'out of loyalty' she had not pursued it. I could not see how unspecified 'crimes against the state' could be so easily absolved, but I didn't argue and instead let her add it to her list of 'personal sacrifices', along with the diplomatic gifts which had all been confiscated, except for a small jade monkey she smuggled out in her handbag.

The drive to the airport, accompanied by a guard, was a chastening and unwelcome reminder of how little had changed over the years. In the fields the dust blew around as thickly as ever, the nation's topsoil vanishing to silt up the rivers and form deltas in estuaries. Seeing this once productive land turn inexorably to barren wastes, even deserts, made me think: is this what we fought for, figuratively and literally? There was also the ambitious public housing project, behind razor wire and abandoned incomplete when government funds ran out; there were the perilous potholes which prompted Serena to tell her favourite joke: 'If people could trust the roads out of the capital, they'd all emigrate.' Outside the airport stood five impressively tall cranes - that lazy mark of economic activity - but these hadn't moved in years, like stranded metal birds, prey to rust and storm force winds. Everything felt like an indictment of weak politicians, well meaning or not, and a democratic government in its last days, snagged up in coalitions and compromise, followed by an autocracy which, up to that point in time, had done nothing but silence its critics. There was even famous old Henry, who could be seen daily, immune to changes in government and weather, on the road outside the airport with his worn out horse and filthy cart piled high with junk, probably always the *same* junk, a sort of one-man anti-modernity movement, raising his battered straw hat cheerfully at the passing cars he'd inconvenienced.

Arriving at the airport terminal, I winced on seeing the soldiers on guard clutching carbines older than they were. Cynics liked to tell me that it was no wonder we had so many border disputes, when visiting foreigners could easily see how ill-equipped our armed forces were, to which my testy retort was always that border wars weren't fought in the airport, and anyway we always won them. If our nation excelled at anything, it was fighting, especially amongst ourselves.

Inside, we met up with others being exiled, many of them friends and former associates. It was a mass clear out. We joked about the privations of the journey there, in our case the lack of air conditioning and the radio soap opera. Serena, uncharacteristically quiet, held my hand. If ever I doubted we loved each other, I thought of this time. She might deserve a doctorate in complaining, but she didn't complain then, and she stoically accepted our predicament. We had to remind ourselves we were not embarking on some extended holiday, and that we would not return soon, if ever.

Our group was segregated from the other passengers in a well-lit room usually employed for customs investigations. We idled our time in platitudes and gallows humour. As was my habit, I conducted a mental exercise on how practical or otherwise it would be for us to rush the guards, grab their weapons and make our escape. I did not dwell on this for long. At least there was a paddle fan to meditate on. And there was recorded music playing - mainly old American country and western, but after a series of ballads, each cornier than the last, I was surprised by the Latin rhythm of bongo drums at the start of one of our favourite songs. Impulsively, Serena pressed her nails into my palm and dragged me to my feet, forcing me untidily into an impromptu dance. The guards were bemused, as probably were our fellow exiles.

I cringed at this memory, but, fortunately, at this point the taxi pulled up at our apartment block.

I found Serena curled up on the sofa. She'd been out with a couple of Ladies Circle friends but came home feeling (her word) 'melancholic'. I told her I'd had dinner with Russo, and when I mentioned the restaurant's name she said, 'Oh, it's not up to much, is it? And the waiters are so smarmy until you ask them a question, and then they make a face like you're something their dog just vomited up. It's because we're foreigners, however hard we try. So, anyway, what's new with him?'

'He's found out he's being followed.'

'Good! Now he knows what it's like for the rest of us.'

'He thinks I should go back home and join the dissidents.'

'You told him, "No", of course. Ridiculous idea. I know he's your friend, but he does come out with some weird notions. And you can bet your life *he* won't be putting his neck on the line. He couldn't even load the bullets he wants you to fire.'

'No, he's talking about getting a gun.'

'Really? Well, thanks for the warning. That's another reason to leave the capital.'

I told her about how my taxi ride home had reminded me of that final journey to the airport. 'Oh God!' she exclaimed. 'That driver wouldn't miss a moment of his soap opera for anything. And that guard in the car stank of onions and sandalwood. I was sure I was going to be asphyxiated. But then I'll always remember that dance we had in the airport. That song was irresistible at that moment.'

'Don't,' I said. 'It embarrasses me to think of it.'

'It shouldn't. The only embarrassing thing was that you were behind the beat. They wouldn't have known, though. The goons standing there with their guns didn't know what to do with themselves. Some people clapped.'

'Don't.'

'Oh, I haven't heard that song in ages,' she said. 'Gloria Estefan. *Como* something. *Como*... Here it is on the internet: *Como Me Duele Perderte*.' She was like an excited child with her find. 'Come on, old boy.' She grabbed my arm. 'Head up. Get with the beat: 1-2-3, 5-6-7. Oh, you're all over the place. How much did you have to drink? Stop. It's like dancing with a pantomime horse. Let's start the song again. Don't grumble - you never know what a dance might lead to. Now let's have one of those big slow turns round to the right, then swing me back sharp to the left. I love that. Those youngsters in the clubs, with their fancy L.A. moves, can throw a girl all over, but for a Cuban casino dance there's no-one for me like my old boy - even if he is behind the beat!'

14
WHAT WOULD FRANK DO?

A few weeks later, Zico and Julia having left for the day, Serena and I were enjoying a typical early evening in the flat. She was preparing herself for going out ('Do you think the blue dress with white spots, or the white dress with blue triangles?' 'Both look perfect on you.'), as we had been invited to another resident's place for drinks to celebrate some award she'd won. I was happy, cooking on the kitchen hob, with our only mild disagreement being the perennial one: choice of music. Serena preferred 'something soothing, light classical would be nice,' but since I was closest to the CD player and cooking our meal, she acquiesced to my choice of random Frank Zappa tracks. It was a warm evening, and the lounge window was wide open. For me it was a sublime few minutes: the aroma of fresh herbs, the bright colours of the vegetables: green, red, and purple, the gentle steam freshening my face, and Frank's untypically sunny *Peaches En Regalia* filling my ears. This spell ended abruptly, as it invariably did, courtesy of Serena. She was standing in the kitchen entrance, hands on hips, with her expression a mixture of fear and fury. I sensed, somewhat reluctantly, that a moment of high drama was about to unfold.

'Someone's firing bullets at the window,' she announced stonily. 'What are you going to do it about it?'

'Bullets? I haven't heard any. Are you sure it wasn't the percussion at the start of this track you heard?'

'Don't patronise me,' she replied sternly. 'Do you think I don't know what a bullet sounds like?'

Grudgingly, I turned down Frank and the pans, left the kitchen and sat in the lounge, well away from the window. I listened hard. 'Could it be stones perhaps?' I said hopefully.

She was unmoved, 'You can tell that to the coroner at my inquest. See how confident you feel then. No, it's bullets - as in, from a gun. If you're convinced it's not, why don't you stick your backside out of the window and see what happens? No don't. Oh, what are we going to do!?' She started to cry.

I listened harder. 'What's that kerfuffle out in the corridor?'

'It's our busybody neighbour. He'll have told half the building by now. At least he'll have phoned the police, so we don't have to.'

'We should anyway.'

'Why? They're useless.'

'Because, if something bad happens, it will help show we didn't want to get involved.'

'The only bad thing that could happen is one of us gets killed or maimed.' At this point she left the room, and I heard something that did indeed sound like a bullet hitting the brickwork outside, just above the window. I went over to the wall next to the window to give myself a partial view of the street below. I felt the slight breeze on my face.

Our flat was one floor up and the block was on a crescent street, shielded from the main road by a private garden full of trees and shrubs. I noted that the section of the street directly in front of the flat was empty, both of cars and people. I went back to my seat; a bullet came through the open window and ended up in the ceiling - more work for maintenance. My sense was that it came from a point in the garden that was directly in front of the window, rather than to the side. I returned to it briefly. Again, nothing to see. I sat back down, and then Serena came in with two loaded pistols from our bedroom and placed them, as though it were part of a formal ceremony, gently on the coffee table before me. She then added a third - nominally hers and bearing a white mark to distinguish it - which she'd removed from a lounge cupboard that we used mainly for storing drinks.

I stared at the three almost identical Glocks lined up so neatly. They looked ridiculous. All that firepower - fifteen rounds in each. And I wasn't even sure a Glock was the weapon we'd need if it came to it. 'Did you phone the police yet?' I asked her.

'Yes,' she hissed.

I felt stupid. Following Serena's fears and criticisms of a while ago, I'd obtained more guns, and they were all kept loaded. I'd toyed with the idea of obtaining an Armalite AR-15 from a black market dealer, the weapon beloved of disgruntled ex-employees, lovelorn students and extremists of all kinds - in other words, mass shooters - but the thought I might ever believe I needed one had frightened me out of it. Sitting there, I felt like a surgeon called to an emergency operation, with a massive hangover from drink or sheer tiredness, terrified of doing harm and staring at his instruments as if he had no idea what they were for. Why was I like this? Was I going gunshy after all these years? I'd had guns all my adult life, and now that their use to me was purely personal, I was nervous of using them.

The problem with a loaded gun was that it almost compelled you to use it. A loaded gun was no better than an empty one until it was used. Suddenly, Serena grabbed her pistol and stood up. She said, 'We can't just sit around. There goes another one. Doing nothing only encourages them.' Irritated, I got to my feet and returned to the wall beside the window. This time I did catch sight of something: a rifle being withdrawn from the wire fence. 'Well?' she said.

'Take it easy,' I replied. 'There's someone with a rifle in that garden.'

'Want me to deal with him? Me with my five lessons. Fifteen rounds - I should be able to hit him once.'

'It's probably a warning,' I said.

'Why are you so reluctant? You're turning into an old man. A cautious, fearful, bumbling old man. I've been noticing more and more how you've changed.'

'Maybe I am, but when you fire a gun in anger, nothing is ever the same again. You can't control the consequences. You can't even be sure what you'll hit. You look out there, and you see an empty street, but the instant the bullet's in the air there might be a pedestrian, a cyclist, a car, a jogger listening to their headphones, a stray dog, even some poor old lady's pet - who knows? And there'll be an audience: people filming it on their phones (do you really want to be on the internet?), people gawping out of windows, newshounds... And then there's the police: "Well, officer, just doing my duty as a good immigrant." It'll be hard enough explaining three guns. If it all goes wrong, and we get deported, you know what that means: it means absolute hell for us.'

She sat down, becalmed. She held my hand. She could understand my dilemma. Then she said, 'Well then, what would Frank do?'

The sheer strangeness of this question tripped me out of my torpor. 'What? Frank who? You don't mean Frank Zappa?'

'Yes.'

'What's that got to do with anything? How would I know? I have no idea... although... actually I *do*, come to think of it. I remember reading once that some kid approached him pointing a gun, and Frank persuaded him to throw it in the pond so the police wouldn't get it. I don't think that would work here somehow. And he didn't phone the police.'

I picked up one of the Glocks and went over to the window. I called out to the gunman. I asked him what he wanted, I encouraged him to leave, I almost pleaded. I told him if he left quietly I wouldn't fire at him. I told him we were two experienced gun handlers with limitless firepower, which was true since we had a whole boxful of ammunition. All he responded with was more bullets, one of which I was sure had hit me but instead went into the wall.

The problem with a warning was that it was an inherent threat, and a threat was an attack, an attack on the psyche. The problem with relying on the police was that it was procrastination. Nothing resolved. The enemy would keep coming back, but the police wouldn't. As for violence begetting violence, the last person to tell me that was a devout Christian who thrashed his kids every weekend for their own good.

I turned to Serena and said, 'How's your tinnitus?' She left the room and returned with ear protectors for us. One thing a Glock wasn't was quiet, and I was glad of them. I threw out some more conciliatory words to our friend, checked the street and then fired in the direction of where the rifle had been. Of course, he could have moved by then. I could waste fifteen rounds quite easily, but I aimed low to try to avoid his head and upper body. Fire came back, and I began to feel the exhilaration, the thrill of it. It was a reminder that no feeling in the world was more intense, more exciting to me than that of shooting while under fire. I had never wanted to feel this rush again, for it was dangerously addictive, but I was feeling it right now. His gun fell silent, but I directed shot after shot at anywhere he might be. I didn't care and quickly exhausted the gun's ammo.

There was a flicker of return fire, but then something weird happened. I was reaching for the second pistol Serena was handing me, when a large white van appeared on the street and parked directly in front of where I thought the gunman was. I couldn't believe it. For a moment I thought it must be full of more trouble, but it wasn't. It was a tradesman. I watched him cross the street and call at the apartment block next to ours. Then a black Ford pulled up. I saw the man with the rifle emerge from next to the white van. He was hobbling. There was little more than a second that he would be in view. My first was lucky - but not for him, the bullet hitting his good leg at or close to the ankle. I fired a couple more around his feet to frighten him. He struggled into the Ford. I muttered, 'Give it a minute, my friend, and you'll be screaming - but I won't hear you.' To my surprise, the car merely limped away. I imagined myself saying, 'Excessive force, Officer? Surely not,' and out of sheer devilry, the kind of thing you can regret afterwards, I dispatched a few more bullets through the car roof.

I took off the ear protectors, put the gun down and hugged Serena. Holding her managed to calm me down. A couple of her tears fell on my shirt. A few yards away, there was shouting and banging on the door. I turned up Frank to drown it out; Captain Beefheart was growling his way through the song about the narcissist *Willie the Pimp*, which seemed oddly apt, but then the smoke from one of the neglected pans set off the fire alarm.

15
THE AGENT

A couple of mornings later, Russo rang me all excited with the news that 'an agent' was intending to visit me.

'Agent of what?' I said. 'Anyway, they've already been, thank you. Left their calling card in terms of damage but took away more than they bargained for.' I explained what had happened. He was surprised and concerned. 'So what did the police have to say?'

'Well, we got off to a tricky start when Serena challenged them, "Why are you even here? We're not celebrities." I gave them a speech about doing what I could to help clear up the streets. I stressed how I'd been careful to avoid killing the man. They seemed quite impressed, although they did suggest I not be quite so enthusiastic about it in future. I assume the attack was a rather cack-handed warning, but of what? It's not as though we needed it. It frightened Serena, though. I think she will leave the capital soon. I can't say I blame her. Maybe her lover can make her feel safer.'

'I always think you're more secure in the capital,' he said. 'Anyway, as I say, the reason I called you is because there's a man wants to meet you.'

'If it's the Grim Reaper, tell him I'm not ready yet, thanks.'

'He's an opponent of the Smooth Killer.'

'There must be millions of us.'

'Can I tell him your address?'

'I appreciate it's on every hired gun's Rolodex, but I like to pretend I've still got my privacy, so I will only meet on neutral territory. My personal security may need enhancing but why make it easy for them?'

I met the agent in an empty, semi-dark bar. I'd taken Zico with me, and as soon as we arrived I made a point of introducing the two men: for practical reasons so that Zico could get in close to give him the once-over, but also as a power play on my part to distract the agent from his inevitable script, and to highlight, without saying it in words that, for the duration of our meeting, my bodyguard would effectively be his as well. Perhaps naively, I had not seen the agent himself as a risk, but who knew what poisonous creeps he'd unwittingly brought with him? Zico sat at a table at an angle, several feet from us, so that he could observe the stranger, but also, probably more importantly, keep a close eye on the car park. Occasionally, he would get to his feet, stretch, and wander ostensibly aimlessly around, no doubt taking a hard look at any movement outside, and I'd notice the agent's gaze distractedly follow him for a moment. When someone entered the bar, Zico would return immediately to his table.

Despite the supposed seriousness of the meeting, a note of comedy was struck by the heavy-set agent's rather eccentric appearance. He was wearing a wide-brimmed red fedora, which at no point during the proceedings did he remove, a Vandyke beard (clearly fake), and a black eyepatch, all presumably as some weird disguise. Even Zico, whose face rarely revealed even the merest hint of an emotion, could not resist a smile, although privately he, like me, must have been wishing the gentleman had chosen a less conspicuous look.

Unfortunately, as well as this issue, another problem was the fact that, for some reason I couldn't understand, but may have been purely out of laziness, I took an aversion, not so much to the agent personally, as to his role as emissary for a faction whose cause I had no desire to engage with.

He offered me a drink. I fancied a beer, especially as he was having one, but chose instead a strong coffee to keep my head clear. Initially during our discussion, he was obsequious to an extent that was embarrassing. After he'd thanked me for the umpteenth time, stressing how grateful he and his masters were for this meeting, and how important it could be for our country, which I knew was nonsense, I asked him sharply, 'So what is this all about?'

He was taken aback by my directness but proceeded to describe how a group within the military ('friends of our democracy' he called them - rather hopefully, I thought) wanted to replace the Smooth Killer with a junta that would 'at the earliest instance' bring in elections. I admired his bravado, even though it struck me as being that of the non-combatant safely out of range of any bullets. I said, 'But I thought all the so-called "friends of democracy" within the forces had been gaoled.'

'There have been setbacks, certainly,' he replied, with a hint of irritation, 'but there's so many opposed to him they can't gaol them all.'

'So what has this to do with me exactly?'

Before replying, he rather portentously took a slow sip of beer. Then he said, 'You, Sir, are held in high regard for your work in government. It is hoped that you and others with your experience could be part of the democratic process.'

I liked the flattery, but on this occasion my self-regard, always a handicap, was offset by my scepticism: 'It's nice of you to say that, but even with *my* vanity I don't believe it. We had a good publicity machine. The fact is, people think all politicians are crooked and / or incompetent, and they're usually right. They don't even say good things about our politicians when they die.'

'They did about your grandfather. He was a good man.'

'I'm not sure he really did much. Maybe in his early days he did. After that it was more like benign neglect.'

'Now your father wasn't in politics, was he?'

I paused before replying, not comfortable with him asking so much about my family. He'd be asking about Serena next. 'No,' I said at last, 'he had a different kind of life.' The image flashed through my mind of my father tumbling downstairs: tray, roses and all.

'I guess it was the son rejecting the father's way,' I said. 'After all, my grandfather wasn't happy in the end. A bit of a mixed legacy.'

'No, his legacy was good. He showed that strong government doesn't need the machinery of violence to rule effectively.'

I was annoyed that a stranger purported to know better than me about it, which was silly on my part because he might be able to be more objective - except he wasn't being objective because he wanted to get on my right side.

I said sourly, 'Anyway, it's a shame this illustrious group of democracy-friendly generals didn't think of this when a host of good hardworking ministers were put under house arrest or in gaol, without charge. It's all a bit late, I'm afraid. But I appreciate things were different then. The sheer greed and depravity of this president wasn't so inevitable... which makes me wonder: how many of these generals were involved in the coup in the first place?' I gave him a few names but couldn't detect a wince on his part.

'That is something I don't know,' he replied with exaggerated earnestness. 'Whatever happens, he will not last for ever. He must be sixty-five or more.'

The agent looked like a man in his late thirties. I could remember when I was a similar age, how ancient anyone in their sixties, even mid-fifties, seemed. 'He could live to eighty,' I said. 'He's got more energy than I have, that's for sure.'

The conversation then turned to the current president's reported obsession with physical fitness, including gym training and his particular enthusiasm for tennis. 'Maybe that's the answer,' I said. 'You need energy to get to the top. You've got to be quick on your feet. When you're launching a coup, if you do it with speed, including quick control of the media, you're more than halfway to the palace. Make sure your friends understand that.'

I didn't think I could trust the agent because, although he meant well, he might just be someone else's 'idiot'. He might say something I liked, such as, 'What we have now is a government of thieves,' but how did I know he wasn't an unwitting supporter of the thieves? Russo was not infallible in his judgement of people. And yet I wanted to believe the agent. I could not dismiss outright what he claimed, so I merely said that, at this point in time I didn't feel confident a return home, even after a new coup by these 'friends of democracy', offered any more security than I had in exile.

'And what if the adventure fails?' I asked him.

'It won't,' he said firmly.

I could at least admire his innocence and we parted on amicable terms, notwithstanding my rejection of his request, although in reality he hadn't requested anything much other than vaguely seeking support. If in fact he was working for the president, I had not compromised myself. Afterwards, I would mull over the idea in my mind. It was both exciting and frightening. I kept reminding myself how nothing ever worked out the way one expected, and it would be the same with this. Democracy was currently broken with not even a plebiscite on the most distant of horizons, and there was a ludicrous, vindictive old man in charge. Who was to say the generals, if they were successful, would stick to their promise of elections? Did I owe a duty to the country that had forced me out? Maybe I did. Didn't they deserve the government they had got? No, of course not. In truth, though, I felt past it, physically and mentally, and yet, notwithstanding my tepid response to the agent, my current situation wasn't making me happy.

'Any thoughts about him?' I asked Zico on the drive back, surprising him because we never discussed anything other than security matters.

'My impression is that he's sincere,' he said. At this point, I heard a slight snigger come from him.

'Did he have a gun on him?'

'I don't think so, no.' At this point he burst out laughing. 'I think the fancy dress shop ran out of them!' His last resistance was now futile, and he realised he could not stop himself, and so he was forced to stop the car instead at the first opportunity. It set me off laughing too, and we both quickly worked ourselves up, bouncing around like two giddy, drunken idiots, slamming our hands on the dashboard in turn, tears rolling down our cheeks, the windscreen steaming up. Goons could have strafed the car with bullets, reloaded and done it all over again, but ours would have been the happiest of all possible deaths. Finally, he was able to contain himself, and we continued with our journey. 'Oh, I'm terribly sorry, Boss. Oh, my God, I can't believe it!'

'Don't worry,' I said. 'I'll just include it in my letter.'

'Letter?' he replied, suddenly serious. 'What letter?'

'I'll start a new page. Page three - and that's just for today.'

'I see,' he said, and he chuckled again but in a forced way. 'When will my company get it?'

'Same as every week - first thing Friday.' I then added with the genuine warmth I felt for him, 'Don't worry, my friend. Excuse my weak jest. It just never occurred to me that a shared sense of humour could be our biggest security threat.'

We proceeded in silence for a few minutes, like two boys caught red-handed in some act of naughtiness, until he startled me by volunteering, apropos of nothing, 'Seriously, Boss, you know there's nothing for you here. If I were you, I would make plans to go back to your home country, but not yet. Oh no, you couldn't do it yet.'

16
CHILD'S GAME

The talk of dictators and the to-ing and fro-ing of generals in and out of power reminded me of a game we sometimes played as children. We would make a soldier out of straw and scraps of cloth. We'd give him a toy gun and shiny plastic medals. He was so impressive that we called him the general, and since he was the best we could possibly make him we called him the general of generals. We wrote him a little speech, and one of us read it aloud on his behalf. The others listened intently - well, I recall my sister at least gave me half an ear - and applauded at appropriate points and especially at the end. When the general wasn't looking, we threw stones at him, called him insulting names, and set fire to him until he was turned to ash. Then we had a parade of mourning with sad patriotic songs, a funeral band, and wreaths. After this we celebrated, happily blaming him for everything bad we could think of, and forgot about him. We enjoyed the wonderful freedom killing him had given us. The next day, we found fresh straw and scraps of cloth and made a new general. We called him the new general of generals and wrote him a new speech, exactly like the old one.

Looking back, I wasn't sure whether we really played this game or whether I had unconsciously made it up. I dreamt vividly, and I found memories of childhood merged with dreams, to such an extent that I had ceased to concern myself with what was true memory, and what was memory of a dream. I could remember asking my sister once, many years later, what she could remember of our childhood games, and she'd said, 'Football. Always football. And occasionally we played a game we called *Soldiers* that we made up. We loved it, but the other kids weren't so keen. It was football. Always football.'

17
RESOLUTION

Serena and I had an understanding that we never lied to each other, although that did not mean we felt compelled to tell the whole truth. I thought if I told her about the meeting with the agent it might make her even more unsettled than she clearly was already. I would not keep it from her, however, if she asked the right question. On the other hand, such was the understanding between us that she instinctively knew when I was holding something back that she might want to know about. No sooner had I arrived back and gone straight to the kitchen to put the kettle on for tea, than she was on me like a hawk on a weasel, or at least that was the metaphor I imagined her using.

'So where did you go today,' she asked from one of the lounge chairs.

'Just out and about in town,' I said. Even allowing for the fact that I was tired, this was the worst possible answer. It sounded like I'd visited a prostitute or gone somewhere to buy illegal drugs.

'Oh dear,' she said. 'I can see it's going to be one of *those* conversations.'

I noticed a slight tremor as I poured the boiling water into the stone teapot. 'Is it?' I said, trying to sound nonchalant. I returned to the lounge.

OK, so who did you meet: some hooker?'

'No, a man who...' I hesitated, not sure how to put it.

She grimaced. 'Look, rather than waste time, why don't you just tell me straight?'

I was too tired to play games, so I merely said, 'OK' and returned to the kitchen to pour the tea. After I'd returned with the cups, I sat down and told her everything about the meeting, albeit in a rambling, probably incoherent way.

She didn't ask questions, but when she thought I'd finished she said, 'I take it you told him you weren't interested.'

'Not exactly. I told him I'd think about it.'

'I see.' She was pensive. 'It all makes sense doesn't it? I mean, the warning we had, if that's what it was meant to be.'

I hadn't seen the two things as connected but could see why she thought they might be. 'You may be right,' I said.

'May be right? Oh, it's obvious,' she said briskly. 'Surely even you can see it.' I did not reply and watched her drain her cup before she said quite slowly and deliberately, whilst clearly aware she was at risk of sounding like a melodramatic soap actress, 'I've been thinking about it for a long time as you know, and I think... now is the right time for me to leave.' She waited for a moment in anticipation of a response, but I gave none. 'I don't mean, to leave *you*,' she said. 'I hope you can understand that - just leave this place.'

'I can understand your feelings,' I said, 'but where will you go?'

I now felt she'd been reciting from a script. 'I have a friend who has a pretty little villa,' she said hesitantly. 'They said I could borrow it.'

'Out of town?'

'Oh yes,' she replied dismissively, as though nowhere in the capital could possibly suit her, ignoring the fact we'd tried several other towns in the past. But of course her real consideration was not *where* but *who with*. She mentioned that the house was in some place on the coast, presumably one without 'all sorts of problems' she'd once expressed concern about.

'I see,' I said with a tinge of sadness. She was having an affair, and this was her opportunity. 'Just for a while,' she said, as if to reassure me, and she reached out to place her hand on my arm affectionately. 'Just while it's so unsettled, so *dangerous*. Of course, it's you I worry about.'

'I'll get by,' I said. I thought to myself, she wasn't so worried that she'd want me moving in with her.

She had the air of an innocent little girl seeking to desert the scene of a small crime, a part she played occasionally and always well. I imagined myself telling Russo, and him assuring me, 'It'll be good for you,' and me not believing it. In fact, I felt oddly ambivalent about it, a feeling I often had when it came to her. She'd said it would be temporary, and I had no reason to believe it wouldn't be.

18
TV

On the evening of the momentous day when Serena had told me she was definitely leaving, we sat together on the old lounge sofa we both despised, sharing a bottle of Pinot Grigio and watching TV. It felt like old times or, more precisely, it felt like old times as I preferred to imagine them. More from a sense of duty than interest, we watched a news channel. One programme included a feature on our home country and showed scenes of poverty and protests. This was pretty typical footage these days; in fact, we'd seen the same pieces of film so many times we recognised the individuals in it - the woman in the purple headscarf at the fruit stall shaking her fist at a portrait of the president, the man in the torn bright blue shirt with blood running down his face denouncing the police. And yet this was different. What impressed us both was the boldness of the people out in Congress Square and the surrounding streets. A large picture of the president was displayed electronically on the wall of the Central Bank, and a section of the crowd shouted, 'Thief!' at it. Serena remarked, 'If they weren't so poor, they'd throw eggs and tomatoes at it.'

A human rights lawyer had just been arrested, and one of the leaders of the protest was castigating the government and stirring up the demonstrators who yelled, 'Shame on you!' in the direction of the presidential palace. But then a large gang of young paramilitaries ran across the square and lashed out at the protesters with what looked like chains, clubs, and even pieces of scaffolding. The TV crew, themselves a target, held impromptu interviews with anyone who'd talk to them. One young man complained, 'Every day, everything's worse. Nothing works in this country anymore. The only people who thrive here are the criminals, the thugs.'

This prompted a sad laugh from Serena, 'Do you remember how the electricity kept shorting out? All those power cuts? And the air pollution? But there's something different going on now, isn't there? A new spirit. Something's happening.' She sounded excited, as though willing it to happen.

I told her, 'This is what the agent was talking about. The people seem emboldened, no longer cowed. They sense change coming, and they want to bear witness to it. I just hope it's the change they want.'

'Or the change they need. But it won't be. It never is,' she said glumly. 'Look at those paramilitaries throwing their weight around - dreadful creatures! What do they want? More of the same, by the looks of it. It's like you always say: nothing ever turns out the way you expect. Imagine all the scenarios you can conjure up, but reality will be different to all of them. No, I'm not being pessimistic, if that's what you think. It could be better or worse, but it won't be what anyone expects. It's like my going to live on the coast: I tell myself it will be a certain way, but it won't be - not exactly, anyway.'

When she talked like this, I almost wished I was going with her. That would qualify as something she hadn't expected, an interesting problem for her to solve. She frowned heavily, as though she'd stumbled upon the same thought. For a moment, it was tempting to speculate that she was not relishing her new life with her lover on the coast as much as she liked to imagine.

'What's the matter?' I asked her.

She paused for a moment, then replied pensively, 'It's just that seeing those pictures makes me feel nostalgic. It's true what that young man says: nothing works there. It's always been the same - the awful water, the terrible roads, the unfinished bridges, the buildings falling down all the time. But it's our home, and it feels like a significant point in its history is about to take place, and we won't be there.'

'You're not missing it, surely?'

'Crazy as it may sound, I am actually. At this very moment I have genuine feelings of homesickness. Not misty-eyed, not rose-tinted, but clear-eyed, recognising the bad things but, I don't know, we were so *alive* then. We had it all once, didn't we? We are allowed to feel sad about it now. When you were in your first government job, Minister of Health and Family Welfare, of all things, we had it all. We didn't know how lucky we were, and that's the truth. We thought, or at least *I* thought, that it would never end. It was important what you were doing, and even your opponents said good things about you.'

'It was all flattery,' I replied. 'And not all of my opponents, probably not even most, said good things.'

'You couldn't do everything,' she said. 'You're not Jesus Christ, and anyway he wasn't available.'

'The truth is, that although in the early days things went not too bad, towards the end I could hardly get anything done. None of the ministers could. But it wasn't our fault.'

'I won't hear of it,' she said. 'Your government eradicated poverty for millions. Now you look back, and you always downplay what you achieved. No, I will not have it. You never used to be like this.'

'We had good PR, of course.'

'Stop it. Stop denigrating what you did. It was a good government with people who cared. I was proud of you and what your government achieved. But now the country's become a criminal's paradise, by the sound of it.'

The rest of the evening we spent watching TV, all the silliest shows we could find. We got drunk, went to bed happy, and made love. It made me wish she told me she was leaving, every day.

19
SOLDIERS AT THE FACTORY GATES

Next morning, there was a photograph from home in the local newspaper which intrigued me. It showed soldiers guarding the gates of a tyre factory. There was a strike taking place, but the soldiers seemed to be guarding the gates more from curious tourists and reporters than disgruntled workers. In the companion piece, the journalist described the scene outside the presidential palace. She mentioned the police showing off their newly imported riot guns and breaking up a crowd of students who weren't even protesting at that moment.

It was as though people were living in the last days of a ruinous dictatorship, a republic of fear. Change was imminent - a revolution, according to the most passionate activists. This interested me because it wasn't revolution that the agent I'd met had predicted, but a coup followed by elections. They were incompatible and it was such differences that kept the strongman in power, for his opponents would never link arms together.

The journalist said that at times the streets were so heavily quiet with anticipation you could hear a grenade pin drop, even hear the thoughts of the secret police.

A woman from the shanty town she interviewed said, 'When they knock on the roof, we run out into the streets in the hope that the neighbourhood will protect us, but we run into more danger.'

The old dreaded one day at a time, dead-eyed and weary, while the young lived like warriors - hyper-alert from amphetamines, fighting in the shadows so that their future children could one day play in the light.

In the pawnshop queue the poor stood in their finest clothes, while the rich were tall, slender and blond and wore dark glasses to avoid the risk of being defiled by the sight of the scruffy, stumpy, and misshapen. Amongst them the rogues shuffled their feet impatiently, perpetually on the lookout for something to steal that someone had once looted from an abandoned mansion. When they had succeeded in their scurrilous endeavours, they paid quick ironic homage to the country that despised them, and vanished into alleyways before the bravest of the police turned up to apprehend them.

20
UNEASE

The day after Serena left, I felt a mixture of melancholy, resentment and relief. At times, I couldn't help thinking I was the biggest fool in the world, and yet I told myself it was right to be understanding. It wasn't the macho way, but it felt like the right way, at least between her and me.

Although we led largely independent lives, even when we lived under the same roof, without Serena I felt vulnerable, insecure. Since she hadn't taken Julia with her, I hired her myself. Julia was inscrutable, which I supposed was a prerequisite for a bodyguard, but certainly I found it reassuring. She was superficially pretty, but there was a hardness about her that was at times quite disconcerting, although it certainly made clear she would stand no nonsense, and there was no prospect of her being compromised by anyone of dubious intentions. She and Zico devised a rota between them to provide twenty-four hour cover. If I slowly withdrew into myself, they would be some company at least, although, on the other hand, the very need for bodyguards made me feel lonely. Even now, I was still not entirely relaxed about having security with me at all times and felt self-conscious when meeting friends not similarly blessed. In restaurants I insisted on sitting in the corner facing the door, and if this wasn't possible I went elsewhere.

I was keen for any news of the old country but was often disappointed by the superficiality of the media coverage. The Smooth Killer had the press on a tight leash, and their copy was timid and sycophantic. Meanwhile, the international press never tired of reporting on his latest eccentricities: his love of Italian Romantic poetry, which he reportedly read in preference to government correspondence, his cancellation of meetings with foreign leaders to plot the cowboy novel he was reportedly writing, or to play tennis with a young female TV soap star who knew enough to ensure she deliberately lost.

As a nation we liked to believe we were so tough that no other country would mess with us. It was a fiction, and in reality other countries never hesitated to mess with us. Much of my career in the military consisted of addressing incursions of one sort or another from the three countries with whom we had borders. Nevertheless, the biggest danger was from our own people by way of coups, assassinations, or popular uprisings.

But now the violence from home had seeped into our adopted country, and I found my daily mental life gradually becoming consumed by imaginary intrigues. Anyone new on the streets near the apartment was a cause for concern. Even with a bodyguard, my mind became overloaded with such threats. Was that a camera in the car across the street pointed at me? Or was it a gun? Who were those two men who walked by just then? I was forever looking through the lounge window to check the street below.

If, when I was out, I saw someone staring in my direction, I wondered, was it at me or through me? In restaurants I scrutinised people one by one, watching carefully for anything that might suggest a listening device or a weapon. I felt ashamed at myself over this. I contemplated seeing a doctor about it. I was increasingly paranoid, seeing enemies everywhere. But even in my doctor's office I would not feel safe; if he went to open a drawer in front of me I'd think he was reaching for the handgun I was sure was there.

It was as though having Serena to look out for had made me less concerned for my own wellbeing. Now she'd gone to someone else's arms, I no longer had that distraction. Thus, rather seeing the doctor, whom, in my madness, I felt I could no longer trust, I decided to spend more time talking to Russo. At least he always had new information about home or had some new racket to tell me about.

21
ROOFTOP BAR

I went to visit Russo, not having seen him since the evening of the snouts. It looked like he'd taken on additional staff, and his team of assistants was different, albeit it consisted of all females as before. He had the same ethnic bric-a-brac, but I noticed a sudden surfeit of ladies' handbags. His main new current interest, he informed me happily, was religious relics - the tooth of a saint, a splinter from the Holy Cross, also antique Jewish artefacts; he even had works from ancient Greece and Rome. I wondered about the provenance of some of this stuff but was reluctant to disrupt the joy of someone for whom the struggle they laboured with day by day seemed, at least for now, worthwhile.

It was as though he'd read my mind: 'People say to me, "How do you know these are genuine?" I tell them I can only go on the provenance. I mean, what am I supposed to do: spend twenty years studying ancient artefacts so I can buy one? I don't know where they've come from originally. If the guy who sells it to me is someone I trust from prior dealings, that's what guides me. It's like a racehorse trainer. If a trainer always tips me winners, then I'm inclined to believe him. Not that I ever gamble, of course. So, Serena's moved on, I take it? Is that what I understand from the text you sent?'

I explained that I believed it was temporary ('Isn't everything?' he said with a hint of sadness,) and that I was relaxed about it.

'Want me to find you a good girl?' he said, reminding me of the hustler he'd been a few years earlier.

'No thanks. If I want company, I think I can easily find it.'

'Yes, but I'm talking about good girls, not tarts.'

He took me to a café I hadn't been to before. We ordered at the counter, and he led me upstairs to the rooftop.

'Another Romantic spot,' I said. 'People will talk, speaking of which...' (at this point I switched to a hoarse whisper) '...where's our friend, the snout?'

'Probably downstairs. Coming up here would be a little obvious on his part, but, you never know, we might see a little head pop round at the top of the stairs. I see them about. I assume they mainly want to see who I meet, so I meet as few as possible.'

'You're like a carrier,' I said.

'Like a virus carrier? Thank you very much. They know all about you anyway. They don't really bother me.'

'They've called round to me,' I said. 'You haven't seen anyone suspicious who's got a limp, have you?'

'I suppose if you'd killed him they'd have been buzzing round me in force. But what about the other fellow, the one I told you about?'

'The agent? I can't say I trusted him. He was buttering me up like an English muffin, which of course works... but he told me there was going to be a coup followed by elections. How often does that combination happen? And with all the purges taking place, who's going to be left to bring the coup?'

We stopped our conversation on hearing someone on the stairs. It turned out to be a dark-haired woman in her forties bringing our coffee and cakes. When she'd gone, Russo said, 'Her sister works for me sometimes. Younger, prettier, unattached.'

'Give it a rest.'

He was suddenly serious: 'No, the reason I wanted you to meet that man was to illustrate that there are people who believe this coup plus elections idea can fly. There's someone called the Squire in the airforce hierarchy who carries such hopes. But no-one I know knows who he is.'

'I don't. But my attitude is, why sign up for something now, which might never happen, before the shooting starts?'

'You're a wise man. By the way...' he was suddenly proud, '...that old Beretta I told you I had, well, it is considered a classic. I went to an expert who confirmed it.'

'Is he the same person who sold you the splinter of the Holy Cross?'

'You're too cruel. I knew you'd be cynical about my new venture. I bet I can sell that. But I realised I missed a trick when I was thinking about what direction to take my business in. I should have thought about old weapons. And not just old ones, but those pump action shotguns you told me about.'

'I think it's not something for the novice,' I cautioned.

He looked momentarily downcast, but only momentarily: 'Think of it:

plenty of potential customers. More exiles coming in. Some old-established families.' He reeled off a few names, then changed the subject: 'I hear Old Smoothie wants to build a new airfield at his home village.'

'Well, I'm all for well-thought-out infrastructure,' I said.

'But it's some little isolated place surrounded by near-desert. And he wants to build a new palace out there.'

'That's reasonable.'

'It will need a new highway for all the trucks it will require going back and forth. Maybe a new railway line.'

'Fair enough,' I said. 'Building projects is the stuff of autocrats. More productive than using statues of former presidents for target practice...'

'Or having racehorses grazing in the palace gardens...'

'... or giving whole villages hallucinogenic drugs as a punishment for witchcraft, and all the other eccentricities of him and all his ilk.'

'But your grandfather was a dictator, albeit a benevolent one.'

'I won't hear of it. Oh no, he was elected. He never had time to go batty. He might have, I'll admit, if he'd stayed in power.'

'Then there was the weirdness of his demise. Officially suicide, I know, but there are stories...'. He stopped suddenly. 'I'm sorry - insensitive on my part - but it has always fascinated me.'

'Yes. Me too. I like the one about him going to see a Tarot reader, and she turned up the Death card, and the shock killed him. But the truth is more prosaic. A bullet that he fired. What I'll never know, and nor will anyone else, is exactly why.'

22
APPREHENSION

A few days after seeing Russo, I received by email an invitation to a prestigious-sounding event. It was a cocktail party for 'prominent exiles' from my home country. I was immediately suspicious. Of course, I liked to be considered 'prominent', but it seemed like a hook to catch the vain and easily flattered. When I mentioned it casually to Zico in the car, he was likewise initially concerned.

'I know you worry about safety,' I said, 'and you're right to do so, but I need to get out more and meet people. Apart from my old friend Russo, I never see anyone.'

It was true: since Serena had left I'd increasingly withdrawn into myself. Worries about security only made me more reclusive. What was the point of living like like this, bereft, not just of danger, but of life itself? The man who'd attacked the flat, even though he'd been injured by my return of fire, had achieved the objective of warning me. I might assure myself I was fearless, but my actions, or lack of them, told otherwise.

I said to Zico, 'At times I feel I might as well be living like a bum in a little wooden hut by the sea, living off fish I could easily catch.'

Zico gave the faintest of smiles and replied unsparingly, 'That is no doubt true.' He paused, slightly embarrassed, then added, 'I can only advise you on your security needs and not your social life. Strictly speaking, it is not my place to give you advice about where you should or shouldn't go, but to avoid telling you would not sit well with me.'

'What bothers you about it?' I asked him.

'It could be a trap to draw you in - in other words, there's no party, merely the bait of drinks and a social gathering, so that someone can browbeat you into joining some crazy scheme...'

'I hear your wise words,' I said.

'Or it could be a target for the so-called Rats, since they will certainly learn of it. Either way, I recommend against your attending.' I was surprised he reached this conclusion so quickly but should not have been. His work must have have taken him to events where the true purpose was hidden from his client, who was thus attending in hopeful innocence.

He continued, 'I happen to know this venue. I had to check it out once. It is not easy to defend. It is small, has multiple entrances, and can be easily attacked from outside, surrounded as it is on at least two sides by inclines, so attackers can easily look down on it. There is also an internal balcony, so someone with a machine gun...' he paused for effect '...could knock them over like skittles. Security is very lax. The CCTV cameras were fake then, and I understand they still are.'

I rang Russo to see if he was going to the party. 'I'm sure my invitation's in the post,' he said sarcastically. 'I never get invited to such things. Excuse me, but I'm not a prominent exile or prominent anything else. Prominent nobody, perhaps. I'm a nobody and I like it that way.' When I mentioned Zico's concerns, he said, 'Impressive. I'd always take what he says seriously. I'm sorry to pour water on your cocktail party career, but it sounds like a prominent magnet for every Rat in the capital. I suggest you save your money on buying new clothes for it and spend the evening with a pretty girl. I can find you one of the best.'

'Best of what? Don't answer.'

'You don't even need to have sex with her if you don't want to.'

'Thank you. That's gratifying.'

'Just enjoy her company. We could make a foursome of it, if you like.' His obvious enthusiasm for the idea alarmed me. 'I can bring one of the girls from the stall. We could have a meal at that Turkish restaurant - belly dancing and everything - and laugh about all the *prominent* people in town. It'll cheer you up. You need it.'

'Some other time, perhaps,' I replied brusquely. 'But you keep trying to persuade me to go back home, to create a new political future for myself. Well, to do that I have to rub shoulders with a few other so-called men and women of the future.' I was beginning to convince myself about it all, although I remained guarded.

'Oh, so you're going then are you, going to meet all the other prominent people?' He sounded hurt. 'You don't need them,' he said. 'You can plough your own furrow, but if you're going to go, make sure you heed Zico's advice.'

23
COCKTAIL PARTY

After due consideration, I decided I would attend the cocktail party, but my necessary compromise with Zico was that I would leave early.

'It will sound good,' he assured me. 'You had a prior engagement, but you were determined not to miss this vital event.'

I was impressed. I said, 'You're starting to think like a politician. Another career awaits you. You should be attending instead of me.'

We arrived at the party early when there were only a handful of people present. I left Zico in the lobby, but, knowing him, he wouldn't stay there long. He'd be wandering around looking for anything or anyone he saw as a potential risk, able to contact me via a pre-arranged phone message if necessity arose. There might be other bodyguards there, but it was not Zico's style to engage in small talk, except the minimum required by normal politeness.

As more people arrived, I was able to renew my acquaintance with several former associates I hadn't seen in years, including a few who'd flown in from other countries especially for the occasion. There were several ex-ministers I knew, as well as former army commanders, all of whom were accompanied by their partners. I was sure I was the only one unaccompanied. Several asked after Serena, and the women, a couple of them ex-ministers, appeared to feel sorry for me, which I quite enjoyed, certainly more than if I'd had one of Russo's escorts with me. Conversation was, nevertheless, quite stilted.

There was one gentleman present whom many referred to affectionately as Our Man. He was the unofficially anointed future leader, which is to say, he was the man they liked to believe could win an election back home, if such a thing ever occurred again. He certainly looked the part: tall, very smartly-dressed, suave and charismatic, glowing with honeyed, almost perpetual smiles. Several women appeared on the point of swooning over him, and even the men were obsequious. Perhaps out of jealousy, I was immediately suspicious and mildly disgusted; it was like the coronation of a pampered prince, a tawdry presentation of him as an absurd (at least in my eyes) leader of a 'cabinet in exile'. I could see his appeal - not merely his appearance, but the way he talked well but said little. But where, I asked myself, was the evidence of inner grit, the sense of deserving through past suffering? His demeanour reminded me of nothing so much as a tranquil pool, serene and shallow. It was as though all trace of the inevitable scars of life had been erased, a man with no past, as if he had suddenly appeared newly formed from the vacant air. He was moneyed, the source of his wealth reportedly the mining industry, although I couldn't imagine his work required significant sweat on his part.

Our Man was perfect for his intended role, but that didn't make me like him. He gave the impression of seeking me out. His handshake was neither firm nor light. He had that knack of making you feel that at that moment you were the centre of his universe, the focus of all his attention. It was more than a knack, it was a trick. Afterwards, I couldn't remember a single word he'd said. He was mesmerising and could easily have removed my watch and stolen my wallet while he was casually talking to me. None of it endeared me to him, although I appreciated the fact that he thought me worth the effort.

Like me, Our Man had to leave early. This fact convinced me Zico's concern was well-placed. I did not want to leave at the same time, as this would probably have embarrassed us both, although probably for different reasons, so I hung around for a couple more minutes before leaving quietly. Zico was in the lobby, talking to the venue's security boss who at that moment was stifling a yawn.

As we exited the front door into the failing light, three men were approaching the building. After we'd passed them, I leaned towards Zico and said, 'Is this it?'

'Keep walking,' was all he said in reply.

A few yards further on, I stopped. 'We should go back in,' I said. 'I've got my gun in the car. I assume you've got yours.' Without waiting for his response, I ran to the car.

The Glock was on the back seat under a blanket. Seeing it in my hands, he said sternly, 'My responsibility is your safety, and we should not go back in. I owe no duty to anyone else, only to you.'

'I'm going in anyway,' I replied, and I strode towards the building. With huge reluctance he followed me, armed with the mini-Uzi or 'the wife' as he called it.

Inside, the lobby was now empty, the security staff nowhere to be seen. I could hear a commotion at the top of the stairs that led to the balcony. We ran up the staircase. I was breathing hard but was determined to be first up, since I had forced Zico into a situation he would have done anything to avoid. Guns started firing, and I could hear screaming. I threw open the swing door at the top of the stairs. Directly facing me was one of the three men, seated on a chair. I shot straight at his stomach. He was starting to slump as Zico burst in and finished him off with the Uzi. He then swung round towards the other two, who were firing at the fleeing guests below. Zico gunned the pair down, although one of them as he fell got a shot in, catching Zico in the arm.

When sure the terrorists were dead, we raced downstairs and, heads covered, ran like crazed dogs for the emergency exit. Once in the car, we sped off. I drove down the road a few seconds, then stopped to phone the ambulance service.

I took Zico to the hospital to get fixed up. As we walked towards the entrance, I apologised to him for what had happened. 'No,' he assured me, 'it was the right thing to do.'

'All of it?'

'All of it.'

24
CRITICS

The Smooth Killer was the nemesis of many, not only me. I feared him, but he had more fears than I did and certainly more enemies. I could never envy him his power because it came at such a price. I felt sure he never slept easily in his bed, not that I did in mine. He could not go out in his car without fear of assassination, all his food had to be tasted before he touched it, and he gave up smoking in case a cigar exploded. In his paranoia he constantly dreamed up new ways in which someone might attempt to topple him.

He appropriated the most opulent mansions he could find, was busy building two new ones, and confined all travel to shuttling between the presidential palace and his various private houses. Even there, I imagined, his fears crowded in upon him. The more staff he had, the greater the risk of a secret assassin at work. It could be someone he'd employed for years who'd suddenly turned against him, or someone who'd joined the staff with the sole intention of finding the right moment for the fatal act.

As time passed, his enemies had, at least in his mind, multiplied. These included squatters demanding land rights, indigenous people claiming back areas rich in natural resources, human rights activists (whom he considered the worst of all), students, union reps, feminists, religious campaigners, communists (the bark of the seemingly toothless dog); additionally, there was everyone that had once been in the public eye who'd gone into exile and, for want of anything better to do, made plots abroad to export trouble back home; there were the scurrilous journalists and commentators, there were disgruntled generals and the men below them who believed their careers had been stymied because of cronyism.

He had friends, of course: big business, multinationals who liked to 'advise' him, the church, and a host of people who paid for their privileges and therefore valued them. There were sycophants who were always seeking ways to be useful. Above all, he had everyone - the common hardworking folk - who wanted order. Some might claim he engaged in oppression, but the alternative was chaos, and, so his supporters claimed, no-one except the anarchists wanted that.

To maintain order effectively required that critics be punished. He saw himself as the divine messenger. Retribution was his speciality. It was a form of creative endeavour he excelled in. Obscure fatal illnesses was a favourite, assassination by road accident, the beauty of defenestration, mysterious disappearances, properties burned down, murder by fake police, livestock poisonings. Gaol was for lowlifes and high-profile busybodies - film directors and the like. A man referred to in the press as an 'opposition leader', although I'd never heard of him, returned from exile to 'negotiate' with the Smooth Killer. Who was this fool's adviser? Of course, he found he had nothing to negotiate and ended up dumped dead by the side of the main highway. Then there was the human rights lawyer who was all too loud and troublesome and whose bullet-ridden body was found at a petrol station. Perhaps it was a wooden autocracy, as some people decried it, but if so it was made of ironwood, and it had survived. Perhaps his time was almost up, but he wasn't listening to the bell. When his time came, he would die in his sleep. Nostalgia for his rule would begin a moment later.

25
AFTERMATH

The morning after the cocktail party incident, Serena rang me: 'I saw it on the news - how awful! I immediately thought of you, wondering if you'd been there, worried whether you were alright. Are you OK? Two of ours dead, oh God! Could have been many more, but they say someone disrupted it, took out the killers. Whatever next!? I'm so glad I'm not there any more. You ought to do the same - I don't mean here where I am obviously but... I do worry about your safety. Do you know anything about what happened?'

'Not much. I was there but left early.' I decided to say nothing else about it, especially about me leading Zico back in. It would only serve to alarm her even more.

'Thank God!'

'Terrible,' I replied blandly.

She abruptly changed the subject. 'It's lovely here,' she said sunnily. 'A villa by the sea. Very relaxing. I need it after reading about what happened last night. So glad to be out of the capital, that fume-filled, Rat-infested place. The gardens here are divine. Reminds me of... No, I won't dwell on it.' After more pleasant talk about how beautiful the gardens were in the splendid weather we'd been having, she said, 'Don't risk it. Staying there, I mean. It's not worth it.' She rang off, happy in the knowledge she'd done the right thing in gently trying to persuade me to leave the flat.

As it transpired, I had been thinking along similar lines and rang Russo to get his ideas. Unsurprisingly, he also wanted to talk about the incident. 'That was pretty weird, wasn't it?' he said. 'I understand the one they call Our Man left early.'

'Like me.'

'Like you? That was pretty astute.'

'It was Zico's idea.'

'Good man,' he said, always keen to compliment Zico, since he had chosen him for me in the first place. I decided I would keep our exploits with firearms to myself - no point putting them into even Russo's portion of the public domain. 'Someone stopped them, though,' he said, sounding excited at the thought of such derring-do. 'Yes, they would have killed the lot, but some guy opened fire on them. That was pretty cool, wasn't it?'

'Do you know who it was who was killed - apart from the terrorists, I mean?'

'A couple of younger men, coincidentally both bankers. So you're wanting to head for safer pastures, I take it? I can't say I blame you.'

'Yes,' I said. 'A new identity would be useful as well. Got to stay at least one step ahead of the bastards now it's turning nasty. But I'm only one of many, and that feels oddly reassuring. What happened last night has given me a broader perspective. There's a real danger, and it affects all of us.'

'Right,' he said, before adopting the air of a real estate agent, 'Now I don't see you as a rural man.'

'Correct. And I do like some creature comforts. I can't see any point being without water and electricity. A small town maybe, but not so small that everything's an apology for not being as good as you'd find in a city. I like a decent selection of restaurants. I like a nice theatre.'

He started laughing at this and, when I asked him why, he said, 'But you never had that back home.'

'Perhaps you're right,' I conceded, 'but at this stage I feel if you can't have life the way you want it, what's the point of living?'

'Not having a point for living is still better than not living at all,' he said.

I pondered this for a moment. 'There is that, I suppose,' I replied at last.

26
NEW CONTACT

While Russo was obtaining a false passport and other ID documents for me, I did research on the internet, looking for a suitable new place to live. I had already told Zico and Julia that I would not need them for much longer. Zico was noticeably concerned, although it seemed this was more for my personal security than his own income. I told him a marksman and bodyguard of his quality would never be short of work, which probably sounded patronising but was genuinely meant.

I decided upon a small seaside town with a vibrant reputation, at least in the imagination of its publicity department, and was looking online at properties there, when I received a surprising call from a woman called Andrea. I'd seen her at the fateful cocktail party and remembered her from my time in government when she'd been a junior minister. She'd been at the party with her husband, an industrialist two decades her senior who looked 'as old as Death'. When I'd seen him at the party, I couldn't resist the thought that he resembled an old cockerel about to have his neck wrung. Andrea was Our Man's choice for minister of education in his fantasy cabinet. I thought he might have other, more carnal designs on her, although probably so did half the men in the room that night. I had swapped phone numbers with Old-as-Death at his request.

Andrea was apologetic about phoning me. I didn't mind, even though, in my current state, all surprises, even pleasant ones, were unwelcome. We talked about that evening; fortunately, she and her husband had escaped unscathed, but she was naturally deeply upset by the incident, and I soon found myself in the role of amateur, and probably very inept, counsellor, a role I did not feel suited for. She asked me about my own experience that night, but, other than saying what she knew already - that I'd left early - I was as evasive as I could reasonably be. I was aware that I was sounding unconvincing, and if the police ever interviewed me I'd have to be more coherent. The call seemed to help her, although I couldn't help wondering what the real reason behind it was. In my paranoia, I speculated that perhaps she was working for the authorities, or had even turned informer for the Rats - after all, someone had obviously tipped them off about the party - but this was incongruous, and it was slightly more likely that it was a date she was after. She was lovely, but I did not need the drama of being caught in flagrante by Old-as-Death.

I was startled out of such absurd musings by her announcing, 'There's someone I'd like you to meet.' I greeted this with silence, which she took as my tacit agreement and proceeded to describe the person. She referred to him as a 'radical' and said he had a 'song to sing' about how the Smooth Killer was imminently about to fall, swept away by a revolutionary insurrection, which would be welcomed by the people, apart from the inevitable odd reactionary not worth worrying about. I told her I'd heard it, or a variation of it, all before, that Messiahs were two-a-penny at the moment, and if I met this character I would likely be rude to him.

Since Andrea seemed to be so au fait with the inner workings of all this 'alternative political universe' stuff, I thought I'd hit her with the obvious question: 'So where does this person you're so keen for me to meet fit in with Our Man?'

'You mean, Sol?' I'd forgotten Our Man even had a proper name, since Russo and I had our own private nomenclature in such matters. 'Sol sees him as useful,' she said, rather disconcertingly. Useful? I wondered if that was what he thought of me. The horses that drew a king's carriage were useful. Even dung beetles were useful. The two people killed and those injured at the party in his honour, which he left early, were they useful? I decided Andrea was naive. Being naive myself, I easily recognised it in others. The more we talked, the more I wanted to continue our conversation over dinner, which felt tacky; I felt as though I was gradually being seduced into the centre of a web, although who the real spider was I couldn't tell. I told her I was leaving the capital soon, without yet knowing when or where to, but I would try to meet the Revolutionary Man before I left. She asked me to let her know when I moved, and I said I would, even though I had little intention of doing so. Being naive, I tried to avoid other naive people, as though they had the Evil Eye upon them and caused mayhem without realising it. In politics the innocent, naive person was sometimes inadvertently like a grenade thrown into a crowded nightclub.

27
POLICE

I did not attend the funerals of the two people the terrorists had killed. I was uncomfortable about not attending, despite the fact I knew neither victim personally, because I prided myself on supporting those who were grieving. No doubt the terrorist I shot had loved ones too that grieved for him, but I felt nothing over that.

My decision not to go arose, not from fear of another attack - from an early stage in my career I had developed the soldier's knack of being ready for anything - but a desire to avoid inevitable questions. I felt I had to protect my secret, whilst avoiding a total retreat into reclusiveness which would be unhealthy. The only way I could see of ending this fear of contact was to go to the police, in much the same way a person burdened by feelings of guilt might go to confession. The only difficulty with that was the fact that Zico would have to go too.

When one morning at the flat I told Zico of my intentions, he was alarmed. I knew little of his personal background, other than his not being ex-army, and I dared not speculate what secrets he might hold. I told him it was inevitable that the police, notwithstanding their lackadaisical approach to their work, would eventually track us down, and that would be worse than if we visited them now. It was the only serious disagreement we had, and it wasn't pleasant. In the end, it was Julia, who had called at the flat with a newspaper featuring a story on the incident, who persuaded him to accompany me. The poor man was terrified that what happened on the night of the party would besmirch his record and hence damage his career. I'd already checked with a lawyer Russo introduced to me once, and he'd verified that we were within the country's laws as regards conceal carry weapons. I asked Zico, 'You do have licences for your guns, don't you?'

'Of course,' he said tersely. I didn't sincerely believe it was as simple as that, but it was sufficient to pacify him, and Julia then removed any resistance on his part by convincing him that if he didn't go to the police he could never move on, because what had happened would play so much on his mind that it would impact on the quality of his work. He gave one final curse, that of someone hopelessly boxed in by circumstance or argument, and then reluctantly agreed.

The next day, he and I visited the main police station in the capital, a bright, showy building that conveyed an air of dynamism and determination to crack the crime menace whatever it took, which was somewhat at odds with the general public's expectations. Indeed, once inside, the atmosphere was not so much of defeatism, but of serene indifference to any measure of success, a place where a quiet day was an enviable success in itself.

We were interviewed by an old-timer. He was heavy, slow and avuncular in a slightly sarcastic seen-it-all-before kind of way. I quickly gathered that for him the cocktail party incident was merely one more reason why his beloved country had too many exiles, refugees, migrants - whatever they were, all fugitives from other people's collapsed legal or economic systems - and it would be too much of a drain on the precious time of the police to expend much effort on the (in his eyes) well-off foreigners importing their troubles into his precious jurisdiction.

As it transpired, the police file on the case, which he extracted from his metal cabinet with a weary sigh, was rather sparse, and I took this as an encouraging sign. Indeed, the attitude he conveyed was one of 'Terrorists taken out, no locals hurt, so why worry?' which of course was what we wanted it to be. Zico and I made statements which the old-timer rattled through.

'So, between you, you shot the whole gang, is that correct?' This thought, which he seemed not to entirely believe, amused him. He beamed with satisfaction.

'Yes, that's right,' I said, not keen to encourage any notion that the incident might simply be the latest explosive salvo in an underground campaign. With our statements written, I wondered whether I'd done Zico a disservice, for I could have claimed to have fired the mini-Uzi myself, since only he knew otherwise, although this might have struck him, not only as braggadocio on my part, but an insult to his honour. It was immaterial now, especially as, on hearing my affirmation, the amiable policeman, with an alacrity previously unobserved in him, stood up, shook us both by the hand and said, 'Congratulations!' with what surely passed for him as exuberance. He then expressed an interest in Zico's skills as a marksman and asked what firearms he liked, and I began wondering whether he was envisaging a possible future career in the force for the young man. He brought us back to reality, however, as he added, 'We might need to talk to both of you again.'

At this point, my concentration lapsed, and my private fears surfaced, such that I made a vague reference to the possibility of a 'network of terrorists out there' and the investigation it might require. This, however, struck him as a novel idea and, perhaps influenced by thoughts he didn't welcome about the number of police officers such an undertaking would need, he did not discuss it with us.

As we walked out, I said to Zico, 'Not so bad was it? You OK with it all?'

'Sure, Boss,' he replied grudgingly.

'Think of it,' I said, 'You could maybe get a job with the police one day. I bet they need marksmen.'

'Are you kidding?' he laughed disconcertingly. 'I get far more money looking after you!'

28
REVOLUTIONARY MAN

I arranged to see the Revolutionary Man in a bar on the edge of the capital. I wasn't much interested in the story he had to tell and was sure this would immediately become obvious to him, but I'd promised Andrea I'd listen. My tactic would be to say as little as possible, even though my mind would be brimful of things I could say, keeping my mouth shut to evade the hook he'd inevitably be trying to slip into it. I'd met this type many times before - promise big, deliver little. Full of hope and even strategy, but low on practicalities. They reminded me of Jesus freaks: the Big Man was always just around the corner. Such people were always on the cusp of something. He obviously thought me vain enough to believe the claptrap he'd come to peddle, and he was probably correct on that point. Fortunately, I knew myself well enough to be on guard for this.

The venue was quiet and dark, sorry for itself perhaps, a bar where business was slow with no-one near enough to eavesdrop. Zico parked himself at a table diagonally between mine and the door.

No-one in life ever looked the way I imagined, and the Revolutionary Man was no exception. My first impression was of a small-town crook in a low budget movie, wiry and young, handsome, and without the wild eyes or air of adventure I'd anticipated. He was of quiet demeanour, a surprising self-effacing manner, and dressed in a dull, dark jacket and trousers. I let him buy the beers, and then he told me, much as others had, that the time was now right for change back home, although it was clear the change he wanted to see was different to that of others. He seemed sincere enough. He told me guerrillas had been training for months, and their ranks were swelling all the time. The unions were ready. Strikes had been held back until the right time, except for those groups of workers who insisted their own battles with management could not wait. Meanwhile, the armed services were disillusioned and demoralised because of all the purges, and the middle classes, often the support base for autocrats, were dismayed by the Smooth Killer's excesses and eccentricities. But what, I asked him, did all this have to do with me?

'The support of prominent exiles such as yourself would be invaluable.' There was that word again: "prominent" which so amused Russo.

'Why so?' I asked him. 'I'm not going to be marching under a red flag and, even if I did, what difference would it conceivably make?'

He was unfazed by my scepticism: 'If nothing else, propaganda.'

'I see. You want me to fight a revolutionary war in the newspapers, is that it?' This was more cutting than I'd intended, but he merely grinned.

'No. More important than that, your knowledge of logistics would be a great asset for us.'

I was taken aback by this. 'But I've never fought a revolutionary war,' I said. 'At least, not on the side of the revolutionaries.' At this moment, images from when I was a soldier came to mind, specifically from the rebellion that we put down violently. They were fearful images that often kept me awake at night. Civil wars were terrible, dirty. Then there was the reminder of that later uprising - the one we in government dithered over, which let the Smooth Killer into power.

'Some of your people would remember me, and not in a good way,' I said. 'They'd want to assassinate me.'

He winced at this, perhaps slightly rattled, but undeterred: 'We have a broad appeal. We want the widest possible support, and this will inevitably include people who have deep-seated resentments, grudges even, or may simply dislike each other, but we hope people will put these things aside for the cause. And I feel your knowledge would be very beneficial.'

Whether from vanity or not, I was beginning to warm to the Revolutionary Man. I felt guilty at my earlier dismissal of him. He declined my offer of another drink, and I wondered whether he was concerned that hostile spies or even assassins might yet suddenly appear. A few more people had entered the bar. They could be tourists, drug dealers, or hired killers - it was impossible to tell. My companion seemed nervous, as though someone had misled him and he now realised it.

'Do you think it's unsafe here?' I asked him. 'After what happened the other week?'

'It's OK,' was all he said.

I sensed our meeting was nearly over. Perhaps he thought it had been a mistake, or maybe his intention had merely been to give me something to think about. I told him I was flattered he'd considered me worth talking to.

I acknowledged he had taken a risk. After all, for all he knew I could have reported straight back to the Smooth Killer's office. I would obviously never contemplate such a thing, but friends and enemies were often interchangeable in a country with politics as febrile as ours.

'I think I know you better than that,' he said (rather hopefully, I thought, since he did not know me at all) in a tone that almost felt like genuine comradeship. If nothing else, he was a good salesman, although I thought him more than that. At least he didn't pretend I was the only thing in the world that mattered to him at that particular moment, the way a huckster would. I was beginning to feel almost fatherly towards him, which alarmed me.

I told him that I could not support a revolution and that, as a man whose main career had been in the services, I did not believe armed struggle was the best course for the country.

He was dismayed, although not surprised, 'But in order to apply pressure, even to force negotiation, not that negotiation is something I would contemplate, of course...'

'Why "of course"?'

'In order to apply pressure you have to take up arms. Without violence and / or the realistic threat of it, nothing changes.' He was animated now, and I was expecting him to quote from history, perhaps the Mexican revolution, the Castro brothers, perhaps Trotsky, but before he could, I said I agreed with his general point but in this instance I was fearful. The prospects for success were still very weak, notwithstanding the support he thought he had. As long as the Smooth Killer could provide the illusion of order in the country, he would always enjoy enough support to keep him in power. It was merely him personally that people did not like.

I said, 'My sense is that his grip on the military and the military's grip on the country are both still strong. I believe you are a good man, a sincere man, but I do not think the job can be done at this point in time. If you are as serious as I believe you are, you would be better to wait and through waiting you may find another, less inherently hazardous path. I do hope so.'

We shook hands and he turned to leave, clearly disappointed. Before he'd gone, I said, 'I hope I have the opportunity to work with you in the future.'

He hesitated for a moment. 'Thank you,' he said. 'The feeling is mutual, although I doubt it will happen.' Indeed, I reflected afterwards, if I were him I would want nothing to do with a patronising old man like me. He reminded me of those I'd known in my youth, who believed all could be cleansed when washed with blood, and if you did not agree with them you were a potential enemy.

29

DREAMS OF REVOLUTION

After the young man had left, I went back to the flat, had a glass of wine and fell into a dreamlike state. The Revolutionary Man's enthusiasm, naivety, determination and idealism reminded me of myself as a young man. In those days, I had bought into the idea of the landless being poor because of capitalism, although then the immediate issue was to rid the country of a despot. To me and many of my contemporaries, the notion of peace under a dictatorship was an anathema: bourgeois and contemptible. I was a student and lived in the city. Although we did not know the term, we were essentially 'cafe guerrillas' and within our ranks were designer urban radicals, mainly sons and daughters of the rich, in Italian suits and blue suede, the Romantic children of the elite. Revolutionary existentialism was our big buzz, although we did not know what it meant. In our minds, we could go amongst the generals like terrorists or like ghosts in a silent movie. We decapitated the statues of the old dictators, we chiselled out new motifs and slogans on the walls of Congress, and found a use for the despot's writings in meeting the perennial need for toilet paper. We marched on the main TV station, and the army opened fire on us. We had no weapons ourselves, except for our cameras, and we ran away.

We had dreamed of 'setting fire to the dog's tail', but there was to be no revolution then. It was to be years later, when I was in the army, that the uprising occurred with almost no prior warning. I had always known one day there would be an attempt at violent change, because otherwise the oppressed would wait around for ever, laughing in their own oppression; the landless were still landless, even when they tore down estate fences in frustration. The poor, tired of being priest-ridden, burned crosses as well as effigies of politicians in the village squares. Their once-loved churches were destroyed. Starving peasants invaded the town centres to plunder government warehouses and supermarkets for food. Yet they had greater ambitions, seeking not only the crumbs from the table, which they never received without fighting for them, but the means to devour even the table itself. Our family neighbour, an old revolutionary, veteran of long-forgotten battles, threw his leg irons into the river and picked up his rifle. Carnival women dressed as the pampered wives of corrupt politicians who were known to scoff at the 'ugliness' of the peasant folk. Banks and luxury car dealerships were firebombed. The opera house, already a rat-infested mausoleum, was torn down.

But the uprising soon lost its spirit and began to wither. Fear and farce plagued it. Personal vengeance and vendettas. Capricious gunfire. Random violence became universal. The army was muscle-bound and heavy, but it won despite itself. The guerrillas were defeated in the forests. The president bribed the Indians to shoot any they encountered, claiming it would be easier than shooting their usual prey. There were massacres on both sides, but ultimately it was a hopeless rebellion, less of a revolt than a media event. The leader of the revolution, inept, had been eclipsed by circumstances. Even small children mocked him as he limped back to his humble little house.

Years later, a rebellion would be more difficult still. Under the veneer of sophistication, amongst the powerful lay the latest version of ancient barbarism. Secret police, detentions, convictions without trial, persecution of all critics - these were now the first rank of artillery, while, because of the constant threat of publicity, the dirty work was done in the dark. Paramilitaries, whose deeds could easily be disowned, or dismissed as overzealousness, never shared any misgivings the armed services might have.

30
MASTER OF SURPRISE

A couple of days after my meeting with the Revolutionary Man, my new friend Andrea rang me to ask what I'd thought of him. This brief conversation led to us going to dinner together. She seemed keen to be away from her cadaverous husband for an evening and told me he had gone to a business dinner. He had a controlling share in an international chemical company, and every now and then he put in an appearance at a corporate event.

I was pleased to see her; I had been going quietly crazy since the cocktail party. I wore a new business suit, and she was in a red and white dress which showed off her figure, though not in a way that was racy or cheap. The venue for our dinner, one she'd suggested, was an expensive Italian restaurant I'd never heard of before, which was a surprise to me because I thought Serena had introduced me to all of them already, especially the pricier ones. I couldn't remember the last time I'd been to a dinner venue with a pianist playing in the background, and it was worth being there for that, regardless of what the food might be like.

'So you quite liked the young man then?' Andrea asked, after we'd ordered. I could tell from her expression that his quiet charm had worked on her.

'He reminded me of myself at that age,' I said, 'which probably sounds awful.'

'Oh, you must have been very handsome.'

I didn't know what to say, blushed slightly, and merely replied, 'I was a bit slimmer in those days.'

'And I'm sure, these days the modern revolutionary doesn't want to look like Pancho Villa,' she said. 'It's a better look to be slightly starved.'

'Well, I liked him a lot but found him rather idealistic, which is a bit worrying.'

'Why so?'

'Idealists do such terrible things in the name of their cause, don't you think?'

'People like Stalin or Mao, you mean, I suppose?'

'No, pretty much all of them. Look for the exception, I say. It's the eternal conflict between the Now, which is unacceptable and in need of improvement, and the Future, imaginary and hopeful, where everything is resolved and better.'

'I never thought of it that way. Hmm.' She frowned.

I continued, 'Take an ambition that is clear, but impossible to achieve, such as to eradicate all poverty, or to make everyone equal, and it can be used to justify whatever action you take in pursuit of it, however barbaric that action might be.'

'I see. Well, I must say, I admire him, idealist or not,' she said, interrupting my flow, which was probably a good thing, since I felt in danger of being boring, which was the worst sin.

'I can tell,' I replied, which brought a beautiful blush to her cheek. 'OK, so we both liked him, but his cause is hopeless, even though our country is probably in a worse mess than ever.'

'Why is it hopeless?' she said, with an air of childish defiance that was quite attractive.

'Because, for all his ideas, I don't think he has the first clue of how to go about it. Technical planning is all. I didn't expect him to share his plans with me - why should he? - but I didn't gain the impression he even knew how to prepare them. I do hope for his sake he chooses another path in life.'

'You sound like a jaded uncle,' she said.

'I suppose I do and that's how he found me. I couldn't blame him. A shame, really. I hope he will mellow with time. But I still don't see what he has to do with Our Man's agenda, whatever that is - does anyone even know? - apart from the desire for power.'

She did not reply immediately, because at this point a waiter brought our starters. 'Sol, Our Man to you, sees him as...'

'Useful?' I interjected. 'That was what you said before. Useful. I'm sure the young man, so willing to put his life on the line for his country, would be gratified at being thought useful by a man like him.' I was being too scathing, a bad habit, and it irritated her. I mentally reproached myself.

'The thing is,' she began, just about to nibble on a small square of toast, 'The thing is, you know just as well as I do, that you have to play every angle in the game. You never know what's going to happen, who's going to be in power, who your friends are going to be. You know what I mean, surely.'

'Only too well. What you really mean is that Our Man would like to ride into power on the coat-tails of a popular uprising, which I doubt will even happen, and be there at the end to claim the big prize.'

'You're far too cynical,' she said in an admonishing manner.

'I know,' I said. 'I try to stop myself. But the truth is, I've seen it all before. I can't help that. If every good cause I've ever been asked to back was a racehorse I'd be a bankrupt three times over. And every mistake there is to make, I've made it. I'm sorry to be so frank. I'm old and tired, and I have a deep-seated reluctance to get involved.'

'And you're bored,' she said triumphantly, as though skewering a darting little fish.

'I need a new purpose in life, that's true,' I said. At this moment I felt I could easily dominate the conversation and, unlike Serena, Andrea probably wouldn't mind, so I checked myself. But she merely sat smiling, sipping her wine. The thought flashed through my mind that she perhaps had other plans for the evening that involved me, but, if so, I wasn't buying, lovely as she was. Home to bed for a nightcap alone would be an entirely acceptable end to the evening for me. She seemed to want me to talk and merely react to what I said, so I carried on. 'Don't get me wrong,' I said, 'he's a good man. It's just that I felt...'

'Patronising,' she said in the tone of a prim English teacher.

'That too,' I replied, 'if you insist. But I don't see anything wrong in feeling a little protective towards him. I felt... paternal is the word I'd use - like giving a younger version of myself some advice. I wouldn't want him to die young out of ignorance, ending up buried in an unmarked grave, courtesy of some paramilitary's bullet. He needs plenty more years to make all his mistakes.'

'I understand,' she said, and I believed she did. We talked a little about the cocktail party and its aftermath. I was as evasive as possible, and, fortunately, she didn't press me on it. We then talked about the old days in government, sharing life stories and anecdotes.

After we'd finished the main course, and I felt satiated on chicken and noodles and a fine Italian red she'd chosen, she took a call on her phone. I excused myself to the men's room and when I returned she was looking pale. 'My husband,' she said sombrely.

I sat down. 'I'm very sorry,' I said, my immediate thought being that the old boy must have suffered a heart attack, or something equally life-threatening, or even life-ending.

'No, not that,' she said, the tiniest wicked smile escaping from her lips. 'No, he tells me there's been a coup back home.'

'Oh, really? So the Smooth Killer...'. I couldn't believe it; was it too much to hope my nemesis was dead?

'Safely behind bars,' she said. So it *had* been too much to hope for. When it came to the Smooth Killer, 'safely behind bars' was a contradiction in terms.

'Well, that's something good,' I said, though unable to hide my disappointment that the old dictator hadn't died in the most excruciating way a new despot or, better, the baying mob, could devise. 'So, who's in charge now? Or is anyone in charge?'

'A colonel, apparently,' she replied, in a tone that suggested she thought a 'proper' coup in our country required at least the rank of general to lead it. She then started laughing, which was a little alarming. 'They call him Elvis. Not his real name.'

I enjoyed the joke, if that's what it was, 'Elvis? You're kidding me. As in Elvis Presley? So how's it been taken?'

'People on the street cheering.'

'They always do. They cheered when the Smooth Killer took over, remember? But if Elvis is anything like his predecessor, they won't be cheering long.' I returned to my feet and raised my glass for a toast, 'Here's to Elvis, whoever he is.'

She stood also. 'To Elvis' we said in unison and took a sip.

'Let's hope he calls off the Rats,' she said. I nodded, even though I suspected the Rats were no longer answerable to anyone.

31

FLASHBACK

Andrea's driver picked her up, and then Zico drove me home from the restaurant. During the journey my mind meandered over the events back home, about which I knew only what she'd told me. The excitement of sudden change in the country brought back to mind another car journey, which had preceded my fall from power as a government minister. It was just such an evening as this, warm with a strong breeze, the smell of tree blossoms and restaurant kitchens, and the sound of fireworks (except on that earlier occasion it was not fireworks we heard but gunfire). Serena and I, both inebriated, were being driven home from an expensive restaurant at which a woman had played piano and we'd enjoyed steak and red wine, feeling good about our lives. But when we arrived home we were met by military police and told we were being arrested. We then had a less pleasant ride to the central police station, during which we learned nothing and Serena repeated over and over, 'I cannot believe this. This cannot be happening.'

At the station we were told we were to be held under house arrest on suspicion of unspecified 'acts against the state', which was a sublimely ambiguous form of words much loved by despots. At the time, I felt as though I had fallen asleep and was navigating my way through a dream, wondering whether perhaps the wine had slipped me into temporary unconsciousness.

Serena's sharp voice was like a jab in the chest. 'How dare you do this!?' she shouted, nearly knocking over a policeman with a sweep of her braceleted forearm. 'Do you know who we are?' When the policeman tried to remonstrate with her, she roared, 'Don't touch me, you creature! You'll pay for this!' and she flailed her arms, an act almost comical in its intensity. It was a bravura performance. The police then held their guns to our faces. There was no point in arguing and no way to seek help, since they had confiscated our phones as soon as they first arrested us, although these were to be later returned.

It was only on the journey back to the house that I became fully alert to our predicament. 'What is this really all about?' I demanded of the military policeman in the car with us. He was annoyed with us, what with Serena kicking his seat like a petulant child and now my question.

He turned to me grimly and stated, 'You're not in charge now. All of you have been arrested. Treat it as a concession that you're not in gaol.'

'Whose concession?' I asked.

He informed us there'd been a coup and told us who the new president was. I knew the man. I knew him well. I'd clashed with him in my latest role of defence minister (which role, despite appearances, I wanted to believe I still held), when he was army chief of staff. His nickname was the Smooth Killer because of his shaved head and reputation for ruthlessness. I'd found him an evil piece of work and a hothead. When factory workers went on strike he wanted us to send in troops to take the works over. He sought to ruthlessly stamp out any first stirrings of public dissent and had wanted to wipe out an entire tribe of indigenous people on the grounds that they 'harboured terrorists'. His attitude was that you did not negotiate with anyone until your foot was holding their throat to the floor. But it had been easy for him to make his demands when he didn't bear responsibility for the consequences.

When we reached home on that calamitous night, there were several military police outside the gates. The one in charge checked his watch and then returned our phones to us. He said we were not allowed to leave the house for any purpose until further notice. In defiance, Serena immediately strode out into the street and shouted with all the strength she could muster at the bemused people peering from their balconies or leaning out of their upper floor windows, 'Tell the world! Bang your pots and pans! Stop this outrage!' Two military policemen grabbed her, and she jostled with them.

'Don't let these pigs and dogs destroy our country!' she yelled. She contrived to fall to the ground, rather like a drunken old actress, grazing her hand negligently in the process. The man in charge told them to leave her alone. As she struggled to her feet, she feigned a spit in the direction of one of those who'd grabbed her. I took her firmly by the arm, span her round and walked her through the gate and to our door. I fumbled for my keys. Once inside, I hugged her, and we both burst into tears as we held each other tight. The alternative life of insecurity we both feared, which had never felt far away from us, was now front and centre.

So began a period of ten months confined to our home. When lawyers tried to intercede on our behalf, they were threatened with arrest too. We were told that if we engaged in any 'seditious activity' our phones and computers would be confiscated and not returned.

Serena was to have a nervous breakdown soon after that evening and was briefly in a secure hospital. I was naturally depressed but soon realised I was one of the lucky ones. Anyone who offered any resistance was beaten up and / or tortured and killed. A reign of terror had begun.

For us house arrest ended when a young, modest-looking governmental official came to visit. He said we could choose exile if we wished, or be formally charged and wait in gaol for trial by a military court, a trial which might never take place. When I said that, put in this way it was hardly a choice, he could not resist a wry smile. Accordingly, our sojourn in exile was about to begin.

32

ELVIS

Andrea rang me one evening to share the latest news. I'd been watching everything I could find on the internet, but the colonel they called Elvis had seemingly come from nowhere to seize centre stage.

'Just what the country needs,' I grumbled, 'another reluctant saviour.'

'So he still means nothing to you?' she asked. 'Nothing triggered from your defence ministry days?'

'No, I confess I don't recognise him. I must admit, seeing him standing outside the palace and the people lining up to cheer, not so much for him but the gaoling of the Smooth Killer, felt rather poignant. Four years ago, it was Old Smoothie coming in that they were celebrating, but I tend to think it was because they were cheering for the end of chaos which they had come to associate with us.'

'You dwell on that too much - don't,' she said. 'You can't base your feelings on the fickleness of the crowd.'

'You're right. And although it's the crowd that has the vote, so many seem not to want it.'

'Do you know why they call him Elvis? Is that really his name?'

'According to the internet, he's an Elvis Presley impersonator. Before he joined the military he used to work the cruise liners.'

'Any good?' she asked.

'I haven't found a video of it. He's a strange one. Eccentric but meticulous, is the impression I've got. An object lesson in how to run a coup. Control of all media early on. That's pretty crucial, as you know.'

'But really it's just one military jacket out and another one in. So what are people saying about him?'

'At random, they say he has a strange reticence, an odd rictus grin, a reputation for drink. They say he walks and talks like a drunk, often wanders completely out of his wits...'

'Oh my!'

'...while in speeches he can lose himself in a tangle of florid metaphors. He has a passion for Jesus, and dope, and guns, and soap actresses. A hard man, they say he eats diamonds for breakfast. He will be the dictator who swoons...'

'What!?'

'He hears the seventh trumpet...'

'I have no idea what you're talking about. You've lost me. Are you drunk? I'm worried about you. So abstruse.'

'I'm sorry. I have had a glass or two, but I'm just reciting off the top of my head some of the things I've read. I've no idea if they're true or not. He likes poetry, a bit like Joe Stalin.'

'And the Smooth Killer. What is it with our dictators and their love of poetry?'

'Yes. I think Joseph Stalin, being a poet himself, is his biggest hero. Apart from Elvis Presley, of course. He wears a tan cowboy hat. A bodyguard places it on his head with the solemnity of a crown.'

'Now I know you're drunk.'

'No, that bit's true. He loves words. He throws them out of his mouth without reference to their meaning. He calls what he's done a revolution. He says, "You may call it a coup, but I know it's a revolution. You can call it what you like. Call it a garden party if it makes you happy." You see, it doesn't matter to him because he's the man in charge now. He does what he wants, and we all talk about it. He loves to remind everyone that he is the soldier. He even keeps a grenade on his office desk, apparently.'

'Oh dear,' she said. 'He sounds just like his predecessor. He sounds like the dictators of old, but even madder.'

'He may be the first Surrealist we've had as president. We've had the ringmaster, and now we've got the clown. Or maybe he's both. Aren't you glad you're not there? I'm expecting lots of military parades, patriotic music. The paramilitaries will never want for work. If the press attack him, he'll shut them down. He's not dull, for sure.'

'Shame,' she said. 'I think I'd prefer dullness. Boring is sometimes good. Were we dull?'

'You could never be dull,' I said. 'But sadly I feel the government in exile is as far away as ever, my dear.'

'Things will change,' she said defiantly. 'We shall will them to change.'

I laughed. 'Well, Elvis is younger than me so I won't hold my breath. But what does it matter to us? We don't have to live there. If it turns out to be good for the people, I'll raise a glass to him. In fact, I'll raise a glass now.'

'I think you've been doing that all evening. You're slurring.'

'For now I'm going incognito.'

'Sorry, was that *incognito* or *incoherent*?'

'Seriously now, I'm not persuaded the Rats will quieten down anytime soon. And I don't intend to take the risk.'

33
A BLOODLESS COUP

It was a bloodless coup, they insisted, and yet all news was hearsay, negotiable. There were reportedly no warning signs, not even a flag in the trees, often a sign of impending change. There were spies in the very stones of the buildings, and yet they did not see it - or they saw but did not report it. To the president they were as unreliable as his dreams. He must have smelt something in the air for he did make a keynote speech that closed the borders. In the frontier towns the rookie soldiers were nervous. They shot at statues; one even hurled a grenade into a passing convertible, because he did not like the expression on the driver's face. Thus, it was not a bloodless coup. That was a lie. The capital was in lockdown, with increased security at major buildings essential. Sirens were heard in every corner of the city. Token riots were calmed with shots in the crowd. When the sacred work was finished, the worthy men of steel left the streets in silence.

All military rulers bore the same smirk, wore the same iron heel, and held the same look of desperation. That's if you could stare hard enough and long enough into their eyes. Behind the darkened limo windows, barracuda-smiling, here were the new crew arriving, quietly littering corpses amongst disaffected generals, or promising adultery amongst their glittering wives.

The season is hot but the country shivers under the new man's thumb. His opponents immediately form a Fifth Column, but he has all the rest, even the Sixth for all those who live in terror of the Fifth.

34
BURGLARY

One morning, I was about to set off to meet Russo to pick up my fake ID documents, when Serena rang me in a state of high dudgeon. 'I've been violated!' she declared breathlessly. 'I shall be destitute!'

'What on earth's the matter?' I asked with studied calm.

'We've had... I've had a burglary.'

'Oh dear. Was much taken?'

'I don't know. Documents. The point is, I don't feel safe anymore. They'll come back, now they've broken in once. It's an outrage.'

I was intrigued as to what documents of hers they might have taken. 'What about your passport?' I asked her.

'No. That was in my handbag which was with me at the time. They came when we... when I was out. In all my life, this has never happened to me before.' I reminded her that there'd been previous attempts.

'Attempts, yes. But they all failed.'

This triggered the happy memory of her once chasing down the street a man who'd tried to rob her. Not content with fighting him off, she did not stop until she'd caught him, knocked him to the ground and held him under arrest until the police arrived. There were other, less pleasant memories. Burglars had visited us several times in the past back home but had always been foiled by the alarm or a security guard. I recalled her saying to me once, 'One of the advantages... probably the *only* good thing about being under house arrest is that I never felt safer.' I could concur with her on that - the military police employed to keep us in also kept burglars out, even though, to be on the safe side, we bribed them.

'I'm glad I've got the gun,' she said.

'Did you get your license?'

'No. I don't think I will just yet. If necessary, I'm sure the officials here are not above being bribed. People here are not above very much, in my opinion. This is truly a desperate place, isn't it? There must be somewhere better we could live.'

'Not back home,' I said. 'That's for sure.'

'I don't know where home is anymore. I feel I don't belong anywhere.'

'Me too,' I said. For a moment I imagined us as two children talking.

I told her I was moving from the apartment. She became alarmed, 'But what about my things there? I have to be sure they'll be safe, especially after this.'

I did not respond and instead changed tack: 'You say they took documents, but you don't seem to know what.' My guess was that the documents were actually her lover's and not hers.

'I think it's another warning,' she said.

'The Rats again?'

'No, I think it's locals. There are a lot of right-wingers around here. Oh, that Elvis Whatsisface would be completely at home. Haters of democracy and especially foreigners. They want to blame us for everything. That incident at the cocktail party didn't help. You'd think they'd be sympathetic but, oh no, they see it as squabbling amongst ourselves on their sacred soil, taking up the time of their precious police - not much time, let's face it. They've got nowhere with their so-called investigation of it, so I understand. They don't care about us, don't want us here, see our culture as inferior and violent, and accuse us of bringing all our problems here to their peaceful, moribund country.'

'Well, do you seriously blame them?' I said.

'Yes, I do. It's not our fault they're so sloppy. I will not be looked down upon by them. And nor should you. We are every bit as good as them, if not better. I thought, naively, that this would be a country of culture and sophistication, but how wrong can you be? For the time being, I think I would like to return to the capital, but I can't if you're moving out. Although, can't you keep the flat on for me? As I say, I have my things there.'

'There's not much,' I said bluntly. 'I was going to send them on for you, if you gave me your address.' The fact was, keeping the flat was an expense I'd hoped to end as soon as the lease allowed.

'Think about it, will you? After all, it'll mean you can come back when you get tired of wherever it is you're going. Where is it, by the way?' I gave her the name of the coastal town I was interested in.

'I see,' she said thoughtfully. 'Probably not a bad choice. Similar to where

I am now, but without all the right-wingers marching every Sunday. And you will retain Julia for me, won't you? A rather inscrutable young thing but very willing.' This was another expense I hadn't contemplated. I stared glumly around the lounge of the overpriced apartment I would soon be leaving - and she would move in, possibly with her boyfriend, and with the benefit of a bodyguard, all at my expense. I looked in the mirror: how had I ever been able to make the cold-hearted decisions required of a cabinet minister? The dilemmas a man in government faced seemed rather easier than those of a husband.

'I do love you,' she said, after what I thought had been silence, but had probably been a monologue of hers that I hadn't listened to. 'You are very sweet, looking after me. Things like this dreadful burglary bring it all home to me.'

35
ADMONITION

I received a call from Andrea unexpectedly. I was interested to find out anything new she'd learned about Elvis, but she had other ideas.

'Whatever is the matter with you?' she demanded, sounding like a bumptious young debutante.

'I'm sorry? I'm not sure I understand what you mean.'

'I'm talking about the cocktail party. You couldn't be bothered to go to the funerals.'

I was bemused. I couldn't understand why she was talking about this now, especially as I'd seen her since then. I said, 'Why are you asking me? It was a conscious decision: I wanted to lie low.'

'Lie low? Like some kind of reptile, you mean?'

I was stunned by her attitude. Was this what she was really like? Serena was never so self-righteously bossy.

'I didn't know them anyway,' I protested. 'As a matter of fact, did you go?'

'I went to one. The other one, I couldn't. But what about the injured? You haven't been to see anyone. People are asking where you are. Why are you hiding? You left early, just before the attack, then you made no contact. What are people supposed to think?'

I liked Andrea. I fancied her. But I didn't need all this. 'I've seen *you*, haven't I? First of all, I wasn't the only one who left early. Our Man, Sol, left before me. Have you had this conversation with him?'

'He had an urgent call. A family matter. I don't know what you're suggesting.'

'I could say the same to you.'

'He went to both the funerals. He's visited all the injured in hospital.'

'I bet he has. Our Man does all the right things. You'll be telling me he healed a few of their wounds next.'

'I do believe you're drunk again. All I'm saying...'

'All you're saying is that I'm a bad person because I left early and I didn't go to the funerals of two people I didn't know. The fact is, my bodyguard, whose advice I almost always follow to the letter, did not like the venue. He said it was too dangerous. He didn't want me to go to the party, and he tried to dissuade me from it. Plus, if I'm honest, I'm increasingly paranoid about everything these days and tend to keep to myself.'

'Yes, paranoid from drinking. It's making you a loner. Reclusive. You're not part of the group, are you?' she harried. 'You'd rather be on the fringe.'

'What group? I don't want to be in any group. What do you want - groupthink? Well, count me out.'

'By the sound of it, you wouldn't make the count. You'd be flat out cold in no time.'

'Call me a maverick if you like, but when I was in government I was the one with most of the ideas. I'm an individual. It's all a fantasy anyway, all this Cabinet of Ourselves talk at a time like this. What are you going to do? Write elegant letters to the press? Raise funds for an insurrection? It's an absurdity.'

I wanted her to ring off before she got any angrier, or I did, but she wasn't done yet: 'So you left early to appease your bodyguard?'

'Not to appease. As I said, I trust him. He felt the place was entirely wrong. So my compromise with him was that I would go to the party but leave early. I was probably the only one there with a bodyguard. What was that about? Where was the extra security? There wasn't any. It was left to the venue.'

'It was only a cocktail party.' Her voice faltered, indicating that she knew she was losing the argument.

'No, it wasn't,' I insisted. If Our Man is supposed to be organising a new political movement, he can start by organising security.'

'You left just before the terrorists arrived. Did you see them?'

'I gave the police a statement. I don't think I need to say anything else to anyone. For all I know, your phone may be bugged. We probably shouldn't even be having this conversation.'

'So would you rather I didn't contact you again?' She sounded hurt.

'I'm not saying that. I need to get away. Too much going on. Now Serena's left me, I need to figure out what I intend to do, and I'm not seeing any answers yet. I'm sorry. Look after yourself.' With that I rang off.

36

MARKET

When I next turned up at Russo's market stall, he was having an argument with a customer. This was a rare occasion as far as I was concerned, not only because I couldn't recall seeing him in a serious argument before, though it must have happened, but also because I couldn't recall ever seeing a customer there. When the unhappy man had left, Russo quickly led me to a nearby bar where we chose a table away from other customers. I bought the beers, and he apologised to me for his mood.

'It's those damned religious relics!' he exclaimed. 'Got me into all kinds of trouble. I knew I shouldn't have got caught up in it. Whatever possessed me to get involved in such a dubious racket? Trade in what you know - why did I ever deviate from that? Religious crooks - aren't they the worst?'

Russo was a true gentleman, and I felt like apologising on behalf of the whole treacherous human race, but he knew better than me that this was an illustration of the world of business - you play it straight all the time and someone somewhere will take advantage of you.

He explained, 'A guy I've been buying from since I started in business - always reliable, never had a problem - told me a monk had approached him, wanting to sell him some genuine Catholic relics from a church needing some cash. So he bought them at "knockdown prices" and was offering me some. He gradually convinced me there was a ready market for this stuff. So I ended up buying the lot - saints' bones, splinters from the Holy Cross, all sorts - all with supposedly good authentication, all in fancy-looking reliquaries. And I sold a few bits, mainly online. Then this man shows up, claims he bought the nose bone of some saint off me, but it was a fake, claims the authentication was signed by a notorious bogus bishop, and even the Latin in the letter is nonsense, the fancy reliquary is actually a cuff-link box, and I'd been well and truly scammed. Then he tells me the bone of St Joan of Arc, which is on my website, is fake because there's no such thing. He says to me: "Didn't you know that she was burned at the stake three times over, and all her ashes were thrown in the River Seine?" Then he tells me that religious relics are notorious for fakes, and says that at one time eighteen different churches in Italy all claimed to have the genuine foreskin of Jesus Christ, and I said, "And since you're so damned smart, I bet you've got the real one on your bedroom wall!" So I gave him his money back...'

'Was that the man who was just here?'

'No,' he chuckled ruefully. That's another story... Anyway, so I return the customer his money and take the nose bone back, but then I wonder if he just scammed me and maybe he swapped it for a fake. So I contact the guy who sold it to me, and now he's out of business. And to cap it all, the monk's disappeared. In fact, there was no monk and not even a church! So now I'm thinking: how do I offload all this stuff? Then this fellow rings me...'

'The one who was here today?'

'Yes. He tells me he wants to see me about these relics, so I'm thinking, that's great, I've got a new customer. You see, I'm still naively believing, or wanting to think, that the stuff's genuine. So he shows up, but instead of talking business he starts berating me. He tells me that the sale of the body parts of saints is not allowed by the Catholic Church anymore, and that it's a disgusting and ungodly trade, and those that engaged in it would get their just deserts and face eternal damnation.'

'Oh Lord!'

'Exactly. Then, to cap all of that, he says that he sees it as his role, on behalf of everything holy, to remove this stuff from the market and, in "furtherance" of that, he'd offer me a hundred dollars for the lot - which is far less than even one per cent of what I paid for it! I'm afraid my patience was exhausted at this point, so I just told him to go to Hell. It's bad enough having to accept the fact that I've been swindled, but to have to listen to these self-righteous smart arses lecturing me, rubbing my nose in my ignorance...'

'Rubbing your nose *bone*...'

'Alright, alright, rubbing my nose *bone* in it... is more than I can bear. Damned thing! I don't know if it's genuine or not. How could I? Saint Someone-Or-Other - I'd never heard of him. All I know is, if I buy something for ten I want to sell it for fifteen, or at least twelve minimum. Simple, you'd think. If I bought it in good faith, I should be able to sell it in good faith. You wouldn't want to buy a saint's nose bone, would you? Of course you wouldn't. That's why I didn't talk to you about it before I got suckered into this. You're such a miserable bastard you'd have told me not to be so stupid, but for once in my life I wished I were you.'

'It's not about the money, though, is it?' I said cheekily.

'No,' he said, and he immediately stood up, grabbed my unpocketed change and threw it at me coin by coin, as I put up my arms to shield myself like a boxer on the ropes, 'No - it - absolutely - *is* - about the - money! And what's more, for the avoidance of doubt, as my favourite shyster lawyer loves to say, it *always* is about the money!'

When he'd sat down again, now flushed, he produced the ID documents he'd obtained for me. I noticed my new identity was Garcia. He said, 'It had to be either that, Smith, or Khan, or something with three 'z's and no vowels, so I chose Garcia for you. You've got your passport, driving licence, bank account, two credit cards and national insurance. All you need now is a life to go with it.'

'Thanks.'

'There's a guy over on the other side of the capital, and all he does is create fake ID documents. He's got a whole factory doing it. The way it's going with this relics business, I might need to get one myself.'

I checked the documents over and then paid him. A little later, he asked me, 'So, you think you're maybe going home now? Now your friend, the Smooth Killer, is in gaol?'

'No. It'd just be my luck that as soon as I got there he'd be out again, strutting about like a peacock. Who's to say Elvis will be any better anyway? I watched his coronation on the internet - did you? I half expected him to start singing *His Latest Flame* or something.'

'Nice words, weren't they?' he said. 'Nice words for a wife beater obsessed with his enemies, Did you hear that "enemies within or without" bit? Doesn't augur well. They're all the same, aren't they, these dictators? By the way, they say he drinks to excess. It puts him into tirades apparently. But he must have been sober enough to organise the coup, so I think people maybe underestimate him. And he hits things. Already smashed up some of the furniture in a rage. Some expensive stuff it was. I said to myself when I heard it, "If only he'd asked me, I could have found him some junk furniture he could smash up and some to replace it with."'

'He's going to be tough, I fear,' I said.

'Yes. Hard on dissidents, communists (if there is still such a thing) and homosexuals. And forget about human rights. No, it's true, it would be too dangerous for you to go back right now. Meanwhile, the Rats could be worse than ever. Go out and hide in the woods if you have to, but you'll need to be well-armed. Not that I need to tell you. You're not taking Zico, is that right?'

'Yes, that's correct. But Serena wants to come back to the capital, and she wants to retain Julia. I don't mind.'

'You mean you're going to be paying for it? Got you round her finger; you're like a fish that doesn't even know it's hooked.'

'I know it alright. She always does it. I know I'm a soft touch. My own fault. I guess I just like a quiet life. Is that so wrong?'

'Oh, don't we all? I would love to give up my stall and sail around the world, but I'd rather sell tat than be a journalist any day of the week. That's one of the most dangerous professions going, especially when you come from our country.' He took a large swig of beer. 'Sometimes I wish I could drown myself in that,' he said ruefully. I was taken aback at this uncharacteristically stark comment. 'Not really,' he said smiling, having caught my look of concern. 'But what if all the religious relics I bought turned out to be fake? It doesn't bear thinking about. Maybe I should take a rifle shooting course or something and become a bodyguard for you.'

'I thought you were going to take shooting lessons anyway,' I said.

He sighed. 'No. Our last conversation put me off a little.'

'You'd be good as a bodyguard,' I said negligently.

'I'd be persistent, that's for sure. Trouble is, I'd chase after them until I knew they were dead.' He drained his glass. 'Well, better get back to it. So the docs are OK?'

'Yes.'

'It's a shame I've got to get back. I'd fancy another. I trust the girls, but they lack confidence, and it embarrasses them to have to ask a customer to wait for me to return. Then there's the difficult ones. Especially if it's some bastard bringing back the Lord's foreskin or something. I could tell them to get lost - caveat emptor and all that - but it's not good for the old reputation. OK, old friend, let me know where you wash up next. I might even take a day off and come and visit.' With that, the best friend I'd ever had hurried back to his stall.

37

INDUCEMENTS

In one of his first speeches as president, Elvis made clear he intended to 'root out' corruption and recoup from the 'thieves' in previous governments their 'ill-gotten gains'. This was standard cheapjack talk that regularly fell out of the mouths of every political leader, whether elected or not, but it gave me some concern. I'd always been as opposed to corruption as anyone else, but had found that in reality it was not so straightforward.

When I had my first ministerial job, every tender for purchase came with the offer of inducements - commissions, service contracts for myself and Serena, gifts, or simple cash bribes. I quickly discovered that, as I'd suspected, this was an area of human enterprise where creativity thrived. At the time, I was aware that other ministers had accepted such inducements, whether they admitted it or not. These were people I held in high regard in all other respects. When I spoke to the then Prime Minister about my concerns regarding the bribes being offered, he told me disconcertingly not to worry about it. It was obvious to me that he himself was a beneficiary of such arrangements. Otherwise, coming from a family of no great wealth, how could he have accumulated three mansions, a Ferrari, three nightclubs and a golf course on only a politician's salary?

With hindsight, I wondered why I'd even bothered to ask him. He poured us coffee and sat down in a chair beside me and patiently explained how, if I were to reject inducements (which he called 'work-related bonuses'), I would be casting unwarranted shame upon a well-established and fair system, from which many justifiably benefitted. It would be insulting to other ministers and, indeed, those seeking contracts with us. I came to realise that the system for handling such rewards was one of the best-run government mechanisms of all.

'Remember,' he said to me in a sagacious tone, 'this is not a country where ministers earn a fat salary. We are like the staff in your favourite restaurant who rely on tips. But they don't have everyone at their door, everyone quick to blame when something goes wrong. If a waiter serves a slightly undercooked fish you complain to him, but you don't demand that he be fired - he didn't cook the wretched thing. We are under terrific pressure all the time. And, let us not forget, it can all end suddenly overnight. You go to work one morning and find a tinpot general - I apologise - a dictator has taken over, and you can end up in gaol - house arrest if you're lucky - whether you've done anything wrong or not. This is not a career where you can plan for the future. Some of us have long careers but, for most of us, our time in office is short and often runs in fits and starts. Therefore such - I would call them *routine* bonuses - can provide some compensation for the risks inherent in our work, the risk of a prematurely shortened career. Do you understand what I'm saying?'

'Yes, I suppose so.' Although I said these words, in my mind I was still unconvinced.

'Have you never bribed a policeman?' he asked. I was initially startled and lost for a reply. He continued, 'Let's put it another way: has a traffic cop never told you your car should be taken off the road because there's a spot of mud on the licence plate, but for a small on-the-spot payment it can be dealt with? You see, it's good for the government because it saves paperwork, and paperwork would mean employing more police, which means more cost to the taxpayer, whereas this way it makes the policeman happy so he'll stay in the job. Do you know how little a policeman earns for doing what can be a very stressful and dangerous job?'

'No.'

'Take it from me, it's not very much, so why deny him that little extra? If we look after the police and, for that matter, the military, they will look after us. Isn't that right?'

'I suppose it is.'

Over time, and through experience and trial and error, I came to an understanding that size of 'bonus' was a good guide to making decisions. Contracts were complex and time-consuming. Weighing up the pros and cons of a particular bid for, say, a fleet of tanks was not easy. There were the technical difficulties, there were budgets, there was the issue of our trade relationships with other countries. Of course, there were civil servants to help, but it was a certainty that they were being bribed as well, so what was a minister to do? If I banned all defence department staff from accepting inducements, I'd soon face a walkout. Besides, the companies we dealt with saw our bonuses as a cost of doing business. To suddenly stop accepting them would seem like a judgement on them, on their past behaviour. Thus, I gradually lost my scruples about it. Not for me great mansions and expensive cars, however. If, as the Prime Minister had suggested, my career might be short, I felt that any bonus that fell into my lap in performance of my duties should, where possible, be in cash. 'Fell into my lap' was the appropriate phrase because I drew the line at requesting a bribe, or negotiating how much the bonus should be. A suitable pause in discussions or a temporary impasse in negotiations always sufficed to remove any resistance to offering one. Such money as I earned in this way was put in safe-keeping in Switzerland, and later in offshore funds, and I took a regular income from it. Indeed, this proved fortuitous since, after being put under house arrest for no reason, I had not earned a penny. Of course, some high-minded individuals put their proceeds into foundations, ostensibly charitable, although everything they put in they took out again in expenses.

Serena was of course aware that I had a Swiss bank account and it became a source of great pride to her. After a while, I even set up an account in her name and she drew an income from that. A third account, however, I kept a secret. I told myself this was not a deception on my part, but a way of preserving a fund of last resort in the event our other funds ran out.

Now we were in exile, I came to see the money I'd prudently stashed away as a form of compensation. Because of the coup, I had wrongfully been denied the opportunity to continue as a minister. With time, I ceased to see the accounts as having any connection with my past life.

Elvis' comments about 'past corruption' did bother me as to what he might intend, however. Then again, the Smooth Killer had likewise promised a thorough investigation into this but, despite punishing all the previous crop of ministers without charge, he did nothing to pursue any specific allegations of corruption, probably because he quickly learned to milk the system for himself. Besides, the people who'd do the investigations would themselves be bribed up to their necks and would pursue their labours with only the veneer of diligence. With luck, any initiative Elvis launched would befall the same fate.

38
GUNFIRE

Because he had toppled my nemesis, I held a fascination for Elvis in the early days of his presidency. He was good at making speeches, although once he started talking he found it hard to stop and tended to veer off into gibberish. There he stood proudly on the presidential balcony in his army fatigues and peaked cap setting out his plans. The future he envisaged was not one that appealed to me, as it sounded like he was taking the country back to some earlier, more narrow-minded time, but I'd long believed that society did not naturally progress along a path towards tolerance and understanding, and instead took a more haphazard, unpredictable track. The underlying human characteristic, it seemed to me, was barbarism, and that didn't diminish; it didn't even become more sophisticated - the means of barbarism merely found a greater variety of forms of expression.

The regal colonel was courting the traditional family, church and nation sector. He considered homosexuality and abortion both abominations. Gays, he said, were responsible for disease and a general decline in moral values. Abortion was an attack on God. When railing against corruption, he proclaimed, 'The termites must not be able to destroy the edifice of state,' which sounded so grand I felt sure he must have stolen it from someone else's speech.

Within a few months, I thought, he'd soon be salting away his share, or rather the share of half of the population. Since I had my own guilty secret in this respect, I had to contemplate the possibility of extradition proceedings. It occurred to me that this might make me safer than before, at least initially, provided the process could be prolonged by an adequately skilled lawyer, since if they wanted to find Swiss bank accounts and offshore tax havens it would be easier if I were still alive.

I abandoned my musings on Elvis' speech, on hearing gunfire outside. I went to the window but saw nothing to explain it. Was this another outbreak of the violence we exiles had imported with us? It was shaming. Our hosts would be all too glad to assist with extradition. It would give their emergency services less to do. Meanwhile, hostile local journalists and lazy politicians would have less to blame us for.

I heard more gunfire and reached for my pistol which, since the cocktail party, now felt as though it were itching to see more action. Its last shot had been a hit. It was like a muscle. If you started using it and then stopped, it got restless. I went up close to the open window and looked in one direction down the street and then the other. I saw Zico, who was on his last day of service with me, on the street, standing relaxed. I called out to him, 'Did you hear the gun? That wasn't you, was it?' He looked puzzled. The gunfire!' I shouted. 'Didn't you hear it!?'

'Gunfire? There's no gunman out here.'

'But I heard it.'

'You didn't.' He started laughing.

'I can't believe you didn't hear it.'

'No,' he said with finality. 'What you heard was a car backfire.'

'Oh.' I was nonplussed, for I was so used to the opposite: hearing a car backfiring turn out to be a gun. Once, I reminded myself, I could tell the difference.

39
ACT

That night, I had a disturbing dream. In it, Russo and I were young students living in the same quarters. It was a very warm evening, and we had no air conditioning. We went outside on to the city street to catch some air and maybe go for a beer at one of the open air bars. We were strolling through Congress Square, deep in conversation, as usual about nothing in particular, when we heard gunfire. We glanced in the direction of Congress House where a man, whom I immediately recognised as the leader of the unofficial Opposition, fell crumpled to the ground. There was no doubt it was him. I recognised his red puffy face, greased hair and ill-fitting suit. It was obvious he was dead. I could see blood spattered on the wall behind him.

His supporters were there, a hundred or so, maybe more. I was conscious of being an observer, a stranger, not part of the unfolding drama. People were crying, angry, shouting, running across the square. Seeing this hysteria prompted us, without thinking, to run. In my head I was grappling with the realisation that I had witnessed a piece of history which I was barely able to comprehend. The act of running with the crowd made us absorb their fear.

Once we were out of the square, we began walking once more. After we caught our breath back, we began to argue about what we'd seen. We could not agree on whether it had been an illusion or not. I believed it was some form of trickery, while he believed it was real. Our argument became ever more heated, so much so that we parted morosely and even took separate trains home. We met up again later. Reconciled, we limped home like brothers chastened for some joint nefarious enterprise.

We returned to our little home in confusion and sorrow. The immediate past was like the air, uncomfortably close. That night, we drank hard and the sweat rolled down our faces. It was a febrile, suffocating night. The mad old man next door banged on the wall and shouted obscenities, not at us but at the heat, the unbearable heat, while we argued continuously about what we'd seen and what we hadn't seen, about our own bravery and cowardice, about believing our own minds, about believing the media, desperate as we felt, frantic for a word of support from somewhere. There was no breaking news on TV about it, nor on the internet which we checked every few minutes. We rang friends and they'd heard nothing, or so they assured us - but could we even believe them? We argued between us about why there was nothing anywhere being said about it. It gnawed at us, and we went over and over what had happened. It could have been a confidence trick, mass hysteria, collective false memory, even a macabre piece of street theatre. Perhaps a film was being made, and we were all extras, even though we hadn't seen a film crew with all their equipment. We couldn't understand why we hadn't filmed the scene ourselves.

We checked the news all next day. Still nothing. And no-one had heard anything. We even thought about returning to the scene to look for any signs, such as the bloodstains, even flowers left for the victim, but we agreed between us there'd be no evidence. We tried to find the victim on social media, but he was not there, no trace of him ever having existed.

40
MOVE

On the evening before my move, Serena phoned me and said, 'I'm worried about you. Are you OK?'

I was puzzled as to what had brought on this latest concern. 'Never better,' I replied heartily and insincerely.

'Only my psychic told me to be watchful, said something ill could befall someone...'

'Something ill? How quaint. Is that how psychics talk?'

'Something bad, if you must.'

'OK and...'

'Said something bad could befall someone I care about. I naturally thought of you.'

'That's kind, I guess. OK. Thanks for the warning. So what do you - or rather, your psychic - suggest I do about it? And what is the "something ill" likely to be?'

There was a noticeable pause until she said, 'Well, you could always consult a fortune teller.' I nearly fell off the chair I was perched on at that moment, taken aback over her sudden interest in psychics, since, despite her exaggerated sense of entitlement, she had always been relatively level-headed. It felt like a bit of a racket to me: a psychic worries you concerning your spouse, and to find out what the spouse needs to worry about they need to consult someone else in the fortune telling business. Work for one was work for all. It reminded me of a lawyer on TV who tells you about some problem you never even knew you had, nor indeed imagined anyone could have, and when asked any question about it replies, 'You need to consult a lawyer on that.'

'You could go and see a Tarot reader,' Serena said.

'OK.' That would at least be more colourful and enjoyable than poking about amongst tea leaves or the first stool of the day, or whatever fortune tellers did. I said, 'Did your psychic give any clues at all?'

She then added that the 'loved one' would be knocked over by a force like a hurricane.

'I see,' I said. 'I think that's enough to worry about for now. Any sign of something stronger than a light breeze and I'll find a basement bar somewhere. But perhaps they mean someone else you care about. I suppose what bothers me is that I might go and see a Tarot person, assuming I can find one, and they'll say something equally vague which could easily be established as true but leave me none the wiser.'

'You're such...'

'I wish I could get into this fortune telling scam. But then I wouldn't be any good at it. I can't bullshit enough - always been my weakness.'

'You're such a cynic.'

'I hear that Elvis is going to ban psychics and whatnot. That and putting the Smooth Killer away shows he's not all bad.'

She ended the call in a huff, and I couldn't resist a fit of laughter. She took it all so seriously. Compared to some things I'd experienced, being bowled over in a hurricane was pretty small stuff. Unless of course the building I was in was being bowled over at the same time. But hurricanes here were not a major risk anyway.

I yawned. It had been a relatively busy day: buying a shotgun under my old name and a car under my new name, a second-hand Mercedes I paid cash for.

My new home was a small cottage near the sea in a rambling town with cultural pretensions. I knew already that it had a concert hall with a reasonable reputation and many bars with music nights. I knew there were a few exiles from the old country living there, but I wasn't especially keen to make their acquaintance. Although it was gratifying to know they were in the area, there was always the potential in their midst for the odd Rat, keen to check any new addition to the local expatriate community against his list of 'legitimate' targets.

41
ART BECKONS

When I wasn't reading, talking or trying to make sense of what was happening in the country of my birth, I continued to wonder what I should do with the rest of my life. As a former soldier and politician, I was not convinced I could be much use to another country. I had considered offering to train new army officers, but was not satisfied such an idea would be well received, or whether such openings even existed. Moreover, if it attracted the attention of politicians in my adopted country, it might not end well for me. The perennial advice of fellow exiles was to keep a low profile, and, following the debacle at the cocktail party, this advice seemed particularly wise.

Other than being able to fire a gun, which I continued to practice regularly, I did not have any particular aptitude. I could not do carpentry or plaster a room. The simple skills of the average householder were beyond me. My mother, who brought me up from the age of three on her own, always paid for such things. Now I rather regretted not having learned those skills. How rewarding to be able to build your own house, or even make a simple chair, enjoying it in the knowledge it was your own handiwork. And yet the tedium of such work was reason enough not to start. I had a low boredom threshold which was fatal to such endeavours.

I could write a bit but had no desire to produce freelance articles, for it would take no more than three sentences for my journalistic efforts to turn into diatribes against the regime back home. Journalism was a hazardous occupation, as Russo said, and was just another way to draw unwanted attention to yourself. Ideally, I wanted to be forgotten.

On reading in the local newspaper that art classes were available at the town's cultural centre, I decided to sign up. Although a hopeless draughtsman, I thought there must be some form of abstract art I could attempt, enough to satisfy my imagination at least. Anyone I'd ever known who'd tried art said they found it rewarding. I could quite happily live in a house full of canvases no-one would ever want to buy. Moreover, if I actually produced a work that someone was prepared to offer money for, the dilemma might be unbearable.

With all this in mind, I purchased a couple of art *How To* books to give me enough confidence to at least turn up for class.

42
DISSENT

While looking at freelance articles about the old country on the internet, I found a statement by a writer friend of mine from the old days who like me was in exile, having suffered at the hands of various crazy dictators. He'd had it tougher than me, having known his share of filthy gaols and solitary confinement. He was fearless, nothing touched him inside, which was where it mattered. We became friends after the government I served in released him from house arrest. More than that, I admired his writings.

The spoken statement he gave was in response to a question he was asked about the scope for dissent under Elvis' regime. It struck me as an odd question, but I was keen to hear his answer, his words typically carefully chosen.

'Under the current government,' he said, 'which does not govern so much as tyrannise its people, we have the dictatorship of the so-called harmonious society - harmonious and, if possible, homogenous - which brooks no dissent. There is no place for the sceptic, let alone something as bold as a critic. They have already arrested the staff of one magazine, imprisoning them for spreading falsehoods about the president's mental health.' He chuckled sarcastically at this point. 'There's a saying that the poor, who have nothing, at least have the Ministry of Information; except that noble department does not give them information so much as take it from them and everyone else - information that results in nightly abductions of democracy activists by the notorious white vans. From outside the disused sports stadium, people can almost hear the accused twitching at trial, and when the music starts they know for sure someone is being tortured. The list of deaths is of course kept confidential.'

After listening to the statement, I turned next to a video of a reading he gave in which he said, 'Democracy is dead, but don't be fooled: it merely turns in its grave. The state belongs to all but has been stolen. We can only encourage the young to wrench it back, for the old cannot be relied upon, since it is they who created this travesty. The old have tamed the visible, but only the young can tame the invisible.'

It reminded me of when I was a young radical, which was when I first encountered him. I was in a group and there were about thirty of us. One night, we stayed up late listening to excerpts from *Open Veins of Latin America* by Eduardo Galeano and other radical writings, read by a scraggly-haired young man none of us knew. Next day, we were a dishevelled army, inspired to greatness as we marched towards the presidential palace. There we shook our fists and shouted, demanding the president appear. But when he did emerge, we hesitated. Seeing him in the flesh on the balcony we became nervous, confused like charging soldiers caught out by a ceasefire order. The police rushed in and we immediately melted away into the city's fashionable coffee bars. Without time to feel foolish, and with no opportunity for real plans, in our minds we would set a hard face to the wind and smash up limousines in darkened side streets, as a rebellion against the ruling elite and, if need be, against life itself. The man who was later to become my friend mocked us, telling us to get back to our schoolbooks and efforts, thus far fruitless, to find girlfriends.

43
ART CLASS

I went to my first art class a week later. The contact for the class said it was easygoing, people turned up as often as they liked, paying what sounded like a modest amount per class. It suited me well. I wasn't sure I'd have the patience for painting, but it was something I was determined to give a proper try. If it didn't work out, it was something I could at least delete from my list of things not attempted yet. Accordingly, having sought advice from the local art shop as to what I might need, I arrived at the class with fresh paints, palette, graphite pencil, eraser and so on, but most of all with the confidence that is sometimes born out of happy ignorance.

The art teacher was a tall young woman, quite dark with a flamboyant flowery dress and jewellery that jangled, a Chinese bob hairdo and jet earrings. She had a distinctive triangular mark on her forehead which looked like a port-wine stain. She seemed friendly but a little nervous. She introduced me to the rest of the class, mainly redundant middle-aged people like me, or pensioners, and she told me what the current topic was, namely a city scene. I immediately knew from her accent that she was from my home country.

I took to the topic with the joyful abandon of a dog chasing a stick into the sea. I chose a grey scene, the capital in the rain. I soon began to think my picture looked rather depressing, however, so I introduced some exotic trees and plants, as well as a couple of brightly-coloured cars. I was hesitant with the brush but felt that confidence would surely grow with time, provided I overcame my initial difficulty. The teacher, Sasha, sat down next to me now and then, which I found a trifle unnerving, especially as her scent had a subtlety that was almost seductive, all of which had the effect of making me concentrate harder on the task in hand. She advised me not to be timid when painting. She showed me how to use the brush to be more expressive with it.

'Don't worry about being too accurate,' she said, blushing slightly. 'There's nothing to worry about. Let go.'

Although the result discouraged me a little, I felt very welcome, which was more important at this stage. Sasha gave us some exercises to do as homework. Claiming to be a 'hard taskmaster', she exhorted us, almost sternly, to 'Practice, practice, practice. Look hard at the colour of things - the real colour, not the colour you initially see, or think you see. Look at faces, buildings - ruins are especially good, or disused buildings - walls, fading flowers. Immerse yourself in it. Above all, don't dabble, don't dither on the edge - jump right in!'

Over the following days, I set about the exercises with relish. I felt like a child again, a child with all the wonder and energy of a new enthusiasm. I kept in mind Sasha's words 'Don't dabble' and her exhortation to practise. I spent hour upon hour working on my rough pictures. One exercise she'd given us was to cut out photographs from magazines of simple scenes that appealed to us, and to paint them as closely as possible in terms of their colour but not their form. It didn't matter about results, she'd said. The aim was to be bold, to take on the challenge without fear. It wasn't about whether you were good or bad; to be able to grow as a painter, which is what would make all the practice feel worthwhile, it was necessary to do as much as possible. It should be a joyful experience, not something to fret over, be afraid of, or procrastinate about. I found it all rather inspiring, enabling me to focus entirely upon something, to immerse myself in what I saw around me, and to relax for once, to forget all about politics, fears of violence, what to do with my life, and everything else that had bothered me in the capital and prevented me from enjoying life. When I wasn't at home painting, I was in the town buying art materials or walking around looking at, not so much objects, as their colours. I worked on as many paintings as I could physically create, usually small works, and by evening I would feel exhausted, relishing every new day and, above all, the next class.

44
DR KIDD

I was saddened to read in an online newspaper that a former president of ours, in later life an exile like myself, had passed away. He was in his early sixties and so only a few years older than me. The paper said he died of natural causes, which was bizarre in itself. He'd cheated death so many times they called him the Cat. After surviving a staged car accident, an attempt to blow up his private jet, and a gunman's bullets fired from within the presidential palace grounds, the idea he'd died in such a mundane way was scarcely credible.

I rang Andrea. This gave me the chance to ask after her ailing husband and mend the metaphorical fence with her that we'd managed to wreck the last time we spoke. I used a phone Russo had given me with my fake ID package. She didn't answer, so I left a message explaining this was my new number. She delayed returning my call, which could have been out of caution - maybe thinking I was someone pretending to be me - or she could have been trying to punish me. I soon grew tired of waiting, however, so I tried again. This time she answered.

'Heard the news?' I asked her.

'About the Cat, our dear old president? Not so old really.'

'Bit of a shock.'

'No, not really,' she said mysteriously. 'We all knew they'd get him in the end.'

'What do you mean?' I felt I must be very naive, perhaps more so than I was accustomed to find in myself, but there were certain news outlets it was my habit to rely upon totally for their accuracy. 'I read it was natural causes.'

'Do you seriously believe that?' she said scathingly. 'Do you think that's really possible? He was, by all accounts, strong and relatively fit, didn't drink or smoke. Parents died in their eighties.'

'Old soldiers, who've escaped death or injury countless times, often succumb to a simple commonplace infection,' I said. 'Nevertheless, it did strike me as rather odd. But he died in a hospital and surely they must know.'

'You really think so?' she said in the tone of someone told something they knew was completely illogical.

'He was in hospital with a respiratory condition,' I said.

'Or rather, he was in a private clinic for tests for a *possible* respiratory condition,' she said pedantically.

'I see. But how...' I scratched my head. Instead of her irritation with me, she was now tormenting me with silence. I said, 'You're toying with me.'

After a pause, she replied: 'OK. His usual physician was there, but a second doctor took over. They gave him an injection, he was discharged, sent home and died.'

'OK. So? What am I missing?'

'The name of the doctor who gave the injection was Kidd.'

'OK.'

'The only problem is, there is no Dr Kidd on the clinic's register. No-one knows who he is.'

'Some administrative error. Some other doctor there. They muddled up the names.'

'No. There is no-one else it could be. And Dr Kidd, so-called, has disappeared.'

'My God!'

'Indeed. Now the family wants an inquest. They claim he was poisoned.'

Before the call ended I asked her how her husband was. 'He's been getting better, thanks,' she said sombrely. 'Although, after this latest news, he's not feeling particularly well.'

45

HOUSE

In my imagination, I soon saw myself as a poor, struggling French artist living in seclusion and dedicated to achieving perfection in art. I was surely the only poor, struggling French artist with a secret Swiss bank account. Meanwhile, I gradually became acclimatised to my new environment. As in other places I'd lived, I soon developed a routine. I started going to the same restaurant and bar every day, where I could gradually get to know the staff and pick up the local gossip. On one occasion in my favourite coffee bar, I recognised a familiar face: it was my art teacher Sasha dressed in a black cape she had wrapped theatrically around her. She was alone and looked nervous, as through trying not to notice me while she waited at the counter. I consciously ignored her and returned to my thoughts on the mystery concerning the demise of the former president. Despite what Andrea had said, I still wanted to believe it was death by natural causes. I did not like to think there was such a thing as a fake doctor assassinating people and certainly not in the country I was now living in. I was grappling with these thoughts when I looked up to find Sasha standing in front of my table. Without saying anything, she sat down to the side of me, which left me completely unnerved.

She apologised and then asked shyly, 'So how's the art going?' My attention was unavoidably drawn to her port-wine stain and, conscious of this, I switched my gaze to her hand, gently resting on the table; it was flecked with little blue and red paint marks and clutched the bag containing her sandwich.

In response, I gabbled: 'If it's all about being prolific, it's going wonderfully. I've never been so productive. Probably never been so happy either. It has taken me over, and I thank you for making it possible.'

'Me?' She blushed. 'Oh, I don't think I've done anything. I can only encourage you to think in certain ways, to not be afraid of it. So you've found it useful then?' She stood up abruptly, disconcerting me again.

'Indeed.'

'I look forward to seeing what you've done. Bring them to class next time.'

'Oh, there's so many. I've gone a bit overboard with it. Some people would say so anyway.'

'Oh, well, that's marvellous...' She was flustered but looked happy. She sat down again. 'Perhaps I could see them anyway.'

'They're in a variety of states,' I said, alarmed at the prospect that she might arrive unannounced at my home, which was irrational since she did not know where I lived. She might want an invitation to visit right away, but being focused on painting so much I hadn't made even the pretence of keeping the place tidy. 'None are properly finished. Some embarrassingly bad, I'm sure. Some hopefully not terrible.'

She crinkled her nose. 'Hmm. So that's a No, then.'

She was about to leap to her feet again, but I instinctively put my hand on her arm. 'Do you have to rush off? Don't you have time for a quick drink?' She didn't answer, I removed my hand and said, 'I only came in here for a snack anyway. They can wrap it for me.'

She turned to face me, eyes wide, studying me. 'OK then. Let's go.'

We both stood up. 'You will excuse the mess?'

'Are you on your own?'

'Yes. No. I mean, my wife's away. The place is quite close by.'

I settled up at the counter, and we left.

I walked her to the cottage. We talked a little about our lives in the old country. I didn't say I'd been a member of the government, or even a senior military officer. For all I knew, she could be an informer for the Rats, willingly or not. She was equally circumspect. When I asked her whether any of her family were still there, she replied, 'No' in a tone that suggested she did not welcome the question and saw her previous life as closed. I did not pursue the issue, however, not wishing to embarrass her.

When we arrived, she seemed fascinated by everything, as though seeing simple everyday objects with fresh eyes. Unfortunately, I'd left the Glock pistol partially uncovered on the table. I saw her stare at it for a moment, and then her attention turned to the paintings.

'It's going well,' she said. 'I'm glad you're in the class.' She was particularly intrigued by an abstract picture that was a crude attempt at depicting a bright scarlet heart being attacked by sharks all around it. I was a little embarrassed by it, since to me it was the kind of thing a confused teenager might produce. 'I love this,' she said.

'Really?' I scratched the back of my head, 'I thought it a bit...'

'Pretentious?'

'Yes.'

'Well it is. That's why I like it.' Was this meant to be a compliment, I wondered?

When she'd finished looking at the pictures and made a few comments about most of them, I made coffee. We sat across from each other on either side of the fireplace. She said, 'Why do you have that?'

'Eh?' I turned round to look at the table. She meant the gun. 'Oh, just a precaution. Dangerous times.'

'Really?' She was genuinely bemused.

'It was for my wife's benefit. She got jittery in the capital.'

'But she's not here, is she? There's no trace of her.'

'You mean the mess?'

'And this is not the capital.' I did not respond. She could not understand why I needed a gun and I had no intention of revealing anything about my previous life. So I said nothing and felt a little sad, as though it mattered, which it didn't. She drained her cup suddenly, stood up and said, 'You don't strike me as a gangster. You're a soldier, aren't you?' Her tone was accusatory. 'I thought so.'

'Was a soldier,' I said.

'I knew it. I can tell.' The brightness had vanished from her face. 'Well,' she said, a little nervously but firmly, 'I had better be on my way.'

46

THE ASSASSIN

The strange death of the former president reminded me, as if I needed it, of how vulnerable we political exiles were. We laughed at the paranoia of dictators, but ours was no less real. To have one's food tasted by someone else before touching it always struck me as the height of pretension, as well as possibly fatal for the poor 'someone else', but its logic was undeniable. To have to take one's own food everywhere and never go to a restaurant would be intolerable. I could easily imagine a 'Dr Kidd' discovering I had a favourite restaurant. He could appear, as if by magic, to take my order and obligingly add a little secret seasoning of his own design to my peppered steak. I had chosen to move in order to be rid of such fears, but they were already once again rattling through the suburbs towards me.

Fear constrained one's life into ever smaller compartments. If I had to check the car for a bomb every time I chose to drive to the supermarket, I'd soon choose instead to have my groceries delivered. No, on reflection, that was impossible, for I could be unwittingly inviting the assassin to my front door! A carefree stroll to the beach was no longer carefree when you were constantly having to check to see who else was around. Any parcel I received was taken into the garden and opened with the care and concentration of a skilled surgeon at work.

On the road, any car in the rear view mirror for more than a few minutes was a potential threat. I looked for obscure routes, back roads, although the isolation of these ways provided their own risks, including the scarcity of potential witnesses to act as a possible deterrent. When walking in town, I always checked to see who was behind me. It brought to mind the time Russo believed he was being followed and the routine I devised for him that showed he was correct in his suspicions. If I was concerned about someone behind me, I crossed the road, and if they did the same I crossed again. Unlike Russo, I wanted them to know.

The former president had known such risks since the first days he was in power, to the extent that he had perhaps become immune, even blasé, about them. As well as the many known attempts on his life, there were no doubt others that had been planned, even started, but aborted. He used to joke about it, saying he was a magnet for any would-be assassin or hitman down on his luck. He claimed not to worry about it. Knowing that his life could end at any moment, day or night, gave him a kind of freedom. It was a genuinely existentialist life he had. He was probably the happiest amongst all of us.

There was I, worrying whether I should hire a bodyguard again, or whether I had enough firepower to defeat a small army, worried about extradition and about murder by a hired hoodlum, while real life passed me by. And yet it wasn't passing me by. Art was giving me a way out of my fears. When the drug-hungry, lone gunman reached town, with the only details he needed about me firmly at the front of his mind, I hoped Fate would ensure he arrived just at the weary but ecstatic moment when I put down my paintbrush, having completed my latest, largest and best work. As he held his gun to my head, assuming he allowed himself such a luxury, rather than simply blasting away with it, perhaps I'd ask him what he thought of the painting. In my fantasy of this moment, he became transfixed by its beauty, or its inherent fascination at least, his brutish mind desperately trying to absorb its sheer power, thus enabling me the second or less I needed to reach for my sacred, emancipatory, loaded Glock.

47

PICNIC

In the weeks after Sasha came to my cottage, I saw her many times, not only at class. I knew her place was only a few minutes' walk from mine, but I was still surprised at how often our paths crossed. It occurred to me that she was following me, and this was disconcerting. I now seriously wondered whether she was a spy. Her art class would not pay her much and, unless she was selling her own work, she might need a source of extra income. Whenever I stopped somewhere for a coffee, she would arrive shortly afterwards. From this I reached the easy conclusion that my daily routine was too predictable. She knew what time I left the house from habit. Increasingly, this bothered me. I had to escape from this routine, but I was scarcely aware how repetitious it was. Even if she was not following me, someone else could easily do so.

Whenever I met Sasha, our conversation was always pleasant and almost entirely about art. It was as though it was the only thing she was comfortable talking about. Whenever I changed the subject, usually deliberately, she always brought it back to painting. This was not boring to me but endearing and, unless it was some clever tactic unfamiliar to me, inconsistent with the notion of her as a spy, since a spy would want me to reveal more of myself, whereas she was learning relatively little. I was not comfortable, however, at the ease with which she had been able to extract from me the fact that I was a former soldier, although, then again, numerically so were most of my male compatriots over conscription age. Nonetheless, the fact that the commonplace, perhaps trivial, topics of conversation, particularly about the past, made her ill at ease, made me curious to know the reason behind it. It was almost as though the curiosity I felt was the result of seduction, drawing me towards her, but to what end?

One particularly beautiful morning, as usual I was at one of my favourite coffee shops, sitting outside enjoying the sunshine, when she approached me, as if from nowhere, and asked me if I fancied going for a picnic. In that picnics were invariably disappointing, I normally viewed the prospect negatively, but such misgivings were easily dismissed by the appeal to my vanity presented by such a lovely young woman wanting to spend a few hours with me. Surely I would learn more about her - she could not spend the whole time talking about art.

'I'll be at yours by one - is that OK?' she said. When I pointed out I had nothing to contribute and so would need to pick up food from the supermarket, she said, 'Don't worry. I have plenty of food. Mainly vegetarian; you don't mind, do you?'

'No. I prefer it.'

'OK. I'll just bring a basket to yours. Lots of different things and... shall we go in your car? Find a quiet spot. There's some nice little secluded beaches along the coast.'

We followed her plan and she introduced me to a quiet stretch of sand which backed on to open countryside and was sheltered from the wind by a rocky outcrop. She'd brought wine, and I had a little of it, whereas she drank quickly as though nervous. At one point, she stood up abruptly, removed her shoes and socks, picked up the hem of her white, mid-length dress and ran into the sea where she paddled like a child. She seemed happy, and I was too.

We spent several hours there, relaxing on the towels we'd brought. When we talked, it was about culture and nature. I wanted to know what she thought about the political situation back home, but she had nothing to say about it and she was right - why spoil a lovely afternoon talking about that? Any questions that approached the personal she pushed gently but firmly away.

As the air began to cool and the tide was quickly coming in, we packed up the picnic things and left. I drove her back to her place. By now she was quite drunk, which concerned me. She invited me in. When I politely demurred, she became a little tearful, which I found odd and so, a little reluctantly, I accompanied her into her home, which was a small cottage, not dissimilar to mine, surprisingly sparsely furnished with an old floral-motif sofa, but little else, in the lounge. I couldn't see any paintings, and I wondered whether her studio was upstairs. She disappeared into the kitchen for another bottle of wine, then poured herself a large glass and drank most of it immediately. We sat on the sofa, she to my right and with her knees pulled up under her chin, her arms wrapped round her legs. Gradually she began to flirt with me. She pulled up her dress to reveal her thigh, then put her feet to the floor, turned towards me and leaned in close to show off her cleavage. It embarrassed me.

'What are you doing?' I said. I was flat sober.

'Whatever do you mean?' she replied. There was more flirting by her. I took a large swig of wine straight from the bottle and was quickly inebriated. Without thinking, I put my arm round her shoulders, then leaned towards her and ran my left hand up her exposed leg towards the top of her thigh while my right hand gently stroked her neck.

'What are you trying to do?' she said sharply, no longer playful.

'I'm just... I don't know.' I was flustered.

'What do you think you're doing?' she demanded, serious, accusatory.

'I'm sorry. It just seemed so natural. I wasn't thinking.'

'Yes, you were. You were thinking of taking advantage of me because I'm drunk. Well, I'm not drunk now.'

'No, I...'

'Were you going to rape me?'

'No, of course not. Why would I do that?' I was bewildered by this sudden change in her.

'Because it's what soldiers do.'

I was annoyed now, 'No. No, what is this - some sort of trap?'

'You told me you're a soldier.'

'Not now, I'm not.'

'You were a soldier, and you're always a soldier. That's what soldiers do.'

'No.'

'Go on then, try and rape me. I can't stop you. You'd be too strong.'

'I don't understand you. Why are you like this?'

'You want to do it. I can't stop you. Do it.'

'No, I think I should...'

'What? Leave and never come back? I agree. You messed everything up. I was so happy for once, and you've ruined it with your stupidity, with your lust.'

'I'm sorry. Forget...'

'No, I can't.'

'Sasha, please, I'm truly sorry.'

'Shut up!' She was becoming increasingly unhinged. Her face was full of rage, her port-wine stain seemed to have turned into a heavy red. I just wanted to be out of there.

'Listen to me,' she said. 'I believe that God is a woman. And I have her wrath. I *am* her wrath. You've done me wrong.' I stood up, annoyed at her, bored with her. 'Yes, you have,' she said. 'You've done me wrong.'

'I'm sorry, I don't see how.' I strode towards the door.

'You have. You don't know how, but you have. Go. Get out. Leave me.' She burst into tears and I left. The afternoon was ruined. I couldn't figure out how it had gone so wrong. Was it really my fault, or had it been inevitable?

That night, I hardly slept at all, but when I did I dreamt I was in court accused of committing an awful crime. I didn't even understand I'd done anything, let alone anything that might be called a crime.

48
JUSTICE

In the strange dream I had during the night after the picnic, all I knew was that I was guilty. I did not know why. From within it, I tried to puzzle it out. There was no incident involving me, but witnesses appeared. There was no crime alleged, but the police were called. No investigation was conducted, but a report was written. There was no victim, but there was a perpetrator. There was no interview, but there were statements. There were no injuries, but there was a room full of claimants. There was no court, but there was a judge. There was no trial, but there were rulings. There was nothing said, but there were press quotes. There was no police file, but the state attached no blame. The case was closed, and yet, to my relief, it had never been open.

49

EXPLANATION

I didn't see Sasha for a while after the day of the picnic. The series of classes were over, and I stopped seeing her around the town. I felt a sense of confused regret. Late one morning, I was gleefully reviewing the latest internet stories about Elvis' actions back home, when I saw a familiar form approaching my door. She was dressed in a long black hooded cloak. I noticed it was beginning to rain, but I waited for her to knock before I got up, thinking she might simply want to deliver a note or something. I invited her in, but she hesitated and merely stood there.

'Are you sure you don't want to come in?' I said. 'No point getting wet.' She came in, removed her cloak to reveal a long, red and black print dress, and sat down awkwardly at my lounge table. I offered her a drink. She declined. Fortunately, I was out of alcohol.

'You've obviously come with something to say to me,' I said. 'I'm sorry that I upset you. I...'

'Don't,' she said. 'It's very difficult for me to talk about.'

'Let me guess,' I said, immediately feeling foolish since I didn't know what words to use.

'I don't think so,' she said. 'You fumbling around clumsily saying the wrong thing. It would only make it worse.' She sighed heavily. 'Oh, go on, if you must.'

'You had some sort of... You had a bad experience back home. A bad experience involving soldiers.'

She stared hard at me. My attention was as usual drawn to the port-wine stain on her forehead. In my imagination it was throbbing with inner rage.

'I confess,' she said after a long pause, 'that at that moment - and this will sound weird - I wanted to dare you to try to... to rape me.'

'A trap,' I said, puzzled.

'If you like to see it that way, yes. Now I felt I should come to try and explain myself. I owe you that at least.' By this point she was talking through tears.

'OK.' I took a deep breath. 'I want you to understand that you can tell me whatever you want. As little or as much.' She had come to talk about herself, but I felt compelled to explain myself: 'I was not going to rape you. I would never. Whether you say you wanted to dare me to - which is something I cannot understand - or not, I won't touch you. I didn't mean... I misunderstood. I'm a bit stupid. I misinterpret. Signs, signals - I misread them.'

'If you see them at all,' she said sharply.

'Yes.'

'That was quite a little speech,' she said.

'I realised afterwards I shouldn't have touched you. You'd been drinking.'

'So you thought you'd take advantage.' I didn't reply. I was condemned whatever I said. She stared ahead and then added starkly, 'I disgraced myself. I can't defend that.' She turned to look at me. 'I'm sorry. I knew you were a soldier. It wasn't only the gun.'

'Anyone can have a gun,' I said.

'But I knew before that. I just knew. And that's why I gave you so much attention. Of course, I was attracted by the fact we shared the same interest - in art, I mean - although for me it's an obsession. It's probably why I have so few friends!' She laughed with a touch of bitterness. 'But I... I wanted to hurt you because you're a soldier. I hate soldiers. I wanted to hurt you on behalf of all of them. I wanted to steal your stupid gun and hit you right between the eyes with it, ram it right into your brain. I know it doesn't make sense. And it's wrong.'

'It's strange,' I said. 'I don't understand it.' She did not respond and, since I had nothing to say at that moment, I went into the kitchen to make coffee. When I returned to the lounge, she had picked up the Glock (which I'd left on the table, partially covered by a newspaper) and was clearly fascinated by it, turning it over in her hands.

'Is this loaded?' she asked.

'Yes. Please put it down.'

'You were careless.'

'Yes I was. Now please put it down.'

She pointed it at me. It wavered in her hand. 'Beg,' she said.

'What?'

'Beg me not to shoot, soldier.'

'You're crazy!'

'Beg.'

I doubted she could shoot straight but wasn't taking any chances. Even a toddler could fire a gun and kill someone. I might survive but be missing part of my face. I reluctantly got down on one knee and said, 'Sasha, I beg you not to shoot me.' I was expecting her to continue the drama by holding the gun to my forehead, but she merely laughed and put the end of the gun barrel between her lips and slid it in and out. 'Sasha, please!' She was trembling with fear as she placed it back on the table. 'Talk to me,' I said. 'Say anything you want. I won't be shocked. I've seen everything.'

She seemed suddenly emboldened. 'OK. Have you seen a fourteen-year-old girl raped?'

'I've seen a girl raped. A teenager.'

'When you were a soldier?'

'Yes.'

'So why didn't you stop it?'

'I couldn't.'

'Did you join in?'

'No!'

'And you know what I'm going to say: I was that girl you didn't help. Soldiers came to our village, looking for dissidents. One of the dissidents' leaders was from our village. My dad had said some things at a meeting in town; someone snitched on him. They sought him out. They took him away - and my mum.'

'Are you sure it wasn't...'

'It wasn't paramilitaries, if that's what you mean. It was regular, trained, supposedly disciplined soldiers. I ran away. They came after me. One of them jumped on me, made some joke about this...' - she pointed to the stain on her forehead - 'and pinned me to the ground. I fought as best I could, but I was weak compared to him. Then one of the others pushed him off, and that one raped me - very violently. The first one then found an old woman and raped her.' She paused, I gave no reply, taking it all in, and she added, 'So that was the end of my innocence, the end of any last vestige of childhood. I felt he was going to kill me, I felt that I was nothing, just a piece of trash. And that feeling stays with me always. So perhaps you can understand, even with your primitive soldier's mind, why I feel hate for you. I can't help it.'

'But do you really hate me, or the fact that I was a soldier?'

'Both. It might seem unjust - and it is - but I do. And I'm sorry because you probably don't deserve it.'

'So why have you come here?'

'To tell you all this. Like I said, I owed it.'

'I see. Well you won't have to see me again. I'm sorry about what happened to you. I really am. And I'm sorry I caused you distress. I certainly never meant to.'

'I know.'

I picked up the gun from the table and took it upstairs, where I kept my shotgun and the other pistol. By the time I'd returned downstairs she'd gone, leaving the front door ajar.

50
IN DEFENCE OF SOLDIERY

Sasha's hatred of soldiers depressed me, even though I could, at least intellectually, understand it. Some soldiers were terrible people - some of the worst, including psychopathic killers. To be effective in the battlefield they had to possess the killing instinct, but it was hard to control in a man sometimes. The army accepted all sorts, including thugs who hadn't been making any money and listless men in need of discipline. The army worked to mould these often damaged individuals into a cohesive unit. Too often the rush to fight ended in anarchic violence, wild destruction, killing of civilians (innocent or not) and mass rapes. It wasn't surprising that some people, who'd never been under attack from a force of marauding outsiders, might consider an army unnecessary, but without an army there would be the risk of the utmost savagery; there would be far more violence and it would be uncontrolled and never-ending.

Every civilian victim of soldiers berated the army bitterly. Criticism went to the top. When I was a senior officer, I often had to discipline men who'd betrayed the people's trust in them, and defend those who hadn't. It was not easy. After some atrocity or other, often not the fault of the armed services, but of paramilitaries, victims banded together and sanctimonious politicians became involved, as well as human rights organisations and lawyers, all together pointing their fingers at the army's leaders.

It was our job to train the men to be more skilled and disciplined soldiers, but also to nurture the support of the country, whom we ultimately served. The worst for an army were internal military campaigns. Everyone could unite against an outside enemy, but when that enemy came from within the country's borders, it was hugely difficult. Today's jumped up teenage terrorist was tomorrow's self-righteous, middle-aged politician. And the whole time, the majority of the public, represented by political leaders and other loudmouths, wanted you to be tougher in order to maintain the peace and order they craved. Any tinpot dictator like Elvis could be popular with the majority of the public if they could achieve that much. Chaos satisfied no-one, except those bent on destruction of the state. Without order there could be no democracy, and to maintain it, in some countries at least, a hopefully brief period of dictatorship was occasionally necessary.

Someone like Sasha had an anger that would never dissipate. She was a tragic casualty of the fight for order. She would never understand the need for the military campaign that had inadvertently ruined her young life. Of course I knew that soldiers raped. As a young recruit what could I do about it? There was no means and no real desire on the part of the military to punish the offenders. Some even saw it as a perk of the job. No-one said anything about it. It sickened me that it happened, and it sickened me that nothing was ever done about it. I once vowed that, if I ever became responsible for the military, I would do something to stop it, but when I reached that position it carried on. The fact there were needless victims such as Sasha did not obviate the need for the military campaign in the first place. To the army the preservation of order was paramount.

I went through these thoughts as I lay on my bed, but I came to no satisfactory conclusion. There was and always would be the need for soldiers, but why did I feel the need to defend them from raped children? It struck me as a travesty upon a travesty, if that was not too intolerably glib.

51
LIST

Russo called me early one morning. The first thing he said was, 'Seen the list?'

I was only half-awake, having just got out of bed. 'What list?'

'The extradition list, of course.'

'What!?' I was fully alert now. 'Why so soon? That's worrying.'

'Is it?' he said.

'Well, I suppose the Rats might be less active. They won't want us dead before they fleece us. They'll want to know where all the loot's buried. Although, having said that, I'm not sure the communication's that good between our government and the Rats. They are their own law.'

'I don't know,' he said. 'They won't get paid if they shoot the wrong person.'

'There is that.'

Russo then revealed that he planned to visit, which startled me. I wasn't entirely comfortable with it. What if he was followed, bearing in mind he didn't seem to care overmuch about personal security? And what if Sasha turned up and made a scene? What would he make of my art? Surely, he'd think I was the pretentious wastrel he'd always believed I was. But he was someone it was very difficult for me to deny anything to. Besides, I needed cheering up and no-one was better for me at that.

Later that morning, Russo arrived in a beat-up Merc he'd got in compensation for some dodgy religious relics he'd been landed with: 'I still made a loss, but what's money when you're happy, right?'

'It helps,' I said sombrely.

'Isn't this is a lovely place?' he enthused. 'Near the sea, too. You're not short of cash.'

'You don't know. You would if you had Serena to keep afloat.'

'Why, is the old boat sinking?'

'She doesn't know she's born. When it comes to getting through money, she's a torpedo.'

'I thought you had her on an allowance.'

'Oh, she's ripped the backside out of that by the end of the first week every month. But I'm not complaining. Not really.'

'Not complaining? That does make a change.' Looking around the lounge, he said, 'What's all this?'

'Just some artwork.'

'Interesting,' he said. 'Avant-garde.'

'An up-and-coming artist,' I said.

'I see. How much did you pay for it all? Quite a collection.'

'Pay? Oh, about five hundred dollars each,' I replied without thinking.

'Really? You were done.'

I said, 'As a friend, I'll offer you one for three hundred. Any one.'

'No thanks,' he said. 'But maybe if I hadn't got this relics racket round my neck, I would. I can't afford to dabble in anything else I know nothing about. I know you wouldn't rip me off, but who would I sell it to? That would be my concern.' He sat down on the sofa, looking at a rock music magazine while I made us coffee. When I returned, he said, 'Are you sure you didn't paint these yourself? There's one over there that's clearly not finished. I know it's abstract, but even I can tell that.'

'The painter sadly died,' I said, trying successfully to suppress a grin.

'If he strung a line like you do, he deserved it. Tell you what, I'll give you a hundred for that one there - those flowers.'

'Flowers? They're people's faces. Can't you see?' He sighed heavily. 'OK,' I said. 'But I couldn't accept a hundred from you.'

'But you'd accept two hundred, right? I always knew you were a hard-nosed bastard under that laconic exterior. Well, to be honest, it's all it'd be worth to me. I haven't a space on my wall and I'd have a hard time selling it.'

'No,' I said, chuckling, 'What I mean is, have it.'

'Really? That's kind. All I'll say is, you have a very good teacher.'

'I do,' I said. 'So you have the extradition list with you?' I asked, keen to change the subject. 'Where did you get it?'

'Government website. I printed it off. I'd have emailed it, but, for all I know, they're watching my traffic. They're watching everything else. I change my phone every other day. They get up late, that's the good thing. I was already ten miles out of town when I rang you from McDonald's.' He handed me the list. 'I may as well tell you right away, we're both on it.'

'Both?'

'So you think I'm not important enough?' He laughed sarcastically. 'It's outrageous to include me, frankly.'

'Yeah, but you're an intermediary. Any exile who needs help comes to you.'

'Yes, but this is supposed to be about finding ill-gotten gains, not settling old scores. What do they want from me - some martyred saint's tibia?'

I perused the list. No real surprises apart from him. My hope was that he'd made a mistake and I'd been omitted. But, no, there I was, well down the third page, well below Andrea and her deathly spouse, and far below the anointed future leader, Our Man. Serena did not appear on it, which she would take as a personal slight.

'If I had any money,' he said, 'I'd just send it to them. But it's not that easy, is it?'

'No,' I said. I didn't want to admit I had salted away cash - I was sure he knew it anyway - and I didn't want to have to justify it, reminding him how the Smooth Killer had robbed me of my career and put me under house arrest without charge, which always sounded self-serving and self-pitying.

'This doesn't bother me much,' I said, lying. 'Maybe it should, but it doesn't. There are so many on this list and many who never served any punishment at all. I was never charged with anything, for a start. A good lawyer... even a mediocre lawyer, could tie this up for years.'

'I worry about our hosts,' he said. 'I don't know why they don't just throw us all out of here. Surely we're more trouble than we're worth. We contribute to the economy in a small way, but think of all the work for the emergency services, the police...'

'I wouldn't worry about the police,' I said. 'They're so slow and inept, they virtually never turn up.'

'Well, they haven't got far with that cocktail party incident. No arrests.'

'I thought all the terrorists were killed.'

'Yes, but no-one believes there weren't others supporting them, waiting to strike at any time. By the way, you didn't tell me about Zico's exploits that night. You kept that quiet.'

'I had to. I hope it's not too well-known.'

'Don't worry, it's not. I find out everything in the end. You must miss him, though.'

'I do, but I like to tell myself I don't need him any more. Don't forget, I'm still paying for Julia, now Serena's moved back to the apartment.'

'Oh, you're such a soft touch. But you did the right thing in changing identity. I sometimes think I ought to do the same, but I can't really be bothered. I've always known when to get out of a situation, and I'm not yet feeling the need, even now I'm on this damned list.' He flicked the page contemptuously. 'I'm tired, maybe lazy, but I can't be doing with any more change. It'll soon be time to lawyer up, my friend.'

Russo had brought some expensive wine with him. We were feeling sorry for ourselves and got drunk. He stayed over. Not once did I feel the need to mention anything further about Sasha.

52

COMPANY

When Russo stayed with me, he commented on my lack of female company and once again offered to provide me with an escort in the usual half jokey / half serious way of his. It was true I was missing it. It hadn't been a concern in the capital because, although Serena had been away so much, there was always such a lot going on, particularly concerning personal safety, that I didn't have time to feel lonely for long. Here there were no such distractions. Of course, most of my time was taken up with art, which was less of a hobby than an exploration of reality, or so I liked to think, but my commitment to it was waning; it was increasingly becoming more of a labour than a pleasurable activity. Russo's apparently sincere interest in my work - in the end, he did take the one he thought looked like flowers but was intended to be people - gave me the aggrandised notion that with practice I was capable of painting masterpieces, or at least a body of work worth exhibiting in an up-and-coming gallery. I knew it was absurd that I should be so preoccupied with success in an activity I'd so recently started; instead of painting whatever came into my imagination, I now chose subjects from the viewpoint of their potential saleability, and this irritated me to an extent that it spoilt my previously entirely innocent enthusiasm.

Apart from the moment of weakness when Sasha had been drunk and flirted outrageously, I had not seen her in terms of a sexual conquest, or any kind of relationship beyond that of tutor and pupil in the field of artistic endeavour. It was not that she wasn't beautiful - she was in her individualistic way - and nor was it our difference in ages, but the notion of our becoming an 'item' was impossible, even in my vainest fantasies. Besides, she was as volatile as a grenade with the pin taken out, and trying to figure out what was in her head at any given moment was impossible. She had been damaged so seriously as a teenager, it seemed, the question of whether it was possible for her to find a happy existence for herself was beyond me. I knew nothing of her suffering, only that it was real. There was nothing synthetic about her. For that fact alone, she was amongst the highest rank of people I had ever encountered, even if our coming together had sent us spinning apart, as though Fate had clashed our heads together for no reason but sheer malice.

Sasha's arrival into my life and her swift departure had left me with a vacuum that had not been there before I met her. In order to address this feeling of absence, and inspired by Russo's half-serious suggestion, I began exploring the possibility of paid-for company.

Following up on an ad in a newspaper's personal section: *Discreet Senior Director Offers Professional Services*, I visited a woman named Chloe who, it transpired, was of a similar age to myself. She lived only a few streets away, and I immediately began visiting her small, slightly dishevelled detached house set back from a quiet road, for talk and sex every Friday afternoon. It was a sublime situation. She naturally bore the emotional bruises of most in middle age, her immediate problem being the need to find an income since her husband had left - hence her new profession. I soon gained the impression that she was popular with clients - and certainly some of the gifts she'd received bore this out - and that most of them were many years younger than her. She was true to her advertisement: discreet and businesslike, but also kind and, at least ostensibly, genuinely caring. The arrangement suited me perfectly. Every week at the same time, I walked through her untidy garden with its high hedges to her door, and once inside we went through the same ritual: talking about how the week had been and then having sex, which seemed to me oddly innocent despite its financial nature.

After Sasha's histrionics and Serena's unrelentingly regal sense of entitlement, it was a welcome diversion. I realised it would not last: I did not intend to visit a prostitute every week for the rest of my life and, indeed, Chloe, undoubtedly a clever woman, clearly saw it as a temporary arrangement until she could find a job in administration or accountancy, which were her preferred areas of work.

I asked her once what she would tell a prospective employer in accountancy about her previous employment for the last few years.

'Easy,' she replied. 'Professional management services for private clients. If they asked for more details I'd make up something relevant, and if they asked for a reference I'd give them your name.'

53
BEING WATCHED

Serena phoned me from the apartment, having moved back in. She sounded highly stressed, which I suspected was her normal state since she'd left me. I wondered if it was a new diet she was on - not enough carbohydrates maybe?

'It's quite intolerable,' she complained.

'What is, darling?'

'I feel I'm under surveillance all the time.'

'But aren't you used to that by now? Wasn't that why you wanted to get out of the capital in the first place?'

'Exactly. To get away from it. And I did, but it's back again. It shouldn't be like this. I don't think you appreciate what it's like.'

'Oh, I assure you I do.'

'I'm aware of something there, something sinister, and I look and there's nothing there. It drives me mad. It's worse than if there really was something there. I'm constantly on edge, anticipating something will happen.'

'Isn't Julia there with you?'

She sounded exasperated with me: 'Of course she is, but she can only deal with what's there. She's very good but she's not a psychic.'

'So it's what is not there that's worrying you?' I felt this conversation was going to be hard work, so I switched on the TV, which was showing a feature on handbag dogs.

'No, it's not only the feeling that there's someone there when there isn't...'

'Right.' I was half-confident I understood her.

'There really is someone watching the flat. I've seen them.'

'As well as the ones you only imagine?'

She could not resist a gentle laugh. 'Yes, if you want to put it that way. Someone stands there looking. A short man with one of those hats - a trilby - and a trench coat.' On TV there was now a girl in a bikini on a beach.

Serena said, 'I don't think you're taking this entirely seriously.'

'I'm trying to, I'm sure.'

'Julia went to accost him and he just walked away. But then he came back. And someone's been calling round at the flat.'

'Same person?'

'Of course not.'

'Well, what do they want?'

'They ask for someone called Mr Close or something like that. Not one of your aliases is it?'

'Oh, I have so many. No, it's not, and who are these people that are calling? I mean, what are they like?'

'Well, there's two of them.' I found I was beginning to feel uneasy. 'Yes,' she said, 'one of them does all the talking. He's short and wiry. Looks like a teenager until he's up close. The other one stands to one side, only just in sight, leaning in now and then almost as a reminder. He's large and heavy and mean-looking, hands big as grave shovels.' On the TV there was now an image of a baker pounding dough. 'It's always the same question: "Is Mr M. Close there?" And always the same answer: "There's no Mr Close lives here and I've never heard of him."'

I said, 'M. Close? Maybe it's the alias of someone else.'

She was silent for a moment, frustrated. 'Why is everything so complicated?'

'There is a simple answer.'

'Go on.'

'Maybe Mr Close, or whatever his real name is, used to live there.'

'Why didn't you say that before?'

'I'm just guessing. But it's a reasonable guess. People often disappear owing money. I might have to do that myself one day. If they call again, challenge them as to what it's about.'

'Yes.' For all her sophistication, Serena could sometimes be like a helpless child. 'The only thing is,' she said, 'I thought we were the first people to live there. Remember the brochure?'

'Hmm.' I could remember it, and it now occurred to me that she was probably right. Who was the dummy now?

'Anyway,' she said, 'I understand there's a list. An extradition list.'

'Yes. So I gather. Anything arrived there about it?'

'Not on that, no. I'm wondering if that's why someone's watching the flat. They're waiting for you. Are you on the list?'

'I am. Russo showed it to me, actually. I'm very well down it, though. Page three, I'm happy to say.'

'Well it wouldn't do to not be on it at all, would it? So what page am I on?'

'I didn't see.'

'Well didn't you check it over?'

'I think you're not on it.'

'Really!?'

'You missed that bullet.'

'That's outrageous! Is your friend Andrea's husband on it?'

'Yes. And Andrea,'

'Andrea too? I can't believe what I'm hearing. I was under house arrest too. They didn't make a distinction then. Don't these people realise? Huh! What an insult! I've got a good mind to complain to the embassy.'

'I wouldn't...'

'No, of course, that wouldn't be such a good idea, would it?'

'I wouldn't have anything to do with them. Probably teeming with Rats. I mean the human kind.'

'I understand. What will happen if... when they try to extradite you?'

'I suppose I'll have to be formally charged first. Hopefully, lawyers can slow it all down.'

'And what will I do, seeing as I'm not on the list? We pretty much lead separate lives these days.'

'You could always divorce me,' I said, tongue in cheek.

'Heavens, no! I do still love you, you know.'

'I thought you wouldn't bite,' I said.

'You don't expect me to, do you? Seriously?'

'No, you're too insecure for that.'

'Yes I am, aren't I? I don't know what to do in a crisis. I either act without thinking or I freeze.'

'But you're not alone there, are you?' I said.

'I am at the moment. Perhaps I should come and visit you.'

Visit? I was immediately flustered by this, especially given the fact she felt she was being watched. They'd follow her car, which wasn't difficult because she always drove sedately, as though leading a funeral procession.

'I take it you want to keep Julia on for the time being?' I said.

'I don't think I could cope without her. It's just a shame she has to sleep. I'd like her here twenty-four hours a day if I could. I had thought of employing Zico as well. He was very good.'

'He's engaged elsewhere,' I said, not knowing whether this was true, but I was determined not to incur the cost of him as well.

'OK,' she said with a sigh, nothing resolved to her satisfaction. 'I guess I'll soldier on. Goodbye.'

54
STATE VIOLENCE

I tried to throw myself into art in order to manage my wilder fears but found it increasingly difficult. Without Sasha's encouragement, the impulse had weakened, the inspiration all but gone. Perhaps my initial productivity had been unconsciously intended to please her. Often I was tempted to contact her, but I feared this would only invite trouble. I had to reacquire the motivation from some other means. Otherwise, I would merely drift listlessly, quietly going crazy. I wondered whether Chloe could provide such an impetus, but the idea was unsatisfactory; my relationship with her, if such it could be called, was compartmentalised. Like good sleep, it refreshed my day-to-day existence but was separate from it, linked only through dreams or random thoughts.

Although I wasn't painting, except for a handful of minutes every day, ritualised in a fruitless search for inspiration, I was at least living the reclusive life of the artist I liked to imagine I had become. My aversion to the prospect of encountering Sasha was such that I avoided my previous haunts - restaurant, bar, certain shops, and most days I stayed indoors, apart from the odd trip to the firing range. Occasionally, I drove out to some fishing village for lunch, but this only made me feel bereft, with no-one to share the experience with, or talk to about it afterwards. I would tell Chloe where I'd been during the previous week, but that didn't suffice. It was like talking to a therapist: it served its purpose, but it was not the same as sharing it with a friend who might want to accompany me another time.

Thus, I spent my time reading, mostly articles on the internet related to developments back home. It helped me come to terms with the fact that the extradition process would eventually uncoil itself and come sliding along a relentless path towards me. What I read about the old country was not reassuring. Whoever was doing publicity for the government was not doing a great job. If the internet was to be believed, violence - which is to say, state violence - was increasing by the week. I was particularly upset to learn that a comedian I remembered fondly, having enjoyed watching him on TV many times in the old days, even been the butt of his jokes when I was in office, had been killed. A motorcyclist had pulled up beside his car as he waited at the traffic lights, taken a pistol from out of his jacket, and opened fire. This was on the outskirts of my old hometown. He'd made a joke about Elvis (the president, not the singer), word had got out, and the president's henchmen had picked it up. The comedian was much loved, but that was no protection.

Nor was it protection for a well-known actor. He'd been drawing attention to the plight of the indigenous peoples, a cause I to some extent shared with him, and had been arrested by the police. They had forced their way into the film studio where he was working and suddenly appeared on the set. The actor was halfway through an emotional speech in a melodrama when they handcuffed him. It was all recorded on film, but the authorities did not care. If anything, it helped them, for what clearer warning could there be about the need to keep quiet? In another incident, a playwright, whose play had been shut down because it was critical of the autocracy, was shot. It was reported that he was depressed at the play's closure. Concerned he might commit suicide, the authorities killed him to save him the trouble.

Such stories were the stuff of my average day. Depressing though they were, I could not ignore them. More than ever, it seemed, the country was being run by thugs and crooks. It was a gangster state. The nation appeared to be cowed and this, more than anything else, troubled me greatly. I could understand why people who had a voice talked so much about change, but the grip of the gangsters was so tight that any criticism was stifled and its author rubbed out. If a much revered comic could be disposed of so easily, what hope did an opposition politician have?

55
CALL

One morning, I found myself stuck staring at an uncompleted picture with my palette in front of me; even the act of picking up the brush was too much, such was my lack of inspiration. I was tempted to ring Sasha but was determined not to convey any sense of needing or wanting her, especially given her volatility. I'd just made my third strong cup of coffee of the day when I received a call from her.

'Were you thinking of me?' she said.

'No,' I lied.

'Only I suddenly had a compulsion to call you.'

'I'm flattered, I think.'

'Don't be.' There was a haughtiness in her tone. 'What did you want?'

'Excuse me, but it's you ringing me.'

'So pedantic. Anyway, I do have news: I'm leaving.'

'Oh.' I was genuinely taken aback. 'Shame,' I said.

'Don't be sarcastic. I'm having to leave.'

'Why?'

'My landlady. She thinks I'm a lesbian.'

'Is she right?'

'No, as if it made any difference.'

'It doesn't. So what happened, if you didn't tell her you were gay?'

'I was with my therapist. In my bedroom. The landlady came into the place demanding the rent. I'll admit I'd been putting it off until the money from the sale of a couple of paintings came through. She refuses to wait. It's just an excuse.'

'Can't you see it as an opportunity? Wouldn't a bigger place be better for your pictures?'

'I don't keep them there. I have a garage someone lends me.'

'I don't understand. Are you not allowed visitors, or something?'

'You're so prurient. You're desperate for the details, aren't you? Typical. My therapist is gay, and I know she fancies me.'

'Some new interpretation of "professional" perhaps?'

She sighed wearily. 'She was giving me a massage, that's all. She said I was full of tension and stress.'

'I could have told you that for free.'

'So she was stroking me, that's all. Tenderly. It was very soothing. And then the landlady came bursting in without knocking and found me kneeling with my back to my therapist as she massaged my neck and shoulders. I had no shirt on, of course. She threw a blue fit and said I had to leave.'

'She can't do that. You have your rights. What are you going to do?'

'I don't know. I don't want trouble. I can't concentrate on my art if I have conflict. I thought maybe I'd go and live in the capital. I could hawk my stuff round galleries. Maybe sell them at a market stall.'

'I'll buy a picture off you if it helps.'

'I don't think you've ever seen them. I don't want charity.'

'Can't you just call it kindness? It'll be a memory.'

'I will miss you,' she said.

'I miss you already.' I immediately realised that saying this was a mistake. A loose line that just slipped out. I knew I'd regret it.

'You miss me now? Why? Like a headache, you mean?'

'You taught me how to paint.'

'I did? No I didn't.'

'You liberated something in me that enabled me to paint.'

'Oh, save me the corn, if you please!' she said sharply. 'It's really about sex. You want me, and it inspires you. Now you know I'm a no-go, you're useless. You have to get over it. It'll teach you that it's never too late to learn anything, as if you needed that. But I'm glad you were inspired for a while. You seemed quite happy.'

'I've even got rid of one of my paintings.'

'Thrown it away? That's a shame.'

'No, a friend offered me a hundred dollars.'

'For one? You took it, right? I'd like to meet this friend.'

'It was the one that looked like flowers but was people. I gave it to him for free. He's an old friend.'

'Tell me something,' she said, closer to the phone as though about to whisper.

'Yes,' I said, feeling like an innocent lamb.

'Were you an officer in the army?'

'Yes. Didn't I tell you that? For many years. Why?'

'It's just that you don't seem like one. You seem a bit, well, soft. Lackadaisical, I guess. I can't imagine you organising an attack or leading men into battle.'

I felt embarrassed by this, flustered. 'Well, it was years ago. I'm sure I've mellowed. Say, do you watch football?'

'I have watched it. But what's that got to do with anything?'

'Certain players appear to do nothing, but once in a while...'

She started laughing. 'I see. No, I think they *really* do nothing.'

'Once in a while, they spring to life, spin round and the ball's in the net.'

'OK, but I think nowadays such a player is just called lazy. I know that much. Maybe you mean you're like a crocodile. Sunbathing all day, motionless, and then suddenly it strikes. I'll call you Croc if you like.'

'I'd prefer to be a lion.'

She sniggered. 'So what were you in the army - a sniper, is that what you're getting at?'

'No, but I could have been. I've always been a slightly better than average marksman.'

'So when was the last time you shot someone? I mean, killed them.'

I paused before replying. I would claim the first terrorist at the cocktail party, since he was already slumping when Zico shot him. 'Just a few months ago, I guess it would be now.'

'Really!? Over here? You're joking now, aren't you? I mean, really?'

'No, I'm not joking. But I don't want to talk about it, if that's OK with you.' Seeking to avoid any further questions on the subject of my military career and recent exploits, I decided to end the call. I'd been tempted to invite her round for farewell drinks, but decided that would be a hostage to fortune.

'So I guess it's goodbye then. Good luck with everything.'

'Goodbye,' she said wistfully and was gone.

56

MARCH

In a country where the people increasingly felt emboldened and determined not to be cowed by the president's repressive policies, it was women's rights campaigners, in alliance with gays, who perhaps presented the biggest challenge to Elvis. I heard about a huge march, uniting these two constituencies, called *Enough Is Enough* and taking place in my old hometown.

I talked to Andrea about it over the phone. 'Why are they so angry?' I asked her. 'I realise I should know already but...'

'The country is so backward, it's embarrassing,' she said, 'and it has always been so.'

'Surely it's worse now,' I said.

'I would not say so.' She had adopted the air of a distinguished university professor being invited on to a downmarket TV news programme. 'We are just further behind, is all, and stupid old Elvis - I'm being kind, I know - he says the law shouldn't change. As you know, homosexuality is still a crime punishable by gaol. But you may not know that it is still not a crime for a man to rape his wife and, thanks to the Church, abortion is a sin. It's not really Elvis' fault. The Church is adamant that the Bible condemns homosexuality, while the woman must obey the man in law. She is still regarded as his property.'

'When we were in power did we not do anything about it?'

'As I recall, we didn't achieve anything, though we did try.' She explained that the Right, blessed by the Church, was too strong. 'We had policies about rape, and domestic violence, and legalising gay sex, but we were hamstrung.'

'Such is the way of coalition government,' I said.

'Yes,' she sighed. 'Sometimes I think a progressive dictator is what the country needs, if such an animal exists. An elected dictator. Someone like your father.'

Later that day, I followed the internet to read about the march. It was marvellous: over a hundred thousand people. This was an impressive turnout, bearing in mind the practical realities: many husbands would have refused to 'allow' their wives to participate, while gays risked gaol even for existing. The march unsettled Elvis so much that he issued a condemnatory statement, claiming it was merely a collection of whores, perverts and foreign agitators and claiming, lest there be any doubt, that God was on his side.

When the marchers approached the presidential palace, the police stepped in with batons to break it up, but there was resistance led by left-wing activists, one or two of whom I thought I recognised from the old days. I watched transfixed as the violence flared. Then a unit of armed police opened fire. Protesters were falling to the ground, some ran away, others ran towards the police, who now launched tear gas. The camera searched frantically for the fallen, obscured by the scrambling bodies and the gas. The commentator was shouting, 'They're using live rounds! They can't even see where they're firing!' Then there was jostling around the camera. It was knocked to the ground. The film stopped.

Later, the government announced that the seven deaths were the result of the victims being trampled on by other protesters. The claim of live rounds was refuted. The government statement said it was an illegal march and the deaths were entirely the fault of the 'ungodly'.

I put down my laptop and went upstairs to my bedroom. For a minute, I stood staring out of the window, fighting back tears of anger.

57
A REQUEST

I returned downstairs and, while I was preoccupied with the news about the march, from whatever source I could find on the internet, Sasha rang me. She wanted to know if she could stay at the cottage as a temporary measure. I did not appreciate the interruption and simply said, 'No' without giving it any thought, before adding, 'I'm sorry, I can't think about it just now. Have you seen the news?'

'I never watch it. I never hear it. I close my mind to it.' I told her about the march and the killings. She was suddenly sombre. 'I would have been on that march,' she said. 'No question, they'd be hanging me for heresy.'

'Why don't you follow the news?'

'I'd never get anything done. I'd be like you: watching the internet all day and fretting about everything.'

'But think of all the different stories on the news. Think of all the ideas for art.'

'I see,' she said, after a pause, perhaps intending to convey the impression of thoughtfulness. 'And have all the stories and ideas made you more productive? Do I even need to ask? No, you have no drive, old man. You may as well go and get a hammock and lie in it all day long, listening to the news and fretting and dreaming up ideas for art you won't create, except once a week you'd drag yourself up and totter out to go and poke the local whore. Don't deny it.'

'What!?'

'I was walking round that way last week, and I saw you and followed at a distance and, sure enough, you looked around furtively and then almost ran through the gate to her door. I don't blame you. You must be frustrated, what with your bitch of a wife away.'

'She's not a bitch.'

'Well, she sounds like it. Anyway, you're not doing anything to take your mind off it.'

'Stop it, will you?'

'So you're not denying it?'

'You seem to know so much about something that's none of your business. Go away. Leave me alone. Don't phone me. You've offended me.'

'Why? Because I know your dirty little secret?'

'She's a good woman. Better than you.' At this point I could tell she was breaking into tears.

'I'm sorry,' she said. 'You think I'm poison. I'm not. I was simply wondering if I could stay for a little while. I won't bother you...'

'No.'

'...just until I'm sorted out and then I'll leave and never...'

'You'll never be sorted out.'

'OK then.' I imagined the tears in her eyes. Words had spilled out of me with scarcely a thought. Mean words.

'Tell me this,' she said, clinging on desperately, 'Since you've been screwing that old whore have you done one hour of painting?'

'That has nothing to do with it.'

'Oh, I think it has. You're bored, dried up. You spend your time worrying about things you can't change, and you have something inside you that you can't express, and so you go and visit that poor husk of a woman, to whom you mean nothing except money, and you call that some kind of life? You told me that I inspired you. Could I not inspire you again?'

'So you think if you stayed with me for, say, a month, a whole month of chaos, as far as I am concerned, with your so-called therapist and whoever else coming round to my place, your landlady banging on the door demanding the money you owe... that it wouldn't drive me mad?'

'No, it could be good,' she said.

'I don't know,' I said wearily, feeling that I could do with that hammock she associated me with, and fall happily on to it. 'Sasha,' I began, in an attempt at being conciliatory, 'if this is really about money, I'll let you have some. I'll lend you what you need. You can pay me back whenever.'

'You don't want to understand, do you? OK then, is that your final word?'

'It is.'

'OK. I'll wait for your next final word then.' She rang off, and I realised I was shaking as I put the phone down and returned to the internet.

58
LOVER

Next day, I drove to meet Serena. She had been in a state of considerable distress, and I agreed to see her, although I would have offered anyway. I insisted, however, that she travel by train, which she considered a great imposition. I explained that the car she'd been using in the capital was almost certainly being followed. She not unreasonably pointed out that they, whoever 'they' were, could follow her on the train as well, but I said it would be more obvious because the place for our rendezvous would have fewer passengers leaving the train. She could confuse any pursuers by getting off and on again at stations along the way.

'I would feel ridiculous doing that. Can't I just bring Julia to be my lookout and take care of any Rats that might be about?' I didn't reply immediately and while I was thinking about what she'd said she sighed theatrically and said, 'OK, I'll do whatever you say.'

I met her in a large restaurant where we could sit in the corner undisturbed. We'd arranged to be there early so there'd be less customers and anyone suspicious would be easier to spot. When I asked her about her journey, she described it as 'not completely execrable, although seeing this odious woman's ugly dog keep licking the seat opposite fairly turned my stomach.'

'Oh dear.'

'Anyway, I took my time in the station like you suggested,' she said. 'I made sure I was the last passenger. I surreptitiously took a couple of pictures of other passengers as they went through the barriers. I was the last person in the taxi queue. I'm getting quite an expert on all this. Intolerable. I can't put up with much more of it.' She looked world-weary, defeated even. What she proceeded to tell me proved to be of great concern and, moreover, deeply upsetting for her. She told me that her 'dear friend' i.e. lover, in whose house she had previously been living, had been assassinated. His house had been blown up while he was there.

'Did you not read about it?' she said.

'Yes. I didn't know who it was, though. Or the connection. I'm sorry.'

'No, I suppose you wouldn't have known. He wasn't an exile like us. Such a lovely man. Like you in many ways.' She paused. 'I don't know what to do with myself now. You're all I have left here.' For a moment she reached forward to lightly grip my forearm affectionately. Spontaneously I placed my palm over her free hand and squeezed it gently.

'You're not giving up the apartment, are you?' I asked.

'No. Oh, I don't know. I don't feel safe there. Even with Julia. I think I need twenty-four hour security, like you had for a while.'

'You want Zico? He's as good as you can get.'

'Zico's not available. You told me that.'

'Oh yes.' I'd lied about it before. Liars had to have a good memory, and I didn't.

'I asked Julia about it,' she said. 'I wasn't sure if you'd made it up to save money, so I checked with her. She confirmed what you'd said. I think he's gone to ground. It's becoming common knowledge about his intervention at the cocktail party. He's a marked man. Your friend, Russo, was getting him a new identity. He wants to be a carpenter apparently. So Julia says. She says there's a big battle going on between different security firms trying to take each other's turf. All very seedy, by the sound of it. And it's turned violent. Ridiculous!' She looked away sadly. 'Oh, what's to become of us!? I'm fed up with not feeling safe. Fed up with having to worry about whether I'm being followed, or someone's listening to my calls, or has planted a bomb under the car. I'm not even on their extradition list - I think they could have at least given me that distinction...' she laughed ruefully, '... since they've stolen my life - any normal kind of life anyway.'

While we ate, it at last dawned on me that the killing of her lover may have been a case of mistaken identity. The thought almost made me bite my tongue. Serena, as if reading my mind, then articulated it for me.

'It did occur to me,' she said, 'that they were really after you. Some mix-up. I know some of those people are pretty clever, but some of the operatives, the ones who do the dirty work, are not always blessed with brains. No, the more I've thought about it, the more I've come to the conclusion that it was you they wanted to kill.'

I stopped eating for a moment while the notion drifted like a ghost through my mind. The irony was painful. There I was, trying, just by being there, to console my wife over the murder of her lover, whose killers thought was me. I almost felt guilty over it.

'I'm sorry,' I said, 'sorry about...'

'It's alright.' She put her hand on my arm once more. 'It was good while it lasted. A dear friend.' She removed her hand, picked up her glass and took a sip of wine. 'But everything comes to an end, doesn't it? We had become less close. That's why I moved back to the capital. But obviously I feel devastated.'

'Of course.'

'Almost as devastated as if it had been you.'

I didn't know how to reply. I felt I wasn't doing a very good job of comforting her, but at least I was there for her. I didn't know what I could do. I didn't want to return to the capital even for a night, and I couldn't see her wanting to move to the cottage. She made no such suggestion, and nor did I.

She was struggling with her grief and my efforts to help her were inadequate. Later, as she waved sadly from the train, I felt she had never looked so lonely and bereft.

59

RUMOUR

From news updates on the internet I learned that Elvis had suddenly disappeared from public view. Was it true, or merely a trap to catch the unwise and the unwary? He had cancelled meetings at the last minute, even with a visiting Head of State. Rumour and wild speculation were rife. Was he ill? Had he been secretly deposed? There were no outward signs of a coup. There were protests against him in Congress Square, but these were met, not by heavy-handed police action, but counter-demonstrations in support of him. Some people said that the police were afraid to go in hard on protesters, following the furore over the killings at the march for women's and gays' rights. There were no reports of violence this time.

I needed someone to confer with and intended to ask Russo but accidentally phoned Serena instead. She showed herself to be remarkably current with the news, and I felt a twinge of guilt at expecting her to be otherwise. I gained the impression she was immersing herself in it as a form of escape.

'I think it's all a bluff,' she said, with the air of someone whose knowledge has come from long and close study. 'You know better than I do how these ex-military politicians' minds work, but I suspect he just wants to see what the reaction is, like Tom Sawyer at his own funeral.'

'So you think this is premeditated on his part and suddenly he'll emerge from behind the curtain and claim in that pantomime voice of his, "Fooled you!?"'

'Something like that,' she said with a sad laugh. 'I don't believe it's a coup. There are rumblings, so I gather from my contacts.' She let this statement hang portentously for a moment before continuing, 'Not all the senior generals are happy with the right-wing policies, but the big concern as always is to maintain stability. The last thing the country needs right now is any more discord.'

I was intrigued by her thinking. Was she becoming a politico at last, or had I underestimated her all along?

'So you still don't think the time's right for us to go and make the country beautiful again?' I asked facetiously.

She answered sombrely, 'There is always time, but if anyone's going to do it, it won't be us from afar.'

That evening, the president appeared on the balcony of the palace and waved his hand in a manner reminiscent of a sick little boy at his hospital window. The camera did not zoom in on him.

'It's a fake,' said Russo derisively when I called him a little later. 'If it's not, why isn't the camera going up close?'

'Body double?' I suggested.

'Would you seriously put it past him?' he remarked.

'It doesn't make sense to me. If he was dead they would put up someone else. Or, rather, someone would leap straight in and answer questions afterwards.'

'They can't decide,' he said.

'That's because no-one else wants it. What are they going to do, release the Smooth Killer?' I shivered at that notion.

As we talked, I noticed some new footage. 'I've never seen this before,' I said. He asked what I was looking at and was able to find it quickly.

'No,' he said. 'They've kept it for just such an occasion. You know how it works. Look, there's blossom on the trees in the garden. There wouldn't be that blossom at this time of year.'

'Wouldn't there?' I wasn't so sure but didn't intend debating horticulture with him, especially as neither of us knew much about it.

'The other thing,' he said triumphantly, 'is that in this latest coverage it looks like he's not carrying any weight. Everyone knows he's got heavy since he's been in power. You'd think they could have been less sloppy. There's no weight-loss programme in the world that could achieve that. I wonder if it's been put up deliberately by his enemies to show he's no longer in charge.'

I scratched my head. 'Maybe it's just the light,' was all I could offer.

We talked briefly about the murder of Serena's lover. 'That's a sorry business,' he said. 'You did well to get out of the capital when you did.'

'Do you think they could have been after me?' As I said this, I thought it sounded vain on my part.

'Mistaken identity? Hmm. Possible.' His tone was sceptical. 'But he was a gunrunner, you know.'

'I didn't.' I decided to share his scepticism and immediately felt relieved, satisfied that the murder was not a mistake. It would teach me to act so self-important - except it wouldn't.

'By the way,' he said. 'I've received an offer for that picture. You know, the one you gave me.'

'Take it.'

'But you don't know how much. This fellow offered me five hundred.'

'Definitely take it.'

'I'll give you half.'

'No you won't. Just give me the hundred you offered - it was really meant as a gift - and keep the rest.'

'OK. And if you've got any more...'

This brought a smile to my face: 'Thank you, but I think it was beginner's luck.'

That night, the government back home issued a statement saying the president had been ill but had now recovered. I couldn't help thinking of the recent death of the former president in exile, courtesy of the mysterious Dr Kidd, and wondered if a similarly skilled physician could exist back home.

60
BESIEGED

It was only a few days after Sasha's call that I heard from her again. Not by phone, which I'd expressly forbidden, but by email. In it she asked me to reconsider and repeated her appeal for help. With a hard heart I found difficult to maintain, I ignored her. After a couple of days, a follow-up arrived. Then, in her third email she said, 'I take it you really do not want to help me, and that makes me very sad. I misjudged you.'

I was pondering over whether to relent and reply to this latest message, while starting a new painting, having at last found a gramme of inspiration following my latest visit to Chloe, when there was a knock at the door. I could tell from the sound it was probably Sasha and ignored it. She realised I was in and simply stood there waiting. Finally, deciding she wasn't going to leave me alone, I opened the door. I could barely look at her face, suddenly ashamed at myself for the way I'd been treating her, and I said nothing, merely ushered her in with the large holdall she was carrying. She sat down sullenly on the sofa. She looked beautiful, a carefully constructed beauty that made her case more strongly than words alone could. I pretended it made no difference but was lying to myself.

'Why have you come?' I asked her. 'Look, we talked about it on the phone. You can't stay here. It's not practical.'

She looked down, as though staring at a mark on her jeans or her lace-up boots, and she adopted a plaintive tone, 'But I've nowhere to live. I've three days left, and I still haven't paid the rent. The sale of my pictures fell through, so I have nothing. I've come to you as the only one who can help me.'

'Why me?' I said. 'Surely you've got other friends who can help you.'

She shook her head sadly. 'No, not round here.'

'What about family?'

'No. No-one here.' Her eyes were full of tears. She knew how to play a man, for sure. 'Aren't you at least going to offer me a drink or something? Are you really so mean? I bet you wouldn't be like this if it was your precious Chloe who came round needing help.'

'She wouldn't.'

She sighed. 'So it really is "No" is it?'

'As I said, I will lend you money. No, I will *give* you money. How much do you want?' She merely gave me a look of disgust as her reply, and I left the room to make tea.

When I returned, she was not there. I felt a pang of regret tinged with guilt. She might be an agent of chaos and a pain to me, but she was a human being who'd suffered terribly in her life and was suffering now. I could hardly claim to be a moral person, which I vaguely liked to think I was, if I behaved like this when someone came to me in need. My mind was momentarily assailed by New Testament stories of Christ's kindness, and I was beginning to feel that I was being unduly harsh, when I heard her on the stairs. I watched her descend them, trying to construct an air of nonchalance, but her face showed desperation.

'There's plenty of room,' she said. 'There's a second bedroom.'

'I know,' I said abashed. I quietly accepted the inevitable. 'Look,' I began, 'there's a couple of things I need to tell you. Risks, if you will.'

'OK, I understand.' I sensed a hint of triumph in her voice.

'First of all, there's a possibility - no more than that - that my wife will want to come and live here.'

'Your wife?' She was clearly perplexed by this prospect.

'Yes. She's had a shock. Her lover has been murdered.'

'My God!' The starkness of my statement took her aback, and she appeared not to know what to say and merely looked uncomfortable. 'I don't mind,' she said at last, recovering her composure. 'How could I? *She* might, though.'

'It's not up to her who stays here,' I said, not wanting to show weakness. 'I realise it might seem absurd, the idea of my wife possibly staying here as well.'

'I guess,' she said vacantly.

'More than that, there's a physical risk too.'

She let out a little laugh. 'She's not going to attack me, is she?'

'No. I haven't told you this, because I wasn't sure I could trust you - and I probably shouldn't be telling you now - but I used to be a government minister back home.'

'Oh. Maybe I should have recognised you, but I've never paid any attention to politics.'

'Well, if the wrong people know where I am, I'm a dead man. I left my apartment in the capital and moved here for security reasons.' I decided against telling her I was using a fake ID. If Serena showed up I could explain everything then.

'Hence the gun,' she said.

'Yes, the Glock you saw, plus there's another Glock, a shotgun and my recent acquisition: an AR-15.'

'I don't even know what that is.'

'It's what every fanatic in the US uses when they've got a grudge and want to kill as many people as possible.' She gave me a look that indicated she thought I was still trying to put her off which, to some extent, I was.

'Do you understand,' I said, 'that you could be putting yourself in real danger?'

'OK,' she said. 'That would be exciting.'

It wasn't the reaction I'd expected. 'Now look,' I said, feeling the need to assert myself, 'I can't put up with any nonsense - no getting drunk, no playing with guns, no craziness.'

'Do you want me under sedation or something?' she said frostily. I did not answer and merely stared at her. 'OK, I promise,' she added meekly, sounding almost convincing. 'If I fail, I realise I will have to...'

'I've got one question,' I said. 'I take it this isn't just for a week or two, is it? You're not looking for anywhere else, are you?'

'You want me to? I realise you want to control me.'

'I don't, actually. OK, forget I asked.'

'Thank you,' she said, relaxing noticeably. 'You won't be sorry about this.'

'I certainly hope not.'

That afternoon, I helped her move her stuff, including her paintings from the garage nearby; I was at last able to see her work, albeit in glimpses. I paid off her landlady; a graceless woman, she merely grunted in acknowledgement. As I carried in the last of Sasha's belongings and closed my front door behind us, I wondered what adventure, what madness I'd let into my world.

61
LOOTERS

The night after Sasha's arrival, there was news of an earthquake back home. It measured 6.8 on the Richter scale. No-one was reported killed, but some people were unaccounted for. The quake hit the centre of a small town far from the capital, and the main buildings affected were retail and commercial.

'I had forgotten about all the earthquakes,' said Sasha, who'd settled herself in remarkably quickly. 'I remember one when I was a kid, right in our area. Several people killed, including a girl I went to school with. I was fascinated by it; I had to go and see the destruction. The whole concept of the earth opening up and the fear that you could fall into it played on my imagination. And there were the aftershocks. Up until then, my parents could pretty much control everything in our little lives. At least, that's what we felt. But now of course I know that what they could really control was very little.'

In the latest quake, hardly had the earth finished shaking than the looters were out. At first, it was a few intrepid young men, then more people arrived; later, it seemed the entire town was engaged in emptying the supermarkets. Of course, cameras were immediately in action; initially, jerky mobile phone videos, then local news, then national TV. Even those employed to guard the supermarkets joined in the fun. 'We are poor,' said one man. 'We have nothing. It's all been taken away from us. Now God is giving us a little bit back. I say, thank God for the earthquake.'

I was bothered by this and said to Sasha, 'I don't remember the looting being as bad as this when I was young - what about you?'

'It did happen,' she said, 'but I don't think my family joined in. It somehow didn't seem right. UnChristian, maybe?'

'Of course, there weren't any big multinational shops, the way there are now, when I was little,' I remarked. 'I suppose there were in your day. Oh no, that grocer's going to be next!' I guessed that the shopkeeper we could now see on the screen lived above his little shop. He stood outside the front of it, beseeching the looters to leave it alone.

'Shame he doesn't have a gun like you,' Sasha said.

He was desperately trying to prevent them smashing the windows. Then a policeman arrived and started firing his pistol in the air. The people outside the small grocer's ran back to the supermarket.

'Does it seem strange to you?' I asked her. 'Here we are, watching looting on TV, as though it's a national sport.'

She sat close to me, and it felt natural to put my arm round her. She didn't resist. It was cozy, like the earliest days of my relationship with Serena.

'It *is* a national sport,' Sasha replied. Sure enough, it was soon revealed that the looting had spread all over the country, even in towns unaffected by the quake, aided by general civil unrest - part protest, part poverty, part pure greed. Elvis had apparently ordered the troops in to restore order.

'Did you ever have to put down a looting?' she asked.

'I do remember one occasion. It made me sick. I was a young soldier on not much pay and some people, some much better off than me at the time, felt justified in stealing whatever they could get their avaricious hands on. They were positively self-righteous about it. Maybe it *was* as bad as now, like the man on here who was thanking God for the earthquake. I recall chasing a squat little man who'd stolen a TV down the street. He tripped on a broken flagstone and injured his leg. Boy, did he curse me! To be honest, the whole thing affected me so much, and the looting upset me more than the earthquake did. I know it shouldn't have. I resolved then and there never to be poor.'

'And then you met Serena?'

'Then I met Serena and she still has the same resolve now as I had then. You could say, wealth (and particularly spending it) is her religion, like yours is art.'

'And yours seems to be sitting looking at the internet,' she retorted.

What surprised me about the looting shown on TV was the brazenness of it. The desperately poor had a kind of invincible courage to them - even if it manifested itself in a rather disheartening way - and it felt like they were cocking a snook at the president, at autocracy in general, at the oppression they faced in their daily lives. It was hard not to feel that if the nation was an animal, that animal could smell change in the air.

62
LEAVING

It was a few days after the earthquake back home, that I received the call I had been silently dreading since Sasha moved in. I had rehearsed in my mind the arguments I would put persuasively to the effect that it wasn't practical for Serena to come and live with me at the cottage, and why I did not wish to return to the apartment in the capital. It would be a difficult conversation if my wife's mind was set on either of these things.

She certainly sounded clear of purpose in her preamble. After asking what I was doing nowadays, about which I was non-committal, she changed the subject to weightier subjects: 'Isn't it awful?' she said. 'I mean, everything that's going on back home. The looters - normally, I'd want to see them shot, but I find myself feeling sorry for them. And that march - live bullets! Whatever were they thinking? Women's rights are such a joke there - a joke no-one could make funny. Anyway, how are you?'

I thought about mentioning Sasha as a lead-in to our inevitable discussion on Serena's future living arrangements, but at that point Sasha slipped into the room so I merely said, 'Fine.'

'Well,' she continued, unfazed by my minimalist response, 'I have something I need to talk to you about. Something important. Now I've been speaking with Andrea - you're not seeing her, by the way, are you?'

I was puzzled, surely she hadn't phoned up to ask me if I was having an affair. 'No,' I replied bluntly.

'Only she talks about you all the time.'

'That's nice, I guess.'

'She's worried about you. Should *I* be worried about you?'

This was such an ambiguous question; I couldn't help feeling like a confused defendant in a police station interview room. I merely said, 'I don't think so, no.'

'Anyway, the two of us agree that something really needs to be done.' I did not like to think what future these two indomitable vixens had cooked up for me. 'Politically, I mean,' she said. 'She and I have become quite close.

Surprisingly so. So what I need to talk to you about - and I don't know how you'll take this...' She paused.

'Go on,' I said, trying to ignore Sasha who was making an obscene gesture with her hands.

'I'm thinking of returning home. Not being on the extradition list got me thinking. Although it's almost certainly a mistake...'

'Oh, indeed,'

'... I see it as a godsend.'

Now the message had gently landed in my mind, I immediately began to feel protective towards her: 'But won't it be dangerous?'

'I can go and stay with my sister. *She* hasn't suffered from the fall of democracy. In fact, if anything she's better off. Her husband got a better job in the civil service, and I'm sure there's more kickbacks than ever. I'd keep a low profile at first; I don't want to embarrass her. But I've been thinking very long and hard. I do feel I need to do something with my life. I see those poor people on the news, I see the women and gays protesting and being shot at, I think about the appalling rape laws, I see domestic violence out of control. I've got to do something...' I looked up: Sasha was miming a well-to-do snobbish woman proudly showing off her breasts in public.

'I understand,' I said.

'...And I realise that what I do may mean nothing in the overall scheme of things...' Sasha had slid to the floor and began pretending to be a well-to-do snobbish woman on her knees giving a blow job.

'...giving something back, running a charity for homeless women or something.' She paused and I, distracted by Sasha's performance, said nothing.

Finally, realising Serena was awaiting a response, I said nervously, 'That'll be more than a small role.' At this Sasha made a circular rolling motion with her index finger.

'Yes, it would,' said Serena. 'But there's nothing for me here - apart from you, of course - and what with the apartment being watched all the time, friends being killed, the fear of being followed... it's intolerable. I feel like a prisoner in this dreadful country.'

'It's not so bad,' I replied weakly.

'But it's not our home. It's not where we should be. We should be back home, fighting to make it better, not wasting our time in this dump we don't even belong in. I want to be there, taking on the gangsters that are running about causing mayhem. Women have to stand up because bad men are running riot, ruining everything. I'm sick of terrible men in power. Oh, I can happily get down in the trenches and fight.' I found this talk quite alarming. I said nothing and merely let her carry on: 'Oh, I'm not afraid of them. I can't wait!'

Although startling, it was very much in character. I still had nagging concerns: 'What if the authorities there interview you?'

'Nothing to interview me about. I won't be doing anything wrong.'

'But what if they ask you about me?'

'Hmm.' She fell silent. I pictured a large balloon beginning to lose air.

'They might ask you where I am.'

'OK,' she said, her voice rising with a hint of defiance. She was determined not to be deflated, and I respected that. 'I'll simply tell them that I don't know. And it will be true. They won't interrogate me.'

'They might.'

'And if they do, they'll regret it.'

'I've no doubt they will - regret it, I mean.' I found I was picking up her enthusiasm. A couple of past incidents flashed through my mind: the time she smashed an umbrella in an over-zealous policeman's face, the time she poured a glass of expensive champagne over the head of a hypocritical politician at a party in his honour. There was no shortage of firepower with her - just a lack of direction sometimes.

'I'll let you know when I go,' she said. 'I'd love to have Andrea come with me. We'd be a formidable team but...'

'She's on the extradition list,' I interjected.

'Things will change,' she assured me. 'And I mean, for the better. We'll get rid of the bad men, however long it takes.'

I looked over at Sasha. She was fast asleep on the sofa with her thumb in her mouth.

63
BAD MEN

It would be easy to think that Serena in her relatively gilded life had, unlike someone like Sasha, suffered little directly from the worst of the male of the species. She hadn't known child rapists, heartless drug barons or crime bosses, and killers surely too evil to have mothers, but she would no doubt reply that the deeds of the various dictators who'd ruled the country for so much of her life had infected the country with a poison that polluted not only the political discourse, but the personal lives of their subjects as well. The concept of the 'bad men' was a preoccupation of hers. She believed men were all essentially bad, with a few tolerable exceptions. For my part, I'd had to confront all types of bad men: violent husbands, pathological liars, psychopaths, murderers, cutthroats, men in gangs or death squads, thugs, traffickers, maniacal cult leaders, cheats of every kind, men driven to evil by drink or drugs or gambling, sex fiends, slavers, Satanists, sadists, torturers, men who couldn't control their libido or their inner destructive rage, or avarice, or jealousy, antisocial men practising every kind of vice and violence, men who treated their women as chattels and controlled every aspect of their lives and told them they had no free will and didn't deserve any, men who trashed women's bodies and lives, men who killed women because of their sex, men so evil they could be redeemed a thousand times over and still be rotten to every molecule of their being.

I was sure I wasn't fit to even step on the same street that a saint had once travelled over, and I had made awful mistakes in life, but I was not a bad man. Elvis and the Smooth Killer were bad, but they were mere kindergarten clowns compared to the school of evil men. Men had always been bad. History was all about them. They had a system called patriarchy to keep them in place. Men in gaol were prima facie bad in the public's eyes. Some stayed bad forever. Many got worse in gaol, while others grew old and tired there until they were no longer a menace to anyone. Some bad men kidnapped rich heiresses and terrorised them, while others kidnapped whole countries and terrorised the people. In war the enemy nation's men were all bad, and even the young boys were bad in the making, but in war all *our* men were good, or at least useful, except for those in gaol. Our brave men went to war with dreams of victory and valour. If they won they returned heroes, the best of men, any war crimes overlooked, but soon they were forgotten and drink and trauma destroyed them, and they became bad men again. If they lost in war, we always knew they were useless, but losing was terrifying because it meant a whole new crew came in, and they really *were* bad, the worst of the worst, because they weren't even ours, marauders high on victory and raddled by toxic doctrines - indiscriminate killers and mass rapists. Some men were bad to spite God, others despite the god they claimed as guide in all their actions.

I decided I should retire to my room to pray for the souls of all bad men - and bad women too - the 'black widows' of press reports, femmes fatales, witches in fairytales, aristocrats bathing in virgins' blood, child killers, 'gold diggers' of the most ruthless kind, women who inspired evil and demanded their men do evil things. Next time Serena complained about bad men, I'd tell her, 'Listen, the man or woman without vice has yet to be born.'

64
INCIDENT

With the threat of Serena wanting to live at the cottage ostensibly removed, the early days of the arrangement with Sasha were innocent fun. She'd made it clear she disapproved of my visits to Chloe, and, admittedly, I was losing interest in my Friday afternoon jaunts, but wisely she did not press the issue. Apart from her therapist's now infrequent visits and the time I spent with Chloe, I was with Sasha, or at least in her close vicinity, constantly. An important part of our time together was spent, when not painting (the enthusiasm for which had immediately returned for me), in finding the best places to dine.

We always drove. Although I had no specific reason to fear for our security in the area around my new home, I insisted on having a pistol hidden on the back seat under a blanket, as had been my habit before.

'Must we?' she enquired on one occasion, after watching me place the gun there as usual. 'I know you've had warnings before, but there's been no sign of it round here, has there?'

'That's the point,' I said. 'You don't think they're going to phone ahead to see if we're ready for them, do you? In a few seconds...'

'I know,' she sighed. 'It's just the constant reminder. I don't feel I can relax with that thing there. It's as though it invites trouble. I realise it doesn't really.' I started to explain, but she simply replied, 'I know,' wearily.

That Sasha would soon tire of my security concerns did not bother me. Much as my affection for her had grown, if she arrived at the conclusion she might be safer away from me and decided to avail herself of my offer to lend her money to live independently, I would not object. The fact remained that only through association with me did she face any realistic danger.

One evening, we tried a new Spanish restaurant in a pretty fishing village along the coast. The food was adequate if dull, but there was a lively bar with dancing upstairs. Neither of us was particularly adept, although I did throw in the odd salsa turn, but we joined in with gusto and soon lost our inhibitions and worries. Afterwards, in the car, she said, 'Thank you,' and put her head on my shoulder. She was a little drunk. I drove us back slowly, enjoying the cool evening breeze off the sea, with the windows down, the sound of the waves crashing, the happy shouts of people on the street.

As we drove through town, I became aware of a motorcyclist behind us. I felt immediately concerned. It was like a sixth sense I'd convinced myself I had. The road ahead clear, I slowed right down to let him pass, but he slowed down too. I put the windows up.

'What's the matter?' Sasha asked dreamily but then was suddenly awake.

'Can you reach for the gun?' I said in a low voice.

'What? Oh God!'

'Quietly, with as little disturbance of the blanket as possible.' I was tense, alert. 'OK. Have you used a gun before?'

'Are you kidding?'

'OK. Don't look behind you. I'm not sure what this joker is up to, but I'm going to drive through town, not home, then I'm going to speed up. I'm going to try and shake him off. It obviously won't be easy.'

I picked up speed. He appeared to wait for a few moments before accelerating. On the outer edge of town, I hit the pedal hard. He opened the throttle.

'Could he be a cop?' Sasha asked.

'Of course not,' I snorted, as if she'd asked whether a unicorn was chasing us, 'but, actually... No, he can't be.'

Out in the country, I took a sudden turn at the last, almost impossible, moment into an unlit narrow road. He wasn't paying full attention and sped on. I turned the car round about a hundred yards from the highway and waited. Sure enough, he came back. I put down my window and inched the car forward while he slowed. As we approached each other, I saw him reach inside his leather jacket. I picked up speed a little, took the Glock from Sasha's reluctant hands and fired. He lost control of the bike and fell to the ground. We sped off.

'Did you kill him!?' She was totally panicked.

'I aimed for his arm,' I replied calmly. 'I'm afraid there was no time to ask him what he was up to, but I suspect he wasn't reaching for his autograph book. So are you sure you want to live with me? This is what life will probably be like.'

'If I have to die, I'd rather die brave,' she replied dismissively, and I couldn't help feeling proud of her.

65

A DEATH

One morning, Russo was on the phone sounding very excited: 'Another one down! Another one dead! The dog has barked its last!'

He'd seen the same news report as me. Another old despot had turned to dust. Elvis had left the proverbial building. Thank you and goodnight. Better, it would not have been the death he'd have wanted. I said, 'He'd have wanted something dramatic: a gunfight with twenty villains, having already killed that many on his own.'

'A brave man who simply ran out of bullets,' he said.

Elvis had been on a trip to the interior to visit earthquake victims, fallen ill and been rushed to the local health facility. I imagined him marooned in a dusty, decaying hospital, lonely, pathetic, cajoled by the overly fussy staff, then stuck in a humid corridor - the great soldier felled by an infection he'd acquired there, or so I liked to believe.

'He had only looked feverish,' joked Russo, 'but now they call it a merciful death. Merciful in more ways than one.'

'Best news in ages,' I said. 'Do you think the fake doctor who killed that other president, the Cat, was responsible?'

'Dr Kidd? Oh, it has to be. I'd rather have him there than over here. I'm afraid to go to hospital now.'

Dr Kidd had become a legend to us, a myth. Any curious death in hospital and he was responsible. We didn't really believe it, but it was an explanation in a world that was becoming increasingly alien to us.

'I see they're saying it was a heart attack,' I said. 'They're not going to admit to it being hospital-acquired are they?'

'There's a big party going on over there: street celebrations, dancing, fireworks, horns honking. Don't you wish you were there?'

'Not while there's an extradition list and I'm on it, I don't,' I replied sombrely.

'Can't you enjoy the moment?' he chided.

'No, because I'm always thinking of the next one. You know what'll happen: another tinpot dictator will replace him. There's never any shortage of candidates, it seems. As long as it's not the Smooth Killer again. If it is, I'm sure I'll want to go and assassinate him, even though I told you I wouldn't. Anyway, Serena's going back. She can tell me what it's like. I heard Elvis' son OD'd again, by the way - fatally.'

'Yes. When he found out there would not be a dynasty after all, he couldn't face life anymore. Some people's expectations, eh? So what will you do now?'

'It seems the Rats are getting worse - I encountered one just the other day around here - but I want to stay. I suppose I could travel. They won't want to be trailing me all over the world. The trouble is, though, if they do follow me I'm vulnerable - and I won't have my guns with me - flights, hotels, airports, so many possibilities to get caught out. Here, out in the wilds, relatively speaking, I can spot a wannabe assassin a mile away. Imagine being in a European capital where you know no-one and every person you see, man or woman, is a potential killer.'

'So despite everything, you're resigned to your current life?'

'I am. My art teacher's moved in with me.'

'Good for you. Is she a honey?'

'Yes, but it's not like that. You should come out and have a look at her work.'

'I will. And we'll drink to the new president, whoever it is, even if in jest. There's some creatures over there make Elvis look like Jesus.'

66

VISIT

A few days later, Russo arrived. He'd borrowed a bigger car for the occasion. He arrived early, Sasha wasn't even up, and I was checking overnight news. We sat drinking coffee under the gazebo at the back with the grapevine entwined around it. He seemed incredibly happy about everything and declared confidently that things back home were bound to improve. Change had been in the air for a while before Elvis' death. You could feel it even amongst the exiles.

I said, 'Now that Elvis has passed on, do you think he'll find out what the real one thought of his act?'

'Did you ever see it? He was pretty good, as such acts go. The one thing he was good at.'

'Not a bad soldier, by all accounts,' I said. 'Of course, he may have written them all.'

'OK, now you're being serious.'

'So his VP is in charge, the one they call the Squire?'

'Yes.'

'Why that name?'

'Because he's very sedate and serious and considers everything very s-l-o-w-l-y, a bit like you.'

'Thanks.'

'Owns a lot of property. Smart guy.'

'Ex-airforce.'

'Yes. A decent man. God knows how he was VP to Elvis. No sense of humour.'

'Like me, I suppose.'

'Yes. But he will get the job done. The only question is...'

'What is the job?' I said.

'Indeed. But we're headed for a national reconciliation plan of sorts.'

'As long as he doesn't let the Smooth Killer out, because he'll steal everything.'

'Realistically, I can't see how they can keep him behind bars. Like you, he's never been charged.'

At that moment, Sasha arrived. She looked stunning with the fresh beauty women have after they've bathed and pampered and prepared themselves for a new day and to feel confident in the world, except Sasha never saw herself as confident. Her port-wine stain served to emphasise her beauty.

'Sasha, this is my friend Russo. I've known him for years.'

'And he still talks to me,' Russo interjected.

'Pleased to meet you,' she said shyly. 'I've heard so much about you.'

'None of it's true,' he laughed.

'That's a relief,' she replied, readily joining in.

In anticipation of Russo's visit, we'd brought her paintings down from her bedroom and unpacked them. He seemed fascinated by them, although I could tell he didn't understand their surrealist nature, any more than perhaps I did. He put on glasses to inspect them closely, one by one, then stood back to gaze on them. It was a great performance as he had no clue what he was looking at, but maybe he knew enough.

'I have this client,' he began, 'I call him a client, but he's more of an occasional buyer. He's rich. I'm moving in different circles these days...'

'I'm flattered you've come to see us,' I said, more sarcastic than I meant to be.

'He wants some art for his new apartment. Anything with vibrant colours. Something like this would work.' He picked out one of Sasha's in which she'd experimented with the style of Miró.

After Russo's inspection of her paintings, which I felt left him all too aware that he knew little about the market he was dabbling in, as if he hadn't learnt enough from his religious relics debacle, we talked some more about politics. Sasha, who said nothing on the subject, was clearly bored at this point, so we went out and had drinks and an early lunch in a restaurant Russo picked at random along the coast.

Soon after sitting down at the table, we drank a champagne toast to the new president, the Squire. Russo entertained us with stories of some of the strange things he'd bought and sold, and some of the customers he'd had ('Did I ever tell you about the old lady who wanted to buy an onyx phallus to cure her asthma?'). Sasha loved it. I was sure she found him more interesting and lively than me, and I couldn't avoid the annoying first signs of jealousy. The thought even occurred to me that perhaps she might be happier living with him in the capital. She could paint for commissions, and he could be her dealer, which, actually, would be a perfect arrangement.

When we returned from lunch, Russo did another inspection of the pictures. He said he would take four of Sasha's and one of mine (out of sympathy, I felt sure). He said he would either give us three thousand dollars for the lot, or he would sell them for what he could get and give himself twenty per cent. Sasha said she would take the cash, of which we then agreed two hundred would be allocated to my picture. Twenty-eight hundred would enable her to get established somewhere else, was the way I privately saw it.

Russo left after doing his own impression of a bad Elvis impersonator which, in our state of inebriation, was hilarious, and we celebrated a successful day.

'I really like him,' Sasha said as soon as he'd gone. 'He's a lot of fun.'

In my heart, I thanked God. I was beginning to realise my own first inklings of love for her, but she needed to move on.

67
IDYLL

In the heady days after Elvis' unexpected death, Serena's move back home was perfectly timed. 'We must all do what we can,' she said imperiously, which I took as a strong exhortation for me to also 'do my bit'. She told me she believed it would soon be possible for all of us exiles to return home. It was all positive in her world now, every light was green. I wondered if she had another 'dear friend', although there was no talk circulating to that effect. I saw her briefly at the airport when she left. She had wanted to visit me at the cottage, but Sasha had objected to 'that old witch darkening our door', so I made an apology that it was impractical.

I heard from her again a few weeks after she'd arrived. She was staying at her sister's. Her sister was somewhat like her, though more toned down and a little taciturn at times, and I could imagine the two of them in concert becoming a formidable force in whatever enterprise they engaged in. If Serena got her charity running, she would be at the front, hobnobbing with politicians and celebrities to get their endorsement, while her sister would be behind the scenes, managing the accounts and suchlike.

Once Serena was back there, however, the idea of a charity appeared to lose its shine. She had thought her arrival would be treated as a major event. It wasn't - the media ignored it. Whereas I, in my cautious mien, considered this a good thing, she saw it as a slight. I asked her if she was happy.

'Not unhappy,' she replied. 'Lots to be done. I will make a difference, but for now I'm having a rest - no, not a rest, I'm assimilating. I'm getting back to my roots.' I felt a little sorry for her. She was never satisfied, and in her voice I could tell that she was realising she hadn't thought through her plans clearly enough. The reality was, she would struggle as she always did, especially with herself.

With the knowledge that Serena was far away and staying there, Sasha became more relaxed. She was protective of the life we enjoyed together. She called it 'idyllic'. I saw it as transitory, and this enabled me to savour it the more, savour it for what it was, accepting its limitations. I sometimes reminded her how precarious it was; the Rat I'd shot would not give up, nor would whoever employed him. We were like a small country protected by guns and prepared for war while enjoying the peace. For me it was the threat that helped make it special.

I stopped seeing Chloe altogether. I told her I was joining the Church, but she queried this, saying it shouldn't make any difference, so I told her I was going to become celibate. Sasha still saw her therapist, who always insisted on visiting her rather than the other way round, which I found distinctly odd. Whenever she visited, I went out to the shooting range. I never asked Sasha about her therapists's now rare visits. I thought she could tell me about it in her own way and time, but she didn't talk about it at all. Increasingly, however, she would lie down beside me in bed, and we would cuddle up close. She would allow me to gently massage her neck and shoulders and back. I began to understand quite clearly what she felt comfortable with. This did not involve sex, and I accepted that. It was not love perhaps, but it was a kind of love.

68
EXTRADITION

One morning, as I was taking a break from painting to have coffee in the garden, Andrea phoned me. She was buzzing about extradition and wondering what I'd heard. 'Nothing,' I replied, adding that I was waiting to be descended upon ('Probably a letter waiting for me at the apartment,') at which time I'd instruct lawyers and let them battle it out with the authorities for as long as possible, at no doubt significant expense. I told her I'd been concerned that Serena's return home might draw attention to me, but in fact her arrival had been ignored. As Andrea immediately showed, my knowledge was out-of-date.

'They're going to end extradition,' she said, delighted that my ignorance meant she could educate me.

'What do you mean: "end" it?'

'They've come to realise that amongst the many exiles all over the world there's actually quite a bit of talent that might be useful.'

'That's never bothered these despots before. They seem to disdain talent in favour of mediocrity, as long as it doesn't ask questions.' I sensed I was sounding bitter, so I decided it would be wiser for me to say nothing further.

She said, 'They want us back, is the latest. Well, most of us, anyway. I say "they", meaning the establishment there.'

'Led by the Squire.'

'Yes.' She gave a little giggle and continued, 'I think they've come to realise that extracting money from the so-called "corrupt" is not going to be an easy task, and therefore they intend to settle with such people. So, let's say, they believe you have stolen five million dollars' worth of assets, they will accept maybe three million, and then you'll be able to go back with a clean record.'

I balked at this. 'Really?' I said. 'Would that be such a good idea for us? Why not just keep the money? I'd rather wait until someone we liked got in and invited us back with no strings, wouldn't you?'

'I don't think that'll happen,' she said. 'You can't wait forever. Do you not think that the violence here comes from our government? We're sick of it.

My husband and I are going back as soon as we can. We don't owe anything anyway.'

This I didn't believe. I'd always held Andrea in high regard, and yet she trotted out such a blatant lie.

'Nor do I,' I replied defiantly, 'but they claimed I did. I suffered under house arrest.'

'For six months,' she said in a slightly dismissive tone.

'Ten, actually, Can you imagine what Serena was like? Anyway, my dear, this is all very interesting, but I can't imagine going back. I'm sure there'll be a few holdouts who want to stay here, not least because they prefer their new life.'

'I should think about it if I were you. Do you want it hovering over you for the rest of your life? I see our return as a new beginning.'

'All I know is, Serena is finding it a bit of a culture shock. She hasn't said as much, but I got that impression from talking to her. It's the things we take for granted here. No blackouts, for example, a fairly vibrant press. OK, there's poverty, but it's not on every street corner. There's a middle class here.'

She ignored this: 'Anyway, we know there'll be lawyers coming over to pursue their claims. The exiles that are interested will have their own lawyers. Don't forget, if you don't settle they're going to come after you anyway.'

After the call, Sasha wanted to know who it was. 'Andrea,' I said, 'a family friend.'

'It sounded like she annoyed you.'

'Did it?' I shrugged my shoulders. She didn't mean to, but she did a little. She thinks I should settle with the government back home and then return there.'

'I'll add her to my list.'

'Of what?'

'Enemies. Anyone who wants to do anything that would take you from me is an enemy.'

69
THE PHILANTHROPIST

At Andrea's urging, I reluctantly agreed to attend a convention to meet a man they called the Philanthropist who was guest of honour. The meeting was at a hotel near the main airport. Dismissing my reluctance, Andrea, who was beginning to treat me like a recalcitrant child, insisted I was 'stuck in a rut' and the meeting would inspire me to get involved.

'Involved in what?' I asked her tetchily, but she did not answer, as though it was obvious and I was merely being awkward.

Thus, with a heavy heart, and despite Sasha's furious opposition, I went to the convention. I'd had a sense of foreboding, given the attack on the cocktail party, but this time the venue was heavily protected. I'd thought about sneaking in my gun, in case we had a repeat performance, but reassuringly the staff inside had metal detectors and conducted body searches. Inside the conference hall there were about eighty people. Andrea was there, looking attractive, younger than her years, glamorous as ever, whilst her husband, continuing to cheat death, looked even older than I remembered. Our Man was there, our great leader-to-be, beaming confidently and fatuously.

The Philanthropist was a middle-aged, thickset man, supposedly a success in everything he turned his hand to; a former nightclub owner and then a newspaper owner, he was now a media magnate on a mission to save our home country. He was surprisingly unflamboyant and instead gave an air of quiet self-possession. My hope was that he was independent-minded.

After Andrea had given brief introductory remarks, we had a minute's silence in memory of the two of our associates who'd died in the cocktail party attack. The Philanthropist then stood up and gave a speech in which he announced the formation of the New Party, intended to be a major force in the 'new politics' that was about to emerge back home. He pledged to put in three million dollars for the campaign and asked those present to also make pledges. I blanched. It seemed like everyone wanted money, especially *my* money. Then he announced what we knew without being told, although it still unnerved me to hear it: Our Man was to be the New Party's leader. I felt disenchanted. Who was this Philanthropist anyway? Some carpetbagger wanting to advance his own interests?

After his brief talk, and a predictably bland contribution by Our Man which ended the speeches, I took the opportunity to approach the Philanthropist and ask him why he was so interested in politics.

'We have got to be rid of the gangsters,' he said, reminiscent of Serena in one of her calls to me. 'There is so much to do, and we cannot do it with such dreadful people destroying the country.'

I couldn't disagree with him on that score. I asked him diplomatically what he thought Our Man's 'main strengths' were.

'He's a natural politician,' he replied, breathing in a little heavily. 'A natural,' he reiterated. I was disappointed by this response, and it must have showed for he added with a twinkle in his eye, 'He's rather bland.' He chortled as though enjoying a joke, 'Blandness works. And he has looks and charm. These can be moulded together to create charisma.'

'Ever thought of running, yourself?' I asked him.

'No,' he replied firmly. 'I have absolutely no charisma and, besides, I haven't the energy - another prerequisite - and I wisecrack too much. I could never take it seriously enough. I do take the New Party seriously, as I said earlier, but I couldn't take myself as a politician seriously.'

I managed to leave the event without committing to anything, which I regarded as an achievement in itself. When I was back at the cottage, I looked up the Philanthropist's name on the internet. I read that he was based in America and was recognised for his charitable work. His business interests were moderately successful and, if what I read could be believed, his charitable donations exceeded what his profits reportedly were. Scurrilous commentators speculated on where his 'real' money came from. I didn't care because I liked him. He had told me jokily that he treated wealth like an invisible force, an electrical current that flowed through him and out into his cherished projects. 'I am just a conduit,' he'd said. 'If I can make good things happen in some small way, I am happy to do so.'

70

POVERTY – A TRAVELLER'S TESTIMONY

Despite Serena's initial 'culture shock', she began to take the first steps towards creating her charity, or at least learning more about the poor, visiting places the politicians tended to avoid. I saw she'd put on the internet a piece of writing, including a fragment by an author who'd made a similar journey:

'I have seen too many troublesome things, going about this country. In the rural interior, subsistence farming would be more accurately called sub-existence. These are people trapped by life, for whom suicide is no way out - people with salt of the earth illiteracy, living isolated in their blighted houses. You see the dust of old farms in the eyes and nostrils of their children, growing up to despise their parents and their poverty.

'People wait for roads to civilise them. In the wilds, the people tell me, "If they knew how dull this forest was, they would not shout with such unbridled zeal, 'Oh, spare those trees! Oh, save that lake!' This concrete's dire - look at the forehead of any child who falls on it - and yet it bears our hopes of quiet wealth in fearful times, or that's what all our great leaders have said, one after the other - so clever, so eloquent, so sublimely sure! We hear them on the news and who are we to carp or question, when every day for us would be a green hell?'

'They still find poverty, even if an elevated form of it, when they move from pitiless countryside to heartless urban streets, to end up drinking street soup in quiet misery. They sleep in the cemeteries amongst the howling dogs of the city. Some go to live in old industrial buildings, with sacking for their bed, rusty metal their furniture. Their only electricity is what they steal from pylons. Children play in ruined restaurants, adults choke on the dust from their own clothes. They are wastrel souls disqualified by history. Once their worry was that they had no rain, and they used to drag their water from the river, but now they are overdosed and left to die on dirt floors, or sleep on mildewed mattresses, their skin maggot-pale. I went to a small town where a man, sleeping on the concrete floor of an abandoned factory, had thrown his meagre possessions from the third storey window onto the street and then thrown his sorry self on top of them.

'They say, if you help the poor man you're a saint, but if you ask why he's poor you're damned as a communist. They debate Third World poverty in luxury hotels. Outside, a man plays piano for the runaways who watch the grey and black limousines arrive. The *World-To-Let* sign is broken, with no bare feet or beggars allowed in. They marvel at all the free stuff the rich people are given, while their own pockets are full of the stale air of desolation. Some of the poor are allowed to be seen on state visits, but there are others we are ashamed of, unless of course it encourages the great nations to give aid without us begging for it, calling it 'financing development' instead. They'll polish the cars of the rich for them, but they will still always smell of their own dirt.'

71
RELUCTANCE

Sasha had been keen to hear my account of the event at which I'd met the Philanthropist, although entirely for her own reasons.

'OK, he sounds sincere,' she said afterwards, 'but why would you want to get involved?'

'I almost feel compelled. It's an adventure. It also feels inevitable, as though I'm becoming caught in a spider's web.'

'Adventure isn't everything.'

'But I feel I don't belong in this country. Other people are gradually moving back, although, don't worry, I'm not going back yet - not all the while they're after my money.'

We were sitting on a wall outside a rundown bar at the time, enjoying the sunshine and watching the people go by. For a moment, I looked at her closely as she observed a young woman walking up the street, bouncing her little son on her arm. I wondered if it was sadness I saw in Sasha's eyes, regret for a life she felt she would never have. It was something I thought I could never ask her, for fear she would emotionally fall apart.

I broke the silence, 'But what are all these wasted years spent here, if not in preparation for a return?'

'But it would not be the place you or I remembered. Full of gangsters, you always say. It will get safer here again.'

"I'd like to believe that, but I never feel safe,' I said. 'And you're not safe with me. By the way, don't forget to start going to the firing range. You'll need lessons if you want to stay with me.'

'No, I don't think so. You know I hate guns. I don't think I could ever aim a gun at someone. Unless I was angry, then God help them. I'd be trouble with a gun. No, the lesson would be wasted, I'm afraid.'

'OK. But all the time you're with me, you're in danger, so you need to be able to defend yourself.'

She made a face. 'I just think you're trying to put me off. It's like you're trying to get rid of me.'

What she suspected was true, although I didn't want her to feel I was rejecting her. I wanted her to be independent. I wanted her to want that too.

'This arrangement can't last for ever,' I said, reaching for her hand, but she pulled it away sharply. 'At some point you'll get tired of it. And you'll soon be able to start doing the art classes again.' She shook her head but I persisted, 'Look how much they've helped me, a pure novice, and you'll also have enough money from your pictures to set yourself up, and you'll be happy again.'

'But I'm happy now. And I thought you wanted a new life. I thought you were tired of guns, and politics, and the old witch, and that other bitch Andrea, who I think you're having an affair with, or want to, or she wants to, or something behind my back. And I thought art was your new life.'

'I thought so too, but I'm torn. It feels like when I was a boy and there would be a big game going on, and I wasn't part of it, just on the outside looking in. Besides, if something happens to you, I might not be inspired anymore.'

'Nothing's going to happen to me.' She laid her hand gently on mine. 'Look, I'll take your damned shooting lesson...'

'You'll need more than one.'

'Whatever... if it's going to make you happy. I assure you, though, that if some creep goes for his Clock, or...'

'Glock.'

'OK. Well, how would I know? If he goes for it, it won't be his arm I'll be aiming for - I'll be aiming right between the eyes! And if you do decide to go back to the old country, I want to be there. So you can tell that damned Andrea to get lost!'

72

LAWYERS

My next visit to the capital was to meet my lawyers on the extradition case. It was a multinational firm whose HQ was in New York and who claimed to be 'marquee label' on such matters. It probably had one of the grandest buildings in the capital, which admittedly was not saying much. The firm was acting for most of the exiles interested in reaching settlement with the old country. The fear of violence and / or forced repatriation was such that there were few who declined to participate.

I sat with my lawyer in a small, square, characterless room. I half expected the cleaner to pop in, looking for a mop. The lawyer, a large, solemn-looking man who looked like he could do with less sitting, was perched awkwardly opposite me with his back to the window. We were on the fourth floor and, through the small section of the window my lawyer was not obscuring, I could see the lake with sailing boats on it - a serene picture.

He asked me, 'So, at how much do you value your questionable accumulated assets, by which I mean assets not obtained directly through work or inheritance? To the nearest million dollars.'

This was a discouraging start. I said, 'Do you mean, how much is allegedly corrupt money?'

He smiled tightly, 'If you like, yes.'

'I have mitigating circumstances.'

'Of course you do,' he nodded. 'So does everyone.'

'No they don't. I was under house arrest for many, many months.'

'Ten, I believe,' he said in a patronising tone.

'It was without charge.'

He gave me a dismissive look. 'A useful offset at best,' was all he'd venture.

'But they can't get extradition if they haven't charged me. They don't get off first base.'

'A detail,' he insisted. 'How much effort do you think it requires for them to formally charge you in absentia? Do you want them to charge you? I could always insist they go through the formalities, but the outcome would be the same, except they will be more annoyed.'

'No, but it just feels like extortion. I lost my career and my pensions, both from my time in the military and in government.'

He paused for a moment, apparently more out of respect than anything else, as if finding a need to slightly adjust his opinion of me, although admittedly this could have been self-delusion on my part.

'How much do you have in Swiss bank accounts or offshore funds?'

'Three million dollars - dropping fast. Are you married? If you are, you'll know what it's like.'

'Not more?' he said.

'I mean, three million the government might claim was illegal inducements, or bonuses, or whatever they call it now. When you take out the pensions they stole from me and compensation for the premature ending of my career, they should be paying me.'

He laughed stiffly. 'I can reasonably predict they won't do that. But if you have three million now, how much did you have to begin with?'

'No more than four. Maybe less.'

'Right, any other questionable assets - penthouses, yachts, gold bars, watches?'

'I was given a villa on the coast by a foreign contractor, although I'd have given them the work anyway.'

'Of course you would. How much is it worth?'

'About a million. I sold it. That's part of the nearly four million I had. The thing is, that would never have gone to the government. In fact, none of these "questionable assets" would have gone to the government. I never stole from the government.'

'Indeed, you didn't. Any cars?'

'Fancy Italian thing. It never worked. Something wrong with the electrics. They can't count that.'

'They will.'

'Now who's being avaricious?'

'Look,' he said, his tone that of an irritable schoolmaster, 'we can make these arguments, but it won't help us. The thing to remember...'

'I know. I know. If I upset them, they'll come after the lot.'

This comment on my part seemed to galvanise him, his expression suddenly determined: 'We will strive to avoid that. No, we *will* avoid that. What puzzles me slightly is that you're on page two of the list.'

'What list is that?'

'It's based on the extradition list but reordered by amount of their claim. Being on page two means you're relative small fry to them'

'Small fry?' I could imagine Serena's reaction of absolute disgust.

Before I could argue that this should minimise their claim, he said, 'But that may be a mistake. Now you were a defence minister, I believe.'

'Yes.' This was only part of my ministerial career, but I saw no value in enlightening him.

'And defence ministers tend to be...'

'I know what you're getting at,' I interjected. 'Lots of big money contracts. But I'm no criminal. I wasn't greedy. That's why I'm on page two, don't you see? Then there's the house arrest and so on to take into consideration.'

'I don't think they take anything into consideration. What they're after is nine hundred and fifty million dollars.' I skipped a breath and he chuckled at my reaction. 'Not all of it from you, I hasten to add.'

'Almost a billion? It makes me wish I'd taken more. Not that I did anything wrong, as I say.'

'As we both agree. I think they understand they won't get all they want. I think, in your case, a million would do it. How would you feel about that? Then it would be over.'

If I'd had a cup in my hands, the contents would have ended up all over my clothes and probably his. I said nothing at first, and he merely sat waiting expectantly until finally I said, 'It still feels like extortion to me. Where do you get the number from? And what's their figure?'

'Ten million.'

Ten million? I did not react. The figure was so fantastical it held no more threat than a fluffy pink unicorn.

'They've done investigations,' he said. 'Of course, much of it's guesswork. They would have expected you to have a lot more than you do. Because you had the opportunity, they assume you took it.'

'Is this what is called being a two-time loser?'

He then produced a spreadsheet the government had provided. I skimmed through it. Two million dollars was from one contract for tanks.

'I never got that. Whose idea was this?'

'So how much did you get?'

'Fifty thousand, as I recall.'

'We could compromise that.'

'No we couldn't. I never got it.'

He gave me a withering look. 'This is a negotiation,' he said. 'Are you wanting to produce all your bank statements? I would advise against that.'

I was sure I'd never felt so depressed, although I probably had. Yes, of course I had. That was the day of the coup, which had been worse, except this felt like a continuation of house arrest - the price you just kept paying over and over.

'Then it will be finished. All closed,' he added helpfully.

'And strictly confidential, without prejudice, with no comeback ever? Full and final?'

'Yes. I know it's tough, but you have to remember that if you don't settle they will, as you say, come after you. Extradition. If that happens, there will be no compromise; or if there is, it will be after a time, possibly a long time, in gaol. The Squire, as people like to call him, is dead set on this process. If there aren't settlements, any political party with an agenda to recover questionable assets will win the election and they may be harsher. It's become that big an issue. And there will be an election: the Squire is adamant about that too. He wants the settlement process out of the way, at least as far as those who will cooperate are concerned, before any election takes place. He himself isn't interested in staying president. Hard to believe perhaps. But he wants a legacy.'

Legacy - always that word. His legacy, my legacy, my father's - that stupid tray of roses. 'Doesn't everyone?' I said to the lawyer. 'But by the sound of him, he's the sort of person the country needs as president.'

'Others have said that too. Right. OK, my friend.' He stood up suddenly, hand extended towards me. I stood up and we shook hands. 'I'll see what I can do,' he said. I was bemused. You couldn't buy a piece of paper small enough to do the calculations.

'It may seem primitive,' he said, reading my expression, 'but remember it is a *quick* settlement. The longer it goes on the more evidence gets produced, the more the number goes up. This is expensive work - accountants, lawyers...'

'Indeed. But it still feels like what American gangsters call a shakedown,' I said.

'I know. But think of what you're avoiding. I'll do my best. I'll work on the principle that for every million they drop I'll go up a hundred thousand, less if I can. If you feel sorry for yourself, don't. You can't hide this. One corrupt civil servant ended up in a monastery in the mountains of Bhutan looking like an Old Testament prophet with a fake ID. Now all he has to meditate on are the flies in his prison cell. And as for the one they call the Smooth Killer, who no-one sheds a tear for, he's looking at a bill for $350 million, and he's already under lock and key.'

I was genuinely shocked. On that basis I really was small fry. 'That's terrible,' I said.

He continued, 'What's more, it's not just a money game. I'm sure I don't need to remind you how corruption costs lives: buildings fall down from cheap materials, gangsters divert money to pollute land and water, cleanup funds go to crooks, small farmers get thrown off their land for vanity projects, charity for the starving buys the elite's luxury jewels.' He paused for a moment. 'Sorry, this work makes you self-righteous if you're not careful. You're doing the right thing, my friend.'

As I was leaving the little room I said, 'Can I just ask: what if some future government comes along and tries to overturn the settlements?'

'Don't worry. It's our job as lawyers to make sure the paperwork renders that impossible.'

As I left the law firm's offices, I had a quick look at the modern art on the walls and thought about where the money for it had come from. I couldn't help feeling I'd just had my pockets picked, but of course he would say it wasn't my money in the first place.

73

ELECTIONS

My lawyer's prediction proved correct. The Squire did indeed announce elections, to take place on a date to be confirmed but within the next nine months. The elections would be for President, with a vote for Congress seats within nine months after that. Nominations for the presidential race were to be made no later than six weeks prior to election date, whenever that might be.

Meanwhile, my lawyer was able to obtain a settlement in principle with the government. All settlements had to be signed off by the Squire. My proposed settlement was for eight hundred thousand dollars, not as bad as feared, though far more than I would have previously thought possible.

I made the mistake of telling Sasha about the settlement, and she was predictably unsympathetic. When I reminded her that she benefitted from my 'ill-gotten gains', she told me that was nonsense: 'That's like saying a beggar given a dollar by a thief is a party to the crime.' I could have argued with her, but thought it would be a waste of breath. She hadn't finished with the subject, however: 'So how much did your friend Russo pay?'

'Nothing. There were no financial claims against him. He shouldn't have been on the list. All he did was upset the government of the day.'

'I could tell he is a good man. Not a crook like you.'

This needled me: 'If you think I'm such a crook, why don't you go and live with Russo? He has a spare room. He could sell your art for you. Perfect.'

'No, because he's a normal man who would want sex with me all the time. He'd be a pest.'

'He's a gentleman.'

'You are a gentleman. You understand me - well, as much as a man can understand anything - any woman, at least. You are patient with me. You are a gentleman crook.'

In the following days, Andrea informed me that the New Party had been formally established and confirmed that Our Man was to be its presidential candidate.

'Isn't it exciting?' she said breathlessly.

I didn't know how to reply, conflicted as I was. Eventually I said, 'I'm thrilled about the election, assuming it's fair - no goons, no guns, no stuffed polling boxes. I'm just not sure Our Man is the right choice. Too lightweight.'

'He holds you in high regard.'

'That's his first mistake.'

'Always the cynic. He sees you as a possible defence minister.'

It was the unquestioning hero worship that came through in her voice when she talked of him that grated on me.

'Really?' I replied, irritated. Of course the idea of political office appealed to my vanity, but therein lay the danger. 'I don't know,' I said.

'Shall I tell him you're not interested?'

This irked me because she was playing the power broker, but then I thought about my father at the top of the stairs, about to fall.

'No,' I said. 'By the way, have you settled with the government yet?'

'Have we...' She was momentarily fazed by the question. 'Yes, we have.' So she'd lied: they did have some 'ill-gotten gains'. I was disappointed in her, disappointed she'd pretended that she and her husband were too good for corruption. It made me wonder whether I could trust her about the defence minister's job. Maybe it was all her idea in the first place. Besides, although the appointment of ministers was within the gift of the president under the constitution, the Squire might seek to change that.

'When are you leaving?' I asked her in a tone that probably unintentionally suggested I welcomed it.

'A few weeks time. We have to find temporary accommodation. We sold our property over there, you see. Be nice to see you before we go.' A gesture of conciliation.

'It would,' I said. I played along. Both Serena and Sasha suspected I'd been having an affair with her anyway, but why prove them right for a casual fling? I'd gladly give Andrea what I thought she wanted, but I'd still like to smack her backside for lying to me.

74
OLD PLACE

After all the endless deliberation about it, in the end my return to the home country was sudden. The sad passing of an old friend there gave me the impetus. I told Sasha I might make plans to remain there. I told her she could stay in the cottage if she wished, or the apartment in the capital if she preferred, since I was still paying the rent there and Serena had left. I made it clear to her I did not want to spend any more time discussing the future, since we said the same things over and over. It was best to let the future take care of itself. She tried to persuade me not to go, but when I insisted that I couldn't feel comfortable missing the funeral, she changed tack and asked me if she could join me. I said she could follow me later if she couldn't settle, but she had to bear in mind that the art market there was quite undeveloped, which she knew anyway. Although I'd now received a finalised settlement on my 'inducements', I was still wary of returning. I took both the real and fake passports with me. I also got word to Zico, enquiring whether he fancied a few days out of retirement to accompany me. As it transpired, he did not need persuading. I made a point of telling no-one else, not even Serena.

We arrived back in the old country on the day before the funeral. The airport felt more unwelcoming than I remembered, and anyone not in a uniform looked like a criminal. Out of caution, I used the false passport, supposedly as a travelling salesman, albeit one not carrying samples. I received no questions, only a hard stare; I felt sympathy for the weary-looking border official: he probably hadn't been paid in months.

The well-attended funeral was on the outskirts of my hometown, the nation's capital, and at the wake in a nearby hotel I was able to spend a little time with my friend's widow. A 'rising star' in the government in which I'd been the defence minister, he'd escaped the purges, always been adept at keeping a cool head when the need arose and was completely incorruptible, which was probably why he never reached a senior role, but also why he avoided gaol or exile. I was saddened that he wouldn't have the opportunity to be involved in the future elections, but his widow insisted he'd died happy in knowing they had been announced.

I also saw Andrea there. I had not expected this, and it took me aback.

'You didn't say,' she admonished, 'You dark horse, you.' I asked after her husband; she said he'd been taken ill. In her black mourning dress and veil she looked unnervingly attractive.

Andrea asked me if, after the wake, I wanted to go for a drive around the capital. I demurred, revealing I intended to look around the area where I grew up. She insisted she drive me there, and in the end I acquiesced. We left soon afterwards in her Mercedes, and Zico followed in the old Fiat he'd hired for the trip ('No car chases, please, Boss'). Andrea's driving was erratic and was made more so when she put her hand on my leg.

'No reason to be uncivilised,' she chided. 'No reason not to be friendly. Oh, don't worry, I'm not going to seduce you. I just want to be near you, hear your voice.'

'Stop teasing,' I said.

'Tell me something... I love Serena, but why do you let her treat you the way she does?'

'She's a free spirit. She does what she wants. She always has. She can't be tamed and I wouldn't want to, even if I could.'

'I'm not a free spirit - I like to be tamed. If the man is man enough.'

'I know what you want. Don't think I wouldn't be interested. Just not now.'

'I can wait,' she said, smiling confidently.

After kissing her goodbye and wishing for a moment I'd spent longer with her - gone to my hotel room with her, or whatever - I started on my stroll around the streets of my youth. Every corner had at least one person who looked like they could be trouble, and I was glad Zico was with me. What had once been an exclusive part of town was now heavily built up, a process that had begun many years earlier. The garden where I used to play had been sold and replaced by two small dwellings; this development had happened since I'd gone into exile, and it saddened me to see the old house looking dilapidated. Its remaining garden now consisted merely of a couple of small cypresses which must have been specially planted - no room for a child to do somersaults or play football.

Seeing a kid on a bike, I was reminded of how as a boy I would ride all over the city, from the villas in the rich part of town on the west side to the slums and shacks built amongst the rubbish dumps on the east. It wasn't safe in the poorest areas then, but now I felt it was unsafe everywhere.

'Let's get in the car,' I said to Zico. I could tell he was relieved.

We drove slowly through streets named after long-forgotten generals, down to the seaport, the early evening melancholy of which I always savoured, then past what was ambitiously known as the financial sector, past a ruined supermarket which squatters had now taken over, then swinging back past the cemetery where my grandfather had erected a mausoleum for the family, then into the smarter section of town where the foreign embassies were all lined up in a row.

In my hotel room I thought of what could have been: a few hours alone with Andrea - Andrea with all her fake confidence and genuine insecurities, who just wanted to be held and loved. Everyone else would say it was wrong, but I was growing tired of doing what others thought was right.

75
PRAY TO GOD

My sudden intense desire for Andrea, which I had never felt for her before, later triggered a feeling of guilt I could not seem to extinguish or ignore. I was so possessed by this feeling that I even went into a church for half an hour, during which I asked for forgiveness from a god I could scarcely believe in. It wasn't only Andrea that I felt guilty about; there was my relative (if rapidly waning) wealth gained in a poor country, my failed marriage (it was only salve to my conscience to call it 'open'), my visits to Chloe, and pretty much everything else I could think of to put on the fire. I told myself that it was because I wasn't really a bad man that I felt such guilt, but that didn't satisfy me either. Most men would take the opportunity to get drunk, visit a brothel and hang the consequences, so why not me?

A night on the town, however, was not a practical option. It soon became clear that the recruitment of Zico for the trip had not been frivolous or superfluous. By the afternoon of the second day, I was finding that I was seeing the same people on street corners, simply standing there looking, not beggars or vagrants but men in smart jackets talking into their phones, and I felt uneasy on the streets near the hotel. Why was it that, whenever I left the lobby, the same man would rise from his seat and be less than a hundred yards behind me whenever I looked? It was not paranoia, for Zico noticed this too. He said a second man was monitoring him. Elvis might be dead and the Smooth Killer behind bars, but the machinery of informers and hoods they'd set up was still in place. Sasha had been right when she'd cautioned me against the trip.

I was sitting in my hotel room feeling trapped, when I received a call from Andrea. 'Don't worry,' she said, indicating from her tone that she thought I was expecting her to suggest we meet. 'I just thought you should know that one of our friends, an exile like us, had his passport confiscated. He's in a similar situation to you: he was on the list but he settled and was led to believe he'd have no problem here.'

'Thanks for the warning. I'm not feeling particularly secure where I am. Still work to be done if the Squire wants the exiles back.'

What Andrea had told me was troubling, and I talked to Zico about it. We agreed the best thing to do was to drive to the border that night. Trying to take a flight out was too dangerous, even with a fake passport.

'Aren't you glad you came out of retirement?' I asked him. He merely laughed. The only potential snag was that he hadn't been able to obtain a gun he was happy with during the time we'd been there, although I hadn't thought we'd need one anyway. It was a stupid error on my part: in times of transition the lowlifes and the gangs were always busy.

As we loaded the car, I said, 'I'm getting sick of this. Nowhere to be free of surveillance. I'm sure if we were out in the wilds of Alaska in a log cabin, there'd be someone hiding behind a snow-laden pine with a pair of binoculars, waiting for me to emerge.' Zico said nothing. My world and his intersected only in his work, and otherwise we were far apart.

We took the main road which ran straight to the border. Zico had bought maps and had studied them to see what back roads we could use as an alternative if we needed to. We were not more than five miles out of the capital when he concluded we were being followed. We turned off but with misgivings.

'I've no idea what these roads are going to be like,' he said. Having at least temporarily lost the tail, Zico picked up speed. 'If they catch us up there won't be a gunfight, so we need to really go for it.'

It was beginning to get dark. He told me there were headlights in the distance behind us. 'We should assume it's them,' he said. As time went on, the car gained on us. Zico regretted not having a more high-powered vehicle. Whenever we drove through a built-up area, he was tempted to turn off into a farm and hide us there, but we decided against it: we'd still have to get to the border and we'd be trapped in some little village which might itself be hostile to us.

We kept on going, still out of easy range of any gunman in the car behind, until we arrived at a small town where we encountered a large procession, hundreds of people with lighted torches. It was a tense situation, and we were not welcome. I could hear the vulgar shouts in our direction, see the angry faces, but eventually they grudgingly let our car in, although we were only able to edge forward at walking pace.

'What's this all about, do you think?' I said.

'It looks like a protest,' he observed.

'Yes. It doesn't look much like a celebration.'

'I bet the whole town is out.'

'I may be guessing, but I think I heard about this,' I said. 'A teenager died. There's a multinational mining company that effectively owns this place. They claimed he was an agitator, and he was murdered. Now the workers are on strike, and every night all the townsfolk march to the company's gates.'

'What's the point, though? Who sees it? TV, I guess.'

'That's how I must have found out about it.'

The car we believed was following us had also arrived at the procession and was beeping angrily.

'You know, I realise now that I saw this on the news last week,' I said. 'All the big agencies must have got it.' I was sweating nervously. 'How are we going to get out of here?'

'Keep calm,' he said.

I looked straight ahead, ignoring the faces. I thought about nothing. After a couple of long minutes, I began to notice the procession ahead was gradually and awkwardly edging out of the way to allow us through.

'Get ready,' Zico said. 'The chase starts again. Pray to God. We have a lousy car and no gun. But, then again, it may not happen. It looks to me like the procession is closing up behind us. They're not letting them through. They're having to reverse out. People are banging on the hood and roof. Marooned in a car you're not going to argue with torches all around you.'

'I know what's going on,' I said. 'I bet it's the same make and colour the paramilitaries use. It's paras that killed that boy. I hope those goons are fearing for their lives. And I don't think there's another road. They'll have to go back to the highway.' I slammed my fist on the dashboard triumphantly and Zico beeped the horn.

'God bless them,' he said.

After that strange episode, we rattled our way to the border. Zico was not relaxed, fearing our pursuers could still reach the border post first. He was right to be concerned. By the time we'd reached the checkpoint, where I showed my false passport and the guard checked his list in search of the name, Zico noticed the paras' car arriving.

'They're going to be following us again,' he said.

We had maybe a minute on them, and when we reached the first town, a couple of miles over the border, we turned off the main highway. We found a small hotel which had the advantage of a car park not visible from the road.

We did not see the paras' car again, although on reflection I wondered if their role could have been merely to see us 'off the premises'.

76
PERFECT SPOT

The landscape on either side of the border was a mixture of mountains, small patches of desert, scrub, pockets of agriculture and, at the base of the mountains, ancient forests. It was regarded by the average metropolitan city dweller as a wild area, crime-ridden and dangerous. I stayed for a couple of days in the hotel in the 'one-mule town' we had stopped in, while I figured out what to do next. I had no mobile coverage and was dependent on the TV to inform me what was going on in the world. Zico needed to return home, so I drove him to the airport and paid for his flight. It was an emotional farewell.

'Any time,' he said.

'I just wish I had a business I could employ you in,' I replied.

'You never know.'

I changed the Fiat for a Chevrolet, just in case the paras were still around. On the way back to the hotel I took a detour and explored the Neighbour State as we referred to it. Maybe my brain was frazzled by the last few days, but I had it in mind to look for a permanent place to live there. As a country it was a sleepy, usually friendly if eccentric, democracy. Its only downside was its enthusiasm for starting border wars with us whenever its populace got restless, border wars they invariably lost, their outcome being the reestablishment through negotiation of the boundary pretty much as before.

I found a little town on the coast. It was a place which I remembered from years previous as having a reputation as a cultural centre. There was a colony of artists and musicians; indeed, a couple of the country's most successful rock groups were from there. I also remembered a famous Englishman, a writer and artist, had set up home in the mountains above the town. As I drove around, the more I liked the idea of moving there, but also the more I told myself to be careful, since I was a sucker for delusions. Just as a beautiful woman could destroy in a man all sensible constraints concerning her attainability, so a beautiful house could melt away any practical constraints in an instant.

I found the perfect spot, a small two-storey white stucco house right in the artists' colony and near the beach. If I was in exile all over again, this is where I would like to be. If Rats came after me, I would change my appearance, my name and my accent, and if they still tracked me down, and I was there without a gun - I had no idea what the gun laws were - I'd be there at my easel, a martyr to my art. With all that in mind, I stopped the car and had a look around. I listened for sounds - dogs barking, children screaming, rock bands practising - but found it quiet. I went round to the back and had a good look through the window. No furniture. Everything about the place was annoyingly close to perfection. Even the garden, though unkempt and desiccated, was beautiful in its way.

I immediately went round to the real estate agent, after enquiring at a general stores how to get there, to ask about the house. A woman dressed more for nightclub dancing than a day in the office, although these were not mutually exclusive, greeted me with a broad smile. She was puzzled by my accent, suspicious since it wasn't local, so I explained it was the result of living so long in other countries but I was now 'returning to my roots'. I told her I'd visited one of her properties, pointing out a picture of it in the window, and told her I was prepared to pay the asking price in full and in cash. She looked at me in amazement, making me wonder if I should withdraw the offer, but finally she said, 'I'm sorry to disappoint you, but the owner was planning to move across the border but has changed his mind, so I heard today.' Thus, the house, lovely as it was, was no longer for sale.

'But it's empty,' I insisted. 'He has moved out already.'

'Yes. That's quite correct, but he's moving back. Where he intended to buy is now part of the disputed area.'

'Along the border?'

'Yes. He thinks it's unsafe there - who knows whether he's right or not? - and being a foreigner over there, who knows? You never know when the bastards will start it up again. It's such chaos over there.'

'Yes, I see. I understand.'

I left immediately, keen to do so before she decided I myself was one of 'the bastards'.

77
BORDER WAR

In the old days, in Grandpa's time, border wars were extremely useful, provided they could be kept limited. Whenever either side was seduced by the alluring spice of conflict, a presidential visit would be arranged. It would all be very diplomatic, but after a sublime meal, fine wines and relaxed conversation, a rekindling of the perennial dispute would be hinted at.

Then, whenever trouble arose at home, such as a general strike or the uncovering of a coup plot, out would come the flags and pennants, and it would be understood amongst the populace that a border war was coming. There'd be long impassioned speeches and parades, and what would follow was neatly choreographed brinkmanship and the occasional theatrical skirmish - essentially bluff and posturing with guns, but little violence to speak of - over a small shaded area on a perpetually and conveniently contested map, a thorn-ridden barren patch of scrub that neither side wanted, except to deny the other of it. Sleepy patrols on overlooks would now and then fire at goats, while diplomats flitted like humming-birds between the capitals. If there were no prisoners to exchange, it did not matter - they could exchange hapless drunks instead.

Those genteel days were gone. Today's border wars were dirtier and more serious, but they were no less useful to presidents and no less futile in terms of land gained.

78

BORDER INCIDENT

Many of the border disputes that I was involved with as a soldier consisted of little more than an exchange of hot air and swearing, getting muddy in the process, and they were soon forgotten. But one episode from when I was a young army officer stayed with me. Everyone's career, whether successful or not, had blemishes on it, but this was deeper than Sasha's port-wine stain and without its beauty. It haunted me ever since it happened and became a spur, forcing me to try to do better in future, as if to make amends.

What made the incident worse was that I'd argued with my commanding officer about the inadvisability of the mission beforehand. We had to take over an enemy post which he believed was lightly manned. I argued that it probably wasn't and that, even if it was, the terrain we had to cross was too open. He was adamant, however; he maintained this little post was of key strategic importance and would help secure an overall victory, reclaiming land that hadn't been part of our territory for fifty years, and which might conceivably have useful mineral deposits beneath the surface.

Having lost the argument because he would not listen, and since every word I uttered made him more determined than ever, I gave up and led my unit towards the post. Unbeknownst to us, it was empty. Instead, there were snipers in the trees to either side of it. For them it was like shooting fish in a dry hole. When we realised what the truth was, we scrambled out as fast as we could. Not one of my men escaped the ambush unscathed. Seven of them were killed, while I was comparatively fortunate in suffering only injuries to my arms and shoulders.

After this disaster, I wanted to quit the army then and there, but three months out of action helped me to see more clearly. The military enquiry that followed absolved me and lambasted my superior. I never had to deal with him again because he was demoted and transferred. He was right in one respect, however: the calamity hastened the end of this particular flare-up, although not in the way he envisaged. Soon afterwards, our government gave up on this piece of land, which was uninhabited, and so it remained lost. So far as I know, no attempt was ever made to extract minerals there. On many occasions, the events of that day invaded my dreams. I never got over it and felt guilty over the deaths. I often thought I should have argued harder over it all. Needless to say, later during my political career when someone wanted to attack me, they would get their press friends to drag up the episode along the lines of "What really happened when…"

79

TRUTH AND LIES

When I was back at the cottage I shared with Sasha, I told her in detail - or as much detail as she insisted upon - about my adventures. I kept nothing back and answered every question with absolute honesty until she enquired, 'I must know: did you *want* to sleep with Andrea? Truthfully now.'

'Alright then,' I began reluctantly. 'Yes. I wanted her very much. She's a liar and I felt I wanted to punish her, but most of all I wanted her. I had so much desire for her when I was with her after the funeral, that I felt disgusted at myself.'

'So you should. You certainly disgust *me*.'

'I even went into a church to ask God for forgiveness, that's how bad I felt.'

'I'm speechless,' she said, although I wasn't sure whether this was a reaction to my wayward desires or to my, previously unmentioned, religious leanings. True to her word, she went upstairs to her bedroom and wept.

When she returned to the lounge, she said tearfully, 'I'm sorry I can't give you whatever it is you want. I don't blame you for wanting other women. It's me, I'm the abnormal one. I'm going to leave. I'm going to get out of your life. You don't really want me anyway. You want me to go and live in the capital, even though you don't want to live there yourself. I get the message. Well, to hell with you!' She was falling apart. It was like watching a piece of precious stained glass breaking up in front of my eyes. So much for the 'I am God's Wrath' speech - there'd be nothing like that again. She couldn't cope with it.

'Why didn't you lie to me?' she wailed. 'Everyone else does. It would have been kinder. Why tell me the truth when it hurts so much?'

'I can't lie to you,' I said. 'Not any more.'

'I can't believe you want to leave me for that filthy dog. Her poor husband ill in bed and all she wants to do - in fact, probably not you, but *any* man - is for him to get her up against the wall. Well, I hope they do put her up against the wall - and shoot her. Oh, I just can't believe you!' She returned to her bedroom for more tears.

When she returned, she demanded, 'What is it you want of me anyway? Tell me, please. No, in fact, I'll tell you. Do you want me to come with you to that place you told me about - with the artists' colony and the beach and the Englishman? Well, do you?'

'Yes,' I said. 'I do.'

'Well then, there'll be no more Chloe, no more old witch Serena, and absolutely no more of that creature Andrea. There'll be Sasha, Sasha and only Sasha. Do I make myself clear?'

'Yes. All too clear.'

She quietened down after this. Although I disappointed her, there was no alternative that appealed to her.

Finally, she said, 'I do love you in my way. I just wish I could trust you as well.'

80
BORDER TOWN

The border town I'd chosen was something of an oasis and atypical of the area. It was like a magnet drawing in all manner of artistic and musical types from the whole region. This gave it an air of fragility which appealed to both Sasha and myself. Following our row, we had settled into a better understanding. Nothing more was said about Andrea and what Sasha called 'her poisonous aura'. I accepted my ad hoc prosecution, not for evil deed but evil thought. Sasha was not going anywhere without me, and we both accepted that. Excited, she worked with me on the practical arrangements for our move. The paintings were passed to Russo for him to sell if he could. This presented him with a challenge in terms of storage, but he did not complain, at least to me. 'I will miss you like a brother,' he said, 'although I never got on with my brothers.'

'I'll see you in the old country,' I said grandly.

'That may be in your dreams,' he said, 'but it's not in mine. I'm never going to return. You'll be back here, you mark my words. Let me know as soon as you're coming.'

After I'd found a new rental place in the town I referred to as the Artists' Colony, I paid off the rent on the apartment but kept the cottage going for the time being.

Once we'd moved in, I bought a car, a beat-up old Ford, but as we explored we soon found the local roads in poor condition and there were few fellow travellers. In the mountain areas, it was often said that the only legitimate visitors were wildlife enthusiasts, and even some of them were suspect. There were lawless villages here and more than one internationally notorious smuggling route. Every kind of criminal lurked on either side of the porous border, light on their feet for whenever the patrols became temporarily interested. These were the margins of the country and society, where borders were trivial, ephemeral. They were contested areas, the balance of local power in constant flux. Tribal lands had diminished with time, much in the the same way that their indigenous ceremonies had been demonised and curtailed by missionaries. Stray dogs roamed through villages in loose packs, chickens scratched in the dry fields. Frontiersmen were now collectors of hallucinogenic plants, or illegal drug chemists. In the bigger towns were counterfeit currency factories and kidnapper hideouts. Meanwhile, on the dusty back roads you could still encounter the odd covered wagon with a mule team that knew the way.

One evening, we stopped for a drink in a small border town. We watched the young hoodlums showing off in their muscle cars in the main square. Here the town devoured the forest, while over there the scrub encroached upon its derelict margins. Two drunken beggars were fighting in a side street. It was desperately bloody and unrelenting, and the onlookers were cheering them on. I was tempted to think they were from another world, and yet I could not help thinking: were they so far from us at heart? Were we really more sophisticated? And that hideous man grimly striding out to shoot wild dogs - could he have been me in another lifetime?

81

ENGLISHMAN

The house we chose to rent was slightly away from the artists' colony itself but closer to the Englishman's cottage. We were told he was very reclusive but had an affinity with the indigenous tribes who still lived deep in certain largely undisturbed (fiercely protected) forest remnants that straddled the border. It was as though, as an outsider, he could empathise more closely with them.

Through someone who knew him, we requested permission to visit. His initial response forwarded to us was 'Not at this time'. We left it a couple of weeks before trying again, and this time received no response, so we decided on a direct approach.

To reach his little house we had to climb a steep, narrow, stony path. We were about twenty-five yards from his front door and on the edge of his garden, when we heard a strident voice, 'OK, stop there!' We looked over to the right where the voice had come from and saw a lanky old man with a straggly beard and a shotgun pointed at us, standing outside his doorway. We told him who we were. 'Never heard of you,' he replied.

'We're friends,' said Sasha plaintively.

'They all say that,' he barked, but he gradually brightened, as though at last recognising the names the contact had given him. He said to me, 'She has a kind face.'

'She does.'

'Otherwise I wouldn't let you in.' He gave us a wolfish grin. 'Come and have coffee. I have all kinds of visitors, most of them unwelcome. The problem of being a recluse in a place like this is that you become an object of curiosity. Something, I assure you, I have no desire to be.' He ushered us in and put the gun in its place on the lounge wall, amongst old photographs of forgotten theatre stars and next to a forlorn-looking stucco statue of Jesus. While he was in the little galley kitchen, and after he'd declined Sasha's offer of help, we merely sat and let our eyes enjoy the lounge. It was like a small flea market with all manner of unrelated objects, some grim items such as skulls, others humorous, some both macabre and comic, also a number of pieces of his own artwork which reminded me of the colourists.

He brought in the coffee with some coconut cakes he'd made. He asked us what we were up to. 'It's a nice area, isn't it?' he said, 'but further out, well, it's not so great.' He started talking about his life, saying he'd been living there twenty years.

'You must love it,' said Sasha.

'I do, but even if I didn't I would never return home. I once read that in old age you should live in a small house by the sea with only the birds for company. You might say that I'm not by the sea, but you'd be wrong. At the back of here,' he pointed, 'there's a narrow path - very dangerous, I might add - that runs circuitously down to a little sandy beach. I don't like the path. I'd rather it wasn't there. I've had one of two try to get in round the back. Hence the shotgun.' He took it back off the wall and made as if to shoot through the window, causing Sasha to flinch.

'When did you last fire it?' she asked him.

'Last week, actually. Some people in the garden. I don't aim to kill, you understand. But it could happen.' He chuckled. We asked him about his old life.

'I hated the pressure to earn money,' he said. 'I got sick of banks contacting me so they could try and make more money for themselves. I was never a miser. I gave away money when I had it, and it always came back.'

'You have a reputation for helping the indigenous people,' I said.

'I don't know if I've helped them. I shot at a few of them for stealing from me once.' He laughed at the memory of this. 'I told them, "I can't be generous to you if you steal everything I'd have given you without asking." I try to understand them.'

The old man explained how the various Indian tribes had been deprived of their territory over the centuries until they were confined to a 'protected area'.

'Even this was invaded by colonists,' he said, 'but these new people, supposedly hippies sympathetic to the Indians' cause, found the area good for growing marijuana. Sure enough, the army got wise and started spraying. This attracted guerrillas who then attacked the army. Thus, the tribes, through no fault of their own, now found themselves caught up in a small-scale civil war.'

'So did it force the Indians to leave their home in the forest?' asked Sasha.

'Yes. Some had to flee for their lives of course. But most of them gradually left the forest for things they needed like medical help, machetes and other tools. They became disenchanted with their life. Some went to work on the plantations in return for food. Sometimes the colonists would "adopt" the Indian children; in other words, steal them. The army then decided to employ those that remained for their survival techniques and this also made them a target for guerillas. Their villages were burned, any possessions stolen and livestock slaughtered.'

'What about diseases brought in?' I asked.

'Yes. The arrival of gold miners led to deaths from TB and influenza, as well as leaving mercury-contaminated waterways - you can imagine what impact that has had. A highway through the reserve was abandoned but left measles behind.'

'So is the army still there?' Sasha asked, glancing over at me disapprovingly, happy to stick me with guilt by association. I looked away and then took a sip of coffee to distract myself.

'Yes. Ten years later, it's still there. Encampments along the river, a hundred or more soldiers. They pollute the river with their detergents, their chemicals, their waste, their trash. You see, the river is central to the lives of the tribes. They drink from it, they use it to wash food, they wash clothes in it, bathe in it. But now the women are afraid to use it and the men are afraid to walk near the encampments to go and tend their crops. So there we are: I've talked too much already. But I do what I can to encourage a better understanding of their plight.' Contented, he raised his cup to his lips.

'We need more like you,' I said.

'I don't know. People say to me, "Why do we need you, an Englishman, to tell us this?" I say, "How many of you have talked to them, have studied them as I have? At least I know these people." Some of the candidates in your election will be advocating genocide. Of course, they won't call it that.' He gripped my hand. 'Don't let them win,' he pleaded.

82
CANDIDATES

Despite Sasha's admonition about contacting Andrea, I found the ability to talk to the latter about politics essential. For her part, Andrea, who curiously spoke as if she already knew of Sasha, volunteered, 'She is not someone I would wish to associate with,' but refused to elaborate. With Russo so far away and keeping his nose out of politics, Andrea was increasingly like a soulmate. I didn't agree with her on a lot of things, and this made it more fun, especially as it was such a time of change.

The Squire came through on his promise. Election dates were announced, candidates for the presidency nominated. Soon there were an absurd number - over thirty hopefuls and rising every day. The Squire was not one of them. He was, according to Andrea who'd met him, by nature what he looked like on TV: aloof. He was determined for the election process to succeed and had no desire to 'reluctantly' give himself ten years in power.

He was benevolent but a dictator nevertheless. Accordingly, he made a speech in which he told the country the winning candidate must be a friend of the army. It sounded chilling, but it was realistic - if the army didn't like the candidate, a coup would follow. He was also not prepared to sit passively by and allow what already looked like a vanity parade become a fiasco, a babble of conflicting voices with the electorate spinning around in confusion. To assist, he set up an 'advisory bureau' to weed out as many candidates as possible. Anyone serving a prison sentence or under house arrest was automatically excluded. By now the Smooth Killer had been formally charged with theft of state property and, given the complexity of his case, no trial date could be set, thereby excluding him. More bizarrely, a leading human rights lawyer was considered a serious contender until he found himself gaoled for making a lewd gesture at a statue of the Virgin Mary.

The official advisory bureau was, however, not the only source of pressure to reduce the number of candidates. One popular left-winger fled the country after death threats, which he ignored, and the twenty-four hour kidnap of his family, which he did not. Another quit when his supporters were routinely beaten up by paramilitaries. Another was shot while posing for photographs with a celebrity fan. Another candidate was arrested in the US for currency irregularities. Another quit when members of her campaign team were attacked with baseball bats and golf clubs and a banner was put up outside her house reading *You're Next*. Another was shamed in the press for drugs and sex parties and arrested for 'corrupting public morals'. It was like a steeplechase with so many early casualties, the fixed-smile reptiles and the tired old crooks of the past all falling by the same wayside. By the time the advisory bureau had exhausted all possibilities, the field was reduced to eight, a number which the Squire still thought too many, according to the TV station he owned. Andrea was excited because her hero and possible lover Our Man had slid through. His bright smile and blandness had not only seduced her, but was reported to be a favourite with the people.

According to Sasha, whose hatred of Andrea had got her interested in politics, her nemesis would bump off her husband if she thought she could be First Lady. When I assured her Andrea's ambitions were confined to being a government minister again, she was dismissive: 'You understand nothing about such women. Why do all the work and get all the criticism when you could have a life doing nothing, except maybe open the odd supermarket, and otherwise spend your time on your back?'

83
NEW LIFE

Sasha seemed to enjoy her new life. She had always liked the idea of an artists' colony, especially one with a local market. Dealers and buyers from all over the region would descend on the small seaside town looking for new works. There were several local galleries. She quickly established herself amongst the group, despite her wariness around other artists. In any group she stood apart, not aloof but separate, and this was no exception. However, so different was her work to that of the others (whose paintings tended towards the strictly representational), that she could not be ignored, and indeed they regarded her with curiosity. She had few new completed works but was extremely productive, mainly painting in the surrealist way she found most natural, whilst incorporating her new environment of sea, arid local landscape and mountains. Her works soon began to sell. Meanwhile, Russo had found a buyer for three of her larger pictures, the owner of a hotel near where he lived, and he forwarded funds from this transaction. He had disposed of most of his original business, retaining a few items more for sentimental reasons than anything else, whilst at the same time expanding his art dealership; he had even signed up several new artists. He had by now established himself ('in a small way' he insisted) as a dealer with 'a good eye', an accolade he accepted with pride.

'I don't always get it right,' he told me over the phone, 'but it is gratifying to me that, coming from a background where the only art I ever saw was in a church, or some ethnic tourist tat, and with no formal education in it as such, I seem to have the knack.'

'You've always had the knack,' I assured him. 'You've always known what would sell, except for your brief adventure in relics.'

'Yes. I'm not going to fall into that trap again. If someone shows up with a "genuine" Rembrandt they found in their attic, I will remember my gullibility when someone produced the nose bone of St Boniface or whoever it was, and say, "No thanks". I still get people trying to sell me that stuff. I tell them, "Take it back to the factory." Biggest lesson I ever learnt. We all need them.'

'I'm still learning lessons about women,' I said.

'That's a scholarship that never ends. And I think you know less at the end of it than you do at the beginning. I steer clear of them, except in connection with business. Relationships is like a whole other world which passes me by.'

'It's a good other world,' I said.

'I do feel I'm missing out sometimes, but then I read about some scandal in the newspapers and I think, "I'm glad that's not me."'

84
KEY SUPPORT

Prior to the campaign, Our Man invited his 'key supporters', namely the leaders of his election team and putative provisional cabinet members, to his house. He lived on a vast private estate far from the capital with five hundred miles of roads, twenty man-made lakes, numerous waterfalls, a replica Spanish galleon and a golf course, plus a host of hundreds of white doves which reputedly created a dramatic sight at night. His mansion with its ornate portico, marble floors, broad verandas and even gargoyles, was a marvel to behold, all courtesy of his family's international gold-mining and diamond extraction businesses. With him in this huge abode was his blonde American Express wife and his kids who, at least on briefly meeting them, had the manners of well-behaved robots. There was not a single thing out of place, not even the suggestion of, for example, a small pile of builder's rubble shoved in the tiniest convenient corner outside. Even while he was in exile, the grounds had been immaculately maintained. Of course, his exile had been technically voluntary and, although nominally on the extradition list, not one cent of the just under a billion dollars the government had sought would have come from him. I had to admit he was a phenomenon of sorts. I doubted a wild thought ever entered his mind and I could not resist the feeling of envy. Certainly, no unwelcome weeds defiled the garden, or so it appeared as I strolled along the path from the car park.

I arrived at about the same time as Andrea, a little early. She was wearing a bright green number she'd probably bought specially, while I was wearing a seersucker suit I sometimes wore to the races. Our Man was busy playing tennis, probably winning without breaking sweat, which seemed to be his motto for life, and when he had finished off his opponent, which took another couple of minutes, and had freshened up and changed, which was another ten, he greeted us, and the rest of the 'gang' now arriving, with beaming beneficence and self-satisfaction.

We were invited into a marquee tent. In all, about a hundred of us sat on wooden seats, with the smell of freshly-mown grass and coffee and an exuberance of patisserie. The main sponsor, the Philanthropist, whom it surprised me Our Man even needed, gave a suitably light introduction. Then our host, looking and no doubt feeling like the consummate champion in his pristine white suit, gave a speech composed entirely of rhetoric and guaranteed to put even the most enquiring minds into a state of sleepy acquiescence. He enumerated every word as if he had just stepped down from a cloud. It certainly confirmed me in the view that there was not one strand of belief he would hold so tightly that he could not let it instantly float away if necessary in favour of another.

Afterwards, everyone applauded with gusto. It had indeed been a marvellous speech, smooth and seductive as soft fur, so much so that I could not immediately recall a single word of it, which presumably was the intention. During coffee I was talking to a pressman from a 'friendly' journal. He told me, 'They say he could sell you measles, although afterwards you wouldn't know if that was what you had or if it was vertigo.' He was soon whisked away for a 'private meeting' with the great man to help with a full-length feature he was writing on him. A TV crew also arrived to conduct an interview. Everyone was happy, especially, it seemed, the communications director, a buzzing, self-important young man, highly-organised and flushed with that fleeting pleasure that comes from everything one touches working perfectly.

When our 'business' was over, we were allowed to explore the gardens. I boarded the little private train, from which I could enjoy the topiary, the waterfalls, the stone gryphons and unicorns, all modelled on a mythical English estate. I got off at the private zoo. After a brief stroll, I sat on a bench and, while my eyes delighted in the splendours of the flamingos and white peacocks, I ate an ice-cream and chatted with a portly American who said he was with the *New York Times*.

'No private meeting for you, then?' I asked in a tone I realised immediately was unintentionally unkind.

'Oh yes,' he replied jovially. 'After lunch. Three o'clock and don't be late.'

I hadn't even thought there'd be lunch, but, sure enough, at one thirty, back in the marquee tent, as we watched a film the campaign team had produced for showing on TV, we were offered all manner of meats, hot and cold, with rice, peas, peppers and various other vegetables, plus a vegetarian option of roasted aubergines and squashes, followed by a cornucopia of desserts. My American friend had a selection of everything. 'I don't eat this well at home!' he enthused. I was tempted to suggest this was probably a good thing but stopped myself.

Andrea came to sit with me when the opportunity arose. 'Hello, stranger,' she said brightly, 'So where've you been?'

'I've been enjoying the peacocks strutting about. Those of them in the private zoo anyway.'

She shook her head. 'You're so damned harsh,' she said. 'Miserable is what you are. You need a good woman to get you out of it.'

'I don't really do politics,' I said, pointedly ignoring her suggestion. 'I can't read people.'

'You didn't say that when you were at the defence ministry. That's the job you'll have again, all being well.'

'Looking back, I think I must have bluffed my way through it,' I said ungraciously. 'I think I'm more like my father than my grandpa. My father did not do politics. He was kind of obnoxious, I believe.'

I looked up at that moment to see Our Man was back in the tent. Champagne was brought in. 'I can't believe all this,' I said to Andrea grumpily. 'Aren't we supposed to be trying to help the poor?'

Andrea was annoyed: 'If you want to be so prissy about it, why don't you give back the rest of the money?'

I flared in response: 'What do you mean!?'

'You settled with the government. It was a compromise. That means you kept the rest. Don't kid yourself; we all did it.'

At this point, Our Man came over, champagne glass in hand - mainly to see Andrea, I was sure. As we talked, it soon became clear it was all Andrea's doing that I would be up for the defence minister's job. He hardly seemed to remember who I was, although even then I could have drowned in all the syrup.

'We feed their dreams,' he said warmly; I only remembered it afterwards because I realised it was the party's mantra. When Andrea left us, presumably so that he and I could get to know each other a little better, it wasn't more than a minute before he pressed my hand firmly to indicate our conversation was over.

85
THIS PLACE

After Our Man's show, I took my new American friend for a drive, as he'd told me he wanted to get a feel for the 'real country'. He said he was tired of politicians and their riches, and comforting words for the poor they would do nothing for. 'Tell me everything you know,' he said. 'Everything you remember.'

'Mostly misremember.'

'That too.'

So I took him on a little trip through the interior. It was many years since I'd explored this area and as I drove it came back to me in images and fragments of memory. I recalled it as a harsh land of disheartening stories and historical evils seemingly embedded in its landscape.

We came to a neighbourhood that was notorious for once spawning a revolutionary movement of sorts. I still remembered the hipster talk of its leaders on a rebel radio station. That would have been enough to put off someone like me even then, but their stated political aims gradually gathered support.

'This lake we're approaching is where they declared a new government on the beach.'

'Yeah?'

'It's true. They drew a map of the country in the sand and marked out their campaign. They filmed the occasion, these half a dozen Castro wannabes. It was a glorified student stunt, but it was enough to wind up the junta. They immediately closed the borders and despatched a few hundred soldiers. The men searched in the forest but couldn't find anyone; they soon grew tired of having only birds and bats to shoot at. Eventually they came across about fifty of these so-called revolutionaries, there was maybe a brief skirmish, no-one killed.'

'So what happened to these "Castro wannabes"? I can't imagine it was a case of "OK, kids, back to your school books!"'

'No. They really were just some silly college kids, but they were all rounded up and never seen again. One was the brother of someone I went to school with. Terrible situation. But even something as trivial as their action seemingly was, had its consequences, its legacy. The fiasco showed the cruelty of the military government. This inspired some real guerrillas into being.'

'And I would imagine it gave the area publicity.'

'Yes. It wasn't long before the latest crop of entrepreneurs came along, seeking the genuinely exotic and its cheaper alternatives. A new destination for the intrepid, rich traveller.'

'Tell me, are there still remote tribes near the border?' the American asked.

'No. There are tribes, but you wouldn't call them remote. The border area was once all wilderness. It still largely is on the other side of the border. And it was home to uncontacted tribes, even in my lifetime. But they soon disappeared, even before the anthropologists had drained them of everything.'

'So would you call this a place of myths?' he asked hopefully. 'That always interests me. Sometimes particular places - mountains, lakes - can be associated with ancient cultures, religions.'

'Amongst the remaining tribes, yes. But in this country it's discouraged nowadays, what with the pressure on land. Myths are seen as a burden, tied up with strange cults and superstitions that can hold back a country and constrain its progress. Like the precious metals buried in the sacred mountain.'

'Now that's a problem for sure.'

'Yes. And the way governments see it, it's like a flotilla of fast boats stuck with a battered old dugout trailing far behind.'

'Yes,' he said. 'It always seems to me, the dominant culture wants these myths to be stamped out until they become safe, no longer a threat, then they become a source of income.'

'And it angers the tribes. They say, "You think we're wild animals who can't think or act for ourselves." I remember one of their leaders telling the Minister of the Interior on TV, "You're like a pederast offering sweets to a simple-minded child. We are not so easily deceived. We once had great riches. Now we're poor because of you and your henchmen, the settlers."'

'Ha! So they don't want the uplift that the modern world can offer them.'

'Right. They just want to get on with their lives, not be treated as objects that need some kind of improvement. But then... you see those young men over there in their shiny white shirts and sunglasses, riding mopeds...' I slowed the car to a stop.

'Driving round and round...'

'Yes. They all grew up in the forest. They couldn't wait to get out.'

'And can you blame them?' he said.

'No, but you can imagine the panic it causes amongst the so-called experts. "How can we preserve their way of life?" they say, to which I remember one of the young men saying on TV, "And how can we preserve yours?"'

'Exactly,' he said. 'Now some people would say it's a shame, but to me... isn't it just part of life? These people are not exhibits in a museum or oddities for scientific research. They want to be mainstream. Or maybe, mainstream with an edge. But it still saddens me, all this pressure on them. Doesn't it you?'

'Yes. It angers me, actually. It's a futile anger, like being angry about children that are born without limbs, but I feel it right enough.'

'Now you were in the army, as I understand it. Did you have encounters with them in that capacity?'

'Some.'

At this point we were distracted by a weatherbeaten, wrinkled old woman in a brightly coloured headscarf and long dress, carrying a basket and approaching the car through the dust.

'How charming!' exclaimed the American warmly. He put the window down and greeted her as she hobbled towards us. 'Some local produce, perhaps? Anyway, you were saying...' I said nothing and merely waited for the inevitable. 'Shall we see what this sweet old lady has in her basket? Fruit maybe? Oh... Oh no, she's begging!' Aghast, he quickly put the window up. 'You were saying, about the army...'

I stepped out of the car and gave the woman a few coins. The American then opened the window and put a banknote in her basket. A word of thanks trickled from her toothless mouth, and she gave us a happy grin.

Back in the car, as we moved off, I continued, 'So, anyway, border wars were often fought over what was Indian land. But I had encounters in other ways too. As a tribe starts to die out, illegal squatters arrive, discord follows and the army is sent in...'

'I can see that.'

'And it grieves me to say, as a former soldier, that the army is no friend to them. Once army officers used to steal their land for themselves and sell it to ranchers for cash. And, of course, like all other armies, ours brought in drink and prostitution with it.'

'The tribes have their own intoxicants of course...'

'Yes, their own routes to the sublime, but drink is easy. And they begin to see the challenges to their culture questioning things they previously saw as facts, as certainties. They feel ignorant and so they drink and despair and eventually a businessman steps in to buy up a village and maintain an "authentic tribal culture" for well-heeled tourists.'

'American tourists,' he observed.

'Yes, but not only them.'

'Could we visit one? Is there one near?'

'We could, but it wouldn't be very enlightening. It's now little more than a private zoo with animals in small pens and a couple of people with tribal heritage left in the middle of a huge ranch. So I heard anyway.'

I pointed in the distance towards a plain in the backlands where a legendary 'lost tribe' used to live. 'The settlers encroached so much the Indians ended up stealing from local farmers, for whom this was an "outrage".'

'And retribution naturally followed,' said my friend.

'Yes. Vigilantes shot the head of the village. It was the beginning of the end for them - or perhaps the end of the end. More slash and burn farming followed. Ranches expanded, growing soy for export. Boom towns prospered. The tribe was reduced to a handful of individuals living next to the old trading posts; their last scrap of economy became some cute religious artefacts made from rubber and imported from China.'

'I remember now: I read about this. The last trace of them disappeared through disease or intermarriage and entrepreneurs created a new 'lost tribe', inhabitants of a so-called Stone Age village. They became part of a tourist trail sponsored by the government. I saw the marketing for it in the States.'

I showed him the beginnings of highways that petered out in the green forest and the abandoned gold mining camps with what were once the workers' bars and brothels. He was impressed by the huge craters left by the goldfields.

'Finally, the government succeeded in building a new road through the forest to nourish the small settler towns. They swelled in size, multiplying themselves every year. Some were like western film sets with gunfights...'

'I can imagine!'

'... in saloons every night, except these were for real.'

We stopped in one of these little towns for a drink. We watched the young men driving their second-hand Mercs around the square, trying to impress the girls, who were as beautifully dressed as in any royal court.

'This place seems to be thriving,' the American said.

'Yes, but in other places you find people about whom there's a saying: "They are too poor to wear shoes in summer."'

We fell silent and my mind wandered. I thought about unending poverty, about dashed ambitions, blighted hopes. The class of veranda dwellers was what many aspired to. Now pathos was all they had left as they looked out over the desolate roofs. The people always complained they were not living in the future the politicians had promised them. For the rural people the metaphorical good luck serpent escaped, never to return, and what awaited them was bad harvests, with the Ministry always to blame.

My friend broke the silence, 'When this circus, excuse me, this presidential election, is over, if you don't get one of the top jobs, why don't you go for the senate to represent these people - the rural poor and the tribal peoples? You clearly care about them.'

'I do. I could see I would soon become the most hated person in the country, though. I'm not ready for perpetual meditation yet. The vested interests, the rich landowners...'

'Like... ?' He raised his finger in the vague direction of Our Man's estate.

'Yes... would want to thwart me and, besides...'

He interjected, 'The rural poor and the tribes don't exactly get along.'

'Right. And they would obviously want a leader of their own. Or two. Hmm. I suppose if they'd have me, I could work with what already exists, give it a boost and then step aside when they got tired of me, which would be after about one term. But I guess the first thing to do would be to educate myself better about them.'

I enjoyed our drink as we watched some kids playing football in a rough field, like kids everywhere before twilight, while my friend told me about his own life growing up in Illinois. It reminded me of the limitless ways of living a human life. Social media made us all the same, even when we argued, but it was the sense of difference that made life interesting. It was the 'other' that we feared which made life worth living.

We were draining our glasses when I heard a kid shout 'Yankee!' angrily. As we walked over to the car, a hail of small stones followed us. It made me feel sick, but my friend said nothing. He was used to it. And, as a journalist, for him it was all copy anyway.

86
THE CONVERSATION NOT HAD

When I returned across the border to Sasha and the artists' colony, and talked to her about what was happening with the build-up to the election, she appeared not to see the implications. It was as though she felt nothing would come of it. She was always to some extent paranoid, believing her current life was in peril, but I wasn't convinced she appreciated what would happen to us if Our Man actually won the election and invited me to join his cabinet.

The conversation we did not have concerned what my life would be like in the event I was in government. I would need to live in the capital, and evenings would be taken up with meetings and dinners, including with people I would not usually want to associate with. I could not imagine her by my side at official events. Moreover, our relationship did not exist in a vacuum. No doubt, Serena would want to come back into my life to take the role of minister's wife and everything that went with it. She would want to combine it with her work on women's rights - and I would want her to. At the same time, Andrea would also be in the cabinet and, although I didn't intend to have an affair with her, if *she* wanted one it might be difficult to resist. It would be the end of my relationship with Sasha, however much I wanted to avoid this, and she surely realised it. It was a conversation we did not allow ourselves to have and perhaps, in her case, it was also a thought she never allowed herself.

87
CAMPAIGN

The campaign began in earnest with the usual mixture of enthusiasm and ennui. Most of the 'laughing stock' candidates had been encouraged out of the race, but there were some bizarre characters even amongst the final eight. One female candidate was a rich aristocrat who claimed to speak for the dispossessed, although she was closer to expensive yachts and offshore trust funds than street kids and poor ghettos. She said she would rule by horoscope. She had been invited to withdraw by influential people supporting other candidates, but she had so much money she was quickly able to silence any criticism. Serena told me over the phone that this woman was a dangerous fake and revealed that she herself was campaigning for the new Women's Rights Party candidate, even though she told me that 'sadly' the party had no chance of winning.

'Why do you say that?' I asked, surprised by her untypical pessimism.

'The fact is,' she said, 'most women vote the way their men tell them. I wish it wasn't the case, but it is. And I assure you, as if you didn't already know, this country's problems are in the main due to the macho culture, and men will not vote for something they see as reducing their own rights.'

'So why bother with the party if it can't win?'

'It's not about winning a bogus election. It's about getting the issues out there - changing the terrible rape laws, introducing abortion rights - there is plenty of work to do.' I was happy for her: she was committed to a cause and clearsighted about its prospects, and that commitment gave her a zest for life she never knew when she was in exile with me.

As the campaign ground on, week on week, three frontrunners emerged. There was Our Man, of course, optimistic and urbane. Females who didn't support the Women's Rights Party, and even some who did, were said to swoon over him, finding him 'charm personified', whereas men I knew tended to distrust his smooth manner, whilst recognising he was what they expected a politician to be: an 'oil slick'. They believed politicians were untrustworthy and enjoyed finding evidence to support it.

My own favourite candidate superficially resembled Our Man. As well as being charismatic, energetic, attractive and articulate, he was, unlike Our Man, clear on policy. He was essentially the candidate of the Left: workers' rights, land reform and anti-poverty measures. Above all, he was hardworking. An honest man in a dishonest age, he was in all respects but one, the perfect candidate. His one blemish was a literal belief in angels. When I mentioned this to Sasha, she said, 'And so what? Most people believe in angels to some degree.'

'No,' I said, 'he really believes in them literally. He sees them in the air, in his car, his office, everywhere. Real Biblical angels with little gossamer wings.'

'A mild eccentricity,' she demurred.

'They come to his study, sit on his desk, look over his shoulder. They talk to him, give him advice, counsel him, protect him, so he says.'

'Has no-one pointed out his mistake to him?'

'It's a waste of time. He only listens to the angels. He's completely nuts. He says, "Without them, where would I be?"'

The most serious opposition to Our Man was the evangelical candidate. He was adored by the military and was as modern as the blunderbuss, whilst at the same time cultivating an image of honesty, simplicity and humility, which both Andrea and I were sure must be humbug. His view of the indigenous tribal peoples was not merely that they were 'backward', but that they were evil, incapable of human decency, their cultures a manifestation of the Devil that needed to be eradicated.

'They were put on this earth to hold back progress,' he said. 'They will never be productive. They are destined to always slow the country down, and to the extent they will not give up their evil practices they must be contained.' He declared that subversives, leftists and dissidents of every kind needed 'a taste of the cannon'. He said under his rule human rights campaigners would be banned. When he was criticised on TV for his fiery language, he attempted to explain that he was only talking metaphorically and it had been 'a quick exchange of remarks' that did not reflect his real views, but in all things he would be guided by God. Afterwards, they interviewed his supporters. One said, 'Of course he's a fool. He says stupid things, but he will keep everything in order, just like God dictates, with civilised people at the top. And that is what we care about.'

I said to Sasha, 'There are millions like this man. They don't even want the vote. All they want is two or three decades of a strongman in charge, a strongman that likes people like them.'

88
BEHIND THE SCENES

During the campaign period I spent most of my time behind the scenes in support of Our Man. I told myself this was out of a sense of duty to the democratic process, as much as the possibility of a reward in the event he won. My work consisted in the main of talking to members of the military I knew from the old days, especially as the Squire had warned that the new president must have good relations with the army. My mission was to persuade them Our Man's policies (which to my mind were effectively non-existent) supported the interests of order and security, which was what the military was supposedly about. Seeing Our Man's main rival as being the Evangelical, I attacked the religious basis of the latter's programme. Faith was admirable, I said, but that did not justify basing society on a literal interpretation of an ancient religious text. I added that the racism of a policy of subjugating indigenous tribes was unacceptable, especially in a supposedly 'modern' country.

'But there is racism everywhere in society,' an old major insisted, as we sat in his office, overlooked by various African hunting trophies.

'But that is no reason to encourage it,' I replied. 'The tribal peoples are citizens too.'

As in this instance, much of what I said felt like a waste of time. In my naivety I'd hoped that one or two of the senior soldiers might make public statements in support of Our Man, or at least demur from the Evangelical's racism, but I got little traction. They had their own private views and, in the main, they were going to keep them private, although one old serving general, who I suspected was a supporter of the Smooth Killer, told me he was an enthusiastic supporter of the Pentecostalist 'except he does not go far enough'.

I challenged him, 'What is it you want: a police state?'

'Huh!' He spat out his coffee with such violence it almost hit me, and I was sure he must have lost one of his few remaining teeth in the process. 'Police state? Pah! What we need is an *army* state! A national emergency, that's what we need. Declare a national state of emergency - it's the only way to govern.'

While I was away most of the time, even at weekends, Sasha, when she wasn't painting, would usually visit the Englishman. She was finding him saddened by events. 'He said, "I read about the election over there and think to myself: who is there to speak for the Indians? No-one. Why doesn't anyone stand up for them? They need their own leaders, of course, but someone could help politicise them. They mustn't give up on politics. All the poor rural people need a political party they can trust." Then he looked into my eyes plaintively and said, "Otherwise, the people of the land will be silent, forgotten. Content to be forgotten perhaps, but it would be wrong."'

'There you are,' I told her. 'Politics may grab you yet.'

'Oh, I hope not! He told me how he once went to a small venue to hear an Indian politician speak. On either side of the speaker was a table, and at both tables sat a man in dark glasses, and behind them was a row of men in army uniforms. He told me, "I realised then it was hopeless." I asked him what happened to the politician. He said that he gave up politics, went to New York and became a record producer, of all things.'

Sasha also told me that in the bars and shops in the artists' colony all the talk was about the likelihood of a new conflict: 'People say the military over there wants a puppet government and a border war to keep its hold on power.'

'I must admit, I've been hearing the same sort of thing amongst my old contacts. A state of emergency is what some of them want. How does it feel being there? Wouldn't you rather be away from all of it?'

'I'm loving it,' she said, 'but I want you here with me. I feel abandoned when I'm on my own.'

89
ELECTION DAY

Election day coincided with the worst weather for several years. High winds and severe floods affected many areas. The Squire declared the vote must go ahead, no matter what. Some polling stations were damaged, several even washed away, and the turnout was unsurprisingly low. Asked on TV why the vote could not be postponed, the Squire replied, 'Many people don't want us to have the vote at all, and we must not give them their chance.'

Not all problems with the election could be explained by natural phenomena. Some polling stations, unaffected by wind or flood, simply 'disappeared' from the count. Some had more votes than 100% of those registered. Some parties complained about such anomalies, but the Squire was adamant that the result, whatever it was, would stand.

In fact, the result was pretty much as I'd expected. Serena told me that she was disappointed the Women's Rights Party candidate had not done better, even though she'd known all along she couldn't win. She came fourth.

The rich aristocrat, for all her concern for the poor, came last, which she called 'the shame of the ruling class'.

Under the constitution the Squire had maintained, an outright winner had to secure more than 50% of the total vote, and any candidate with over 25% of the vote could participate in a run-off. Accordingly, Our Man, the Evangelical and the Angel Man went through to the next round. Supporters of the Evangelical tried to persuade the Angel Man to withdraw, but he would not hear of it. He told a reporter, 'An angel told me this morning as I was getting into my car that I had to see it through. I would not dare to disobey.'

'And where was the angel at the time?'

'He was standing on the dashboard. He is one of the more vocal ones. He is not one to be trifled with, I assure you.'

A border war, having been anticipated for weeks but not forthcoming, did at last occur a week after the election. One country 'stole' ten square miles on the northern end of the border, and an hour later the other country 'stole' twelve square miles at the southern end. Large contingents of troops were deployed on both sides, although they were hampered by the adverse weather. Loud music was the main weapon employed, much to the annoyance of the local hunter gatherers who found their favourite prey had fled. Migratory tribes thus moved camp. Guerrillas came down from the mountains to attack the soldiers, and so the border war threatened to become a civil war. It was a double state of emergency that the Squire reluctantly declared, exactly what many of the Evangelical's supporters had wanted.

The main problem the war caused me was that I was cut off from Sasha because the border was closed. During this time Andrea kept asking me where I'd be and what I was doing. I gave her the usual runaround, and in the end I went to see Serena who was resting after campaigning hard for her candidate. I was delighted to discover that she had a new boyfriend and a rich playboy at that. When I saw her she looked tired but happy. She had a number of projects in mind - charitable campaigns, even TV work - and she shocked me by telling me she no longer wanted her monthly allowance: 'I don't need it and, even if I did, I think it's time I gave you your freedom (I don't mean divorce, of course), because money's not everything. I've never been happier; well, not since our early days. And I receive reports - oh yes, my spies are everywhere - that you're shacked up with a grubby little gold-digger....'

I was shocked and embarrassed. 'What gold?' I said at last in an attempt at levity. 'I assure you, it's all been dug. And not by her.'

She gave me a look of weary disapproval. 'Be that as it may,' she sighed, 'she'll fleece you for everything. There, I've warned you - ignore me if you wish. Anyway, I don't want to be a further drain on you. Be careful, though, she's not who she claims to be.'

'I think you've got the wrong person there. Your spy is not very good.'

'Oh, I don't think so. Time will tell. But at least you won't have me to worry about.'

In the end, I rang Andrea and invited her to dinner. She wasn't free, but of course the revelation of my interest played into her hands. I thought if Serena knew something about Sasha's story, then Andrea probably knew more.

90

RUN OFF

The presidential runoff vote took place two weeks after the election. A ceasefire in the border war was declared in order to assist, although some polling stations remained out of action because of the weather, and others closed early after 'extremist threats'. The guerrillas did not declare a ceasefire, since they did not recognise the election, and they burned down a few polling stations as part of their own campaign. Overall turnout was down to under a third of the electorate.

The result of the runoff vote went according to the military's plans and the Evangelical won with 51% of the vote. Depressing though this was, I gained some private consolation from the fact that Our Man was beaten into third place by Angel Man. Andrea was devastated and her misery was compounded by the fact there was widespread gossip to the effect that she was having an affair with Our Man. At least the two of them could take solace in the artificial lakes, the tennis courts and the English estate tat, assuming his American Express wife was out of the way. I felt sympathy for Andrea, however, because, for all the criticism she might deserve for her dalliance with the odious man, she had worked extremely hard for the campaign, certainly far more than he had. I also felt for her because she now had a salacious reputation, and in my heart I did not believe the rumour true, even though perversely I wanted to believe it.

Having been voted in, the Evangelical's next step, (other than to thank God and 'pledge allegiance to His Will' and make a speech on TV so interminably long and boring that on my hotel TV I switched over to a programme on cheese-making instead), was to choose his cabinet. He appeared to dither, however, and only a handful of appointments were announced. Meanwhile, the ceasefire in the border war was put under strain after a few small skirmishes. The biggest worry was that the guerrillas were becoming emboldened and causing mayhem, whilst recruiting new members in the remoter areas that always felt neglected by the politicians and bureaucrats in the capital. Some of the leading military figures made worrying statements to the press to express concern that the election had led to increased instability, and that perhaps the country had been better off with one of them in charge.

I met Andrea for lunch in my old hometown, the capital. It was a restaurant I once used to frequent regularly, but now, years after my previous visit, I couldn't help thinking it relied too heavily on its reputation, and the waiters had a breezy arrogance about them that I disliked.

'Things are not looking hopeful,' I said, referring to the service, although she thought I meant something else.

'Indeed, they're not,' she said. 'You were right, though.' I gave her an interrogatory glance. 'You were right about Sol - Our Man as you call him. He wasn't the man I thought he was. He couldn't win an election, and he couldn't run the country.'

I was dying to know, but couldn't ask, whether this was inspired by a lover's tiff or was a genuine change of heart.

'I'm just glad the Squire's still there,' I said. 'But he won't be for long.'

'No,' she said. 'The Squire wants to relinquish power as soon as possible and it is well-known he does not like living in the palace.'

'I expect the Evangelical to move in within days. Rather him than me. I wouldn't want to live in the palace after the Smooth Killer was in there. You might open a wardrobe and find the odd cadaver or two.'

'Ugh!'

'Sorry.'

I felt bad for her. Her husband was hanging on to life by his last trembling fingertip while her relationship with Our Man, however serious it might have been, appeared to be over. In addition to that, the country had elected a right-wing government, which was an anathema to everything she believed in, and the country, instead of enjoying democracy, seemed to be regretting it.

'Have you seen Serena lately?' I asked her, keen to change the subject.

'We work on some things. She wants me to join her women's rights movement, which I probably will do. She told me she was worried about you.'

'Why?'

'None of my business.'

'Won't you tell me anyway?'

'I don't like to spread gossip. Especially since I'm in my own share of it myself.'

'OK.' I was tempted not to pursue it. If there was something bad about Sasha, I'd be the last to know. So be it. Right now, she was the the least of my worries.

Andrea, however, had a different priority. 'How much do you know about this Sasha?' she said.

'She had a terrible thing happen in her teenage years. She became an artist to help her get through the trauma.'

'Is that all you know?'

I was annoyed now. 'What is this? First Serena, now you. What are you getting at?'

'If you want to return to public life, you will need to be rid of her.'

'Jealousy,' I said. She shook her head and, clearly offended, promptly changed the subject to the election.

When I kissed Andrea goodbye, I wished the best for her husband. He was a kindly man. I was only glad he was too far gone to know about the gossip concerning his wife. The irony that it could have been me she was having an affair with did not escape me.

As I walked across Congress Square I felt the weight of the country's troubles descend upon me. Why couldn't I be carefree like that couple of young lovers over there? Instead, I was ill at ease, the same as I'd felt in the last few months of exile. 'Here we go again,' I said to myself as I made my way warily to an illicit back street gun dealer's shop.

91
VOLUNTEERS

When I told Sasha over the phone that I'd bought a gun, she sounded downcast: 'Oh, I thought you were through with all that.'

'I know what you mean, but the city does not feel safe. I still feel like a marked man, even though I should be happy, relaxed.'

'It seems to me like it's any excuse and you get one, the answer to every question. I should have realised that life with you would be all about guns. Guns, guns and more guns. People die and the guns go on. I dream of a time when the guns die out and the people go on.'

'Dream on.'

She told me she missed me. I couldn't bring myself to reciprocate. Perhaps it was what Serena and Andrea had suggested about her but not said outright, perhaps it was the frenetic situation in the capital, but I did not miss her and her loveless attention.

'When are you coming back?' she asked.

'I don't know. I have to stay here until things are resolved.'

'What things? I don't like it when you're not here. I don't feel safe. And don't tell me to get a gun.'

'Ask the Englishman. He'll find you a gun if you need one. I'll be back in a day or two anyway.'

'You just said...'

'I know but if you're hurting...'

'OK.'

I stayed in the capital. There pressure was growing on the Evangelical to appoint a defence minister without delay. It was generally agreed, which is to say, agreed in the media, that a hardliner was needed, a man to 'bring violence to the violent and retribution to the rest'.

Serena told me over the phone, 'He could appoint you. You wouldn't stand any nonsense.'

'I'm no hardliner,' I said. 'I could never be the person to follow through on the Evangelical's policy on the Indians, for example. I'm not even neutral: I support them. It would never work.'

'You're a bit of a hypocrite there, though. You liked your little border wars, you told me once, and yet the Indians are the ones who suffer the most. Has that never occurred to you? Oh, I do wish he would make a decision! This man was voted in, he's appointed half a cabinet, all the easier ones, and the most important decision he can't make. What's up with him? Is his pipeline to God bricked up? He'd better hurry up or there'll be a coup to add to the border war and the war with the guerrillas we've already got bubbling away. It would only take the army to spring the Smooth Killer from gaol.'

She was in a prophetic mood. Her Tarot reader had told her a man on a horse would be unseated and therefore it was settled that the leader would fall. It was only a matter of time: this could be today, next week, even next year. Whenever it might be, the Tarot reader's prediction was certain to be proven correct.

As it transpired, events moved very quickly. The Squire quit, the Evangelical was formally sworn in, and he moved into the presidential palace. Even then, he still made no decision regarding the new defence minister. When guerrillas shot a well-respected army major, disenchanted officers stormed the gaol holding the Smooth Killer. I immediately knew that I was in great danger. I turned on the news on my hotel TV and there he was, my nemesis, making a speech, officially to his supporters, but in reality to the whole nation: 'We need strength at the top. The country is under threat. Enemies in our midst.' Etcetera. I went to bed and when I woke up I learned that the Smooth Killer had been offered the defence minister's job.

To any reasonable person this would be enough, but not him. It merely fuelled his ambition. Instead of accepting the job he again appeared on TV, this time declaring he was the strong leader the country needed. I believed, however, from the admittedly dwindling contacts I had in the military, that only a minority of officers would support him in this. The circus show continued. With Sasha constantly sending texts pleading with me to return home, I watched on TV another speech, this time by the Evangelical. Appealing directly to the people, he called for 'Volunteers for Democracy'. I had only a vague idea what this meant, but I decided I would go and see him.

Getting past the staff at the presidential palace was uncomfortably easy. I kidded myself it was my name that opened every door to him. Of course it reminded me of my many previous visits - the ornate Italianate style of the interior, the atrium, the marble floors, the murals depicting events from the nation's history, the portraits of previous presidents, including my grandfather - I bowed before the old man and then looked hard into his grey eyes, as if for inspiration.

When I encountered the Evangelical, he was moving boxes around in his study. He was frailer than I'd expected. He had a TV on, with the news channel giving updates, which he'd been half-watching forlornly. Fortunately, he knew who I was, although disconcertingly he asked me, 'Do you want the job, is that it? You want to be defence minister, is that why you've come?' He seemed overawed, as though he hadn't expected to win the election, as though he wasn't sure, deep within himself, whether it really had been God guiding him - what if it had been a demon instead? Or what if he was merely losing his faith?

'I don't know who I can trust,' he said. 'Everyone wants power, don't they?'

'Not everyone,' I replied. 'Some of us just want our place in the world. The right place.' For reasons I hadn't even thought of, I offered to be part of his presidential guard. 'OK, I'm not as quick as I once was, but I can still fire a gun. You asked for Volunteers for Democracy. Well, here I am volunteering.'

'But can I trust you?' he said. 'I believe I can, but I have to wait for God to guide me.' He seemed lost, isolated. I looked into his eyes but could see nothing behind them. Here he was in the position of supreme power and he was impotent.

I said, 'I am personally and indefatigably opposed to the man who now threatens you. The one everyone calls the Smooth Killer.'

He appeared not to know this name: 'You call him the Smooth Killer? That's interesting.' He laughed gently to himself. It impressed me how this Indian-hating, God-fearing fundamentalist was, underneath the paraphernalia of faith and worship, a vulnerable creature. I couldn't understand why I was even interested in helping him. Perhaps, however, if I were made defence minister, I could divert some of his more offensive policies. Under the sheen of fire and brimstone, he was malleable, suggestible.

At the end of our conversation, he thanked me for my offer to join the presidential guard, but said he had enough men already and beyond that

'God will provide'.

'Besides,' he said, 'You should be behind a desk, not standing, guarding the palace. I mean that not as a slight on the skills I'm sure you have. Neither of us are young men.'

Disappointed, I returned to my hotel. Nothing had been achieved and I felt frustrated.

92
DEMONSTRATION

The Volunteers-for-Democracy campaign was essentially an attempt to establish a mass movement of ordinary people to prevent a return to dictatorship. I did not hold great hopes for its success, but this kind of thing had sometimes worked in the past. The two main losing presidential candidates called upon the people to demonstrate 'in support of the president'.

'Not because you agree with his policies,' said Our Man on TV, 'but because you believe in what he represents: the democratic process'. He gave a fine speech and I told Andrea so over the phone.

'I know,' she said predictably, 'You realise that I wrote it.'

I did not believe that fine words and demonstrations were enough to prevent a coup, so I asked a long-established, high-ranking friend in the army to keep me informed. On the morning after Our Man's speech, I received a call at six a.m. on my hotel phone. It was not from my informant but the person he'd told me would call on his behalf. The voice said that a small commando unit would imminently make a raid at the back of the presidential palace, intent on arresting the new president, but it would be stopped.

Filled with excitement for I knew not what, I took my pistol, ran downstairs, out of the hotel and towards Congress Square. A demonstration was planned for that day and people were already arriving. Food vendors were opening up their stalls for the day, a sign I always found reassuring. There was no obvious sign that anything dramatic had happened yet or was imminent.

Suddenly I heard gunfire from the direction of the palace. The demonstrators panicked. I immediately ran round to the back of the palace. I watched out of sight and from a safe distance. I could make out a group of uniformed men strong-arming an individual, presumably the new president, away from the gates. They bundled him into a car. The arrest had been successful, but then soldiers emerged from the shadows and prevented the car from moving off. The coup had been averted. All was well. Exactly as I'd been informed, the plotters had been thwarted.

I retraced my steps and lingered a moment or two, watching the front of the palace. I was about to leave when an armoured car arrived and drove in through the gates. Intrigued, I ran to a raised area at the side and stared through the railings. I felt uneasy and took out my pistol. Emerging stiffly from the car was the man of my fears, the Smooth Killer. I would recognise him anywhere - even, no, *especially* in full army uniform. He smiled confidently - gaol had made him stronger, fitter, indestructible. For a single moment he was stood facing towards me in all his self-regard and glittering medals, and out of instinct I fired. As though in a film, I saw him begin to collapse to the ground. His frightened guards began shooting in my direction, but I was gone like a ghost. I ran for my life down an alleyway. The exhilaration at what I'd done gave me the strength and the pace of a young man. Once I was sure I was out of immediate danger, I began to slow down.

93
STREET

I made my way through the back streets towards the hotel. The city was becoming vibrant. The morning markets were getting busier. The criminals were also up. I had to go through an alley notorious for pickpockets, but there was no-one around and besides, at that moment I felt I could take on anything. Landing a hit with a bullet always had that effect. It was euphoric but dangerous because it could make you careless. Suddenly, round a corner came a young man, probably late twenties, in a suit. He didn't look like a pickpocket, more like the next victim of one. Then I saw four kids run out. Street kids, the bane of the average city-dweller's life - feral, damaged kids who'd known no love. A menace. In no time they were on the man. They pulled at his clothes. They were hyenas upon their prey. They were quick workers, and their victim was struggling to fight them off, desperately trying to escape. If Zico were with me he'd tell me to get out of there fast, but he only cared for my welfare, not anyone else's. I couldn't leave a man to suffer at the hands of these urchins who lived underground in squalor. Any sympathy you felt for them, and I did feel it when I was sitting in my armchair at home, had to be put aside if you encountered a group of them on your own.

I rushed over to them. I wasn't thinking. I must have imagined my appearance on the scene would panic them, or at least disturb them sufficiently to enable the young man to escape. Not one of them so much as flinched. Indeed, the four were now joined by another two. But the young man did break free. I saw him run past me, his coat slashed by the large knife that one of them carried. They ran after him but then switched their attentions to me. I immediately realised the young man had simply run for it, leaving me alone with them. I could almost hear Zico's words of concern for me in my ears. I could not outrun them. I pulled out my gun. Still they were undaunted and they ran at me. I fired the gun in the air, all the time shouting at them to go away. They did back off for a moment, but then they went for the gun. I was fighting them off with my other arm. They stank. They were like rats in human form. I felt the knife slash my jacket and pierce my skin. An image of Sasha flashed through my mind - who would look after her if I died at that moment? With no other thought, I shot the kid attacking me with the knife. He slumped. I had shot him in the head. The others drew back. I ran off, leaving the limp body where it lay. I heard a policeman shouting, attracted by the sound of gunfire. At that moment, I heard sirens and guessed they were heading for the palace.

I ran in the direction of the hotel. Blood was running down my arm and dripping from my hand. I stopped for a moment and wrapped my scarf around my wrist. I must not leave a trail. By the time I reached the lobby of the hotel, I felt ready for a heart attack. I took my time and made my way to the lift. I wanted to be alone but a well-to-do-looking woman with her two little kids joined me. I was still breathing hard, but I tried to slow it. We reached the third level, and, as I turned to exit, I noticed the little boy staring at the floor. I glanced down. There was a fresh bloodstain. I put my foot there, pretending to be unaware of it.

At that moment I hated all kids. I read a story once about a man who would throw toys out on to a highway so a street kid would run out into the path of a truck to collect it, and at the time it appalled me. It still did, but back in my room, as I inspected the long cut in my arm and gradually stopped the flow of blood, I could understand why such kids were so feared and hated.

94
EXIT

I washed the wound and, with my arm no longer bleeding, changed into a different shirt and put the torn and bloodied one inside a plastic bag in my suitcase, along with the torn jacket. As always, the problem was what to do with the gun. My concern was that I might get stopped by police once I'd stepped outside the hotel, or be held at the airport, or I might encounter street kids, either the same ones or different, and have to fight them off whilst still holding my suitcase. In the end, I put the gun in a drawer in the bedside table, placing it behind the Bible there. It was a dilemma, but I thought that whatever I did I might regret it, so I did not change my mind.

I checked out. I'd originally planned on a longer stay, and the person at the desk asked me if everything had been in order, and I said, yes, explaining that I needed to get back for business reasons.

I took a cab to the airport. As we drove through town, I noticed there were a lot of soldiers on the streets, and the city felt a little quieter than usual - quiet but tense The market was as busy as ever though. After a minute or two, I tried not to look out of the window because I did not want to see street kids. It would be very much my luck that we'd be stopped at a traffic light, and one of those that had attacked me would be there, and they'd shout in recognition and call me murderer, and only God knew what would happen next. I found if I did not look, I did not have the worry over whether they could see me or not, or whether they were even there. Instead, I concentrated on the driver who, I noticed, had put up little plastic skulls and skeletons above the dashboard, presumably as some kind of good luck charm. I had shut off my phone and avoided the news. The driver had the radio on but at such low volume that I could barely hear it. Instead, he gave me his own running commentary: 'This country is going to the dogs, isn't it? Never known it so bad. Even the election was a farce. We ended up with three candidates: a man who believes in angels, a religious fundamentalist, and a man so slippery, if you put him in gaol he'd slide through the bars.'

'Well put,' I said, delighted to be able to laugh again, especially at the expense of Our Man.

'Now I hear, the one who made it worse, the dictator - we always called him the Smooth Killer - is out of gaol and has taken over. I can understand why, because the one who won the election doesn't impress me much, not that any of them do. They say he...'

'The dictator?' I could not bring myself to say even his nickname.

'Yes. They say he's launched another coup.' I said nothing, happy as anyone bearing secret knowledge. 'Well he didn't improve things last time,' he said.

'It must be time for the weather report,' I said hopefully, tired of hearing about my nemesis.

He ignored me. 'It proves we can't even keep anyone in gaol.' He hesitated for a moment, wisely mulling over the possibility that I might be a spy on behalf of the Smooth Killer. It was his own fault: I hadn't asked for his opinions. But he was irrepressible: 'Now, crime... I've never known anything like it. I can't stop anywhere for more than a second in case some kid tries to wrench off a piece of the car. Keep the window up, Sir, we're approaching the lights. We don't want some ruffian sticking their hand in. It happened last week. Some poor woman had her fancy necklace stolen. How he did it, God knows. Took it right off her neck. Mind you, the police are no better. The latest is, they get you to pull over on some pretext...'

'They've always done that.'

'No, this is different. A new scam. They pull you over, find nothing, then charge you an administration fee for their trouble. They don't even have to dream anything up. So what do you do, Sir? Are you here on business? You look familiar, like a face I vaguely recognise from way back.'

'Just visiting,' I replied perfunctorily.

Not wishing to deprive him of conversation, and more particularly to distract his mind from trying to trace me from amongst his memory's pantheon of 'failed politicians', I added, 'I'm an art dealer.'

He then treated me to his opinion on Picasso whose works, to my surprise, he liked: 'I say, if you want an exact replica, take a photograph. Although that's not true, is it? A photograph is always different, always selective. They say a picture tells a thousand stories, but the picture's often a lie. I'd rather have the thousand stories and make up my own mind. No, I like an artist who explores the human mind. That Freud had some good ideas...' And on and on he went, with me contributing the odd word, praying there wouldn't be some police message come up on the radio about someone they were looking for, that might throw him off his happy trail of opinions about psychology, into philosophy, then art again and back to psychology, by which time we'd arrived at the terminal and he said happily, 'I think we've covered a lot of ground between us. Thanks for the interesting chat.'

95
FAILURE

At the airport I bought a ticket for the first plane across the border. Some international flights, especially transcontinental ones, had been cancelled, the airlines having pulled out, and the general mood amongst the passengers was tense and, in some cases, furious. There was a heavy presence of soldiers and military police, which had the effect of adding to the anxiety in the crowd, rather than calming it. I checked in the suitcase; I showed my fake passport. There were extra security checks. The man in front of me was detained. I realised now the stupidity of putting the bloodied shirt in my case - what if they wanted it opened at the other end? I could sense myself sweating already. I had my story lined up: that I was hopping across the border to visit a sick uncle, a story I hopefully wouldn't need as it sounded pathetically weak. I was too stressed to think up anything better. The man in front was so vociferous in his protests prior to being led away, that the security staff were visibly annoyed. In the process of calming himself down, the official who would have spoken to me merely waved me through.

In the departure lounge I watched the TV News. I could hardly believe my eyes. On the screen was a hospital bed with people standing round the patient. Could it be the last rites? No, it was the Smooth Killer being sworn in as president. I was devastated although I was not alone, as was evident from the faces of other passengers. Some even groaned in disbelief.

He'd been hit in the shoulder and was shortly to be operated on. The man who'd shot him was described as a terrorist. It could not have worked out better for the despot. He was the supreme patriot. Shot by an 'enemy of the state', he was triumphant. How much better than an old soldier was an *injured* old soldier who'd carried on, made stronger by what had befallen him? Weak democracy defeated; terrorism defeated. He spoke briefly from his bed, including a defiant message to the demonstrators: 'Get back to your luxury mansions and your cushy rich lives and let the armed forces protect you as they always have.' The one reliable thing in this country, he said, was the community of selfless men and women in the armed services. He called for 'unity amongst all right-thinking people'.

All I could surmise was that the arrest of the car involved in the kidnapping of the Evangelical had been a sham. This meant I'd been lied to by a trusted confidant. Or, as was more likely, he had been lied to himself. Whatever the situation, my nemesis had prevailed. And not just prevailed, but won the whole game of cards from being in a position of having no hand to play. Even a bullet hadn't stopped him. My bullet. Failure. Whoever said Heaven was a fleeting and fraudulent place was right. Certainly the heavenly moment of glory was.

I listened to what was being said about the 'terrorist'. The police had spoken to some of the demonstrators and they'd given a description of a possible suspect. *They'd* given a description!? The demonstrators? So much for standing up for democracy - standing up for whoever's taken charge, more like. I listened to the description and looked at the made-up picture of the 'terrorist' on TV. It wasn't me at all. Either deliberately or unintentionally, they'd given a faulty description. All was not lost.

I had been dreading arrival at the other end of my plane journey, fearing they would want to inspect my case. I was fortunate, however, because the customs officers' time was taken up with a group suspected of carrying drugs. It was not until I was in the cab from the airport that I checked my phone texts for the first time in the day. It was all messages from Sasha: Where was I? When would I be home? Why hadn't I phoned?

When I arrived home, she was cold towards me - sullen and unwelcoming: 'Why didn't you phone me? I felt abandoned. Is this what it's going to be like from now on?'

'I couldn't call you.'

'I was texting you like mad, pleading with you to contact me. I don't expect you to love me - you couldn't anyway - but you could at least pretend that you care.'

I was exhausted and didn't want to argue, so I changed the subject to her strange appearance. 'What have you done to yourself?' I said. She was dressed in denim shorts and a torn T-shirt and had tattoos on her arms and legs and on her neck and upper chest. She looked outlandish.

She said defensively, 'There is a great tattooist here. I have been to see her every day since you've been away. Spending all your money.' She sniggered. 'I've got roses, bats, a scorpion, a bird of paradise, a sun god, shells. By the way, I saw the news. I never used to watch it before I met you. The man who fired the shot, was that you?'

'If it was, I was just doing my bit for democracy, ma'am,' and I raised an imaginary hat.

Seeing my arm wound, she said, 'Who did this to you? Was it security staff or something?'

'A kid brandishing a knife. A street kid.'

'My poor soldier! Tell me what happened. Did you fight him off?'

'I don't want to talk about it.'

'You must tell me. Please.'

'There were six of them in the end.' I recounted the whole incident.

'You killed a child - how terrible is that!?'

'You can imagine how I feel about it.'

'If you hadn't still got your gun with you, you wouldn't have intervened. The poor man would have been robbed, but the kid wouldn't have died, wretched though his life might have been.'

'Did you ever have an encounter with them? Did you ever have them threaten you with a broken bottle in your face?'

'No.'

'And do you know what the police do with them? They shoot them. That policeman was likely a part-time death squad member. He'll claim fifty dollars for that kid's corpse.'

'And for all your politics, I bet it's got worse. But you do care, don't you?'

'Sitting here in this safe little lounge, yes I do, But when you've got six of them on you, at least one with a large knife, you don't have the luxury of your high opinions.'

She put her tongue along the wound.

'What are you doing?'

'I want to taste your blood. And I want to taste your sweat before I clean you up. I still care for you, even though you're a bad man. I always wanted a man with a wound that I could care for.'

96

A DEMAND

She cooked us a quick meal. I noticed she was becoming angry - she threw the pans around noisily - but I sensed it was herself she was angry with. She was hiding something from me.

During the meal we were silent until she suddenly pushed her plate aside, took a gulp of wine and demanded, 'You have to take me over the border. I can't live here anymore. I don't feel safe.'

'Why? I'm here now. What's the matter with you?'

She banged her fist on the table. 'But it's when you're not here! I feel abandoned to all these horrible men. Men want to proposition me all the time. I can't walk to the shops without some guy wanting to grab me. Either that or they simply stare. They can tell I'm on my own. I can't sleep for fear someone's going to come in and attack me.'

'I'm sorry, it never occurred to me.'

'No, it wouldn't because you're a man and because you're full of yourself and your nonsense. If you want us to live here, you can't leave me on my own like this. I thought this place would be magical, and it is on the surface, but underneath it's like everywhere else, which for a woman on her own is unbearable.'

I was perplexed: 'Surely, you realise I can't go across the border. I'm a wanted man. If I get recognised, I'm going to end up in gaol. I might as well kill myself.'

'Don't be so melodramatic.' She poured herself another glass.

I stood up and went over to the window. Nothing outside took my attention. I turned to face her. 'No, seriously, I can't do it. Why do you think I just left there?'

'To see me, was what I was hoping. Obviously not. But can't you just do it for me? I have to get away from here.'

I approached the table and looked closely into her eyes. She was scared almost out of her wits. Her hands were trembling. I put my arm around her but she shook off my embrace.

'Why are you acting like this? Why are you so anxious? It doesn't make any sense. I'm here, and I'll protect you. Let's see how things go for a while. We don't know what's going to happen over there, so it's better that we stay here for a bit.'

She was adamant. 'No. I have to go. *We* have to go.'

'Tell me what happened,' I said. 'You're obviously not telling me something.' I was becoming irritated with her so tried a different tack: 'Look, I tell you what: I'll put you on a plane and you can go back to the cottage.'

She stamped her foot. 'No. You have to come with me.'

'Whatever's the matter with you? I intend staying here for a little while, so I'll take you to the border and give you some money and you can stay over there until you want to come back.'

It was then that she stood up, walked over to the cabinet where her bag was and pulled out a pistol. 'Stop arguing,' she said. 'I will use it if I have to.'

'You're kidding!'

She pointed it at my head. 'Take me across the border. I know you can easily overpower me. I know you can trick me. You're as cunning as a rattlesnake. I don't trust you, but please do it for me. If you care - if you ever cared for me the tiniest bit, you'll do it.' She was distraught and the gun wavered in her grasp.

'Then put down the gun.'

'No. Right now it feels like the only friend I've got. If you weren't so stupid you would accept the situation. If you cared more about me than your stupid politics and your precious Andrea you wouldn't argue with me.'

I shook my head, laughing sadly in disbelief as I conceded defeat.

97

CROSSING

She was right: I could easily trick her out of it. I could distract her in order to wrest the gun off her. But if I did that I might fail and she could open fire. I wanted to slam her against the wall and yet, at the same time, I didn't want to hurt her. Rather than take the risk I decided to play the obedient dog. I loaded as much of our stuff as possible into the car, which was suitcases of clothes, the paintings and not much else. Sorting out what was left would await another day, a less frenetic day. I knew I could stop the nonsense at any moment, but, assuming I was able to disarm her, I would be none the wiser as to what this was about. I had my dark theories, but I did not wish to think them through, let alone articulate them.

'Hurry up or I'll shoot,' she said contemptuously. 'Besides, I've always wanted to make a soldier suffer.'

'Go ahead then,' I said, irritated. 'Right between the eyes. You know you won't, because you can't.' After this, I said nothing. I had teased Fate by telling her she couldn't do it, but it was better to play along with this little drama, whatever it was. She wanted to be in control, so I would let her - for a while.

Once the car was loaded, I got into the driver's seat. She sat directly behind me and stuck the gun barrel hard into my neck. I protested but she ignored me, and I accepted that this was how we would pass the few miles to the border crossing. I tried to drive slowly in case we hit any bumps, but when I did decelerate I felt the gun pressed even harder. As we approached the border, she hid it. I showed our passports, mine being the fake one. Once we were through, she told me to drive another thirty miles and find a motel that had a bar and restaurant nearby. I felt the gun on my neck again, but after a few miles she removed it. She'd achieved what she wanted. I'd been her willing slave, at least in her eyes, although like a slave I was seething inside.

98

CONFESSION

We pulled in at a motel and I paid for a room for the night. She asked if she could keep the car and I agreed. I was heading back to exile so didn't need it. We therefore removed only my things and a few of her clothes.

We found a bar nearby. It was a sleazy, downbeat place with guys in biker jackets and truck drivers playing pool and leering at the women, no doubt bemused by the colourful creature in denim shorts at my side. The atmosphere between her and me was tense and nervous. When we were seated at a table, I said, 'What's all this about, Sasha? What have you done? Why did you treat me like a dog?'

'I'll explain and I hope that you will understand that I meant well.' She took a swig of beer but remained nervous. 'When you were away, I used to spend a lot of time going to see the Englishman. He was someone I could relate to in some strange way, relate to his ideas. But not only that, he was like a friend. His place is quite isolated, as you know. The path to it is quite secluded here and there. I didn't feel safe, so I asked him if I could borrow a gun.'

'But you've never fired a gun. You were going to have lessons but...'

'I started having target practice with him up there. He gave me a pistol. The gun gave me confidence. I began to realise that a gun can be a great equaliser. A woman only needs the strength to pull the trigger and to not be sent flying by the recoil. And I'd been starting to see suspicious people along the path, usually young men just hanging around. I became scared. I kept seeing the same men. Sinister-looking men. Then one day one of them started pestering me. He started saying abusive things, horrible things that he'd like to do to me. Of course, I'd heard them all before. All women have. Then he grabbed me and threw me to the ground, he tried to pull my dress down, then he jumped on me and started ripping at my clothes. I was so determined that I managed to break free...'

'How did you do that?'

'I got him with a straight two-finger poke in the eye. He screamed, raised his hand to his face, and that enabled me to get clear. I took out the gun from my bag. As he tried to grab me again, I shot him. I shot the piece of trash three times. And, yes, I killed him.'

I had my head in my hands. 'And so what did you do with the body? Or was it too heavy to move?'

'I got my foot under it and was able, with some difficulty, to pitch it down the slope into a stream. Then I walked away as though nothing had happened. You think I'm terrible, don't you?'

'No. But were there any witnesses? Didn't anyone hear the shots?'

'I don't know. But I bet on the day of my trial there'd be witnesses - suddenly out of nowhere there they would be. And the jury would be full of them. Witnesses to the shooting but not to the attempted rape. I knew he was dangerous before it even happened. I can usually tell a potential rapist. There were lots of them there. What was I to do: stay indoors all the time? I told you I would be trouble with a gun. I couldn't tell you what I'd done before because I didn't want you to become an accomplice. I wanted you to be able to say that I held a gun to your head, which I would tell the court. I don't want you caught up in it.'

'I can understand that, but we could have just pretended. It's not like it would make a lot of difference to a court, frightening me like that.'

'Except I didn't think for one minute you were frightened, although I'd like to think you were. But, anyway, apart from wanting to protect you, I don't give a damn about what happened. For once, I wasn't going to be a victim... be *the* victim. I did it and I don't care. Besides, there's no extradition treaty here. They wouldn't send me back.'

'Is that everything you wanted to tell me? Or is there more?'

She took another swig. 'You must have heard rumours that I'm no good, that I'm not what you think I am, not what I told you, haven't you?'

'Maybe. Hints, suggestions.'

'OK, I'll tell you straight. I wasn't always an artist. Maybe I never was.'

'Nonsense. Stop saying that.'

'Anyway, after the attack on my village my life just fell apart.'

'You mean, when you were fourteen?'

'Yes. I managed to get to a town in the district where my aunt lived. She helped me, she nursed me, got me medical help. She made a new life for me.'

'What happened to your parents?'

'I never saw them again. My father died in prison, my mother never recovered and ended up in an institution. She later escaped and disappeared. I like to think she's out there somewhere, maybe living with an Indian tribe on the border, or in some commune. My aunt did her best, but I was a mess. I got mixed up with some bad people. Then I got rescued by a sugar daddy, or so I thought, until he got bored with me and pimped me out to his friends. I got out of that situation, lived on the street. Then one day I wandered into a modern art gallery and I thought: I can do this. So I read about it, looked at lots of pictures, read about the lives of some of the artists and thought: that could be me. So I learned how to paint a little and conned my way into teaching it. Was that so wrong? I'm not a wicked person.'

'I don't care what you say, because to me you are an artist. You're not a con. You were a good teacher. You helped everyone in class. And people buy your art.'

'But why do you think I was there in the first place, abroad amongst the exiles? Because I was sent there from here. I'd been working as an escort for a while, which I hated. I was arrested and thrown into gaol. Then I was sent abroad to spy on exiles.'

'So you worked for the Rats?'

'Yes.' She was staring into my eyes as though pleading for forgiveness. I looked away. 'So I would cozy up to wealthy exiles, go to their houses and then pass on what I learned to my minder. If the exile was working against the state back home, they would deal with him. The trouble was, worthless as I maybe am, I couldn't do it. I hated it. Then my minder beat me up because I wasn't providing anything useful to them, and I told him I wouldn't do it anymore. So he got mad, said he was going to rape me, and I smashed him over the head with a stone statuette of Venus he had, and I fled. Then I quickly gathered together my stuff from my flat and left. So then I moved to the other side of the country. I don't know what happened to him. Maybe I killed him, I don't know. But I lived in fear after that, fear that he'd turn up, or someone who'd been sent to avenge him would. So when you appeared in class, I thought to myself: maybe he can help me, maybe he'll protect me. And I did feel safe with you. And when that guy on the motorbike chased us, I thought it might be me they were after. So I felt glad to be alive. And then we moved to the artists' colony and I thought: that's it, I'm even safer now. But when you were away, it felt like all the danger, all the fear had come back.'

'And what was it all about when we went on that picnic, and you got drunk and flirted with me outrageously, and when I responded in my clumsy way - in my defence the drink went straight to my head - you challenged me to try to rape you?'

'I was drunk. But at that moment it felt like a test. If you'd tried to rape me I would have fought you off, and if I could I would have killed you, To kill a soldier for what a soldier did to me once would have been sublime. But I had chosen wisely. And once you let me in to explain myself, I knew you were hooked.'

'So what's with all the tattoos?'

'Like my beloved Frida with her clothes...'

'Let me guess: Frida Kahlo?'

'Yes... with my tattoos I prepare myself for death.'

'Please stop saying things like that. And before that distant day, how will you live?'

'Work in bars. Sell my pictures if I can. Sell my body if I have to.'

'Don't be ridiculous, that's not for you. Why does it have to be you against the world? I hate to tell you, as if you didn't know, but it's a mismatch. You won't survive like that.'

'I don't care. I feel worthless. I feel like I'm trash. I put on a brave face, but in my heart I feel that I deserve to be treated like it.'

'The way I see it, we could live in the cottage in exile like we used to. We can both be happy. It'd be like it was before.'

'No it wouldn't. That's over. It was based on an illusion anyway: the illusion that we were both artists.'

Later, she held my hand and said to me, 'Tonight for the first and last time I will give myself to you - utterly. It'll be something to remember. Something for me to remember anyway. I know it's Andrea you want and not me. That doesn't matter. You could never break her like you can break me.'

'I don't want Andrea.' It was a lie but my desire for Andrea seemed a mere fantasy when confronted by the reality that was Sasha. 'I thought you found making love painful.'

'I don't want to make love. I want you to use me like all other men have done. There's never been any love in it for me. The only person who opened me up with tenderness, who showed me love, was my therapist - and I'm not even gay. Sex hurts me, but don't try to be gentle because it won't work.

It's because you're a man.'

'I can learn, can't I? I'm not stupid. I'm not some brute.'

She stifled a laugh, 'No, you're not stupid. There just isn't time for you to understand me in that way.'

After a few drinks we went to our room and straight to bed. I was tired and wanted to sleep, but she wasn't going to allow it: 'Come on, old man. You can sleep tomorrow. I want you to ache for me. I want you to be wiped out. I want to make you feel like there's no-one else for you in the world but me. And I won't be there, but you'll have your memory, more beautiful than reality could be, a beautiful never-ending longing. I may be terrible inside, but I can still make something beautiful.'

She lay naked on the sheet, propped herself up haughtily on her elbows, and taunted me as I gazed on her beauty and her tattoos. 'I want you to use me, soldier. Prove that you can.' I was gentle with her, but she merely laughed, indifferent as a trashy whore. I tried to kiss her, but she resisted. 'Don't waste time trying to please me. I'm not worth it, and you can't. Just use me for your pleasure like everyone else has. Pretend I'm your precious Andrea, except I mean nothing to you.' She was a lazy lover, but for all her cold-heartedness she could not resist now and then a sigh, even a shudder of pleasure. At one point I merely stared at her, with her port-wine stain, her gently desperate eyes, and her strange, beautiful tattoos. I wanted to tell her I loved her but knew it would be wasted words.

'Stop it,' she said.

'What's the matter?'

'Stop thinking. Stop staring at me. There's nothing there behind my eyes. I'm nothing. You can think afterwards all you want. For now, use me. You want to. Do it.'

Every time I fell asleep, she would wake me again. 'Come on, soldier. Wake up. Live, can't you?' and she would begin kissing me and then admonish me, 'Hurt me. Make me suffer. I'm the worthless thing you want to destroy. I'm every piece of trash you ever wanted to exploit and then be done with.'

She woke me once too often. Seeing her looking down at me demanding more attention, I was suddenly and inexplicably enraged and pitched her off the bed onto the hard floor. She hit her head and groaned. I stumbled out of bed and when she tried to get up I dragged her back down. I held her face hard against the thin, filthy carpet. 'You want to be hurt, I'll hurt you.' She tried to fight me off but I easily overpowered her. She pleaded with me to be gentle but I took her like a drunken, angry cuckold with his cheating wife. Then I thought of how she'd forced me to cross the border with a gun to my neck, and I thought of her working for the Rats who'd almost killed me, and I bit her neck hard, causing her to squeal in pain. I returned to bed and left her on the floor.

She was crying. 'You really hurt me, you bastard! You didn't have to be so rough. You might as well have killed me. Did you even understand what you were doing to me?'

I was angry again: 'Listen, bitch, if you keep telling me to hurt you, I'll resist and resist but will eventually hurt you. And I'll hurt you bad, even if I don't mean to. You got me mad. You got what you deserved. You worked for the Rats once. You're rotten. You can't help it, but you are. You're messed up. You've treated me like dirt. That was your mistake. Now shut up and go to sleep where you belong - in the dirt!'

She lay there whimpering as I quickly fell into a drowse.

And, next morning, as I rubbed my sore head I wondered what had happened. If love was a battlefield, both sides had won and lost, both sides had been destroyed.

99
LEAVING

I left first thing in the morning. Sasha was asleep on the bed. No point in sham ceremony, I felt. I put two hundred dollars for her on the bedside table, then hesitated. I heard her stirring. I heard her say, 'I don't want your money, soldier.' I checked my wallet and put down another hundred. Still more than plenty left for a cab. I took one last glance at her. It reminded me of every last glance at someone I'd ever loved.

The airport was buzzing and there was a queue at the ticket counter. I figured a lot of people must be heading out to avoid the return of dictatorship and all the paraphernalia of oppression that went with it. Who could blame them? I assumed the volunteers for democracy must have given up already, but that was unfair of me. There was nothing on the news about the Smooth Killer in hospital. I wondered if they had operated on him yet.

I was beset by guilt. I rang Sasha. I wanted to try again with her. She was not happy to hear from me, especially as I'd woken her up. 'I just wanted to ask you to rethink,' I said.

'What?'

'I don't want to learn in a year or two that you're living on the street - hooked on heroin, working for a pimp who's your dealer and keeps you working to pay for it.'

'Don't worry. You won't know. I'll just disappear like my mother.'

'A pimp will drag you into his car, stick a needle in your arm, and you're his property from that moment on.'

'Go get your flight, old man. I hope you feel proud of what you did to me. I can look after myself, so stop worrying about it. You've hurt me enough. I'm not your responsibility. I didn't want your money and I don't want your remorse, not that you express any. And when I'm some general's trophy mistress and you're desperate, lonely and ruined in your own filth, I'll send you your money back with my photograph. I look forward to that day.'

'You're deluded,' was all I could utter, as much to myself as in response to her.

100
THE INTERVENTION

When I arrived back to exile and the cottage, it was dark. The place seemed sorry for itself to the point of reproachfulness. It felt cold and damp. I made a fire in the grate. I wandered around the place, looking for signs of my former life there with Sasha. I already felt sentimental about that time. I was beginning to feel the unwanted ache, the longing she'd promised.

I was so tired I went to bed early and slept late. Next morning, I reacquainted myself with the town and called into the coffee shop where I would often meet her. I succumbed to the temptation of a newspaper. The main story was a local one about the discovery of a drug dealer's corpse in a construction site. My eye was next caught by a small picture of the Smooth Killer. I was speculating that he'd chosen his cabinet and I was wondering who was in it. All military men or the odd civilian? So many questions. What had happened to the Evangelical? Was he in prison? If so, was it a physical one or a prison of his own mind? Would the exiles who'd returned still be safe? What would the Squire do? What would the Smooth Killer do about *him*? Had there been any leads on the 'assassination attempt'? My mind was in a frenzy, but I managed to put off reading the paper until I arrived home.

I sat down in my lounge with a coffee and perused the newspaper. On closer inspection, the picture of my nemesis looked like a new one, perhaps taken at the hospital. He was still not back at the palace, unless this 'news' was out-of-date. I read the article and learned, to my astonishment, that he was dead. Was it possible my bullet had killed him after all? I was in a daze. Euphoria.

I phoned Andrea: 'I can't believe it,' I said. 'He's gone. He's really gone. I don't know, though. He's so slippery. It wouldn't surprise me if it all turned out to be fake. That's it: he's faked his own death!'

'He didn't,' she said calmly. 'He really is gone. Some complications from his treatment. He was having surgery on his shoulder.'

'How could it happen from a bullet in his shoulder? How did he really die? A heart attack?'

'No. But can you believe it? They say Dr Kidd has struck again!'

I called Russo. I was barely able to contain my joy at the news: 'You've heard the latest, haven't you?' I said.

He sounded subdued, however: 'I have indeed. An injection. Dr Kidd came through again. Wish he could do something for me.'

'Why, what's up?'

'I could be deported, believe it or not. That damned gun got me in a jam. I got in trouble with the police. Unlawful use. I had lessons, like you said, and was really enjoying it. So much so, I started showing off the damned thing. Then I fired it in the air to celebrate the Smooth Killer being shot, damaged a window and an undercover cop tried to arrest me. I just thought he was some hoodlum and threatened him with it. So now I'm in trouble. A friend bailed me out. Now your nemesis is gone, are you going back?'

'Everything's looking up, now the Smooth Killer's finally out of the way.'

'Incidentally, it wasn't you fired the shot, was it?'

'Yes, it was. I couldn't lie to you.'

'You should feel proud.'

'I do. Now the Evangelical will have to form his government and there might be a role for me. But he's having some kind of personal crisis. He can't make a decision. But I don't really care. At least Serena's taken care of. I phoned Andrea and she's saying: "When are you coming over? When are you coming over?" I don't want to stay here. I only came here to get away from the Smooth Killer.'

101
FEVER

I became obsessed with the fact that it was me that had fired the shot that had put the Smooth Killer in hospital. It reminded me of the conversation I had with Russo once, when he said that it would only take one bullet to make a difference. I'd laughed it off at the time, but he'd been right. One bullet. It was enough to make me a national hero. I was full of it; it made my head swirl. The stars seemed brighter at night, and in the morning the sunshine was warmer, the birds sang louder, and even the trees seemed to leap out of their roots to salute me as I walked into town.

My mind raced over the possibilities. I'd take the defence minister's job when it was offered. I'd be the best defence minister ever. Although was I not that already, from my previous time? In that position I'd continue the fine tradition of winning all the border wars. There'd be no more trouble with guerrillas. I'd educate the Evangelical about the Indians. I'd force him to change his policies towards them. If he didn't, I'd set up a political party to help them, like the American journalist had suggested. Later, I'd run for president myself. I could launch my own coup. I would revive the great days of Grandpa's time. I'd rule for twenty years like he did. Longer, if mortality allowed. I'd modernise the country. Literacy and poverty levels would be the best in the world. I would end all violence in society. Leaders of other countries would visit to find out how we achieved it.

I'd work with Serena to improve women's rights and end discrimination of gays. It would be a golden age. I'd give back the rest of the money I'd hidden away. I never wanted it anyway. I only kept it as compensation, but now I wouldn't need it. I'd be president, and I could pay myself whatever I wanted. Except I wouldn't take much. I'd be one of those rare men who lived modestly while in power. I'd set up a foundation, a charitable foundation for street kids, or maybe a general anti-poverty movement. It would persist even after my death. It would become the greatest charity in the universe. My name would live on around the world. I'd divorce Serena and marry Andrea. Life would be exhilarating, perfect. My legacy would be secure and golden for ever.

And yet... and yet there was a flaw in every plan, a worm in every apple. The world wasn't going to open up so easily for me. Younger, more ambitious people weren't going to let an old man boss them around. I'd had my chance, and I'd taken it, for better or worse. Some things had gone well, others not so. I could not expect another chance. Everything was complicated, conflicted, untidy. And what if I was president and became ill? I'd be terrified of hospital. If I saw a doctor I didn't recognise I'd probably die of shock. I was sure Dr Kidd did not really exist. It was a coincidence, the kind of coincidence that became a myth. But what if he did exist? Waiting years if necessary for his next victim - waiting for me.

102

REPRISE

A couple of days later, Russo came over, and we had a party. He brought booze and dope. Despite his legal worries, he was exuberant: 'You did it, man. You got him!'

'It was Dr Kidd. Without his intervention...'

'Sure. But without your bullet he wouldn't have been in the hospital in the first place.'

'At least they're looking for two people now and not just me.'

He grabbed my hand and hugged me. 'You're a hero, man. You're my hero.'

It felt like our old college days. We played some of the favourite albums from our youth: Frank Zappa, the Grateful Dead, Santana, the Doors' *L.A. Woman*, Led Zeppelin, the Stones, and albums by rock acts from home.

When we were both half-drunk, he asked me about Sasha.

'I said goodbye to her,' I said. It was her idea, not mine. I don't want to think about her anymore. I came to the sad conclusion she was immune to kindness. She's the antithesis of the woman who wants to be told you love her all the time. She believes she's unloveable and that she can't love.'

'Is she right?'

'I don't know. Probably. I sometimes thought I loved her, but maybe I was kidding myself.'

'I liked her,' he said. 'I thought she was a lot of fun. A little quiet.'

'Nothing wrong with quiet. I think you took a shine to her.'

'I take a shine to everyone. She'll be back.'

'I hope not.'

'She knows what's good for her. You're her meal ticket. I don't know how many meal tickets you've got on the go nowadays.'

'None, actually. I don't pay Serena an allowance anymore.'

'Yes, but that was her idea, right?'

'I confess that's true. But Sasha coming back would be the end. We'd have to stay here. I could never go back. No career. No money. No Andrea.'

'There'd be no Andrea anyway. I didn't think you'd ever get with her. I hate to say it, but she was and always will be a tease. Everyone knows that - except you, it seems. But why couldn't you go back home with Sasha?'

'I wouldn't tell anyone else but you this. The fact is, she killed a man. It was when we were living in the artists' colony in the border region. She claims he tried to rape her.'

'God! But why do you say "claims" - don't you believe her?'

'Of course I do. But I start to think how the police would see it - and from that perspective it doesn't look good. You can bet your life, it'll turn out to be a family with money and influence. She's looking at the rest of her life behind bars in some filthy gaol. She's suffered most of her life, and I don't doubt she'll suffer the rest of it too.' I told him about the drive across the border and the rest of her 'confession' to me. 'So you see the problem: she wouldn't be able to live without me, her reputation would destroy me politically, and there'd be the risk of her being kidnapped. It would be a hopeless situation. Anyway, I upset her on our last night together. She's a mess, but I was way too rough with her.'

He grinned. 'You're a bad man.'

We stayed up late, talking and drinking. Russo was increasingly feeling sorry for himself because of his court case, whereas I was excited about a future without the Smooth Killer or Sasha to have to worry about.

Despite the drink, I slept poorly. I dreamt I went to a fortune teller who predicted someone would try to kill me and succeed; I was then immediately threatened and would have died, were it not for the fact that I woke up. At least three times I awoke after a version of this dream, until at about five I finally slept soundly and did not wake until past nine. When I got up, I found that Russo had gone home, leaving a note: 'Thanks for a great evening. Pray for my luck in court. Or a corruptible judge!'

I went onto the internet, keen as ever for the news from home. There was the latest on the cleanup from the storms. Meanwhile, the Evangelical was back in the palace.

Andrea had sent me an email: 'When will you be arriving?'

I was in the process of replying when I heard someone at the door. The thought flashed through my mind that it might be Sasha. I extinguished that thought immediately. I looked towards the door, then heard a breeze blow some leaves against the window at the back of the house.

In truth, I knew it was Sasha there. I could see her now; she was wearing a thin floral print dress I recognised and no coat, which made her look vulnerable. I hesitated to answer. In my mind's eye my ambitions were falling apart like ramshackle buildings in a storm. When I opened the door, I just stood looking at her.

She was staring at the ground. 'I have nowhere else to go,' she said plaintively. I placed the back of my hand under her chin and gently raised her head. She looked exhausted. She didn't smile. She bore the look of a woman who'd been slapped about the face several times by an uncaring man. I tentatively stroked the side of her face and her forehead.

'Why are you here?' I said. 'You can't be here.'

'Well I am. And now that I've come all this way, are you going to let me in? Or will you turn me away?'

Once inside, she appeared a little more relaxed and said, 'I wanted to touch the hand of the man who shot a dictator dead.'

'Stop.'

'No, I mean it. I wanted to kiss the hand that held the gun. I wanted that hand to caress me. What you did changed history.'

'I thought you didn't want to be with me anymore.' I pulled her towards me, but she resisted, insisting her back was hurting, as if to admonish me. I slipped my fingers inside the top of her shirt to gently caress her neck which felt cold. I enjoyed her scent. I pressed my lips to the mark on her neck I'd put there on the last night I spent with her.

'Don't,' she said. 'You really hurt me. I know why you did it, and I forgive you, even the biting which was vicious. Even if I deserved your anger, your cruel words, and to have my face pushed in the dirt, to have you nearly break my back - it still hurts, thank you - and the brutal sex without any hint of tenderness, I did *not* deserve to be bitten. You assaulted me, you bastard. And I bet you wouldn't do that to your precious Andrea.'

'So why have you come? I don't understand it. I thought you wanted to make your own way in the world, your own peculiar way.'

'I soon realised I couldn't do it.'

I ended my caress and she followed me into the lounge and sat down, now nervous again. 'I got scared,' she said. 'I was going to go with a trucker. I thought he couldn't treat me any worse than you. I was following him to his cab. One of the whores standing nearby urged me not to. I knew he was a killer. I didn't care at that moment. I'd be just another disposable female body in a world of them. But when he opened the cab door, I had a panic attack and just ran away. Does that make me a coward? I don't care if it does. My last ounce of self-preservation kicked in. I decided to return to the one person I thought would always protect me, bastard though you are. You may be turning macho just like all the others, but you wouldn't reject me. You tried it once - do you remember? And you couldn't do it then, so there's no way you could do it now. Or were you lying when you said you wanted me to come with you?'

'No.'

'Then why are you not happy? I can tell you don't want me here now. I can feel your hostility. You're turning mean. You were sensitive before, now you become angry easily. I'm thinking that you never meant anything you said.'

'It's not that. Things have changed.'

'What things? I just decided I wanted to be with you, like you said you wanted. Or was I mistaken?'

'You said yourself there could be an attempt to extradite you from here.'

Her face brightened a little. 'Only if they find me first. But I couldn't be in the old country with you. You wouldn't be there most of the time. You'd be away doing your politics, and I'd be alone, and it would begin again - all the staring and the dirty comments and the groping and grabbing - and, worst of all, someone might come and kidnap me and take me back across the border. I realise what I need, what everyone needs, is a place they can feel secure in. I thought here you could hide me. I could change my appearance. I could get a fake ID. You could get me pregnant. That would slow it down. You could get me a top lawyer to fight the extradition if it comes. I don't deserve to go to prison. I killed a rapist, a man who would have raped me and others. A baby, that could be our legacy.'

'Take it easy.'

I went into the kitchen to make coffee. My head was pounding, made much worse by her volley of wild ideas. Her mention of legacy made my mind wander. I thought of my father. He had no legacy, just that stupid video of him falling. It suddenly didn't seem to matter anymore. What good had my grandfather's political legacy done for him? I thought about the street kid I'd shot. What had he cared about such things? What did millions of people care? They only lived for the next day, or the next meal, or the next fix. The only legacy the street kid left was a bloodstain on the ground, a corpse for someone else to dispose of.

When I returned, she started again: 'I once thought that maybe you were right all along and I should have gone with Russo. He seemed a good man. I sent him my latest paintings, and I thought about sending myself. He doesn't have big ideas about saving the country, he's not cursed with an obsession about his legacy, he's not going to be shooting dictators and street kids. Sex in return for security, that's all. But I don't really know him. He might turn out to be as big a bastard as you're becoming, so I'll stick with the one I've got. Now you're not going to turn round and deny what you promised are you?'

Sex for security. Everything with her was transactional. I said, 'Do you mean, what I promised you, or what I promised myself?'

'What are you saying?' Her eyes widened in such alarm that I almost laughed. She was so brittle that I could break her in an instant with a single word. Part of me wanted to do just that, and yet it was her vulnerability that made her addictive to me.

'No,' I said, 'I won't renege on it - despite everything.'

'So you would give up your ambitions and protect me, and when they ask you to go back to do politics again, you will say "No" because you've dedicated the rest of your life to the pursuit of art?'

I grinned. 'Yes, I guess that's what I'd say.'

'OK, and so when you're old and drooling with your teeth falling out, I will look after you.' She smiled innocently. 'Do you believe me? Maybe you don't.'

'It's not the most appealing future I could imagine for myself, I must admit. I take it I'll be gaga as well?'

She ignored this and her expression hardened. 'Maybe, instead, you'll merely wait and see and you'll still go to the one you wanted all along - that bitch Andrea - and you'll abandon me. You know in your heart you want her, but you try to deny it. And if I have my way, you won't have her. And her husband won't die. He'll hang on for ever. I *will* him to live. He could outlive you, even me. In my case, I hope he does.'

'Why do you say things like that? Why do you talk sometimes as though you've given up on everything?'

She paused, as if mulling over her response. 'I don't mean it,' she said. 'Not really. Although if I get caught, it would be better that I died. And if you turn into a bitter old man...'

I let her sentence trail off unheard as I walked upstairs and into my room. I picked up one of the Glocks, which was on a bookshelf. I turned it over in my hand. A gun had its own solutions. Two bullets. One each. I couldn't help thinking we were both doomed in our own ways. What future did we have here, trapped? I feared becoming the man she saw me turning into, perhaps the man that in her heart she secretly wanted, a man who would ultimately destroy her, a man who would end her suffering only by ending her life - a man I could only despise as I stood there in my room staring at the gun in my hand.

But a gun was not a neutral thing. It had its own agenda. And it was a stupid thing. It provided solutions when you didn't need one.

I carefully placed the Glock back on the shelf and returned downstairs.

103
THE CURSE

Sasha was draped over the sofa, looking settled, yet still nervous. 'Cheer up,' she said. 'I thought you'd be glad to see me. I'm disappointed you're not.' As I approached her, she gently pulled me towards her and stroked my cheek with her fingertips. 'Don't worry, old man,' she said tenderly. I kissed her on the lips and then pulled away from her.

She said, 'Why do you worry so much? Take me out to lunch, can't you? Pretend you're happy my being here. Look, you never know when something will end, so why do you worry? You only know that it *will* end. Nothing endures, so why fret about it?'

'Platitudes,' I replied morosely.

'OK, you're right, but platitudes can be true.'

I looked at her smiling, genuinely happy. What did she have to smile about? Damn her, I thought. Damn her. She'd ruined everything. I went to fetch my coat, then paused. 'Is it cold out?' It sounded so ridiculously trivial.

'A little chilly... I guess.'

I checked myself in the mirror. I looked exhausted and my face was not that of a kind man, as I used to believe it was. Caring about legacy was a curse. Maybe a witch had cursed me once. And a legacy was never clear, or certain, and was always negotiable, partial. She had killed one man, maybe two, maybe caused other deaths. I had shot a dictator, I'd killed a street child and an unknown number of men. Who was to say what was good or bad amongst all these killings? Even the dictator had an innocent, young granddaughter who loved him; even the street kid had a future I'd deprived him of.

I turned to look at Sasha again, watched her for a moment picking at a thread in her dress. She was trouble for sure, but she was my trouble. She couldn't help ruining everything because everything had ruined her. And she could not help but dismiss her own death in a throwaway comment, as if nothing mattered, and that I couldn't help but admire. But the future she now wanted for us was too restrictive.

'I've changed my mind,' I said.

'Have you got food then?'

'No. I mean, I have to go back to the old country. I can't stay here the rest of my life.'

'I can't believe this!' She slammed her forehead with her palm in frustration. 'Why did I ever believe you!? Why did I believe a word you said!?'

'Hear me out.' I sat down next to her, put my arm round her. She leaned towards me, submissively resting her head on my chest. I said, 'I remember that Englishman we got to know - especially you - telling us to speak up for the indigenous tribes. Then, when I was part of that idiotic politician's campaign team, I met an American journalist. Nice man. He wanted to explore, so we drove around the interior. We talked about the tribes and he suggested I should maybe work for them politically to give them more of a voice. Now I'm not suggesting I could do that, and maybe that would be inappropriate anyway, but perhaps I could at least find out more about their problems, make their situation better known in the world, do what I can to help their cause. Or, if not that, I could find out more about the street kids, see what I could do for them. The thing is, Sasha, sweetheart, listen to me...'

She was not taking my talk well and she raised her head away from me. I persisted, 'Look, we can either stay here for ever in isolation and one day someone will show up with a gun or a warrant, or we can go out in the world, explore it, try and make a difference if we can. Whatever the situation, we can still paint - think of the opportunities! We'll be OK for money. They'll give me my pensions back, we can live off them. And if they try to get you, we'll stop them. We'll tough it out and we'll win.'

She looked at me quizzically, trying not to smile. 'You're serious, aren't you?'

'I am.'

'You're mad.' She sighed. 'Go on then. I'm in your hands.' She leaned in towards me again, put her arms loosely round my neck and then held me close. She was silent for a few moments and then said, 'Will you promise me one thing?'

'Depends what it is.'

'Will you ask Serena for a divorce?'

'Yes, I will.' I kissed her gently and then we both got to our feet. I noticed my phone had a new text - 'Welcome back!' it read. I did not recognise the number and so immediately went upstairs. I returned with two loaded Glocks. Sasha, who would have once flinched and demurred, now matter-of-factly put one of the guns in her handbag.

We took a cab to a fishing village on the coast. I wanted it to feel like old times and it did. We went to a seafood restaurant we'd been to before. She was subdued, but after a glass of wine she relaxed and became quite animated as we talked about practicalities. Back in the old country I'd buy a house by the coast or in the capital - I would let her decide - and then I'd sort out all the arrangements. And although I didn't mention it to her, I had to hope that by the time I formally moved out of the place in the artists' colony, any police investigation wouldn't have connected it with the strange couple who'd suddenly left town: the tattooed young woman with her distinctive port-wine stain and the older man. We'd buy a 4x4 and explore the country. I'd decline any offer of a government job, and I'd steer clear of Andrea.

I gave back to Sasha what she'd said to me - about nothing being permanent or predictable. She accepted this with good grace.

I asked her, 'One thing I've always wanted to know: what did you do with the gun? Having had the thing stuck to my neck for a while, I feel a certain affinity towards it.'

She half-smiled and put down the wineglass she was holding. 'I thought about throwing it into the back of a pickup truck, I thought about hiding it somewhere in the motel - I soon gave up that idea! - and in the end I drove out to the woods and hid it in the ground. What do you do with a gun? It saves your life and then it condemns you, unless you can somehow destroy it or hide it forever.'

At that moment, I experienced a feeling of inexplicable and intense love for her that I had never known before. Perhaps it was the effect of the wine, but I was rash enough to believe she felt something too.

But looking around the restaurant a few minutes later, I couldn't help noticing my old insecurities begin to resurface. Why was that young man in denim jacket and jeans seated by the door at that poky little table when others were free? And the heavyset, smartly dressed man over in the corner, wasting time over his coffee: what was he carrying in that canvas bag?

Later, when we were leaving to go and wait outside for the cab, I saw in the corner of my eye the heavyset man also rise from his chair. I told myself it was pure coincidence. I pressed Sasha's hand tightly in mine. As we walked through the empty bar with the man now unnervingly close, I deliberately slowed my steps. She instinctively knew. I suddenly nudged her to one side, causing the man at our heels to lose balance. He bumped into my shoulder and then apologised in an insincerely courteous manner. I took the opportunity to glare in his face. As he walked away grumbling, I told myself it had been the innocent stumble of a hurrying man. I assured myself he was not removing a gun from the bag he carried and would not be waiting for us outside. I pulled the Glock from my pocket as a precaution; Sasha was already holding hers.

Printed in Poland
by Amazon Fulfillment
Poland Sp. z o.o., Wrocław